Search for the Holy Grail
The Complete Series

Search for the
Holy Grail
The Complete Series

By MJL Evans and
GM O'Connor

Table of Contents

Only the Stars Remain Constant

December 20, 1689

The Christmas market was in full swing in a village nestled within the snow-covered hills of Hanover. Vendors in the town square filled steins with mulled wine and offered their handcrafted Advent wares of blown glass, wreaths, and seasonal foods like Backfisch and Stollen for sale. Evergreen garlands had been hung between buildings, and street lanterns bathed everything in a warm, golden glow.

Just beyond the festivities stood Oskar's Metals. Inside, oil lamps burned, and Helena Braunschmidt stood peering through a telescope aimed through the window at the constellation Orion. She often wondered what it would look like to see flames flickering off its shoulder. Ares, an aged German mastiff of pure steel blue, lay sprawled at her feet, soaking up the warmth from the nearby kiln. "Only the stars remain constant," Helena murmured.

"The stars will be there." Oskar, in a leather apron, stirred up the fire.

"Though they may appear upside down," Helena quipped, waiting for a laugh that didn't come. "Remember when I was little, you promised we would build the world's largest telescope? One that can see so far…" Her warm brown eyes gazed at the sky. "You could see someone looking back at you from another world."

"Careful. I could be stoned just for *hearing* that," Oskar said. "Cardinal Grimaldi has been seen in town. He's had it out for you since he heard of this 'moonraking' you speak of. Traveling in dreams—nonsense like that only adds fat to the fire."

"Are you scolding me? It is not nonsense." Helena stared out at the sparkling blue snow on the Deister mountains. *I wonder if I'll ever see them again?* Moving to Aragua sat heavily on her shoulders. "I'll miss snow."

"*Ja*, no snow." Oskar patted his perspiring bald head with a piece of old cloth. "I don't like the heat, you know."

"Says the man with a kiln."

"At least I can cool off when I'm done here. The thought of a never-ending summer does not appeal to me." Oskar placed a telescope shell alongside the others, and then sidestepped to a sink containing fittings and rings.

Helena picked up one of the telescopes and aimed it out the window, not at the sky but at the Christmas market.

"You're not giving the coating time to dry," said Oskar.

She carefully returned it. "Perhaps Aragua is not ready for fine telescopes. Maybe we'll become pirates. Pirates of the Caribbean. Stranger things have happened," Helena said.

"You and your fantasies."

"This one is warped." She indicated one of the many telescopes.

"I make the finest lenses in the world," Oskar said with pride. "That has to count for something. We have everything the colony needs to be successful."

"Except snow."

"Doesn't your countess need you?"

"She's the Snow Queen this year. She's not going to miss me for hours. She's probably on her third bottle of brandy by now. I'm glad she can carry on as if nothing's happening."

"That explains it. You're hiding here so you don't have to go to the fancy-dress ball tonight at Angelin Castle. I'm flattered."

"She's oblivious," Helena said. "She couldn't care less about politics."

"It's her way of coping. She did send Catharina and Natalia on ahead to check it out. You know how close she is with Fred and Max. She must be torn up about it."

"Catharina's letter just arrived. She said the temperature was so high that lead was peeling off the windows. She had quite an adventure in the Jamaican Blue Mountains, but I'm not inclined to believe it. Though, apparently, they did meet some Maroons. She said Natalia found them fascinating."

"Natalia hasn't written? You did have an argument before she left."

"Nothing that dramatic. Catharina said she is compiling a body of work first. She must try to show me up. Besides, there's no point in trusting anything to seagoing mail now; it would take two months to arrive, and we'll have left by the time it does." Helena glimpsed a device on the table. "You finished it!" She investigated the astrological mechanism with its spinning parts, wheels, and miniature comet.

"Not quite yet," Oskar said. "It needs adjustment."

"You included the comet. Good. I tell you, it will come back." Helena peered through another finished telescope, looking across the village again. Houses were festooned with boughs of evergreen and multicolored lanterns. The nearby lake lay frozen beneath a fresh blanket of snow. "I always like the lights this time of year." Snowy banks led up to the castle. Torches flickered, illuminating the stone building, with its towers and grand entrance guarded by the statue of a gilded, double-headed eagle.

"Which color represents which gods or planets? Red for Vulcan or Mars?" Helena pondered. "At least we won't have Cardinal Grimaldi there to tell you what we can and cannot see through our lenses."

"No, only the Spanish Inquisition, the Dominicans, the Huguenots, the Quakers, Protestants, Catholics, and Jews. Cardinal Grimaldi spent time in the New World."

"*Ja*, he couldn't stand the heat, either. That's one thing we can learn from the cardinal." Helena aimed the telescope across the valley. "Oskar, look at this. There are lights out there."

"What, more flying lights?" His mouth curled into a smile, and he aimed a telescope of his own. "Where are we looking?"

She adjusted his aim. Lights from the valley grew in number, forming rows.

"Soldiers are across the lake, with cannons!" Oskar's shaky hands collapsed his telescope. "It's an army!"

More lights ignited, moving towards the castle. Horse riders appeared out of the darkness, heading into town.

Ares barked.

"Stay with Oskar." Helena looked into the dog's eyes.

"We should hide you. I'll send someone to warn the countess." There was a pause.

Helena was already out the door and could hear Oskar mutter, "I hate it when she does that."

She snapped the reins, and the wheels of the carriage squeaked over bumps. Helena's heart pounded as the horse almost stumbled over itself getting up to full speed. She turned into a tunnel of trees, ducking to avoid being smacked in the face. Out of the corner of her eye, lights continued to cross the river. Once free of the tunnel, she came to a clearing next to a stone wall. Angelin Castle stood before her. She halted next to the entrance. The double-headed eagle glistened beneath the torch light, and raucous laughter and music carried from the grand hall.

Helena gave the guards a nod of acknowledgement and went inside. Within the grand hall, half a dozen trees stood decorated with shiny red apples, silk flowers and gingerbread. A feast of roast duck, roast goose, potato dumplings, sautéed mushrooms and apple and sausage dressing had been laid out on a banquet table.

She watched as a *Feuerzangenbowle* was delivered to an area covered in evergreen boughs. The scent of cinnamon and cloves emanated from the mulled wine. A pair of tongs was laid over the bowl and a cone-shaped sugar loaf was set between the metal pincers. White rum was poured over the sugar and set on fire. The caramelized mixture dripped appetizingly into the wine in the bowl.

Helena navigated through partygoers, all dazzling in their sequined costumes. Though they all wore ivory and gold masks, she recognized the Mayor of Hanover and the Baron of Leipzig by the gold pendants pinned to their collars. She pushed through a shimmering sea of blue, green, gold, and burgundy fabrics until she caught sight of sparkling white.

Countess Aurora of Calenberg stood laughing with Ariel, a gray and white turtledove on her shoulder. Her porcelain skin was pink from copious sipping of Cognac brandy and her plump frame sparkled in a bejewelled gown. An ostrich-feather headpiece bounced as she disappeared through the crowd.

Nearby was Dodo von Knyphausen, who painted the countess's portrait. Clad in a long, dark cloak, a black beret, silver wig and matching beard, he did a passable impression of Leonardo da Vinci. He threw up his hands as the countess shuffled away. "No, don't leave! How am I to paint under these conditions?"

Dodo sat with his paintbrush in a cup of turpentine while he took a long drink of white wine, admiring the canvas perched on his easel.

"Where is she?" Helena asked.

"Mentally or physically?" Dodo scratched beneath the false beard and absentmindedly mistook the turpentine for his drink.

"How many has she had?"

"Glasses or bottles?" Dodo scrutinized her attire, which comprised a moss-green skirt and matching bodice jacket with gold embroidery. "Bottles. A few."

"Dodo, I said don't let her finish the fourth or the fifth. She'll be spread like butter by midnight." Helena scanned the room. "Who did she go with?"

"She's off with the new guard captain. The dashing one in polished silver. She's probably just showing him the ropes."

"Pack your things; we're leaving," said Helena. "I'll get the countess." She pushed her way through the crowd and reached a short, deserted hallway that led to a private sanctuary that both women shared since childhood. As children, they played hide-and-seek within the secret wall passages that would gradually lead to the secluded promenade.

Inside the study, the countess was lying on a wooden desk, legs in the air, with the guard's head buried between her thighs. Aurora released a loud moan before he thrust into her.

Dodo clambered up behind Helena, his paints and easel packed. "Are we setting up here? Shall I paint her in the upside-down position, or is she going for the just been ravished look?"

Helena coughed and banged on the door. "Countess, there's an emergency."

"Oh, Helena, there's always an emergency with you. Oh, Captain Helmut, harder!" Aurora clutched the guard and he grunted. "No, no, don't. You mustn't!"

"My lady, there's an emergency," said Helena.

Helmut tried to pull away, but Aurora's legs locked around him. Her hat fell askew as she writhed against him. "No, you mustn't come in me. Don't come. Don't come."

"Come quick!" said Helena.

Aurora and Helmut both gasped, finishing.

"You shouldn't have," Aurora said.

"Sorry, my countess," Helmut said. "I didn't mean to."

They slid apart and began putting their costumes back together.

"That's all right. You performed magnificently. This is your future bride, my handmaiden." Aurora indicated Helena. "I had to make sure you were a man of quality first."

Helena and Dodo both looked at him as Helmut refastened his trousers and then his breastplate.

"Not bad," Dodo remarked.

"Countess," Helena said her voice rising impatiently. "There are soldiers coming."

"Oh, you're so right." Aurora giggled.

"We have to leave; it's not safe. We're under attack! I've seen horsemen."

"I'll go see what's happening. Stay close." Helmut departed.

"I for one could use a smoke." Aurora took out a marble pipe and tin of tobacco from a jewelled pouch, then went to the fire and lifted an ember from it with tongs to light the pipe. She returned, inhaling deeply before exhaling with a sigh. She reattached her headpiece and retrieved her bird, then led the way to a side gallery, which opened onto an outdoor promenade.

"Now, what do you think of Helmut? He's got a big angry one, like a large bratwurst. Exactly what you need, a damn good prodding."

Dodo stood beside them, drinking from a crystal goblet.

"The Baron of Leipzig wants me, but I intend to play hard to get until I know if Duke Eugen wants me, too." Aurora adjusted her corset. "All these men will just have to keep their codpieces on."

"What about Charles II?" asked Dodo.

"I thank all the gods that he was unable make it due to poor health." Aurora eyed Helena. "What is it you were on about?"

"Hanover is under siege," she said, trying to maintain her calm.

All three glanced around at the evergreens, which sat silent within drifts of shimmering snow.

"We may not be able to see it from this side," Helena said.

Dodo readied his pipe. "Have you been seeing flying lights again?"

"Aunt Sophie said we're safe here. Has she ever been wrong?" Aurora replied. "Relax, have fun, and stop your worrying. I promise everything is fine."

Suddenly, orange and red light ignited the sky and a rumble vibrated through the air, shaking snow from the tree branches. The music in the ballroom came to a grinding halt, and partygoers scurried for the exits.

Helena crossed her arms and gave a dry cough.

"Oh, you're right," Aurora admitted. "You're always right."

"We had better do as she says," said Dodo.

Aurora threw her hands in the air. "Can't I have one night of pleasure?"

"What's going on?" asked a nobleman who'd just come out.

"War, apparently, sir," Dodo replied. "Puts a gloom over the whole evening."

Soldiers and diplomats were assembling outdoors, chattering loudly. Captain Helmut, who had found his officers, reported to the noblemen before leaving again with an assigned guard.

"See, look at that bulge." Aurora elbowed Helena. "You should leave with the servants," she added to Dodo.

"Servants? I'd like to remain with you if you don't mind."

Helmut returned with three officers and the mayor, who announced: "Transylvania is under attack by the Ottomans. The Prinz Elector Frederick is calling all our armies to war."

"Hanover is next," added a nobleman. "We must yield to Emperor Leopold, or the Ottomans will destroy us."

"Where is Prinz Maximilian's army? He'll protect us," said another.

"Prinz Maximilian has declared that our houses now belong to the Holy Roman Empire," said the Baron of Leipzig.

"He can't do that," Aurora stammered. "Freddy said he couldn't do that."

"Maximilian's army is here now," the baron argued. "He's declared that all pagans and atheists be removed from the fatherland."

"It's not like we didn't see it coming," Dodo said.

"Countess, you'll have to come with me." Helmut and his men guided Aurora and Helena away, with Dodo trailing behind. "You are in danger tonight, Countess. Cardinal Grimaldi ordered that you be arrested for the crimes of witchcraft and sexual deviancy."

"Witchcraft?" Aurora and Helena said together.

"Were you not arrested for dancing naked in a pagan ceremony with several other women?"

Aurora thought a moment. "Possibly."

"Uh, the countess was never implicated in the *pagan* aspect of it," Dodo countered.

Helmut led them to a recess beneath a grand stone staircase and tapped a panel that triggered an opening. They followed him into a cave-like room. The opening to the passage shut, taking with it the light. Fumbling in the dark, they descended a short staircase, where the flicker of a lantern could be seen ahead. Helena's heart rose into her throat as she came face to face with a stone likeness of Odin, the ancient god of war, and then Frigg, the goddess of marriage. Other shadowy figures danced in the candlelight.

They turned a corner to the spot where a death shrine housed wax renderings of ancestors.

"The dead give it away." Dodo gave a nervous laugh. "I bet if you smoked enough opium, you could make the walls come alive."

They turned another corner. "Your Aunt Sophie anticipated this move by Maximilian. Ready a carriage," Helmut said to his lieutenant. "Something inconspicuous."

"Where are we going?" asked Aurora.

"I'm to deliver you to Calenberg." He paused at the bottom of another staircase. "This will take you up to your chambers. Dress warmly, both of you, and be ready to go in five minutes."

They climbed the stairs, entering a passageway that opened into the countess's chamber.

Helena began filling a valise with all the practical items she could find.

Aurora put Ariel in her gilded cage and stuffed a satchel with perfume. "Orange blossoms or rosewater? To hell with it, I'll take both."

Dodo removed his costume and slid on his overcoat.

"You're not wearing *that*, are you?" Aurora said.

Dodo brushed imaginary dust off his red and gold cloak. "Hey, this is real Venetian velvet. It doesn't grow on trees, you know."

"Please hurry, Countess!" Helena said. "Dodo, keep a lookout."

He stood reluctantly in the hallway, rocking back and forth in his black polished shoes.

Aurora opened her wardrobe to peruse her travel cloaks. "Blue lily or the sapphire shimmer?"

Within minutes, Dodo rushed back in, pushing his way behind one of the wardrobe doors next to Helena.

Metallic clanging of guards rattled the hall.

Aurora sighed extravagantly. "Just be quiet for a moment. Let me think!"

Soldiers burst in; swords drawn.

Aurora glanced around the wardrobe door. "Uh, come in."

"Countess Aurora, you are under arrest."

"Can I not get changed first?"

"Come with us now."

"Aunt Sophie's not going to be happy with you." Aurora was escorted away at blade-point.

Moments later, Helena peeked out as Helmut and his lieutenant entered. "Where's the countess?" he asked.

"They took her."

"The scenario we feared," Helmut told his lieutenant. "On Sophie's orders, she must not fall into the hands of our enemies."

Countess Aurora of Calenberg was dragged, complaining, to the east entrance of Angelin Castle. Soldiers roughly herded her to the point where townsfolk were being prevented from leaving. A figure in a red robe approached her as a lavish carriage arrived, delivering Prinz Maximilian, clad in full blue steel armor studded with gemstones. With him was Count Molke, looking sullen in a long, shimmering robe.

"Oh, Maxi, you really had me going," said Aurora.

"Silence, witch!"

"Witch?" Her mouth turned down. "Maxi!"

"Countess Aurora is to be burned, immediately," said Count Molke.

"I agree." Cardinal Grimaldi's lips curled upwards into an evil grin. "Make an example of her for Emperor Leopold. Be sure the townspeople all witness the execution. This should send a clear message."

Guards were dispatched to round up more townsfolk.

"Execution?" Aurora's heart pounded. "Maxi, what are you doing?"

"She cannot be burned without a trial," the Baron of Leipzig put in.

"God decides when to execute justice, Baron. God wants to burn her right now."

"With pleasure." Maximilian indicated a sheltered terrace. "Right over there."

"Maxi, you don't want to hurt me." Aurora's heartbeat thrashed in her ears. "The terrace? I remember that's where I said it was tiny. I was joking. I didn't mean to laugh. It was cold out! You know what happens when they get cold!"

Guards dragged her to the wood structure, which was now being doused with oil.

"Maxi, I was always there for you!" Aurora's breathing grew shallow as her eyes darted around, seeking escape. Soldiers dragged her forward and threw her to her knees. Before her was a drift of unblemished snow, sparkling in the moonlight, which led down the sloped barrier wall, into some woods beyond which, she knew, was a cliff and a creek.

"Do you confess to being in league with Satan?" Cardinal Grimaldi demanded.

She gave him a cold stare. "I will if you will."

"Confess!"

Aurora's breath hung in the air as she scanned the snowy woods again. "A hex on you, you bastard!"

"Confess, witch!" the cardinal yelled, eliciting angry shouts from the crowd.

Aurora gathered up her skirt and, momentarily freed from the soldiers, darted for the snowbank ahead. A mighty leap put her at the mouth of the woods. She straightened her white ostrich-feather hat and plowed through the thicket of trees ahead of her.

"Halt!" Maximilian bellowed, as his men stood uncertainly. "Well, seize her!"

Gunpowder ignited and shots flew in Aurora's direction. She crouched down, the white shimmer of her ballgown blending into that of the sparkling snow. She unpinned her headpiece and placed it on a tree stump. Then, keeping low, she went on, navigating quickly around bushes, fallen branches and mossy rocks coated in frost. Suddenly, her footing gave away and she stumbled down an embankment to the creek.

"There!" Maximilian shouted and a barrage of shots was accompanied by the metal clang of soldiers fumbling in the snow. "Move!" There was more clattering of metal and several thuds. "Set up a perimeter around the grounds. Do not let her escape."

Aurora regained her footing and crossed a clearing into another heavily wooded area.

Echoing behind her was Cardinal Grimaldi's voice. "You've lost her!"

"Time is of the essence," Count Molke reiterated.

"Surround the woods and cut her off," Maximilian ordered.

Helena drew a pocket telescope from her sleeve. From the chamber balcony she was able to follow Aurora's movements as she made it to the creek and into the woods beyond, which would lead to the village.

Helmut borrowed the telescope. "It's only a matter of time before they find her—and us."

"I should have gone to Italy," Dodo said.

Helmut led them back inside the chamber. He seized a blue gown from the wardrobe and rooted about for a matching headpiece. "Quick, put these on."

Helena scrutinized the peacock blue gown. "*This* dress?"

"Yes. I have an idea."

She quickly disrobed and Dodo helped her into the gown.

"I can still get you out," Helmut said. "You'll be the decoy, and Dodo can do what he always does."

Dodo gave him a scathing look. He grabbed the spare portable easel from the wardrobe that the countess kept handy for orgy nights.

"Where the hell will we go?" said Helena.

"To Hamburg, to meet the ship. I'll slow them down while you get away. It's the only way to get you out." Helmut leant into her. "You know she intended to set us up tonight. She said you fancied me."

She met his gaze. "I never set eyes on you before tonight." Her full breasts strayed from the corset, giving him an eyeful. "You seem to perform well."

"I'm pleased," he said. "I do?"

"We'll bring it up later." Helena finished lacing the bodice.

"You fancy him," said Dodo.

"*Ja*, so do you," said Helena.

Fighting erupted in the hallway, and then there was gunfire. They departed the room swiftly through the secret passage, retreating to the south stable house, where a carriage waited with provisions.

Helena pinned the fascinator, with its tall blue peacock feathers, onto her head. Helmut, seeing her shiver, covered her shoulders with a fur cloak. "I can't do it," she said as she climbed onto the driver's bench of the carriage, trembling.

"All our lives are in danger; you must do your best," Helmut said.

Helmut's lieutenant arrived. "I have news from the city. The Braunschmidt guard has been attacked. They're falling back to the village."

"Maximilian's defied his mother's orders," Helmut said. "I advise you to leave; there is no chance. Protect the Braunschmidts headed for Hamburg."

"The Christian armies may attack the convoy."

"They have more pressing matters." Helmut handed Helena a leather pouch filled with gold coins. He removed an Athame dagger from his belt and put it in her hand. "I sharpened it," he said, looking into her eyes. "Keep it with you at all times."

Helena admired the silver ceremonial blade, which had a polished ebony handle engraved with two crescent moons and one full.

"And you," Helmut addressed Dodo. "Drive safe."

Dodo's shoulders dropped as he set his art supplies in the back seat and begrudgingly thrust himself onto the bench beside Helena.

"Remember, turn left before the checkpoint. I'll have someone there waiting." Helmut stood off to the side.

"Move out, men," the lieutenant called. "Let's go."

Helena released the brake and cracked the reins. She glanced back at Helmut, who knelt to pray beneath the pre-dawn stars. "Odin, my old friend, I need you most of all. Nerthus, please accept this blood as payment." He cut the palm of his hand. "I, Helmut of the Braunschmidts and the last of the Semnones Guard, give all that I am to you. Deliver us from our enemies."

The carriage sped off along the south road.

Helena snapped the reins as she heard shots being fired, and Dodo melted into the seat. "This is not what I had in mind when I said I wanted to travel," he said.

Helena caught a glimpse of the Reiters, clad in shining black armor, galloping on horseback towards them.

Inside the dungeon of Angelin Castle, Captain Helmut von Eindringling knelt before an elaborately carved wood altar with burning candles and incense. He chanted to the gods and goddesses. He awaited his enemy's arrival, and thus his fate.

Helmut had already become a decorated soldier by his early twenties, when he joined the Konigsberg Dragoon Academy to become a captain. He defended the western borders during the Franco-Dutch war. Then served Prinz Frederick in defending Germany from the Ottomans. At the Battle of Vienna, he participated in the largest cavalry charge ever seen. Afterwards, Helmut was sent to protect the Calenberg realm.

Helmut's remaining two guards gripped their axe pistols, keeping watch at the base of the stairs. The mayor and three noblemen paced, vigilant, brandishing swords.

Footsteps neared; then all was silent, broken only by the gentle hiss of armor plates sliding upon each other. Then Maximilian appeared out of the shadows, a flashing demon in the torchlight.

"Where did she go?" Maximilian demanded.

"You won't get away with this, Maximilian," the mayor said. "I know this has nothing to do with a witch-hunt."

"I have officially declared our land to belong to the Holy Roman Empire. I'm here to claim it in the name of Emperor Leopold."

"Your mother should have something to say about it," a nobleman said.

Count Molke's tread was much lighter as he arrived at the base of the stairs. "The other houses voted ten to one. I don't think she'll have much to say at all."

Cardinal Grimaldi arrived too, followed by half a dozen guards. His attention was drawn to the statues in the room. Odin, the god of war and death, stood in armor, a winged helmet on his head and a raven on his shoulder. His wife, Frigg, the goddess of marriage and motherhood, stood next to him in a gown with elaborate sleeves, also wearing a winged helmet. Nerthus, the goddess of fertility, stood apart from them, a cascade of hair over the shoulder of her robe and clutching an orb in her hand.

"Look at this heresy," Cardinal Grimaldi said in disgust, holding out his cross. "I will have you all arrested and burned for crimes against God. Satan worshipers, all of you."

"You speak in the presence of Nerthus!" Helmut exclaimed. "Before the goddess herself."

"Blasphemer! Captain, you are under arrest for witchcraft," the cardinal said. "Guards, seize him!"

Helmut leapt towards Maximilian. Their swords clashed. Blades swung and slashed, but enemy guards quickly deflected Helmut's attack, propelling him into a corner.

Helmut's guards fired their flintlock pistols and raised their axes. Two of the enemies fell, decapitated.

Maximilian's guard threw a dagger, piercing Helmut's shoulder.

Helmut withdrew the blade and tossed it away as he collapsed. No one noticed the trajectory of the dagger until a horrified cry came from Cardinal Grimaldi. The enemy guards stood agape at seeing the blade piercing the cardinal's red shoe. A string of obscenities flowed through the cardinal's lips as Count Molke tried to extract it.

The noblemen took advantage of the distraction to charge the remaining enemy guards, and Helmut couldn't help but release a dry laugh even though blood was now saturating the fabric of his dress uniform. "There's one thing our gods have in common. They demand blood!" He rose to his feet, propping himself against the wall. His sword came up just in time to deflect another assault.

This time Maximilian came in swinging two swords, each slicing into Helmut's sides. "Where is she going?" he demanded as Helmut again crumpled to the floor, blood pooling around him.

"Answer your prinz," said the cardinal.

Maximilian plunged both swords into Helmut's chest, leaving him gasping desperately for air.

Maximilian readied to attack again.

"Enough!" Cardinal Grimaldi waved his hand.

Maximilian nodded to his remaining guard to arrest the mayor, who had raised his hands in surrender, relinquishing his sword.

Leaning on Count Molke, Cardinal Grimaldi limped over to Helmut, knife still embedded in his foot.

"It's imperative that she die immediately," said the count.

"Not until I break every last bone in her body," spat Maximilian.

"The handmaiden knows where she is," said the cardinal. "Where is the handmaiden?"

Helmut gurgled and spat blood onto the cardinal's face as everything grew dark.

Cardinal Grimaldi wiped his face with his broad collar. "This hasn't been my day. You heathen bastard!" The cardinal tried to kick Helmut with his good foot but recoiled. "Did you arrest the handmaiden?" he demanded again.

"No. Baron Gretsch's Reiters are in pursuit of the handmaiden," a guard said.

Count Molke continued to prop up the cardinal. "Get a move on!" he ordered, as Helmut exhaled his last breath.

Aurora clambered on through the frozen woodland, huffing frigid air into her lungs. Beyond a broad tree, she caught sight of the first tinge of orange dawn invading an inky blue sky with a smattering of stars. Yonder sat the town square.

The countess continued to the road, nearing Oskar's Metals, where the glow of a kiln glimmered through dark windows. She tried the door. Unlocked.

She crept inside, half expecting Maximilian's guards to leap from the shadows to seize her. *Maxi, you traitorous pig!* she thought. *Aunt Sophie's going to be furious*. Something nudged her leg: Ares, wanting his ears scratched. "You daft dog." She reached down. "Where is everyone?"

Ares followed a whistle to the back of the shop.

"Now, push," Oskar was saying to his assistant Gustav as they slid crates of telescopes onto the back of a cart.

Oskar looked up at her approach. "Where's Helena?"

Aurora's bosom heaved. "I lost her." She sniffed hard. "She's with Captain Helmut, last I saw."

"We must prepare to leave," Oskar told Gustav.

"Yes, sir." Gustav peered out the window through a telescope. "Reiters! Maximillian Gretsch of the Braunschmidts."

"The wolf in bear's clothing," Oskar mused. "We have to get you out of here right now, Countess."

"We could disguise ourselves as a married couple on honeymoon," suggested Gustav.

Aurora stared blankly at the youth, who was scarcely of age. "You want me to pretend I'm married to Lord Lackbeard?"

"Sorry, my lady, I meant no offense. The crate it is, then."

"Crate?" Aurora said.

Oskar indicated one of the double-sized crates.

"They'll search the convoy, so she can't go to Hamburg," said Oskar. "Sophie will make arrangements. We'll send you to Calenberg."

Oskar and Gustav picked up the empty crate and set it on the cart.

"Get in," said Oskar.

Aurora's mouth hung open. "Are you serious? I'm not getting in a crate. Not in a million years."

Gustav revealed a bottle of Cognac. "Countess."

"Oh, thank the gods!"

Gustav tossed it up into the crate.

"Not the Cognac!" Aurora leapt onto the cart, only just catching the bottle at the crate's edge.

Each man reached up to give her bottom a push and she fell in, screeching.

"Please, Countess. If they arrest you, they will burn you alive!" Oskar filled a leather pouch with water from a jug before collecting a dark travel cloak and wool blanket. He placed them inside the crate.

"They already tried!" said Aurora, sitting up.

"Gustav will escort you to Calenberg."

"Can I trust him?"

"Umm, yy…nn…well, yes. I'll only put two nails in, so you can get out easily. They'll be looking for you, so stay in it as long as you can."

Two nails in my coffin! Aurora thought. "Wait, my smokes!" She fished inside her cleavage. "Oh, there it is." She pulled out a clay pipe, a pouch of tobacco, and a Cuban cigar.

Together, they pushed her head down and closed the lid. The loud bang of a hammer sealed her in.

She heard the creak of a gate as the cart was rolled out into the yard and hitched to a horse.

"Go now, mix into traffic," came Oskar's muffled voice. "I'm going to look for Helena. Come on, Ares!" He whistled.

"I can't believe it actually came to this," Gustav said, and the cart shifted as he sat down in the driver's seat.

"I'm not. The veil has fallen over us. Once you're out of town, lose the convoy and head directly for Calenberg Castle. A river barge will be waiting for you."

The brake clicked.

Reins snapped and the cart vibrated as they drove along the hillside before slowing. Aurora carefully forced open the lid a crack and saw they were in a line of caravans trying to leave the city. In the distance, she saw that the west wing of Angelin Castle was on fire—her chamber. The flames reached such a height they seemed ready to pull it down brick by brick.

Aurora choked back a sob.

"What are you doing?" Gustav said. "Keep the lid down."

"Are you not seeing this?" she snarled.

"I do. But we must leave here as quickly as possible."

She stared at him coldly.

"Sorry, please, Countess. Someone will see you."

Aurora did as she was told.

Roads Less Travelled

The snow glistened in the mid-morning sun as sparrows and robins flitted through branches of the peaceful forest, seeking food. Now and then, a red fox ignited the landscape as it chased down some small animal, while the frozen lake reflected the light with hints of blue. Just beyond, the west wing of Angelin Castle still smoldered. The east wing buzzed with workmen smashing pagan statues and dismantling any articles deemed sacrilegious.

Maximilian sat at a heavy spruce-wood desk in the library, thumbing through documents. He wore a dark blue dress robe with a silver sash. Before him sat a plate of leftover duck with apple and sausage dressing. He drank mulled wine from a pewter mug.

Sitting opposite him in a large, cushioned chair was Cardinal Grimaldi, his bandaged foot propped on a stool. He was sipping wine laced with laudanum and enjoying a slice of Stollen. He winced at the movement of his foot as he reached to take a magnifying lens from the desk. Shifting the lens into various positions, he remarked, "This is useful. The handmaiden made this at her uncle's shop. Clever girl. It's a shame Satan got to her first."

Count Molke entered, looking pale in a black robe. On his way he glanced at a pile of debris.

"I'm having the place redecorated. What do you think?" Maximilian asked.

"Were there any secrets hiding in the walls?" Count Molke wondered aloud.

"It's not here," the cardinal said. "The Braunschmidt contribution is not here."

"Impossible!" exclaimed the count. "Where did it go?"

Maximilian rose, walked to the fireplace and picked up a metal poker. "Good question. You were responsible for securing it." He brought the poker up and drew it violently across the mantel, smashing all the ornaments placed there.

"I'm telling you, it has to be here," the count replied.

"The plan is flawless—that's what you said," Maximilian grumbled. "Pick up the treasury and kill Aurora and the mayor and all our enemies in one fell swoop. Flawless, you said! Smash it all down. Find the money!"

"We're out of time," the cardinal replied. "The pope and Emperor Leopold will not wait. They are mobilizing, and so must we."

"The trick is convincing the other houses in Hanover to unite their treasuries and join the banking Fuggers," said the count.

"We should transfer the Hanover treasury to the Vatican to show the Fuggers we have the security," said the cardinal. "We need the Calenberg treasury as well, but how do we get your mother to agree?"

"She will not have a choice," said Maximilian. "Calenberg Castle is being dismantled. I will have the treasury emptied."

"In exchange, the pope will recommend to Emperor Leopold that Maximilian be made crown prince over all of Germany," the cardinal told the count. "The Braunschmidt contribution is merely a drop in the pond of our conglomerate. It's time we claimed Calenberg itself."

"You're right," said Maximilian. "Mother has had long enough to respond to my ultimatum."

"Prinz Maximilian, we must not make any hasty mistakes," said the count.

"No, only well-planned mistakes. Aurora is obviously responsible for this, and I want her found."

"Her handmaiden is also a witch and must die," said the cardinal.

"She and the painter were used to trick us," said the count. "Now, both got away, thanks to your incompetent guards." Maximilian smashed a vase standing on a nearby table with the poker. It fell and shattered, sending a fragment flying into Cardinal Grimaldi's eye. He shrieked, cradling his face as he reeled out of the chair.

Count Molke, reaching out in a vain attempt to save him, instead caught the cardinal's injured foot, making the man howl as he fell to the floor.

"Are you all right?" the count asked. "We haven't time to fight among ourselves."

Baron Gretsch's Major Krieger and two Reiters came down the stairs to report to Maximilian.

"My Prinz, Baron Gretsch is following a lead to Hamburg," said Krieger. "I'm in command of the unit until he returns."

"Hamburg? Did Baron Gretsch go after the carriage alone?"

"Yes, sir."

"He must know where it is," said the count. "It's not like Gretsch to go chasing a stick."

Cardinal Grimaldi eased back into his chair. "Leave the countess and her handmaiden to Baron Gretsch for the time being. Prinz Maximilian, it's time you claimed Calenberg and the Hanover treasure."

"Mobilize your men," Maximilian said to Krieger. "We take Calenberg next."

Aurora awoke to a violent jolt that nearly shook the lid off the crate. She shoved it off and looked out, blinking. It was daylight and snowing. The cart disembarked from a river barge and turned onto a road before coming to a stop.

Gustav leapt down.

Aurora tried to stand. "Hello? A little help, please."

He offered a hand.

"Oh, my back!" she groaned.

"Is there anything I can do?"

"Yes, find a better plan than hiding me in a box!" Aurora bent backwards and forwards, then stretched her arms above her head. She reached for the nearly empty bottle of Cognac and downed what was left. She shivered and put the cloak back over her shoulders.

Gustav headed behind a tree.

"Don't worry about me; I went in the crate. This better not be permanent, or I'll have to become a common mushroom picker!" Aurora climbed down, still trying to straighten her back. "Pretending to be newlyweds would have been better than hiding in that crate. We'll stop here for a bit, then?"

Gustav returned.

"You nap. I'll take us the rest of the way," Aurora said.

Gustav climbed onto the bench and closed his eyes.

They wheeled along a tree-lined road until it reached a battery tower, next to a bridge. A moat surrounded a castle of stone, brick, and wood. A steep incline marked the path to the outermost fortress, which appeared to be in the midst of a planned destruction.

"What the hell is happening?" Aurora said.

"What is it?" Gustav asked.

"We're here. And the castle is being dismantled." She steered the cart to the main entrance, where they both dismounted. The guards, recognizing Aurora, admitted her but blocked Gustav.

"He stays with me," she insisted.

"Not possible, Countess," said the guard.

"It's fine, let him in," Aunt Sophie's voice came from somewhere inside.

They entered to find Aunt Sophie—Sophie Amalie von Braunschweig-Calenberg—sitting in a grand chair, wearing a deep burgundy gown with silver accents. "Aurora, I'm so glad you made it."

"Yes, me too." Aurora exhaled a sigh. "What has happened here?"

"Your cousin has taken advantage of his father's condition. He's seized power through bribes and betrayal. To think Maximilian would betray us to Emperor Leopold. My own son. I said if this was to happen, we'd leave by ship. But only a few reached Hamburg." Sophie rang the servants' bell. "And those who did were arrested. The Braunschmidt army is to be sent to Transylvania to aid Frederick."

"Helena. I lost her. I don't know where she is."

"I have no news of her. Maximilian's army is on its way here. He'll be here in days," said Sophie.

Aurora burrowed her fists into her waist. "He wants to burn me as a witch."

Sophie's eyebrows rose sharply. "You must leave at once."

"Where will I go?"

"South America, as planned. I have a ship waiting for you in Friesland. It's all been arranged with Lord Van der Hagen. I'm sending you with a special squad of my best men, disguised as merchants. They will deliver you and all your belongings to a transport ship."

"I must find Helena first," Aurora insisted.

"If she's alive, my agents will find her."

"What about Gustav?" said Aurora.

"He should return to Angelin and cover your tracks."

"I'm running a little low on provisions," Gustav said.

"My men will see to your needs. There is no time to waste," said Sophie.

"Thanks, Gus. I owe you one."

"You could pay me."

"Of course." Aurora looked to Aunt Sophie. "Make sure he has a heathy stockpile for the road back."

"He'll be looked after; I'll see to it. Now go pack."

Aurora was escorted to her room, while Gustav followed the guards outside.

"Where's the Cognac?" Aurora asked a servant.

"She said to take only the essentials," the servant said.

"*Ja,* so where's the Cognac?"

The servant vanished to retrieve some, while Aurora examined perfume on her dresser. "Now, lilac or lavender? Oh, the honey water is a must!" She grabbed all of them and put them in her case.

Next, she packed her jewelry into neat little boxes. And finally, she ordered the servants to pack her dresses in a travel crate.

By evening, she was travelling along the Calenberg Road in a caravan. She ate a picnic of roast goose and potato dumplings, accompanied by Cognac. Afterwards, she opened a travel bag and drew from it a portrait of herself and Helena, smiling together. She clutched it to her heart.

Snow tapered away to freezing rain. Gloomy gray clouds hovered over the port of Hamburg, where in the distance docked ships were being unloaded of their cargos of cocoa beans, sugar, spices, and fabrics, and loaded again with crates of lager and Riesling wines.

A carriage neared the city's massive defensive wall. Helena snapped the reins, while Dodo shivered beside her, trying to sleep. They had taken turns driving all the way, stopping occasionally to feed and water the horse.

Helena pulled her fur cloak closer around her face as she slowed the carriage behind a procession of merchants entering the city.

When they came to a stop, Dodo roused. "Finally." His teeth were chattering. "We must get inside somewhere."

"Look for Das Brauhaus; it's near the docks."

"How the hell do we get to the docks?"

"The ships are straight ahead. I just have to navigate this maze."

Once through the main gate, they continued their journey along bustling streets. Evening was fast approaching, and the streetlamps were being lit. Evergreen branches hung from doors and Advent wreaths glowed on windowsills. Colorful lanterns were left to burn on shop doorsteps in honor of Christmas. Garlands of silk flowers were strewn on wrought-iron gates. Trees had been brought inside homes to be embellished with sparkling decorations.

The carriage slowed as they neared the waterfront. Through the wall of rain, a white and black building came into view, *Das Brauhaus* painted across its front in large letters. Helena navigated the horse into a public stable, thankful it had a roof. She gathered up her extravagant peacock blue skirt, now drenched with rain, and climbed down. She grabbed a communal bucket and filled it with well water. The horse drank gratefully.

They gathered their belongings and went next door to the tavern and inn. Wood shutters covered the windows of the upstairs compartments. An old weathervane listed to one side on the peak of the roof. Inside, a roaring fire was blazing in the fireplace of the tavern, which was filled with a series of long golden spruce tables with benches. A built-in cellar sat in the wall behind the bar.

Dodo staggered over to the fireplace, peeled off his Venetian velvet cloak and hung it on a nearby hook. He sniffed. "It's ruined. It'll never bounce back!"

Helena went to the bar and ordered them mulled wine, scalded knackwurst with mustard, and kirschwasser. After paying, she hung her fur cloak next to Dodo's and took a seat in the corner next to the fire. The rain was still pelting down, threatening to flood the whole city.

When supper arrived, Dodo embraced his pewter mug, inhaling the spices in the wine. "Never thought I'd be so happy to have a cup of wine." He eyed Helena. "You look like shit."

"You do, too." She held the mug, warming her hands.

"Who the hell is supposed to meet us?" Dodo asked.

"I don't know."

"I just love being informed, don't you?" He dipped his knackwurst into mustard and took a bite.

"Since you came back from England, I don't understand you," Helena spoke irritatedly.

"I picked up a bit of English humor while I was there."

"Well, it's horrible. Please say what you mean."

"I'm melting. I feel as oily as a Rembrandt. Can I say that?"

She shook her head in disgust. "At least my hair has thawed." Helena gathered her brown locks over her shoulder before dipping her sausage in mustard. "But I can't stop shivering."

"You're shaking like a leaf. Have more wine." Dodo took another mouthful. "The countess says if you drink enough, sometimes things just work out by themselves."

They drank and ate as slowly as possible. At the end of their meal, they downed the kirschwasser. The cherry brandy warmed Helena's insides. "Should I get us another?"

Dodo nodded. "I don't like this one damn bit. I see myself getting put on a boat for the Barbary Coast."

Helena waved her empty glass at the barman and took more coins from her purse.

"She's probably on to the next ball, with a new painter and a new handmaiden," Dodo said. "Ah, maybe not. She'd be lost without us. I just hope she has some Cognac to get her through."

"She's fine. Probably on her way to the ship as we speak, and Helmut said someone will meet us." Helena periodically glanced out the window.

Polizei skulked about outside.

The barman brought over their drinks.

"*Scheisse*," said Dodo. "Maybe they aren't looking for us."

"They're just doing their rounds."

Dodo finished the kirschwasser in one gulp.

Helena finished hers. "Okay, they are looking for us."

"Maybe we should slip upstairs?" Dodo suggested. "There might be a back exit?"

"My body's too heavy to move." Helena glanced out the window, then back around the tavern. The only ones drinking were half-conscious dock workers.

A constable and a man clad in black entered Das Brauhaus and made straight for Helena and Dodo.

Dodo massaged his face. "I knew I was destined for the Barbary Coast."

"They're frozen. Lucky to be alive, for now," the constable said.

The man in black towered over them. His chiseled face bore a slightly downturned mouth, and his dark eyes probed Helena. She recognized Baron Maximillian Graf von Gretsch, an enigmatic family guardian who did Aunt Sophie's biding.

"Take her on board with the rest of them," Gretsch's deep voice rasped.

"Others? Is Oskar with you?" Helena pressed. "Aurora?"

"Her friend can go," Gretsch said.

"Go?" Dodo challenged. "Where exactly will I go?"

"He stays with me," Helena said. "He's a friend of Countess Aurora."

Dodo put out his hand. "Not a close friend."

Gretsch glowered. "Take them away."

After collecting their cloaks, they were prodded forward by a wooden truncheon down a ramp to the docks.

Gretsch followed but paused to speak with another man.

"Captain Fuchs," Gretsch acknowledged. "I'll take these two with me. We sail for Friesland immediately."

Guards began to lead Helena away, but she swiftly grabbed Dodo and dragged him along.

"I can't get on a boat!" Dodo was sweating in the cold.

"Shut him up, or I'll leave him to freeze," Gretsch said.

"When he gets like this, it takes all night. Aurora usually gives him a tonic," Helena said.

Gretsch opened his satchel and took out a tincture. Dodo's mouth fell open and two full droppers were dispensed. Gretsch capped it and put it back in his bag before boarding the ship.

Within minutes, Dodo swaggered aboard with Helena's help, and the ship sailed away into a wall of rain.

Stars twinkled in the deep blue sky and blankets of snow glowed in the moonlight. Maximilian's carriage arrived at Calenberg Castle, and he and Count Molke disembarked.

Maximilian strode alone into the dining hall, where his mother sat eating supper by candlelight. He pulled out a chair and sat. A servant brought over some wine. Silence hung in the air.

"Mother, kindly tell me how you managed to empty the treasury without anyone noticing?" Maximilian said.

"With so many work crews around, it could have been anyone," Sophie replied. "I don't know what happened to it."

"I wouldn't have expected you to resort to thievery, Mother."

Sophie took a mouthful of stew. "Thievery?"

"Yes, it belongs to God now."

"So, my youngest son can be crowned prince over all of Germany? Hardly. What silliness has Count Molke been filling your head with? Whether your father wakes or not, the law is the law; only the eldest son shall inherit."

"Father will never wake, and Frederick can't even hold Transylvania. I rule this house now."

"Nevertheless, your God will have to wait a while longer."

Maximilian smashed his wine glass to the floor and stormed out. In the treasury chamber he found Count Molke reviewing a document.

"It's gone," Maximilian spat. "All of it!" He drew his sword and, spying a portrait of his mother hanging on the wall, slashed the canvas. "I can't believe she did this to our family!"

"Do you have any idea how much this could cost us? The transfer of funds must be completed on time as agreed," said the count. "This is not tulips we're investing in, but a Vatican bank."

"I didn't bring an army and six oxcarts here for fresh air." Maximilian took out his freshly sharpened knife. "I will flay my mother alive until she divulges the location."

A guard brought them another pile of documents, which Count Molke snatched up. "Perhaps she sent it along with that godless bastard child of a countess?"

"With Aurora? Ridiculous. She's nothing more than a stupid aristocrat."

The count discovered, tucked between two pages of a publication, a bill of sale for seven crates of Cognac to be delivered to Van der Hagen Shipping in Friesland.

"You can ask her yourself; we know where she's going," said the count.

De Heilige Graal

Aurora opened her big brown eyes to a cold blue Friesland sky. Seabirds echoed overhead, catching the breeze beneath their wings. The caravan rattled along a wooden dock. After two days, she was eager to stretch her legs. Her transport came to a halt next to a busy warehouse. Aurora exited, her satin sapphire gown gleaming as she draped a length of white fur around her shoulders.

De Heilige Graal, an exquisitely carved East Indiaman, sat tied to the dock, the figurehead of a haloed Virgin Mary at the bow. A red, white, and blue flag fluttered at the ornate stern, while its three masts flaunted cream-colored sails with Dutch patterns. The exterior of the stateroom had over a dozen windows and was painted indigo with orange molding.

A man with silver hair, wearing an ostentatious purple suit, came down the gangway towards her. "Welcome to Friesland, Countess." He tipped his hat and bowed.

"Thank you, Lord Van der Hagen. I'm *incognito*." Aurora followed him to the ship.

"Not exactly low-profile, but you are my guest here, not a fugitive." He signaled a crewman. "Your shipment of Cognac brandy arrived this morning and is already loaded." A handsome man with golden hair came down the gangway. "This is Captain Nicholas van Gelder."

"Sir," the captain said.

"Get everyone on board. We're leaving now."

Van Gelder signaled the officers on the top deck, then to the crewmen on the dock. Crewmen loaded travel cases and a wooden wardrobe onto the ship.

Aurora went on to the main deck, escorted by the captain.

"Welcome aboard *De Heilige Graal*, Countess." Van Gelder smiled and continued up the stairs to the quarterdeck.

Aurora gazed up at the vast rigging, her mouth agape. Hundreds of lines were strung above her head.

"That sky doesn't look good," said the first officer. "We should wait a day or so."

"We'll depart as soon as we're loaded," said van Gelder.

"Stand by fore and aft," said the first officer.

Viscount Van der Hagen approached Aurora with two extravagantly dressed young women. "Countess, may I introduce my daughters, Katrina and Persephone."

"Hello," Aurora said.

"Hello," responded Katrina, the dark-haired one, with a curtsey. She wore a pale pink gown with an elaborate skirt embellished with lace and pearl accents.

"You've never been on a ship before, have you? I can tell." Persephone's blond curls whipped her cheeks as she shuffled over in an iridescent green frock.

The crew was now clearly readying for departure.

"I've made this crossing twice already," Persephone continued. "You can ask me anything about any part of the ship." She pointed forward. "That's the bow, and the forecastle. You might get sick for the first while. Though I didn't."

Katrina leaned towards Aurora. "No."

"No, what?"

"No, she never stops talking," Katrina said.

"Have you picked your cabin yet, Countess?" Persephone pointed aft. "I prefer the starboard side for the trip over." A huge sigh escaped her lips. "The view is breathtaking in the evenings!"

"Release the moorings," shouted van Gelder.

The sky darkened as the gangway was raised. Crewmen climbed into the rigging to release the sails. Longboats pulled lines and the hull moved. The sails unfurled, blooming in the breeze. *De Heilige Graal* sailed away from Friesland.

At the shipyard, a Brandenburg yacht with triangular sails slid into Friesland's port, docking next to a time-worn cargo fluyt. Baron Gretsch emerged on deck from the main cabin. The gangway lowered, and he disembarked.

He checked around the vicinity of the warehouse and found only an abandoned caravan with a few crates left behind in it. Dock workers and crewmen were busy loading the fluyt. A man puffing tobacco stood watching Gretsch.

"Where are the other crates that came on this caravan?" Gretsch asked.

"On that ship there." The man pointed to a vessel on the horizon.

"What's it called?"

"*De Heilige Graal*. She's owned by Van der Hagen, bound for the West Indies."

"I must follow it. I commandeer your vessel."

"My ship?" The man raised an eyebrow. "On whose authority?"

"Is your ship prepared for sail? Captain—?"

"Bohn, Victor Bohn."

"I will pay well."

Bohn refilled his pipe. "That's an East Indiaman; she's faster than us. It would take some innovative sailing just to keep up."

Gretsch tossed over a bag of gold coins. "You can keep up."

Bohn reconsidered. "As it is, my ship is for hire. Aye, we can keep up. Make sail, boys! We have a commission."

"Tell Captain Fuchs she's on a ship headed for the West Indies. Tell him to bring my ship to St. Eustatius," Gretsch told the yacht captain.

"Yes, Baron Graf von Gretsch," the yacht captain said.

Helena and Dodo were brought out.

"Get on that ship," Gretsch said.

"So, Aurora's out there? What will you do with us when you catch her?" asked Helena.

"Get aboard, and if there's any trouble from you or the painter, I'll throw him in the sea."

"We're sailing, Doorman, let's get going," Bohn ordered.

"What about Dover?"

"Our intended destination is now St. Eustatius."

"The West Indies?" Doorman grimaced. "We don't have enough provisions."

Bohn coughed. "Ready to sail. St. Eustatius is the intended destination, is that not correct, Baron Gretsch?"

"Just follow that ship," Gretsch said.

Thunder boomed across the night sky, alternating with lightning on the horizon. *De Heilige Graal* tossed about in the waves. The chandelier inside the state room rattled, while trays of food slid around on the dining table.

Aurora stood at the door, holding the frame. Her stomach rumbled from hunger and nausea. Clutching onto anything well-fixed, she made her way to the table and sank heavily into a seat. She patted her bruised left eye with a saltwater compress.

Van der Hagen set down his drink. "Are you well, Countess?"

"She doesn't have her sea legs yet," Persephone said. "The dress looks nice on you."

"Thank you. You made it?"

"Handmade by Persephone herself." Van der Hagen beamed at his daughter.

"It's beautiful. Thank you. Could use a little dazzle, though. Dinner smells very good."

"Wine?" Van der Hagen offered. "Or Oranjeboom lager from Rotterdam?"

"No, thank you, not just now."

They filled their plates, except Aurora, who made a half-hearted attempt, but her plate slid away. She caught a slice of bread as it coasted by.

Katrina grabbed Aurora's plate and put a few slices of cured mutton on it, handing it back.

"Thank you, Katrina," Aurora said.

Thunder boomed overhead.

Persephone laughed. "That was a good one!"

Van Gelder offered Aurora a green bottle. "Chartreuse?"

"Thank Frigg!" She grabbed it. "Yes." She poured a generous measure and took a throatful. "That's better."

Van Gelder got up for another bottle.

Aurora ogled him with her shiny, drunk eyes. Her cheeks warmed. "Ladies, let's go on deck. I want to see lightning."

"You can't go on deck in a storm like this, my dear countess," van Gelder said. "You couldn't see anything right now."

"I lost a telescope that way," Persephone said.

"You've lost several," Van der Hagen remarked.

"Sorry, Captain van Gelder." Aurora twirled her hair. "The only thing I know about ships is they float. Let's hope."

"They should make telescopes that float," Persephone said.

"Huh?" Katrina frowned.

"They should make telescopes float, so if the sailors drop them in the water, they can retrieve them."

Van Gelder stifled a laugh. "You can't stop a ship to look for a telescope, my dear."

"What if you had wood, captain?" Aurora asked.

"Sorry?"

"Would a wooden telescope not float?"

"Not necessarily," Persephone said.

"It would float," Van der Hagan added. "But it's not practical if you have to make a lot of them."

"My handmaiden's family makes fine telescopes." Aurora stared out the window into the darkness. "Helena."

"Is she your slave?" said Persephone. "Father said you were filthy rich. You're a countess, but it seems you don't have slaves. No slaves? How do you exist? I'd die without my slaves. I've had Brown Holly since the day I was born. She's my nanny. I love her more than anything. I miss her already."

"Did you have to leave her behind?" Aurora drank more Chartreuse.

"No, she's here. She's in the hold. Slaves aren't allowed on the upper decks unless they're working."

"They're only allowed on deck once a day," Katrina said.

"Health regulations." Van Gelder shrugged. "They carry scurvy. Most ships don't allow them on deck at all. I think we're being quite liberal."

"Captain, can we disregard the class rules just this once?" Katrina pressed.

"I think a nerve has been struck," Aurora said.

Van der Hagen sighed. "Katrina has taken up a cause, I see."

"Yes Katrina, it's good to have a cause." Aurora gave a thin smile.

"Those anti-slavery braggarts are nothing but trouble. If they had their way, they'd ruin the colonial economy. I tell you, the trade in slaves is the future," Van der Hagen insisted. "Don't let anyone sway you into investing in tulips. Transporting slaves to where labor is needed, that's the way of the future."

"And what's your cause, Countess?" Van Gelder asked.

Aurora poured more alcohol. "Tonight, Captain, Chartreuse."

"We could have a ship celebration where everyone dances and sings, and nobody cares if you're rich or a slave." Persephone raised her glass.

Aurora thrust her glass in the air. "I'll drink to that."

"Allowing slaves on deck will piss off the crew," said Van der Hagen.

"We never worried about pissing off the crew before," Persephone said. "Oh, it could be grand. We could set up the main deck with lanterns and tables."

"See," Van der Hagen began. "You let women have too much freedom and they run amok."

"Women shouldn't even be speaking of this." Van Gelder turned to Katrina. "I hear you're engaged to the magistrate on Curaçao. You must be very happy."

"Sorry, Captain, no."

"Katrina's upset because she had to leave Hans," Persephone cut in, and then sighed. "I miss Klaus."

Van der Hagen raised an eyebrow. "Who's Hans and who's Klaus?"

"Can we not talk about this now, please?" Katrina snapped.

"Hans is from the village," Persephone continued.

"He is?" Van der Hagen said.

Katrina shushed Persephone.

"She doesn't like being promised to someone she doesn't know," Persephone continued. "Personally, I can't wait."

"Are we there yet?" Katrina said.

They all laughed.

After another hour, everyone agreed it was time to say their good nights.

"Don't worry," Persephone said. "You'll get your sea legs, Countess."

"Goodnight, Captain," Katrina and Persephone said simultaneously and retired to their cabins.

"Goodnight, ladies," van Gelder responded before accompanying Aurora to her cabin. "Now, about your sea legs." He caught her arm.

Aurora frowned at him.

"That's better, but not so rigid." He let go of her. "Relax your knees a bit."

They both rocked with the motion of the ship.

"Like this?" Aurora wobbled.

"Well, almost. The Chartreuse is working."

"It'll do in a pinch, but I'm a Cognac countess at heart."

"I'll open a crate when the storm clears." He gave her a warm smile. "Practice that before you go to bed and before you start walking in the morning. Goodnight, Countess."

"Goodnight, Captain, and thank you." Aurora went into her room and shut the door, then clawed her way to the bed and collapsed.

Helena adjusted an oil lamp, illuminating the cabin, which had been divided in half by a makeshift screen. She and Dodo shared one side, while Gretsch kept the other. *Salamander* slammed down into a series of waves.

Gretsch went to close the porthole, but Helena took out a telescope and braved the spray to peer towards the horizon. *De Heilige Graal* flickered in the distance.

Dodo groaned. "Please, close it."

"Yes, close it," Gretsch agreed.

Helena, her dress now soaked, snapped the porthole shut. She shook herself and the telescope. "We should make these more water-resilient." She glimpsed Gretsch staring at her.

He returned to cleaning his weapons. "You should change into dry clothes."

"I have none."

Gretsch opened a satchel and passed a long nightshirt and linen cloth to Helena and indicated the water barrel nearby. "Clean up and dry off."

"Thank you." She took the items and went into the corner. Feeling his eyes on her, she turned down the lantern. After putting on the nightshirt, she hung the damp peacock blue dress in a corner wardrobe and knelt beside Dodo, who couldn't stop shivering. "Is there something I can do?"

"Just don't open the window again," Dodo chattered. "How do you know if she's even on that ship?" He pulled the blanket closer around him and sat up. "When do we eat?"

"The crewmen said they can't cook in this weather."

"That's fine. I'll freeze to death long before I starve."

Gretsch unwrapped a cloth to reveal a slab of dried meat. "The captain said we can have this until we're through the storm. This will get you by, Painter." He took out a knife and sliced it. "Here. Schinkenspeck."

Helena took the slice of meat as well as the canteen Gretsch handed her.

He returned to his seat to clean a hakenbüchse musket.

Helena sat down with Dodo and turned up the oil lamp, in part to increase its heat.

"Eat it, it's delicious," Helena said, relishing the smoky meat.

Dodo took a bite. "This *is* good." He finished a slice. "This is so good I could live on it."

"The captain gave it to him. I heard him say they ship it, so there's lots."

"It is divine." Dodo finished eating but then began coughing, while continuing to shiver.

Helena wrapped herself in a blanket. "Ares would love it," she said of the meat. Tears welled in her eyes and she sniffled. "At least I know he and Oskar are together."

"So, what's the plan?" Dodo rasped. "Or is there one? Does Baron Gretsch hold us for his master, the emperor? Or Maximilian? Or does he plan to dine on us for the trip over?"

Helena waited for Gretsch to respond. He didn't.

"We're following the countess," said Helena.

They huddled for warmth while lightning flashed outside.

"But are we prisoners or passengers?" Dodo wondered.

Helena eyed Gretsch on her way to her hammock. He seemed asleep with a book in his hands. She climbed into bed. Curiosity got the better of her and she watched Gretsch's droopy face. She pulled a double chin and scowled, imitating his tired features. She pushed her bottom lip out and bent her lips into a frown.

Gretsch turned his head to look at her.

Helena turned over in the hammock, but not before he shook his head.

Cardinal Grimaldi limped along with a crutch beneath his left arm. It was a sunny day in Vatican City, and he was happy to be away from the frigid German landscape. He trod on the lawn outside the Sistine Chapel, drinking in the Roman heat.

A monk approached. "Cardinal Grimaldi, the pope will see you now."

The cardinal entered the rectangular chapel, slowly crossing the opus alexandrium pavement of marble and colored stone. A vaulted ceiling divided frescoes depicting scenes from the book of Genesis, and vibrant Raphael tapestries graced the walls.

The *pièce de résistance* depicted hundreds of figures, a glorious heavenly world floating over the unbridled earth below. *The Last Judgement* by Michelangelo was indeed a splendid fresco. *Someday this will all be mine,* the cardinal thought as he continued to the pope's chamber.

A papal guard met him. "Wait here."

An excited voice echoed from the room. "You see, the light of the sun harvested in a series of chemicals where it can be stored and transformed into energy. I call it solar power!"

"Yes, yes, leave the plans with us," came the pope's voice. "And we shall peruse them thoroughly."

The papal guard escorted the man out and signaled another guard.

"Take him away to be executed."

"What?" the man exclaimed.

The papal guard shook his head. "Inventors! When will they ever learn."

"Indeed," said the cardinal.

"This way," said the papal guard.

Pope Innocent wore a cotton bandage over his right eye, and angry red welts swelled down both his cheeks. His head hung to the side, as if from a laudanum stupor. The papal guard gently nudged him awake.

"Why do you disturb us?" asked Pope Innocent.

"Cardinal Grimaldi to see you, Your Holiness."

"Show them in."

The cardinal bowed.

The papal guard departed.

"What news have you?" the pope demanded.

"I'm afraid we didn't receive the funds as expected from Germany. It seems the Calenberg countess has run off with the goods, so to speak."

"We are confused. Did Prinz Maximilian not take care of the situation weeks ago?" the pope asked.

"He did, but unfortunately Maximilian is not in complete control of Hanover," said the cardinal. "Without the Braunschmidt and Calenberg Treasury, there is not enough to pay the Fuggers's Bank. You know what happens when you don't pay off the Fuggers. The countess escaped to Holland with the entire Braunschmidt payroll. Whilst the Hanover treasury is headed to the Caribbean on a ship called *De Heilige Graal*."

"We cannot believe our ears." The pope's hands flapped. "All of God's plans are going to shit! Where are they now?"

"Our spies say she is on her way to South America, a German colony called Aragua, near Caracas. They have a small port in Lake Maracaibo called Little Venice."

"Lake Maracaibo, in the Caribbean? Oh, fuck us," the pope exclaimed. "We are currently weak in the Caribbean."

"The English have sent agents after her as well, I'm afraid." The cardinal took a step backwards.

"The English? Oh, Jesus Christ! We grow weary of their incompetence." The pope grabbed a blank parchment from his desk and began writing. "Send this at once. Our fastest avisoes. We must have the help of privateers in the Caribbean."

"I will see to it."

"Of course, you will. You will go with them."

"B-but I have an intolerance to heat," the cardinal stammered. "That's why you sent me to Germany."

"Are you questioning us?"

"No, Your Holiness. I meant, I miss Jamaica, oh so very much."

"Don't you forget who we are! We are the pope! You can tell Maximilian that if he ever wants to see the inside of this papacy, he better get down there and find us those thieving witches." The pope's nostrils flared. "And you, Cardinal Grimaldi, shall be responsible for completing the financial transaction with the Fuggers. Go at once and be gone from our sight!"

The cardinal moved to the door.

Pope Innocent spun his wooden globe. "Why must the Caribbean be such a thorn in our sides? We do not trust Cardinal Grimaldi, do we? No, we don't."

The cardinal raised an eyebrow and quickened his pace.

"I have notified Don Medina in San Juan. It's time they paid for their mistakes. Why must the Caribbean haunt us so? Now, bring us some panforte with marzipan and a couple of harlots!"

The Plight of Corsairs and Privateers

An eight-horse carriage clopped along the stone road to La Fortaleza, the executive mansion in the city of San Juan. Guards opened the wrought-iron gate and directed the vehicle to the main entrance. Don Medina, in a red and black doublet with matching breeches, passed through, his aide following.

Governor Santos Carlitos emerged; his white ruff collar quivered as he hurried to meet him. "Don Medina, how wonderful it is to see you again."

They shook hands.

"A pleasure, Governor Carlitos," said the don.

"Bring refreshments to the garden," Carlitos ordered the servants.

The don was escorted through the interior patio, past two circular towers: Homage and Austral Tower. They followed a walkway through a maze of manicured hedges until they reached a babbling stone fountain. Just beyond sat the Bay of San Juan and the mighty fortress of El Morro, currently under construction.

"May I apologize again for the slight misunderstanding with the monkeys," said Carlitos. "It was meant as a gift. I'm not sure what happened."

"Yes, of course it was. Pope Innocent is recovering. But that's not why I'm here. My business is urgent."

They pressed on to the garden, where the sweet fragrance of multicolored roses mixed with the salty sea breeze. Bright red heliconia, resembling lobster claws, flourished in the well-maintained beds. Palm trees provided shade that the governor and the don took full advantage of as they sat down on a stone bench.

"How may I be of help, Don Medina?" Carlitos said.

"It's you who needs my help, Governor. It has come to my attention that King Charles has ordered your execution and that I am to be appointed governor."

"My execution?"

"He has already dispatched a letter to the viceroy. The executioner's delegation from Cuba should be here within the week. I'm to have you arrested today."

"I swear on the Bible, I did not know those monkeys were baboons," insisted Carlitos. "They locked them in a crate for weeks without food. They were happy and smiling on the pamphlet."

"For your dealings with pirates and your botched treasure ship salvage. You reported finding no treasure but flaunt a lavish lifestyle. I warned you."

"For appearances only, Don Medina, I assure you," Carlitos said. "The hurricane wiped us out."

"You asked the king for more money to finish construction on El Morro, then invested in a slave enterprise without approval from myself or the council."

"An investment, as you said. An investment in San Juan."

Don Medina relaxed in his seat. "El Morro was to be completed by now; that itself was to attract investors, to save San Juan from French pirates. Your corsair, Miguel Rivero, is also implicated. You both made good on that wreck without telling us. He's a known pirate. He was almost hanged last year in Santa Catalina."

"Rivero is retired. I swear to God! I merely keep him close by for added protection from pirates and English privateers," Carlitos explained. "It was Sánchez in Santa Catalina who is to blame for our misfortune. He lies."

"I have no desire to be governor, but your life can only be spared by direct intervention from the pope. I have received communication from Cardinal Grimaldi, formerly of Port Royal, now in Germany."

The don's aide passed him documents from a pouch.

"A situation has presented itself that will solve our problems. There's a ship, *De Heilige Graal*, an Anglo-Dutch–owned East Indiaman, which left Friesland carrying a German countess. And she's a witch."

"A witch?" Carlitos said.

"A witch who may be carrying a fortune in gold claimed for the treasury of the Holy Roman Empire. To help appease a strained relationship, His Holiness and Emperor Leopold ordered all resources be allocated to bring this witch to justice and recover the Hanover gold. If you agree to bring me the countess and any gold or documents she may be carrying, then we would be under contract with the Vatican, and you ineligible for execution."

"I would, of course, need to cover expenses."

"Of course. I think four thousand gold pieces is sufficient, don't you? And you take whatever booty the Dutch have on board. To be clear, there can be no link between me, you, and your pirates. There can be no trace of Spanish involvement. I assume you will involve Rivero?"

"He is our most successful corsair. He will bring us the countess and *De Heilige Graal*. I will ensure that the capture of the ship cannot be traced back to us."

The don extended his ring hand. "Thy will be done."

Carlitos knelt to kiss the emerald ring.

The corvette *San Antonio* sailed towards Santo Domingo, tailing several small galiots. Something about one of the ships caught the eye of Corsair Jorge-Miguel José Rivero. He peered through a telescope at *Lamb*, a long, thin barco-luengo galiot. His mouth spread into a grin. "At long last, you shall have vengeance, Father."

Rivero gave the signal, and a red flag was raised to the top of the mainmast. His men readied for attack as Captain Silvestre Soler gave orders.

San Antonio sped up alongside *Lamb* and deployed grappling hooks.

"The ship is yours, Captain Soler." Rivero grabbed a rope tied to a yardarm and swung across, followed by his officers.

Lamb's captain and crew held guns and cutlasses but were outnumbered.

"I am Jorge-Miguel José Rivero. I claim this ship in the name of my father, Miguel Jośe Jorge Rivero."

"I'm Captain George Cole out of Port Royal. I bought this ship legally and am here in Santo Domingo on a mission of commerce. We're just picking up some cocoa, here."

"You will tell me where I can find the buccaneer John Morris," Rivero said.

"With certainty he's probably on his fifth wormwood wine right now, sitting on the privy at the Four Feathers. I can take you to him if ya like?"

"You mock me," Rivero spoke coldly.

"Morris is long retired, my friend," Cole continued. "Now, I insist you let us be on our way, or I shall formally protest."

Rivero drew his rapier. "The ship is mine. You will all surrender."

"That's piracy. You have no legal claim on this ship."

Cole dropped to his knees when the rapier pierced his chest. Burbling sounded in his throat before he fell dead on deck.

Cole's crew were shocked.

"Kill them all," Rivero ordered, and his men dispatched them, dumping their bodies overboard.

"For my father I rename this ship *Fama*, as it was always meant to be," Rivero said. "For those who took her I shall give no quarter."

Off Santo Domingo, beneath the afternoon sun, *San Antonio* sailed alongside *Fama*. An aviso approached and a messenger passed Silvestre a scroll. Rivero swung over.

"Message from Carlitos in San Juan," said Silvestre.

Rivero read it. "We are now working for His Holiness. Under no circumstances may we engage in any acts of piracy against the English. Use the French privateer to find *De Heilige Graal*."

"*De Heilige Graal*?" Silvestre said. "The cup of Christ?"

"No, a ship. A ship carrying untold riches and a German witch," Rivero said. "Sail at once. I'll refit *Fama* myself. Call the men for a pirate attack and meet us there."

"How do we explain this in the log?" replied Silvestre.

"We'll say they were carrying stolen goods from that hell-pit, Port Royal. I'll meet you at Isla Cangrejo."

A blanket of stars reflected against the Bermuda water. The long galiot, *Rascal*, with its devil figurehead, seemed to claw its way forward. Its oars propelled along the shallow coast until lights twinkled from the nearby town.

Major Thomas Paine stood on deck with the moon behind him. His wide-brimmed hat cast his face in complete darkness as he pointed off the starboard bow.

The pilot, Jakob Fokman, adjusted the tiller. Waves splashed off the reef as the ship drew closer to land.

Paine made the call of a sea bird, and the men readied their weapons. *Rascal* maneuvered to a dock next to an inn. From inside, a fiddler churned out a tune, while silhouettes danced beneath the warm glow of hanging lanterns.

"Return in one hour, if you please, Mr. Fokman," said Paine.

"Aye, sir." Fokman climbed up to the tiller.

"Let her run," Paine said.

The oarsmen pulled their oars from the water and the ship glided in silence. Fokman turned the tiller, steering towards a small wharf. Paine's knees cracked as he swung from the deck to shore.

Fokman signaled.

The men smiled in silence as they dipped the oars back in the oily water.

Paine proceeded toward a three-level house, sitting next to a drawbridge. He lit his cigar. Two shadowy figures emerged from a stable.

Paine turned down a narrow passage to the fishing dock, creeping in the shadows behind the cleaning station. He waited. Cutthroats were searching ahead.

Paine's hands shook, trying to grip his gun. Then came an explosion of gunpowder and sparks. He staggered from the recoil of the blunderbuss. The bodies of the cutthroats fell into the sea. The blast from the gun echoed for miles, while smoke wafted over the bay. Fiddling resumed and drunken laughter continued.

Paine drew his pistols and crossed the drawbridge to Sandys Tavern. Once inside, he scanned the room. In a dimly lit corner sat Lieutenant William Kidd, a pewter stein on the table in front of him. Kidd's head hung low as if asleep.

Paine approached; blunderbuss visible on his belt.

"I know that gun," Kidd said. "I'd know that gun anywhere."

Paine sat opposite.

Kidd's beard was overgrown and bedraggled. His clothes reeked of perspiration, brine and ale. "I didn't expect ya. Yer supposed to be defending Newport from French bastards. Who were your friends outside?"

"French bastards, who else. Why are you still here?" Paine probed.

"I'm cursed." Kidd managed another mouthful of ale. "That's what it is. Cursed. Yer doctor cursed me."

"I left you in charge of the good doctor." Paine raised an eyebrow. "I warned you, my old friend. You let your crew get the better of you, and here you are, smelling and looking like ya crawled out of kraken dung."

Kidd waved his hand. "Your doctor ran off with my ship."

"Your crew ran off with your ship and my doctor," Paine corrected.

Kidd tipped forward, half conscious. With one eye scoping the table, he corralled his remaining coins.

"Perhaps you should retire?" Paine said.

"Coming from you? I'm in me prime, laddie. Maybe they'll elect you admiral of the Brethren. How'd ya like that?"

"Then I'd be obliged to turn it down. I'm home to retire." Paine signalled the barmaid. "Another round of drinks and his accommodation for the night."

"I'm retired, he says." Kidd laughed. "You said that in '83 and '85 and '89. Retired, my buckled shoe. You're retired and I'm Mary, Queen of fuckin' Scots."

Paine handed over a gold coin to the barmaid who delivered the drinks.

"Much obliged." Kidd revived and took a mouthful.

"I want you to command an expedition, Billy," Paine said.

"On the morrow, I sail for New York. My benefactors want a report on my progress. Ever been in a gibbet? I'll stay here and help you—you're gonna need it." Kidd gestured for

Paine to come closer. "I intend to demand the bastards fund me a new ship so I can track down the scum who betrayed me. Nice knowin' ya." Kidd finished his drink.

"Incidentally, those men you blew away belong to your old friend Pierre le Picard. It's not a rowdy bunch of renegades but a major force, under a letter of marque by the governor of Acadia," Kidd continued. "They're waiting for the English to move so they can lure 'em out. Then they'll try for Newport, my source says."

"The job I got for you is in the Leeward Islands," said Paine.

"I'm not particularly fond of the Leeward Islands, don't ya know. Madagascar's where it's at now."

"Don't forget we both owe the same bank. Our investors in New York insist, and they're willing to forgive and forget if this gets done," Paine said.

"What is the deed that needs done?"

"A Dutch ship carrying a German countess. You must capture the ship and the countess alive. Alive," Paine reiterated.

"Alive," Kidd said. "That tends to complicate matters these days."

"She's important. It must be done legally, or, if that's not possible, then under a pirate flag. It's top secret."

"Top secret?"

"I can't say it any clearer. You must capture her safely and alive!"

"Got it." Kidd belched. "Top secret, alive, capture the Dutch countess in the German ship."

"Don't make me put ya to bed, Billy. I left the plans with Fokman; he'll remember on the morrow. Yer meeting Gilbert and Tewsteps on *Amity*. *Rascal* will be here in an hour to fetch you. Your payment is on board." Paine finished his drink and patted Kidd on the back. He departed, tipping his hat to the barmaid.

"*De Heilige Graal.*" Kidd laughed.

"What's humorous about that?" asked the barmaid.

"It's a joke, lass. It's the *Holy Grail*."

South by Southwest

Aurora stumbled downstairs from the main deck and worked her way aft. She advanced to a stack of barrels, expecting to find tobacco. Aurora held up her candle to read the label. It indicated *highly explosive*. She backed away carefully before blowing out the candle—and backed right into an officer.

"Ah, good!" she said. "Which way to the grand cabin?"

"Aft. Right through there."

"Aft right?"

"Come with me, Countess." The officer led her up a staircase.

Once back in familiar territory, Aurora found the grand cabin. She knocked and entered.

"There you are." Van der Hagen took a sip from a crystal glass. "I thought you'd run off."

"I got lost."

"It can happen. She's a big ship."

They sat down to dinner and slaves served them. Holly, Persephone's nanny, was dressed in white linen; the letters VH had been branded on her arm. She brought over a bottle of Cognac for Aurora.

"I'll pour myself," Aurora said. "Our houses are very different, Viscount."

"Aboard *De Heilige Graal*, you'll find only the very best in comfort and luxury. I'm sorry we haven't had a chance to speak privately so far. On this trip I've been kept busy. I hope your cabin is to your liking?"

"It's fine, thank you. Your ship is charming. Though I wonder if I could access your ship's store. I seem to be out of tobacco."

"Yes, I underestimated. Two barrels wasn't enough. I will send for another." He gave her a smile. "Despite what Katrina says, my ships are clean, and I don't mistreat my slaves. Prepare my pipe," he said to Holly, who did as instructed.

Aurora took a mouthful of dinner. It stuck in her throat like a wad of cotton when she tried to swallow, so she took a gulp of wine.

"You may not remember, but we have met before. I knew your father."

"At least one of us did," Aurora said. "Yes, I remember. I was seven and I saw my father off at the ships when he left me with Aunt Sophie. You were taking him away to war. I was very rude to you, if I remember?"

"Oh, yes. You told me what you would do to me if your father did not return. Fortunately, he did. At least for a while." Van der Hagen sat back, letting his legs splay.

Aurora stared at her glass. "That was the Battle of Vienna?"

"Yes, it was back in '83. I was to transport demi-cannons to Trieste to reinforce the Hapsburg lines. We sailed all the way down there, only to find out the Ottomans besieged Vienna in July." He lit his pipe and inhaled deeply.

Aurora wondered if there was more Cognac.

"The Polish, Lithuanian Holy League and armies of the Holy Roman Empire were ready to drive them out," Van der Hagen continued. "Calenberg's armies were fighting alongside the Polish armies, side by side, while Gretsch's Reiters reinforced the Viennese Garrison."

Van der Hagen rattled off more leagues and nations while Aurora listened to the sound of her finger stroking the rim of her glass.

"Well, we drove those fuckers out of Europe for good in Vienna," said the viscount.

"What an amazing battle strategy. You mentioned Maximillian Gretsch?"

"Yes, Baron Maximillian Graf von Gretsch commanded Calenberg's Reiters."

"Baron Gretsch's Reiters were there that night."

"The night you fled?" Van der Hagen paused. "You fled from Reiters?"

"Sophie didn't tell you?"

"No, she didn't. This is most disturbing. Gretsch is not someone to be trifled with."

"He serves my cousin Maximilian, the Prinz Elector, apparently. Maxi hasn't been in his right mind lately, I'm afraid." Aurora prodded her supper with a fork. "I don't know what scheme he's concocted now. He's not the same as he was when we were young. He's crueler, power-hungry."

"Gretsch is fiercely loyal to the House of Hanover. Sophie currently sits in that chair. I have a palace in St. Eustatius. When we get there, I'll hide you away for a while. At least until your privateer arrives from Aragua."

"I hate to impose, but maybe just until the others arrive?"

"No imposition at all."

Shrieks of female laughter resonated from the cabin above.

Van der Hagen finished his drink and poured another, topping up Aurora's glass.

"Well, the girls are certainly enjoying Captain van Gelder's company tonight." He rose and used his walking stick to hit the ceiling. "Behave up there!"

More laughter.

Aurora sat silent for a moment, drinking, and listening to the barely audible voices. Swiftly, she brushed away a tear, remembering Helena's face. "Sorry."

Van der Hagen held her hand. "Your handmaiden?"

"Yes, how did you know?"

"Persephone told me. She knows how much you miss her. Therefore, it's so important to have slaves; you don't want to be emotionally attached to the help."

Aurora glanced at Holly, who looked away before eye contact could be made. "Helena's not my servant. She's a Braunschmidt. She's been my best friend since I was little. I've never been away from her. The last time I saw her, we were at the annual Christmas ball. I never even said goodbye." She poured herself another drink. "Forgive me, I'm not good company tonight. Let's join the girls for some cribbage, shall we?"

"Certainly."

Aurora took his arm, and they went upstairs.

Aboard *Salamander*, Helena sat in the corner under the bowsprit beam of the forecastle. The boat rocked briskly. She opened the porthole to enjoy the fresh morning air.

Gretsch evidently had the same idea, as he stood just outside.

"Bleah!" Helena shuddered and relatched the porthole.

Later in the morning, Helena joined Dodo for a painting session at the ship's forecastle.

Gretsch emerged from the forward cabin to join Bohn and first officer Doorman on the quarterdeck.

"She's very beautiful," said Doorman. "Like a Renaissance girl."

"You're just lonely. She's too plump and lumpy for me. The countess, I assume, is more beautiful," said Bohn. "*De Helige Graal* is no longer in sight, Baron. Please join me in my cabin for dinner this evening. The three of you."

"Certainly. The three of us?" Gretsch said.

"Yes, please."

"*Scheisse.*"

Dodo protected his paints and brushes as the wind picked up.

Helena's hairstyle began to unravel, and she held it in place with her hand. "She sailed off without us. She didn't even want to go."

"She can hardly be blamed as the brains behind the plan," Dodo said. "You're hurt, but you shouldn't be. She's probably worried sick about us."

"You think so?"

"Of course. She loves us both, I know it."

Helena snorted. "She loves Cognac, cock, coca-leaf and tobacco."

"And us, I tell you. She is lost without you."

"That is true," Helena said. "She is hopeless."

The gust of wind came, and Dodo clutched the easel.

"We're going to have to wrap up soon," Helena said. "I'm making dinner for the whole ship."

"You are? That's absurd," Dodo said. "Why?"

"The captain said some of the vegetables weren't stored properly and were going to get thrown over. I looked through them and found some that were still edible. We can't waste good food, as we are in danger of running out."

"I agree. I love your cooking."

"Then you'll help?"

"Help?" Dodo lowered his brush.

"Yes, help."

"Help cook?"

"Yes."

"Uh, no. I'm an artist; I only cook on canvas."

"Fine, you can spend the afternoon with Baron Gretsch."

"I'm surprised Baron von Grouch approved."

"He didn't. So, let's keep it between us."

"This is getting interesting," Dodo said. "If Max Grouch doesn't approve, then I'm in."

"We need to keep him far away from the galley until later this afternoon."

"How do we do that?"

Gretsch was charging along the deck below on his way to the forecastle.

Dodo knocked his tray, and it was almost caught by the wind. He yanked it back, sending a jar of paint thinner spilling over the rail.

Gretsch cursed loudly, going back the way he came.

"How was that?" Dodo said.

"*Wunderbar*!"

Later, inside the cookhouse, Helena filled a large pot of water and cranked it over a fire. She added spices and started chopping beet roots.

"Borsch?" Dodo cringed.

"Sometimes it's the only thing Aurora can eat after a long weekend. We had to live off this for weeks, back in Transylvania. Keep cutting."

"Me? These are disgusting. People don't eat this part." Dodo reluctantly picked up a knife.

"Yes, they do. This is the Polish recipe. It's not my favorite, but it'll do with what we have."

"You learned a Polish recipe in Transylvania?"

"*Ja*, I was born there. Aurora and I spent several years there with Freddie and Max, fighting against the Ottomans," Helena said.

"Do you remember your mama?"

"No, she died when I was a baby."

A look of horror filled Dodo's face as his hands turned a deep purple. He scraped more into the pot. "This could make a good dye. Purple is a difficult color to get the pigment just right." As an experiment, he dipped his sleeve in the pot.

"You can paint, but you can't cook. Both are messy."

"Yes, well, one is art, and one is woman's work."

"Woman's work?" Helena gave him a stony stare. "You're going to have to do these things yourself, sooner or later. Woman's work? You make women's dresses!"

Dodo thought a moment before both laughed.

When dusk arrived, Helena and Dodo went to the captain's cabin. Helena knocked.

"Come," Bohn said.

Inside the cabin lay a spread of bird trimmings and dried meat. Gretsch stood up at Helena's presence.

"Come in, Dame Helena." Bohn kissed her hand.

"She's not a dame; she is under my charge," said Gretsch.

Helena gave him a sideways glare.

"All the same, she graces us with her presence," Bohn said.

"How do you do, Captain?" Helena said. "This is Dodo von Knyphausen, the countess's portrait painter and dress designer."

"Fashion designer extraordinaire," Dodo insisted.

Gretsch snarled as he sat.

Bohn closed the cabin door and patted Helena's shoulder. "Please join me."

Helena recoiled and sat next to Dodo. They were served wine as both eyed the plate of dried meat.

"I see you are acquainted with Schinkenspeck," said Bohn.

"Yes, indeed. It's divine." Dodo helped himself to a slice.

"Thankfully, we have enough. I had a shipment to sell, which didn't come to pass. There's enough for weeks, and I would not have sailed without it."

"I am grateful," Gretsch said.

"So am I." Dodo chewed happily. "I hear the soup is delicious as well."

"Yes, the young lady made it."

"She did?" Gretsch stared at Helena.

"Yes. I hope you are not offended, Dame Helena, but I had fire control on standby," said Bohn.

"You should have checked with me first," Gretsch said.

"Sorry, but we can't have food spoiling," Helena replied.

"It's not appropriate. I give you too much freedom on this ship."

"She's done us a service," said Bohn. "Provided we're not shitting our guts all over the side by daybreak." He laughed. "I won't ask you why you're chasing *De Heilige Graal*, but I do insist on knowing what dangers may lie ahead for my ship and crew. So, why are you chasing *De Heilige Graal*? Who am I going to tell?"

"The countess of Calenberg herself is on that ship," Gretsch said. "I must contact her. I believe her life to be in danger."

"Is there a chance we can catch *De Heilige Graal*?" Helena asked.

"Not unless she stops. You didn't give us much time. We'll have to stop in the Leeward Islands," Bohn said. "*De Heilige Graal* is the superior ship, I'm afraid. You might have been better off if you had kept looking for a faster vessel. You have no idea what I'm putting this ship and crew through just to try to keep up."

"I understand, Captain," Gretsch said. "I will pay extra for the inconvenience."

"It's not the money. But you're welcome, of course. There are hundreds of places she could go to in those islands. What will you do if they aren't there?"

"I will need to hire another ship," Gretsch said. "To continue the search. Preferably a faster ship than yours."

"I understand completely," Bohn said. "I'm in need of a new ship. *Salamander* has seen better days, as the English say. She's past her prime."

Helena glanced out the window, searching for her countess.

After a stormy night, sun broke through the clouds, drying the deck of *De Heilige Graal*. Aurora entered the grand stateroom whistling. She joined Katrina and Persephone at the breakfast table.

"You're cheerful this morning," said Katrina.

"I saw Helena last night in my dream," said Aurora.

"Was she a ghost?" asked Katrina.

"No," Aurora snapped. "She's trying to find me."

"Perhaps it's witchcraft," said Persephone.

"She calls it *moonraking*," said Aurora. "She believes she can travel in her dreams."

"Do you believe she came to you in the dream?" said Katrina. "Or was it just a dream?"

"My moonraker came to me."

"There are moonrakers on the ship," Persephone said.

"How do you know?" said Aurora.

"The topmost sail is a moonraker. That's what Captain Van Gelder calls them."

"Can you climb that high?" asked Aurora.

"I've been to the crow's nest. Not on this ship, but the crow's nest is at the very top."

After breakfast they went on deck, taking advantage of the periodic sunshine. Aurora put up her hand to block the glare as she looked up to the top of the mast. The crow's nest beckoned. She could tell Helena all about it. With the help of Katrina and Persephone, Aurora was fitted with a makeshift climbing outfit.

Van Gelder and de Britt stood at the wheelhouse watching the horizon.

"Have the watch," van Gelder said to de Britt. "Careful on deck, Countess."

She gave him a quaint smile before leaning on the rail, watching the crew maneuver through the rigging at shift change. She took a deep breath and ventured downstairs to the main deck.

Aurora tucked away her raincoat in between rope lines. She felt naked wearing trousers, a buttoned shirt, and boots. When no one was watching, her shaky hands clutched the rigging, and she began her ascent. Very slowly she moved, knowing everyone was watching—waiting for her to fall and break her neck. She was determined not to give them the satisfaction.

Aurora eventually reached the platform of the mast and took a break. The cool sea air saturated her skin. Helena, she thought, would love to do something like this. *Don't look down,* she told herself. Her eyes betrayed her.

The crow's nest wasn't far now. She grabbed the rigging and finished the climb. It felt like being at the top of the world, surrounded by deep blue ocean and floating gray clouds. A moment of vertigo had her clutching the lines. "*Scheisse!*" Below her, *De Heilige Graal* looked miniature. *Now, how do I get down?*

Sunrise on the Atlantic Ocean bore tones of turquoise and brilliant orange, with foamy crests churning on the water's surface. *Salamander* parted the way serenely on its course towards the Caribbean. Helena marvelled at the view, while Dodo snored softly behind her.

After breakfast, Dodo ventured outside to paint, while a copper wash tub was brought in for Helena, large enough to kneel in. Crewmen brought pitchers of hot water from the cookhouse. Once full, Helena disrobed, sinking into the warmth.

Helena massaged a sea sponge across her arms, then over her upper back, stopping to scratch a pimple on her shoulder.

Footsteps approached from the cookhouse. Gretsch's footsteps. They stopped abruptly. His reflection appeared in a mirror hanging on the wall. His dark eyes invaded her.

Her first instinct was to cover up, but instead she continued to bathe. She stood, teasingly washing her backside. After sudsing her entire body in olive oil soap, she crouched in the tub, using a pitcher to rinse off.

Gretsch entered, going to his corner to work, his back to her. He appeared to be brooding.

"I didn't hear you come in," she said, quickly finishing the bath and grabbing linen to cover herself. She slid on a cotton shirt that hung down to her knees. "I fixed your telescope for you." She ventured out from her side of the room and went to his table.

"Fixed?" He extended it and looked through. He seemed impressed as he tested it through the porthole. "Quite clever."

While she was getting dressed, she felt Gretsch's eyes upon her. It was so peculiar to hear anything complimentary coming out of his mouth that Helena had no idea how to react to this attention. She scratched absently at a scar on her chest.

"Does it hurt?"

Helena was unable to think what he meant for a moment. "What?"

"The scar?"

"Oh, that." A scar between her breasts. Its origin was something she had no memory of. It had always been there, and she always kept it covered. "How do you know?"

Gretsch set down the telescope and took her hand in his. "We've both been inches from death." They were face to face now, mouths so close they might have kissed.

A chill crept up her spine, and she withdrew. She headed to the forecastle, where Dodo was painting a seascape.

"I heard a crewman say we're almost there," he said. "We should see land tomorrow."

"*Ja*, I heard the same thing."

Helena sat on a chair and struck a pose. He switched canvases.

"Think she'll be there?"

"In St. Eustatius? I hope so."

"What do you think they'll do to us?"

"I don't know. Maybe they'll sell us to the Dutch or Spanish," Helena said. "Or, maybe they'll execute us for being witches."

"I have pondered that possible outcome." Dodo watched her for a moment and continued to paint.

"Anything's better than being prisoner to the foul Baron Gretsch."

"Oh? I thought you were warming up to him. He's taken with you."

"Don't make me sick. He's unsettling."

"I was joking. He might settle for your painting."

"The man is utterly repugnant." Helena laughed.

A door swung open and Gretsch emerged.

They fell silent.

"Arm higher, please," Dodo said.

"That's as high as it's going."

"You two are expected at the captain's table tonight. Your dress is clean. Seven bells. Be prompt." Gretsch walked on towards the aft.

Helena stuck out her tongue.

"What was that?" Dodo asked.

"Zat vas Baron Maximillian Graf von Gretsch of das Calenberg Reiters," Helena replied, doing her best imitation.

Dodo pointed to the sea. "No, that!"

Helena looked to the water. A porpoise jumped out at the bow, then another.

"Perhaps we should go inside?" Dodo said.

"Inside? Are you mad? These are dolphins—or porpoises!"

"And they can jump out of the water. I don't want to be breakfast!"

"Paint this!"

"It's hard to get the pose just right."

Helena's eyes lit up as the creatures followed alongside the ship. Playing and chasing each other along the bow. There came a loud crack. One of the animals spurted blood. It veered off, disappearing into the tide.

Helena stormed to the railing, where Doorman and other crewmen were laughing as they aimed muskets.

"What are you doing? You stupid fools, why?" Helena slapped one of the men upside the head. "Stop it, right now!"

Doorman yanked her arm.

Gretsch appeared, a pistol and an axe-pistol aimed at Doorman's head. "Unhand her, or I shoot."

Bohn bounded down the stairs from the quarterdeck. He aimed his pistol at Gretsch. "You're aiming a weapon at one of my men, Baron Gretsch."

"This girl is under my authority. These men will not touch her," Gretsch hissed. "Ever!"

"She attacked us!" Doorman said.

"Shut up," Bohn said. "You'll speak when spoken to. Baron Gretsch, you'll lower your weapon, or I will fire. Let her go."

Doorman released her and Gretsch lowered his weapon.

"What the hell is this all about? What were you doing to the girl?" Bohn asked.

"As I said, she attacked us," Doorman said. "Over a fish."

"Those animals are not yours to kill," Helena asserted.

"Baron Gretsch, take the young lady inside and keep her there. Then join me in my cabin. I want a word."

"I won't let them harm these creatures."

"We'll be arriving in the Leeward Islands in two days. You'll stay in your accommodation till we get there. Baron Gretsch, I command the ship." Bohn addressed his crew. "To your stations. Trim the sheets. We must maintain speed, damn it."

Doorman and the crew got to work.

Gretsch escorted her to the cabin. He said nothing, but Helena caught a thin smile as he opened the door for her.

Inside, Dodo waited, brush in hand. "I told you we should have gone inside. May we continue?"

Helena resumed posing.

Later, beneath the crescent moon and the stars of the glowing Milky Way, Helena snuck out to the bow, with Dodo trailing.

"You realize we'll be flayed if we're caught?" Dodo said.

"I just want to see the stars. It's the first clear night in ages." Helena's mouth was ajar as she stared up.

"Do you really believe there are wonders and far-off places out there?" Dodo looked up.

"I'm sure of it."

"How will we get there?"

"Magnetics."

"I don't believe in magic-netics."

"Magnetics isn't a belief; it's science," Helena said. "The magnets, like in a compass, can be used to propel us to other worlds out there someday."

"Magnets can't do that." Dodo smirked.

"It's a magnetic force which makes the moon go around the earth. And the earth, and other planets go around the sun. Even comets can go around the sun." Helena sighed happily. "We can make ships that sail on magnets to go around all of them."

"This is why they want to burn you as a witch." Dodo pursed his lips. "You're quite the dreamer."

"I bet you, a hundred years from now, we will have ships that sail through the sky, propelled by magnets instead of wind. Those ships will be able to take us anywhere we want to go. Anywhere."

"You're on. How much are you betting?"

Helena smiled, catching a glimpse of Gretsch lighting his pipe next to the porthole.

"It is a nice dream. I hope someday you will see your flying magnet ships, Helena," Dodo said.

"So do I." She lay back to enjoy the stars.

By sunrise, *De Heilige Graal* was east of the Leeward Islands. Another brilliant sky came and went, and mountainous islands appeared ahead. After breakfast, everyone lounged in the grand cabin next to the open windows, drinking a Dutch beverage called *koffie*. Aurora enjoyed the smooth, bitter drink and poured herself another. Slaves cleared away the dishes while Van der Hagen peered through a telescope out the starboard side.

"I know!" Persephone jumped up and down, flapping her elbows. "Well, what am I?"

"An idiot?" Van der Hagen offered.

They all laughed.

"Come on. I'm a dodo!"

"Yes, you are," her father agreed.

Katrina looked at the window. "I, for one, am very sad for the dodo."

"I miss my Dodo," Aurora said.

"You had a dodo?" Persephone asked.

"He paints me."

"Your dodo can paint?"

"No, Dodo's my painter," Aurora said. "But I did have a pet dodo as a little girl."

"What happened to it?" Katrina said.

"I had two. A boy and a girl. We took them with us to Transylvania. They got out one night in a blizzard and froze to death."

"Any bird that can't even fly deserves to die. It's God's will," said Van der Hagen.

"I heard that there's only two left, and they're both male," Persephone said.

"Helena thinks maybe it wasn't quite a bird. She said maybe it's a creature trying to become a bird but hasn't learned how to fly. Or a bird that no longer wants to be a bird."

They all stared at her.

"She can be unconventional at times," Aurora said.

"Aurora says Helena visits her in her dreams," Persephone said.

"Pure fantasy, I assure you." Van der Hagen lit his pipe. "Now don't let me hear you girls talking such nonsense. Katrina, if all the dodos die, it's God's will, and 'thy will be done.'" He sighed. "Why didn't I have sons?"

"Hey!" Persephone smacked her father's arm.

Katrina looked out the window with a telescope. "What kind of ship is that?"

A small ship with triangular sails sped by.

"It's so fast." Aurora pressed her face to the window.

"That's a mail runner. You can cross the Atlantic in less than half the time with one of those. My father has three of them, going back and forth all the time," Persephone said.

"Why didn't we take one of those?" asked Aurora.

"Oh, they're dreadfully uncomfortable!" Persephone looked mortified. "You'd be lucky to get a hammock."

"I only sail on my flagship," said Van der Hagen. "Besides, you need protection."

Another ship appeared in the distance.

Aurora looked closer. "I don't see anything."

"Let me take a look." Van der Hagen used his telescope. "Another ship. In fact, more than one. And trouble. I'll be right back."

"I'll come, too," Aurora said.

They went upstairs to the captain's cabin and knocked on the door. Inside, van Gelder and de Britt were reviewing charts.

"Viscount Van der Hagen, and Countess, it seems we have reached the Caribbean only to find ourselves in a war," van Gelder began. "A mail runner informed us of the formal declaration between France and the alliance."

Van Gelder led them to the side window gallery with a mounted telescope. Both looked. At least forty ships sat within a blanket of smoke, some aflame, some sinking.

"You can see our dilemma," van Gelder said.

"What do you recommend?" said Van der Hagen.

Van Gelder consulted the charts. "We should turn south. There's no way to get through to St. Eustatius from the eastern side. We can see how it looks down around Guadeloupe, and, if it's clear, come up here from the west."

"And if it's not?" Van der Hagen asked.

"We could go straight on to Tobago."

"Very well, turn south. Make for the Guadeloupe Passage."

Van Gelder headed back on deck.

Flames and plumes of smoke engulfed St. Kitts. Dozens of English warships in a line formation across the eastern horizon bombarded the island.

Pirates Raid St. Eustatius

Baron Gretsch rose from his desk. Helena was in the copper tub behind him. He approached and she rose. Droplets of water fell from her breasts, and he tongued them away. His manhood stiffened and he caught her mouth with his.

Helena guided him to the cot in the corner and lay down, her legs parted, beckoning him to enter. Gretsch unbuttoned his trousers, member throbbing, almost bursting as it brushed against her silky thigh. He entered her, engulfed in warm, wet pleasure. He thrust into her, flicking her nipples with his tongue. She groaned, biting her lip, and her insides spasmed.

Gretsch pumped into her, harder, faster, until he finished. Visions of blood plagued him. Raped and murdered women, impaled bodies and heads half severed at the neck filled him with nausea. Mutilated corpses and horrific screams on the battlefield rampaged through his mind. Helena tried to scream, but all that came out was a burbling of blood. Gretsch looked down at the knife in his hand; he had cut her throat.

There came a knock at the door.

Gretsch woke, his face wet with tears. He gasped, trying to get air into his lungs. There was another knock. He quickly wiped his face before answering it. But when he got there, whoever it was had left. Composing himself, he went up to the dark deck.

"Lights out," Bohn ordered and scanned the horizon through a telescope. "Join us, please, Baron."

Gretsch peered ahead. Below, at the heads, Helena and Dodo snuck out for a look as the ship went dark. Gretsch exhaled at the sight of Helena.

"Those are ships of the line," said Bohn. "How many I can't tell."

"Too many and too scattered to count," Doorman replied.

"This is no small engagement. There are French, English, Dutch, maybe even Spanish in this fight." Bohn's mouth was downturned. "Now, Doorman spotted a large East Indiaman in the early daylight hours heading in this direction. He's positive it was *De Helige Graal.*"

"I'm certain it was her," Doorman said. "That would put her on course for St. Eustatius."

"And it would put me on course for captain of the year, getting you there. But it could have been another ship; there's a lot like her around. There's also a good chance she made a turn," Bohn said.

"Which way would she turn?" Gretsch asked.

"Pick a direction: St. Martin, St. Barts, Barbados, or Tobago. What we don't have is food, only Schinkenspeck."

"Please, no more Schinkenspeck!" Dodo groaned.

"Quiet down there," Bohn said. "You should be inside."

"Helena," Gretsch spoke, not unkindly. "Go inside."

Lights flashed ahead and a deep rumble vibrated the sea and sky. Fiery shots lit the heavens, revealing another line of ships.

"What exactly are we running away from?" Dodo asked.

"There's also the possibility that *De Heilige Graal* is sunk or taken," said Doorman.

"I was going to mention those possibilities as well," Bohn replied. "We'll remain on course."

"We will?" Doorman said.

"Yes. You see, it's too late to turn to port or starboard. The French are turning to go back around St. Kitts. The English, I'm assuming, are heading for St. Barts. They won't be turning against the wind; their lines will move off northwest. We land on St. Eustatius and find out where *De Heilige Graal* went."

Later that night, *Salamander* continued its course towards St. Eustatius. A battle went on around them. Ships of the line fired at each other, igniting the sky with smoke and gunpowder.

Helena emerged on the forecastle.

"Go to bed!" Gretsch insisted.

"I'm just getting some fresh air." She coughed. "Who the hell can sleep, anyway?"

"I will, if you give me more of that tonic," Dodo added.

"Dodo, you have to see this," Helena said.

"No, I don't. Where's that bottle, Baron Grou—Baron Gretsch, may I have some more of that bottle?"

"Helena, get inside and stay down," Gretsch said.

She complied, closing the door, but continued to monitor the scene through the porthole while periodically tending to Dodo.

Sainte Andrew, a new East Indiaman, sat in the harbor next to Fort Orange in St. Eustatius. Her cannons sat ready, anticipating trouble, while the town continued its usual business. *Salamander* waited offshore.

Helena peered out of the porthole at a smoking town, hectic with ships coming and going. People scurried around loading carts, preparing, as if expecting disaster. It was very much how Hanover had looked when she left.

Gretsch entered the cabin.

"We going ashore or what, me hearties?" Dodo swung breezily in a hammock.

"How much did you give him?" Gretsch asked.

"More than the recommended dosage."

"Good thinking. You carry him when it starts to wear off. I'm going ashore. *De Heilige Graal* is not here. Doorman is a fool. You wait here. I must find out where she went and arrange another ship."

"Are we safe here?" Helena looked him in the eye.

"No. Don't leave this room." Gretsch departed.

Helena withdrew the recently sharpened Athame dagger that Helmut had given her.

Dodo clumsily climbed out of the hangmat. "Is Baron Grump gone?"

"He is."

"Then let's get out of here. We'll be safer away from all this." Dodo packed his portable easel. "We must bring the paintings."

"We can't carry them," said Helena.

"But they're my best work! I can't leave them."

"They must dry."

"That's true. I'll send for them."

"Yes, send for them. Grab the blanket and that big coat the captain lent you."

"Oh, the big coat." Dodo deepened his voice. "Hi there, I'm a big sailor!"

"Keep it down!" Helena changed into the shimmering peacock blue dress that gathered at the back.

"Fancy," Dodo giggled. "They'll see you."

"I can't go running around town in a night shirt."

They finished packing and snuck onto the deck at the bow. Longboats sat waiting below. Helena threw her satchel down first, then climbed over.

Dodo handed her his easel and case of paints. "How far is it?" His legs hung down, dangling like a frog.

"Only a few feet." Helena grabbed his foot.

"Whoa!" He let go, nearly landing on her.

"Quiet!" Helena hissed.

Dodo belched loudly. "That doesn't count. It was involuntary."

Before grabbing the oars, Helena untied the other two longboats, and they drifted away.

"I'm just fitting in," Dodo asserted.

She began rowing.

Behind them she could hear Doorman shouting. "They're getting away!"

"That's right. We're just big happy sailors heading into a war zone," said Dodo.

Doorman cursed. "She untied the boats—get them back!"

The harbor was so littered with ships that Helena had to navigate around larger vessels. The fort fired its guns and the haze from the explosion wafted along the coast. Boats landed on the beach and armed men charged into the village, shooting, stabbing, and throwing grenades. A cart blew up in the street, sending townsfolk running for cover.

"Amazing!" Dodo exclaimed. "Am I imagining all this?"

"No." Helena snarled. "Artists!"

They reached the beach and scrambled out of the way of running people.

"Where do we go?" a fleeing townsperson chased down a dock official.

"French pirates have taken the island," the official said before shouting through a trumpet. "We must all leave. Board the Sainte *Andrew*. We must evacuate."

Helena and Dodo followed the crowd through the fort gates. "Try to blend in," Helena said. "Look like a married couple."

Dodo put his arms around her. "Just you and me, honeypot."

"Not happily married, just married." She caught sight of Gretsch and Bohn rushing to the *Salamander*, while Doorman led a longboat coming ashore. She pulled Dodo aside and they detoured through a warehouse that reeked of fish.

Helena pushed Dodo ahead onto the gangway.

"I'm going to need another bottle, if you're going to get me on this ship," Dodo said.

"Those crates are labeled *Calenberg*." Helena pointed. "It's from Calenberg Castle. This is one of the ships taking the castle to Jamaica. We must board. I can contact Sophie through her business associates in Port Royal." She prodded him along, with her fist in his side.

"Ouch, what are you doing?"

"Looking like a married couple."

Halfway up the gangway, they were stuck in a long line of people. Helena glanced back at the dock. Captain Bohn was retreating to *Salamander*, while Gretsch was nowhere to be seen.

Eventually they boarded the *Sainte Andrew*, trying to be inconspicuous. People pushed and shoved. Helena felt as though she were drowning in other people's sweat and fear. The tension grew as screams erupted and people shouted "pirates!"

Helena and Dodo headed for the bow of the ship but were halted at blade-point and herded back to the main deck with the rest of the townspeople and the ship's captain.

"This ship is ours!" a young, fair-haired pirate declared.

His accomplices cheered.

"You are all hostages of the freebooters of St. Kitts. Set sail!"

The lines to the ship detached and longboats towed the ship from the harbor. By evening, *Sainte Andrew* had drifted away from St. Eustatius.

Rascal glided into the docks of St. Eustatius; its deck full of angry rogues ready to disembark. Captain William Kidd stood among them. A cutlass and a brace of pistols hung on a leather belt around his waist, while a blunderbuss was ready in his hands.

Gunfire came from French freebooters using the warehouses for cover. The nearby sloop, *Amity*, fired five cannons at the warehouses. Fokman led the charge. Thirty men swung from ropes onto the dock, brandishing weapons. They swarmed the freebooters, cutting them down one by one.

"We have the dock," said Fokman.

"Time to call for *Assistance*," Kidd said.

Flags were raised.

HMS Assistance sat offshore. At the signal, longboats were deployed.

Kidd and Fokman waited at the dock.

Amity landed. Captain Gilbert and Tommy Tew "Tewteps" joined Kidd, while the Rhode Island Rogues waited in anticipation.

"Right on time, Gilbert," Kidd began.

"This is not the job I signed up for, says I," Gilbert replied. "How's one to find a treasure ship in the middle of war?"

"It's already found for you, Gilbert." Kidd indicated *Salamander* in the harbor. "Look, two Dutch ships."

"'Tis a Dutch port, Kidd," said Gilbert.

"Take her."

"But Major Paine said we're looking for a Dutch East Indiaman. That's a West Indiaman," Tewsteps pointed out.

"Aye, she's in disguise. The west is fixing to go after the east, and she's close, I know it," Kidd said.

"It's not the right ship, is it?" said Tewsteps.

"I'll take it," Gilbert said.

"Gentlemen, let's go," said Kidd.

Everyone rushed out to their respective ships to navigate the busy harbor. *Amity* fired a shot across the bow of *Salamander*, while *Rascal* came alongside. Kidd's crew hooked onto the Dutch vessel before swinging across to commandeer the ship.

The Dutch crew lowered their weapons.

"I seize this ship in the name of King William," Kidd said. "Fokman, search the ship."

"We are not carrying anything you want, and we are not part of the pirate attack," said a Dutchman. "We are peaceful merchants."

"Yer a wee scunner, ain't ya," Kidd mocked. "Are you captain of this ship?"

"I am Captain Bohn." Bohn glared.

"Pleased to meet you. Are you harboring a German countess, Captain?" Kidd asked.

"I know nothing of a German countess," Bohn said.

Fokman brought out a painting from the forecastle.

"Careful with that," a man said. "It's drying."

"Who's the lovely lass we have here?" Kidd inquired. "Who's yer model? Is she also a passenger?"

"She's not aboard this ship," said Bohn.

"Kidd, Thornhill's landing," Gilbert said.

"Find the lass; she may be aboard," Kidd ordered.

"We lost the girl. I think she may have been taken on that ship." Bohn indicated *Sainte Andrew*.

"Then, God rest her soul. Search every inch of this ship and hold them here till I get back," Kidd told Fokman.

Kidd took a longboat over to Fort Orange, an island unto itself. The stone fortress overlooked the waterfront, and its walls were lined with cannons. Crewmen hauled the boat up the beach.

"Wait here," Kidd ordered, before hiking up the bay path to the courtyard.

Major General Thornhill was standing next to a palm tree, conversing with his aide. The major general's decorations glistened in the sunshine.

Foolish land lubber, Kidd thought.

"Make note of the time and record that I have liberated St. Eustatius," said Thornhill.

"Aye, sir," replied the aide.

Kidd approached. "The island is secure, General."

"I know it is, Kidd. Why did you allow *Sainte Andrew* to escape?"

"We're working on a recovery plan."

"The situation is that French freebooters are holed up in St. Kitt's. They have nothing left to fight with," Thornhill said. "Just what is your interest in this, Kidd? Last I saw of you, you were on your way to face your backers in New York. It didn't take long for them to send you back."

"Begging the General's pardon, but this is all top secret." Kidd took Thornhill away from his aide. "This is all very hush-hush, but I'm searching for a German countess. I'm charged to find her. Orders from King William himself."

"May I see these orders?" Thornhill held out his hand.

"Nay, it's all very hushed. This German countess traveled on a Dutch East Indiaman. I say she came on *Sainte Andrew,* and I plan to take her."

Helena crouched down behind other passengers aboard *Sainte Andrew*, while Dodo used his oversized coat as a private sanctuary.

"Drop anchor off the bar," said a pirate. "And sort the hostages, men from women and children, and take slaves below."

Freebooters herded the women and children.

Dodo, seized by terror, yelled, "Helena!"

She ducked away from the group but came face to face with a pirate, one with curly dark hair with fringes of silver. "What a pretty!" He seized her arm and took her to the quarterdeck. A fair-haired pirate swung down on a rope, practically colliding with Helena and her captor. Blades clanged, cutting Helena's hand.

"The ship is mine, Barns," said the fair-haired pirate.

"Stick to the plan, Ding Dong," Barns replied. "The women go to the bar."

The pirates ushered women into longboats and lowered them into the water.

"The English are predictable. They won't see this coming," said Barns. "Are the charges set?"

"Aye, it's all set to blow," said Ding Dong.

"The moment they board, light her up. They'll bring *Assistance* in closer and send men to put out the flames," Barns said. "That's when you blow her to kingdom come and we take the prize. We'll turn her guns on their own lines."

"What will you do with them?" a freebooter said.

"Human shields," Barns said. "Who'd want to shoot these?" He cupped Helena's breast.

Ding Dong licked his lips, turning to Helena. "I want this one."

"She'll keep me company with the others for now." Barns inspected Helena, stroking her hair. "Hear that, sweetie? Ding Dong likes you."

Barns pushed her into a longboat, and Helena landed on her knees.

Gretsch sat on a rickety wooden bench in a barred cell, his ankles and wrists in restraints. Guards patrolled the hallway, clanging the bars with truncheons. Doors slammed with an echoing rattle, and screams could be heard behind a solid wood door.

After Captain Kidd raced away to find *Sainte Andrew*, Bohn and his men were transferred to the city lockup on St. Eustatius. The jailor panicked when the group arrived, struggling to sort French freebooters from innocent crewmen. Bohn convinced the jailor with a bribe that his crew was indeed innocent, and they were allowed to return to the ship.

Gretsch, on the other hand, remained detained. He shook his head, making color rise on his cheeks.

"Captain Kidd seems to want to handle things his own way," Bohn said, standing outside the cell, awaiting Doorman's return.

"Stupid English," Gretsch snapped.

"I think he's a Scot."

"Stupid Scottish." Gretsch manipulated the restraints roughly, applying a metal pick to the lock. "They're all stupid. Stupid and greedy. I must escape. I cannot sit here. I have a mission to complete."

"I'm with you," Bohn said.

"Are you?" Gretsch freed one of his hands.

"Yeah. But I'll have you know, if you escape, you'll be considered an outlaw and a pirate."

Gretsch released his other hand and started on his ankles.

A guard returned with Doorman, holding Gretsch's royal Calenberg seal.

Gretsch put his wrist restraints back on.

"Gretsch. Baron Gretsch?" the jailor said.

"*Ja.*"

"Baron Maximillian Graf von Gretsch?"

"*Ja*, that's me."

The jailor unlocked the door. "Baron Gretsch, you have been ordered released. The charges are dropped."

Gretsch shook free of the shackles and retrieved his seal.

They returned to *Salamander*.

"How long do you need, Baron?" Bohn asked.

"No time at all."

Gretsch went to his cabin. Papers had been scattered all over the floor. He cursed.

"I'm leaving you in command," Bohn told Doorman.

"In command of this ship?"

"My confidence is already fading," said Bohn. "Gretsch and I are going after the girl."

Gretsch returned his Calenberg seal to its wooden case and hid it within the papers. Next, he lined his leather belt with knives and a pistol.

"Am I to wait for you here?" Doorman asked.

"No, it's too treacherous. Take her to up to St. Martin and wait there. Fill the stores for the voyage home."

"Shall I peruse their goods?"

"Load the ship as you see fit, Captain. Oh, sell off the last of the Schinkenspeck," Bohn insisted. "I never want to see that stuff again."

When Gretsch returned to the main deck, he was fully armed, including an axe-gun strapped to his body. He and Bohn climbed down to the longboat.

"The ship was headed for St. Kitts," Gretsch said. "Which way is that?"

Bohn indicated the next island and the ship next to it. "There she be."

Full On Nasal Assault

Kidd and Gilbert arrived in the smoking town of Basseterre by afternoon. Pirates and freebooters were running amok, using women, children, and clergy from *Sainte Andrew* as hostages. The women's clothes were torn to reveal their breasts, and everyone was tied together with ladders behind their backs.

Kidd remained at a distance, down at the beach. "I don't believe it," he said as Billy Barns came into view.

Kidd and Barns had sailed together under Coxon's privateer ship with Bill Mason and were once known as the Three Bills. Once the letter of marque was revoked for pirating and war broke out between the French and English, chaos ensued and Coxon moved on. Barns became an unpredictable drunk who erupted into violence every night. Mason had had enough but was unable to lead, so Kidd was the top pick. Barns refused to give up command, so they marooned him on a desert island away from shipping routes. And now Barns and his pirates' brandished torches as they stormed the town.

English soldiers took up positions on the wall, aiming their muskets and cannons.

The gate captain manned the tower, shouting, "Stop where you are, or we open fire!"

"I trust you can see for yourself that these are indeed women and children," Barns shouted back.

"We will do what we must. Ready to fire," the gate captain ordered.

Barns hovered a torch near one of the women. "I'll light these beauties up."

"Now, now, let's not be hasty," Kidd bellowed. "We can work things out."

"I'll not be intimidated by lowlife freebooters," said the gate captain.

"Safety of civilians is our concern," Gilbert said.

"Dutch migrants. Be done with them," said the gate captain.

"And one German countess," Kidd said.

"A countess? Which one?" asked the gate captain. "Hold on a moment. Do you have any aristocrats?" he asked Barns.

"No, but we have a bishop," Barns said. "Wait, did you say a countess?"

"Not so loud," said Kidd. "It's top secret."

"Hogwash," said the gate captain.

"Well, walk the plank—it's Billy the Kidd!" Barns let out a laugh. "Can it be?"

"Let's talk, Billy, just you and me," Kidd said.

"We got nothing to talk about, Billy," Barns replied.

"I ask for parley, as per the code."

Barns paused. "Very well. Turtle Bay. Midnight."

"You'll meet with him? What for?" said the gate captain. "You're not in command here."

"We bide our time, Captain. I'm experienced in these matters," said Kidd. "Barns has no trouble killing hostages, so if ya don't want their screams to haunt the rest of yer days, listen to me."

Oars extended from *Fama* like the legs of a centipede treading through water. Rivero caressed the rail, relishing the grain of the wood. Two decades earlier, *Fama* had been taken by the buccaneer John Morris, who killed Rivero's father and renamed the ship *Lamb* as an insult. Rivero resorted to piracy to restore his family's name.

Fama sailed alongside *San Antonio,* trailing a Dutch ship heading north, fleeing a battle at St. Eustatius. Soon they closed in. Rivero raised a speaking trumpet. "Stop and surrender."

"You have no legal right to stop us. We're bound for St. Martin," the Dutch captain replied.

"You carry a wanted criminal and a potential witch."

"We carry no passengers."

Rivero, alongside several men, threw grappling hooks and swung over to *Salamander*, while *San Antonio* aimed swivel cannons.

The Dutch captain and the officers rushed downstairs to the main deck.

"What is this?" the Dutchman demanded. "Get off my ship."

Rivero unsheathed his blade and drove it through the Dutch captain's chest. More of Rivero's men swung over. *Salamander's* crew surrendered their weapons.

"Mr. Doorman," a crewman said, trying to assist the Dutch captain as he staggered, blood gushing from the wound. The captain gasped and fell face-first on the deck.

Silvestre swung over unexpectedly. "What happened?"

"It was necessary," Rivero insisted. "He was resisting."

"This is not correct," Silvestre said.

"Search the cabins," ordered Rivero, dismissing him.

Men scoured the forward section, and paintings were discovered in the forecastle.

"Bring them here," said Rivero.

Portraits of a young woman were delivered to the deck alongside various weapons.

"That's her," a crewman confirmed. "The men say she's a countess and may be a witch."

"Whose weapons are these?" Rivero inquired.

"They belong to the German witch," the crewman said.

"I want the paintings in perfect condition; they are evidence," Rivero said.

Silvestre grabbed him by the arm and took him aside. "What are you doing? This is piracy! We'll both be hanged."

"She is the countess. I'll bet everything."

"Which is exactly what you have done," Silvestre said.

"It could not be helped. Have this ship sent to Carlitos in San Juan. I shall pursue the countess."

"Tread carefully, my friend," Silvestre said. "I am not a pirate and don't want to be hanged as one."

Kidd stood at *Amity's* bow, his men rowing towards Turtle Bay. A crescent moon shone through a layer of rain clouds, illuminating the blackened ruins of the once-popular tavern, The Turtle's Shell. Barns waited nearby.

Kidd approached with caution.

"Oh, the nights I thought of what I would do to you when I found you," Barns began. "And here you are, walking right to me."

"Here we both are," Kidd said. "If it were anyone else, I woulda run you through and the men would have followed me. I gave you a fair chance. I spared yer life."

"You left me on a desert island to starve to death."

"As per the code. It was war, mate. The men wanted me."

Barns looked around. "And where are the men?"

"Treacherous bastards, all of 'em," Kidd barked. "Not worth the mention."

"You have an offer?" Barns said. "Let's hear it."

"A treasure ship, Billy. The Hanover treasury is comin' our way, and I'll split it with ya. *De Heilige Graal.* An East India boat with all the trimmings. Even a German countess."

"What do you want from me?"

"Join forces. St. Kitt's is a lost cause, and they've been fighting over this island for a dog's life. And Turtle Bay— what turtles? *De Helige Graal* brings riches enough for us both to retire. I need good men, and yer as good as it gets. What do ya say, Billy?"

"You asking me to trust you? And you can hold my dick when I piss, too," said Barns.

"We was best mates once, Billy, but war broke us apart. Let's unite again for an old-fashioned pirate attack."

"I'll discuss the offer accordingly with my men. You'll have my reply at dawn. If this is a trick, you'll be the first to die."

"Glad to have you back, Billy," said Kidd.

Helena sat tied to a stake within an encampment along the sand bar of Turtle Bay. As she slipped in and out of consciousness, her dreams were studded with explosions and cannon fire. Instead of snow, there was sand, and instead of evergreens, there were palm trees. Her nostrils stung from smoke and the stench of sulfur. She tried to move her aching arms, but they were bound behind her. When her eyes opened, raindrops slid down her cheeks.

It was after midnight when Barns returned. He uncapped a bottle of rum and took a swig. He released her bonds and allowed her to secure her bodice. Helena stood up to stretch and massaged her wrists, as Ding Dong's longboat landed on the beach. He charged over to the camp, took a swig of rum, and began combing her hair with his fingers.

"Pretty thing, ain't she?" Barns said.

Ding Dong brushed his balls against Helena and spat on the sand. "Hello, sugar lumps. Call me Dong."

Barns raised the rum bottle like a defensive weapon. "Keep your hands off her."

"You met with the English. Why do you delay?" Ding Dong raised his sword to Helena's throat. "I say we rape her and get on with it."

The air escaped from Helena's lungs, and she struggled to fill them up again. A paralysis seized her, and she was unsure if she'd be able to defend herself. She would rather die than have her body defiled.

"Kidd wants to join forces to capture a treasure ship," said Barns.

"He's off his head—or it's a trap," said Ding Dong.

"He says the ship is called *De Heilige Graal*." Barns slipped his fingers spider-like along the blade, lowering it from Helena's throat. "A ship of that name and description was spotted just days ago, sailing south off Guadeloupe."

Helena tried not to react, but her eyes gave her away.

"That name means something to you?" Barns said. "She knows something. Is there a countess on board? Is it a treasure ship?"

"I don't know," Helena said.

"She's lying. For all we know, she may be the countess. Are you the countess?" Barns pressed.

"No."

"It's been a long time since we've seen the likes of a treasure ship by her lonesome." Barns pondered. "Stick to the plan. What better way to capture a treasure ship than with a ship of the line?"

They grinned and grumbled in agreement.

"I'll take this countess." Ding Dong cleared his nostrils. The mucus just missed Helena as he took her arm.

"The young lady is going to stay close to me," Barns insisted. "At least until we know more about her."

Within the hour, they moved her onto a nearby fishing barge. The salty stench of decay turned Helena's stomach. Ding Dong gripped her neck so tightly it cracked, and she was unable to call out to Barns. They entered a cramped cabin.

Ding Dong released her and lit an oil lamp, revealing crusted mucous all down his sleeve.

Helena caught her breath, sneering.

Barns gave orders on deck.

"I'm going to have some fun with you." Ding Dong's spittle shot into her eyes as he laughed.

Helena squinted, trying to generate tears to wash it out. "Barns won't like it."

Barns pushed through the cabin door. "No, he won't. Hands off."

"If it's money you want, I know how to get you money," Helena offered.

"She *is* the countess!" Ding Dong said.

They laughed and brought out a quarter bottle of rum.

"No, I'm not a countess, but I know wealthy people."

"But, tonight, you're just a girl," said Barns. "If Ding Dong is a good boy, I might let him have you."

Ding Dong set a deck of cards on the table. "I'll play you for her." He shoved a knuckle over his left nostril, firing a yellowish green stream out of his right. The residue showered Helena and the table.

"Not on the table or the cards, ya filthy pig!" Barns wiped down the cards and table, not noticing the stringy congealed remnants on the wall. "Did yer father fuck an alpaca?" He offered Helena a used handkerchief, which she refused, using her sleeve instead.

"Lucky night, girl—you get nailed no matter who wins."

Both pirates laughed.

"Deal." Barns shuffled the cards while wiping. "No more of that, Ding Dong. Ya know I hate it when ya do that trick with yer nose. Sorry, Yer Worship. He's a pig. He can shoot a bottle off a stump from twenty feet using only snot."

"If I'm the countess, you won't rape me?"

"If you're the countess, we won't make it hurt as much." Barns gulped back the last of the rum. "Just be a good girl and you'll still be able to shit on the morrow."

"Speak for yerself. I'm going to wreck her." Ding Dong put his knuckle to his right nostril.

Helena turned, shielding herself. Another barrage was released, clearing the table and hitting the bulkhead. This time, Helena received only a smattering on her sleeve.

"Not on the cards, you vile, rancid swine!" Barns exclaimed. "This bottle's empty. Get us another one, girl. Down there." He pointed to a crate full of hay, wedged between piles of netting.

Helena fetched a new bottle and uncorked it. The men played a few hands and argued over the way Ding Dong shuffled cards and regularly showered the room with sputum. At one point he spat upwards, so that it landed on his own head.

Helena thought that must have been an accident.

Barns shielded his hand. "I said, not on the cards!"

Helena waited for the next expulsion from Ding Dong before extracting a tincture from a hidden pocket in her dress, having swiped it earlier from Gretsch's things. She emptied its contents into the rum before tucking it away.

"Bring that bottle here," Ding Dong said.

Helena handed it over.

"Sit tight, sweetheart, you're in for a fun night." Barns gave her a self-satisfied smile.

They played cards for over an hour, and Helena was beginning to wonder if the tincture had expired. Nothing seemed to happen until Ding Dong fired one of his nasal assaults, then dropped to his knees.

"What was that?" Ding Dong waved away the trailing string of mucus. "It's coming out of everywhere!"

"What?" Barns looked out the porthole.

"That flash! There, see it?"

"Flash?" Barns turned his cards upside down.

Ding Dong stumbled forward until his face hit the doorframe. He leapt to his feet and raced onto the deck, screaming, "Fire rain!"

Barns followed in quick succession, claiming that the stars were turning green.

Helena saw her chance and climbed through the porthole. Ding Dong's longboat was tied up haphazardly alongside two others. She untied them all, climbed into one and pushed off with an oar.

Ding Dong chased after a pirate smoking a cigar. He snatched the smoke and began writing in the air.

"What are you doing?" Barns asked.

"I can spell letters in the air!"

"Something's not right," Barns said. "We've been tricked."

Helena could hear them stumbling and crashing back inside the cabin.

"Where is it?" Barns said.

"Where's what?" Ding Dong asked.

Their feet slammed against the floor, racing on deck again.

"What am I looking for?" Barns said. "Oh, the girl."

"There was a girl?" Ding Dong licked his finger, checking for a breeze.

"A countess!"

"You're right, a countess. Where'd she go?"

"You were supposed to watch her."

"That was hours ago," said Ding Dong. "She could be anywhere."

Barns checked under the netting. "She's gone!"

"Who? Oh, her!"

Ding Dong finally noticed Helena and fired his pistol.

"What?" Barns leapt into the air, pulling out his weapon. "Where? Who?"

"There she is!"

"You're right. Get her!"

Ding Dong ran straight off the deck into the water, making a mighty splash.

Their curses and obscenities grew fainter as Helena slipped away into the darkness.

Kidd was awake all night, taking refuge inside the ruined tavern, The Turtle's Shell. He sat with his head in his hands at one of the remaining tables. "I know we don't talk much, God. It's as much your fault as it is mine, but we can work together on this one. I'm on my knees here, so to speak, God, so if ya can hear me—"

Gilbert walked in.

"Don't ya fuckin' knock?" snarled Kidd. "Sorry, not you, God!" He put his hand up. "I'll be right with ya. What now, Gilbert, can't ya see I'm talking to God?"

"Come quick," Gilbert beckoned. "They're up to something."

Kidd's knees cracked as he stood. "Oh, God, what now?"

The pre-dawn light silhouetted the wall of St. Kitt's. The gate captain fumbled with his belt, securing weapons. Kidd and Gilbert ran up to the wall, to find Barns there with the hostages, as they were the day before. He held a flickering torch.

"He's going to light it," the gate captain said.

"Is this yer answer, Billy?" Kidd called.

"She's a witch," Barns said. "And witches should be burned."

"He's going to light it," said Tewsteps.

"Nay, he'll take the deal," Kidd said, downplaying Barns's actions. "He's just theatrical."

"He's going to light it," Gilbert reiterated.

"Barns, you know, if it means that much to ya, you can have the island," Kidd offered.

"Where's the countess?" Barns asked. "We want her back."

"What countess?" Kidd checked his pockets.

"Burn it all and go," said Ding Dong.

"Aye," said Barns. "Burn it all and take to the sea!"

Ding Dong ignited a torch and threw it in the midst of the bound hostages. People screamed and flailed as flames rose. Freebooters retreated, running down the sandbar.

Gilbert and Tewsteps led men over the walls using a rope. They doused the flames and cut the people's bonds.

"The French are retreating!" the gate captain called.

Kidd climbed the tower. The hostages were freed, and freebooters were on the run. "Time to call for *Assistance*."

Rivero stood at *Fama's* bow, scanning the dark water with his telescope. Many boats were being rowed away from St. Kitts while *Sainte Andrew* was arriving. He would search her next. A signal flashed from *San Antonio*. Rivero directed his telescope. Silvestre indicated the coastline where a boat was tossing in the waves. A girl was rowing but unable to land. As they watched, the boat smacked the rocks and took on water. Rowboats from *San Antonio* came to the girl's aid, while *Fama* continued.

Rivero watched from the canvas-covered command deck. His father's old captain's chair had been brought out and now sat in its rightful place. As sunrise approached, the French war canoes left the island. Rivero heaved a sigh of relief; he did not want an encounter with *les flibustiers*.

Fama and *San Antonio* docked side by side, and Rivero and Silvestre boarded *Sainte Andrew*.

"Who is captain of this ship?" Rivero called.

"The French rigged the ship to blow," a voice replied. "We have most of the traps; your men are a godsend."

"The French bastards left plenty of surprises," said Silvestre.

The girl from the sinking boat was brought aboard. She was pale and shivering, wearing a disheveled blue dress. Silvestre offered her his hand as she reached the top of the rope ladder.

"What is your name?" Rivero demanded.

"Helena."

"Did you come from this ship?"

"No...well, yes. My friend—husband is on this ship."

Silvestre's men reported that there were no more bombs that they could see.

Civilians were brought up on deck.

"The fight is over. This ship is not ours to take," Silvestre said to Rivero.

"Get your men together; get ready to leave," Rivero said.

One of Silvestre's officers boarded. "The French have captured *Assistance*. They are far from finished here."

Helena staggered, taking panicked breaths.

"Calm, *señorita*. I am here to protect you. I am the famous Cuban Corsair Jorge-Miguel José Rivero, at your service. You will come with me."

"Ships approaching," Silvestre said. "English. A galiot and a sloop. We must leave."

"Keep her with you; keep her safe," said Rivero.

Silvestre took her aside and wrapped her in his cape.

"*Scheisse*," uttered a voice in the crowd.

"Dodo!" Helena exclaimed.

"Get her dodo," Silvestre told one of his men.

An officer interrupted: "The English are here."

Rivero gripped his sword. "It's too late to leave."

A wild-eyed man in a burgundy coat swung over with a handful of rogues brandishing blunderbusses and muskets.

"I claim this ship in the name of King William," a Scotsman declared.

Rivero relinquished his sword. "The ship is yours, Captain. The danger is past. All the bombs have been defused."

"And you are?"

"I am Cuban Corsair Rivero."

"No, her—over there." The Scot indicated Helena.

"A hostage. The rest are being recovered from the hold."

Kidd jerked his head to the side and winked. They stepped aside to speak privately.

"She's a German, that one. The lovely thing there." Kidd's voice lowered. "Good job, Cuban. Keep her safe. Just between us, this is top secret. This woman is very important."

"Is she?"

"Aye. She may be nobility. But first, we're taking back our *Assistance*. See the girl and the ship safely to Nevis and I'll make sure you're rewarded."

"There is a reward for her?"

"Aye, there's a reward. More pesos than you can count. Do this right, and your own king will want to thank you."

"If she's that important, I'll guard her with my life." Rivero saluted.

"Fort Charlie, Nevis. It's the large tower. You can't miss it. I'll be along presently with *Assistance*."

The Scot and his men swung back to their ship, which swiftly departed.

"Royalty, is she?" Rivero smiled. "Take her to my cabin. You are safe now, *señorita*."

Spanish soldiers took Helena aboard *Fama*.

Silvestre and Rivero spoke quietly as the English ships moved off.

"Another lecture is not welcome," Rivero said.

"No. This time, fortune smiles on you," said Silvestre.

Dodo was brought to them.

"Where is the dodo?" asked Silvestre.

"I am Dodo," said Dodo.

"Oh," said Silvestre.

"*Señor*, you may join your countess on my ship," Rivero said.

"You found the countess?" Dodo said. "Thank the gods."

Dodo was taken aboard *Fama*, still carrying an easel.

"This is not the right ship," Silvestre said quietly. "It is a cargo ship meant for Port Royal."

"This time you are right, my friend." Rivero grinned. "I have her. I have the countess. That Scot just confirmed it. This may not be *De Heilige Graal*, but nevertheless, she switched ships; it's her."

"Fortune smiles on you."

"Prepare to make sail," Rivero said. "We'll steer south as not to arouse suspicion, then escort us back to San Juan."

Men staggered out from below. The ship's captain fell to his knees, coughing. "We did it," the captain gasped. "The ship is secure."

"We will leave you to your ship now, Captain. I trust she is well in your charge."

"Aye." The captain waved. "Thank you for your help."

Rivero swung back to his ship. *Fama* and *San Antonio* rowed away from the rising sun.

Rascal rowed hard to the beat of a drum, followed by *Amity*. Kidd gripped his blunderbuss, while Fokman manned the tiller and Tewsteps inspected weapons on the main deck, where rogues readied grappling hooks. Ahead was the ship of the line, *HMS Assistance*, commandeered by French pirates.

"Keep us behind her, Fokman," Kidd barked. "The French bastards can't aim her big guns behind."

The ships closed in. French sharpshooters fired muskets.

"Keep yer heads down," Tewsteps ordered from the bow, not taking cover himself.

Kidd smiled. "That's captain material yer showing, Tew. See, men? Tewsteps has no fear. Ready to board."

On the upper aft decks of *Assistance*, Barns and some freebooters aimed muskets.

"Fire!" Barns shouted.

Gunfire burst from the poop deck, killing many men aboard *Amity* and *Rascal*.

"To hell and back!" roared Kidd.

Grappling hooks deployed from *Rascal's* bow, latching on to the ship. Kidd followed his army aboard. On the main deck of *Assistance*, the French and English fought for control.

"Take her back," Kidd ordered. Two French freebooters challenged him with swords. He fired his blunderbuss, blasting them away.

On the poop deck, Tewsteps shot freebooters with his pistols. Gilbert and men from *Amity* entered, wielding weapons.

"They're all around us," Ding Dong cried. "Scorpions!"

"It's hopeless," called Barns. "Let's get out of here."

The pair ran for the heads.

Kidd drew both of his pistols and fired, but Barns and Ding Dong jumped into the sea.

Freebooters and pirates panicked and fled, but most were shot in the attempt.

"We have the ship!" Tewsteps said.

"Finish them off!" Kidd ordered.

Shots were fired at the men in the water.

"Signal the island and all commands," said Kidd. "I've reclaimed *Assistance*. Gilbert, tie the longboats and weigh anchor."

"Signal from Thornhill," Tewsteps reported. "The island is secure. The battle is over."

"Aye, we are victorious," Kidd proclaimed. "Barns jumped. Bring him to me."

A search was made for the missing man, but no trace of him was found.

That evening, Kidd sprawled on the plush chaise longue in the captain's cabin of *Assistance*. He admired the stained-glass window and lit a Cuban cigar, inhaling deeply. Gilbert and Tewsteps entered, also smoking.

"No sign of Barns yet," said Gilbert.

"Keep looking," Kidd said. "Ya never know where he'll turn up. I'll not make that mistake again."

Tewsteps relit his pipe with a candle.

Kidd's shiny black boots kicked the chair. "Don't smoke in here, ya ingrate!"

"Shame that the commodore was killed," Gilbert said. "Now there's no one to command *Assistance*."

"Aye, a shame. 'Tis a fine ship he had here. She'll be mine for this."

"You think so?"

"Of course," Kidd affirmed. "You capture a ship from an enemy, then that ship is yours. It's an almost certainty. Gil, how about you be her pilot, and Tew, her first officer."

"And I suppose you be captain of the ship," Gilbert said.

"Is that so hard to fathom, Gilbert?"

"Merely advising caution. Don't count your chickens, says I."

"Have faith in me, Gilbert," Kidd said. "I'll take you to fame and fortune."

A lively celebration flourished at the governor's mansion in Charlestown, Nevis. At Fort Charles, torches were lit, and the terrace was adorned in flowers. Musicians played

Pachelbel's *Canon in D Major*, and in the harbor, English warships displayed colorful glass lanterns, their reflection dazzling on the water's surface. Partygoers flocked to the festivities, arriving in fancy dress.

Major General Thornhill marched up to the fort, victorious once again. He'd spent the past two years kicking the French out of the Leeward Islands, losing two fleets and hundreds of men in the process. His tactics had included murder, kidnapping, poisoning and starvation, and now he was confident the French were gone permanently. Waiting to meet him on the terrace were Governor Codrington and other highly decorated ship captains.

Amity and *Rascal* towed *Assistance* to the dock below.

"I say, Tim," Codrington began, "she doesn't look all that bad."

Thornhill looked down at *HMS Assistance*. "Indeed, she came out of it fairly well, I'd say."

"How long for repairs?"

"Not long at all. I should be able to complete them right here."

"Splendid."

On the platform below, Lieutenant Kidd was first off the gangway, waving to a cheering crowd.

"Now, who's this again?" Codrington asked.

"Kidd," Thornhill replied.

"Kidd? Oh, that dreadful Scot. I thought he was thumbing a ride to New York."

"Seems New York didn't want him either." Thornhill gave a mirthless laugh. "He says he's on a secret mission to capture a German treasure ship. A countess."

"I didn't know Germans had treasure ships," Codrington said. "I assumed it was all farmers and butchers."

"I heard something in the news," Thornhill said. "I thought your wife would have told you. Seems a countess has run off with the Hanover treasury and is on a Dutch ship."

"Then it's certainly worth looking into. Bring Kidd up here at once."

Kidd strolled triumphantly on the pier, flanked by Gilbert, Tewsteps and Fokman, who had donned their best clothes for the occasion. Kidd was searching the harbor for Spanish ships.

"Where be the Cuban and the countess?" Gilbert asked.

"He better not be up at Newcastle," said Kidd. "I told the simple Cuban, it's the fort with the large tower. Ya can't get any fuckin' clearer than that. They must be here."

Assistance moored behind them.

"Behold our new ship, men," gloated Kidd.

"'Tis not a certainty, says I," said Gilbert.

"'Tis a certainty, Gilbert. We just saved the bloody flagship. How soon can you be ready to sail?"

"No sooner than a week," Tewsteps said.

"That's not good enough. I want my countess to travel in style," Kidd said. "I'll stay here with *Assistance* and the countess and get her fit. Gil, you and *Amity* go down to Barbados, while Fokman scouts the southwest. See if the *Holy Grail* is running for the Spanish Main."

An aide came out of the fort gate.

"That's more like it," Kidd said.

"Lieutenant Kidd?"

"Aye, Captain Kidd, laddie."

"Governor Codrington wants a word."

"Of course he does; lead the way. Give the men the night in the tavern," Kidd said to Gilbert.

"Aye, they could use it. Would you care to organize that, Mr. Tew?"

"It'd be an honor and a pleasure, Captain Gilbert, sir. We'll all celebrate Kidd's new command—and the countess."

"Shh! Remember, hush-hush," Kidd said.

Tewsteps mimed buttoning lips and hurried back to the ship.

"Now come with me, Gilbert. Fortune and fame await."

Kidd, Gilbert and Fokman traveled along the causeway and up a flight of stone stairs until they reached the terrace.

"Lieutenant Kidd," Codrington began.

"Cap—aye, yes, sir."

"I understand you played a small part in the recovery of our *Assistance*."

"Aye. By no means small, sir. We fought hard for her, sir."

"General Thornhill thanks you for recovering her."

"Indeed, Kidd," Thornhill added. "Well done."

"Quicker action might have saved the life of Commodore Leake, but war is war," Codrington continued. "I'm sorry to say, *Assistance* has lost all her senior officers. So, I've decided to give command over to General Thornhill."

"General Thornhill, sir?" Kidd questioned.

"Yes, thanks Kidd," said Thornhill.

"Beggin' yer pardon, sirs, but has the general ever commanded at sea before?"

"Not at all, but what better way to start than with a ship of the line." Thornhill grinned.

"Very true," Codrington agreed. "Now, what's all this about a secret mission? Let's have it."

"I am indeed on a secret mission," Kidd said.

"Yes. A secret mission to capture a countess and the Hanover treasury, if I'm not mistaken."

Gilbert and Fokman exchanged looks.

"Uh, well, it's hush-hush, you see. I have the countess and now I'm in need of a ship of the line to pursue and recover the Hanover treasure in the name of King William."

"And what are you to do with the Hanover treasury once it's been recovered?" Codrington asked.

"I'm to hand it over to King William's authority."

"And, who is King William's authority here?"

"You are, sir."

"Yes, indeed, Lieutenant Kidd. I charge you to carry out your mission and bring the Hanover treasury and *De Heilige Graal* to me," Codrington said. "Now, bring me this countess. I want to speak with her."

"She's with the Spanish captain. Captain Cuba."

"Who?"

"The Spanish captain," Kidd said. "There were two Spanish ships in the battle; they came here."

"No Spanish ships were involved," an English captain said. "And none are here."

"What?" Kidd felt an invisible noose tighten around his neck.

"They're not here," the English captain said.

Thornhill cleared his throat. "Captain Jorge-Miguel José Rivero is wanted for piracy and murder."

"Oh, God," Kidd said.

"Shit," Gilbert added.

"Is he the man you handed the countess over to?" Thornhill asked.

Kidd could scarcely speak. "Captain Rivero, son of Rivero, the pirate."

"Oh, well done, Kidd." Thornhill laughed. "You handed her over to a wanted murderous pirate. Congratulations, old chum." He gave him a thumbs-up.

"Then I charge you to clean up your own mess, Kidd," Codrington said. "Go out and recover the Hanover treasury and the countess. Bring them both to me, along with the pirate Rivero."

"Such a task will require a warship. Should I not be granted command of *Assistance*?"

"That's *HMS Assistance*," Thornhill corrected. "And you are not officially here, remember?"

"That's right, Kidd. Without an official mission, there can be no official decoration, and hence, no command." Codrington smirked.

Thornhill leant forward. "It's all very hush-hush."

"Now get out, before I strip you all of rank for gross incompetence," said Codrington.

Kidd's face was flushed, and he turned to leave. His men followed, staring at him.

"It's not my fault!" Kidd protested. "Goddamn aristocratic bastards!"

"What's that?" Gilbert asked.

A commotion came from the harbor.

"Oh no, my ship!" Gilbert rushed down.

"What have you got against me, God?" Kidd closed his eyes. "What did I ever do to yew, ya fuck'n bastard!

Goddamn bloody patchwork pigeon-brained scobber-lotching sons of bitches!"

Kidd raced down the steps to the causeway, where *Assistance* and *Amity* had both burst into flames. Fokman rolled on the ground, extinguishing his blazing clothes. Men were scrambling, trying to save him and the ships. At the edge of the water, *Rascal* was being rowed away with Barns aboard, waving back at him.

"Billy!" Kidd screamed. "I'll get you, you low-life scum! I'll tear you limb from limb! You slimy, flea-bitten mongrel bastard sucking sack of flaming worm fodder! Next time I'll feed you to the sharks!"

Bocas del Dragón

Islands appeared as large black formations in the water. Only a few pinpricks of light gave any indication of settlements. The moon slipped in and out of the clouds, while the faint sound of music carried on the wind, unworldly and chilling. Aurora noticed a distinct male scent: herbal cologne mixed with saltwater.

"Good evening, Captain," she said.

"Hope I didn't startle you," he replied.

"You didn't. I sensed you were there."

"Let me guess, you were moonraking?" He gave her a smile.

"Sure." Aurora held her breath a moment while the downdraft blew his sweaty scent at her. "It's so beautiful here. I'm tempted to jump off and live on one of these islands. They're so tranquil."

"They can be hideous and ferocious. Then, the very next day, be a beautiful dream. Like you."

"I heard one of these is Guadeloupe."

"We passed Guadeloupe, and Marie-Galante just back there." Van Gelder pointed. "Dominica over there, and over there, that's Saint Marie, otherwise known as Murder Island."

"Sounds like my kind of island. Were you looking for me?" Aurora leant into him.

"I had to be sure you weren't smoking. And to bring you inside. It's time for curfew."

"It's time for Persephone's astronomy lesson, anyhow." Aurora followed him. "She's quite a little navigator. She loves the stars and wants to know each and every one."

"Do you know each one?" he asked.

"Of course. I'm a countess." She winked, tailing him up to the main deck and aft, where Van der Hagen was attempting to smoke his pipe.

"Viscount, good evening," van Gelder said.

x

Van der Hagen rushed to conceal his pipe. "It certainly is."

"They're out there," van Gelder said. "Sorry sir, total blackout tonight. You understand?"

Van der Hagen gave a shaky laugh. "Hiding on my own ship. May I walk you in, Countess?"

"Thank you, sir."

De Britt came up to the rail. "I see a light."

Telescopes trained in that direction. There was a tiny light beyond Dominica. Two more lights appeared.

"That's them," van Gelder said.

Van der Hagen's shoulders relaxed. "Thank heavens."

"Yes, you can relax. They're still heading southwest. Note in the log that three French ships are heading southwest. They are completely unaware of our location."

"Well done, Captain van Gelder."

"Give the good news to the girls. Goodnight to you both."

"Goodnight, Captain," Aurora said.

"Try to get some sleep."

Van der Hagen escorted Aurora to the grand cabin, where Persephone and Katrina sat by the window, peering through telescopes. "You'll be pleased to know that Captain van Gelder has once again outsmarted those French ships. They're searching west of Dominica."

"Persephone said," Katrina said.

"Is Aurora going to show us more stars?" Persephone asked.

"Life's so much simpler when you just stay inside and watch stars," said the viscount.

Aurora went over to them. Mars shimmered red and gold. "Come explore the stars with us," she offered to Van der Hagen. "I know most of them. My Helena has been boring me with it my whole life."

"You know most of them?"

"Most of them on a bright night like this, when you can't see so many."

They all laughed but quickly silenced, remembering to be quiet.

Katrina peered through her telescope. "You're right. Mars flickers red, gold and silver."

"I often found my father speaking to Mars when he was going off to war, when he thought I wasn't looking."

"Did Mars answer back?" Katrina asked.

"Unfortunately, yes."

"Papa, are we going to Tobago?" Persephone asked.

"Captain van Gelder is just following procedure, that's all. We're perfectly safe."

"What's in Tobago?" Aurora asked.

"It's a dreadful place," Persephone said. "It's where they torture slaves."

"We don't speak of such things, not in front of the countess," Van der Hagen reminded.

"No, please. Is this one of your places?" Aurora said.

"It may be the safest place for you right now," said Van der Hagen.

"We can't go there," Katrina added.

"No, Papa, we can't go there," Persephone chimed in.

"We will speak no more of it." The viscount crossed his arms. "I'll see you to Aragua, but where this ship goes when in danger is up to Captain van Gelder," Van der Hagen said. "Come, Aurora is going to name all the stars for us."

By sunrise, *De Heilige Graal* had anchored off Tobago.

Aurora woke before then. It seemed she was awake early most mornings now. She watched as they approached the city and saw that it was smoking and cursed. There would be no way to go ashore now. How she longed to walk on land again. After pacing around her room, she went to the grand cabin.

The viscount and his daughters were already there. Katrina and Persephone looked forlorn.

"Captain van Gelder is going ashore," explained Van der Hagen. "Women are not allowed out of their rooms. I'm sorry."

De Britt arrived to escort all the women back to their quarters.

And again, Aurora paced.

By late afternoon, the women were allowed back out and congregated in the grand cabin once more, watching as boats returned to the ship.

"Captain Van Gelder has returned, Papa," said Persephone.

"Excuse me, I must speak with him."

"I'd like to go, too," said Aurora.

"Absolutely not. Stay here." Van der Hagen closed the door.

"What do you think happened?" Aurora asked Persephone.

"A battle. When I was little, my father told me about a huge battle which took place here between the French, English and the Dutch admiral, De Ruyter."

"I've heard of him," Aurora said. "My father liked him."

"He's dead though, now," Katrina said.

"He died when we were little," Persephone said. "I hope we leave soon; I hate it here." She got up to stretch. "The smoke is choking me."

"So, this is the slave capital?" Aurora loitered at the window.

"Father says there's three slave capitals in the Caribbean: Tobago, Curaçao and Port Royal. But he says they're all awful like this one, and Port Royal is undermining the cost, to put Curaçao out of business," Persephone said. "And there's talk of building a new one, bigger than all of them, to put Port Royal out of business."

"They can all end up like this one," said Katrina.

"Why no Spanish slave capital?" asked Aurora.

"Papa says it's because the Spanish are always being attacked, so they just buy their slaves," said Persephone.

"What about the French?" Aurora said.

"The French don't buy slaves; they steal them."

Van Gelder and Van der Hagen entered.

"The island is practically deserted," van Gelder said.

"What happened here?" Aurora asked.

"An Indian attack."

"West Indians, I assume?"

"Yes. Indians from Bocas del Dragón," said van Gelder. "There are hundreds dead. Some fled by boat. They didn't discriminate. Women and children were plenty. It was gruesome."

"But not unexpected. A sight I've seen many times," Aurora said. "When can we leave?"

"Soon, Countess. I must check on my business associates," said Van der Hagen. "And determine exactly where they went. I do have other responsibilities. We'll get you to Aragua presently."

Inside Aurora's chamber later that day, she heard voices above her. She opened the window to hear them.

"We know our business partners left for Samaná Bay, but not if they arrived safely," van Gelder said. "I think we should stop at Margarita for news."

At sunset, Aurora went to the grand cabin for supper. They were just getting settled when a bell rang. Then a whistle blew, and soon drumming began.

"Battle stations!" an officer called.

"Here we go again," said Katrina.

Van der Hagen entered and escorted the women to the side gallery lounge. Slaves cleared away the food and table in seconds and crew unlocked the cannons. Slats opened and the cannons were slid into place.

"Are they Indians from Bocas del Dragón?" Aurora asked.

"No. Three French ships of the line coming from the north," said Van der Hagen. "Van Gelder has no choice but to turn south and go around Trinidad and into Bocas del Dragón."

"Sail astern!" called the lookout.

"It looks like a frigate," said de Britt.

Van Gelder aimed his telescope, scanning the coast of Trinidad, then across the horizon to a frigate with French patterns in pursuit. "*Cheval Marin*. Have the rest of the cannons loaded." Van Gelder collapsed his telescope.

"Is she giving chase?" said Van der Hagen.

"Unless we can gain speed, she'll have us," said van Gelder. "Sound general quarters!"

"Sound general quarters!" de Britt echoed.

"We have forty cannons on this ship," Van der Hagen boasted. "We could stop her with one shot."

"That ship is just too fast," said van Gelder.

Some crewmen rushed up the rigging while others prepared the cannons.

"Will we make it?" asked Van der Hagen.

Van Gelder shook his head. "I'll try and hold them off until we reach Whale Gulf."

Inside the gallery lounge, Aurora met up with Katrina and Persephone. They sat in silence, catching glimpses through the window. Aurora could see the outline of mountains go by, and the occasional canoe.

"We're in Bocas del Dragón," said Persephone.

The ship turned sharply, and the women grabbed hold of whatever they could to steady themselves. Paintings and decorations fell from the walls. Cannon fire boomed and the smell of sulfur wafted through the room.

Panicked voices echoed through the decks.

"Ready to fire full broadside," said an officer.

The ship righted itself.

"Fire," the officer exclaimed.

The floor and walls rumbled and shook with the concussion.

Aurora covered her ears and closed her eyes. When she dared open them, Van der Hagen was there to check on his daughters. The ship turned again to the other side this time. Aurora was thrust against the window. Two more ships emerged, one with a seahorse figurehead.

"Which ships are those, Papa?" asked Persephone.

"*Émerillon* and *Hazardeux*," said Van der Hagen. "That's what's left of the mighty French West Indies Line. They are faster, more maneuverable, and better armed than we."

De Heilige Graal swiftly turned again.

The rest of the night was spent like this. The French ships chased while *De Heilige Graal* turned or periodically fired, to slow the enemy.

By dawn, French ships were in the distance, being attacked by the canoes and piraguas of native warriors. *Émerillon* and *Hazardeux* fought, while *Cheval Marin* turned north.

"I think we've seen the last of them for a while," said Van der Hagen.

Aurora exhaled for the first time in twelve hours.

Later that day, they docked off Margarita and had a brief respite. The women went for a stroll on deck that was short-lived. Soon, bells chimed, and crewmen rushed to their stations.

"And we do it over again," said Aurora. "I know, I know, back inside."

Sunset in the gallery lounge featured dinner and a show. The ship twisted and turned around swampy islands. In the distance was *Cheval Marin.*

After supper, Aurora yawned, not having slept for a few days now. "Not that it's not an exciting battle, but I'm going to bed."

Persephone snored gently beside her.

"That explains why things have been so quiet." Katrina yawned.

Aurora shut her eyes briefly and was asleep. When she opened them again, it was morning. Her neck cracked and she tried to straighten it. "*Scheisse!*"

Persephone and Katrina were both awake in the chairs beside hers. They were anchored in Margarita, next to a quaint village with a church sporting a tall steeple.

Van der Hagen entered the room. It had been transformed back into a grand cabin, and breakfast was already on the table.

"I hope we didn't rock the ship too much for you?" he said.

"It was terribly exciting," said Persephone. "Every time we thought we lost *Cheval Marin,* there she was again."

"Exciting?" Katrina said. "They were trying to kill us!"

"She was so close I could almost spit on the figurehead!" Persephone fanned her face.

"Yes, that was close, indeed," van Gelder said as he arrived. "Did you have time to tell her?"

"I was going to." Van der Hagen turned to Aurora, his face somber. "I must speak with you, Countess."

"Bad news, I'm afraid," said van Gelder. "We got word here in Margarita of a tragedy. We intended to land in Little Venice, but it has been destroyed by an Indian attack."

"Destroyed?" Aurora felt tears prickle her eyes.

"I'm sorry, yes. There are no known survivors. The Spanish in Maracaibo city say it was a massacre. I wouldn't hold out hope," Van der Hagen spoke gently. "As it is, there is no longer a port of call for Aragua. The colony no longer touches the ocean waters. The only way to get you into Aragua now is through Caracas."

"Caracas is not welcoming anyone who isn't Christian," added van Gelder.

"What do you suggest?" Aurora's voice quavered.

"It's best to take you to Curaçao and wait it out there."

"Are we not stopping here at Margarita? I could wait it out here."

"Sorry, Countess. It's for your own safety."

"If you say so." Aurora went to her chamber and stared out the window as *De Heilige Graal* drifted away from the gorgeous island.

A Spanish aviso came alongside the ship, and Count Guillermo Hernández watched from the balcony, high up on his razeé galleon. He hurried inside the captain's cabin to his desk and plunged his nose into a box filled with white powder. He sneezed, covering his grand mustache in powdery residue. His red eyes watered, and he opened the window. Shuddering, he ventured back for another helping of coca-leaf powder.

"This is the most wonderful discovery in all of the New World!" The frilly cuff of his purple suit dipped into the mound on the desk. Hernández licked it until his tongue was numb.

A knock came at the door.

Hernández raised his head trying to respond, but only managed to moan. "Is that news from Sánchez?" he forced.

Captain Iglesias entered, wearing an ornate metal cuirass and morion helmet. An aviso carrying a satchel was beside him.

"From San Juan," said the aviso.

"I don't take requests from that *serpiente*, Governor Carlitos." Hernández rubbed his shiny face.

"This request comes from Don Medina."

"Let's see."

The aviso opened the satchel and handed over a scroll. It was a poster indicating the Countess Aurora was wanted for witchcraft.

"By the grace of God and all that is holy, we will not let this come to pass!" Hernández re-rolled the document. "You will return to San Juan at once." He wrote on a new parchment. "You will take this to Don Medina, and you will tell him that I am coming with all speed." He poured wax and stamped it. "A German witch thinks she can just move into the Spanish Main."

Hernández took another pinch from the box and shivered. "Go-go-go-go, at once! God be with you. Iglesias, come here!"

As the aviso left and Iglesias approached, he dusted powder off his eyelids.

Hernández shook the wanted poster. "She's heading for Aragua. Make for Caracas with all speed!"

"A witch, truly?" Iglesias said.

"*Si*. A German witch! They are the worst. She's coming here to start a colony of pagans in the Americas! We must stop her." Hernández took a small silver spoon from his pocket and brought another helping of white powder to his nose. "By the grace of almighty God, we cannot let that happen. We will capture her alive and bring her to Don Medina to be burned!"

Captain Iglesias saluted and then departed.

Hernández looked at the wanted poster again. "What are you brewing, German witch?"

The sky ignited into a fiery sunset, drenching *De Heilige Graal* in dazzling red light. Aurora opened a case of Cognac using an iron wedge, while slaves set the dinner table.

"Where did you get that?" Van der Hagen asked.

"I used my broomstick." Aurora uncapped a bottle and drank.

"Please be careful. Don't roam the ship. These are dangerous times."

"Curaçao should be visible in a few hours," van Gelder said. "Then dry land for you, Countess. At least until we have a way into Aragua."

"If you don't mind, I'd like to go to Little Venice to see it for myself."

"Out of the question," Van der Hagen said.

"There's nothing left. It's all gone. The same thing happened to Gibraltar. Henry Morgan sacked it, l'Olonnais sacked it, and Laurens sacked it. Now it's gone. It's not coming back," van Gelder said. "The great Lake Maracaibo is unforgiving and famous for intense lightning storms."

"You were hired to take me to Little Venice; I insist you stick to Sophie's original plan," Aurora asserted.

"She needs to find out about her friends and family," Persephone said.

"Her friends have died," van Gelder said. "The plan has changed."

"How so?" Aurora burrowed her fists into her sides. "If you are not willing, then turn south for Caracas, and I'll walk from there. I've been on this boat for ages. I've seen a few maps."

"I won't risk my daughters," Van der Hagen said.

"I'm not asking you to," Aurora countered. "I'll hire a ship in Curaçao."

"We will take you on to Little Venice after we stop at Curaçao," Van der Hagen said.

"That is not advisable," said van Gelder. "But I can get us in there."

Aurora gave a thin smile.

A bell rang, and then another. Followed by drums.

Aurora maneuvered past crewmen and cannons to reach the deck where Van der Hagen, van Gelder and de Britt stood.

"You should be inside, Countess," van Gelder said.

"Who is it this time?" Aurora asked.

"A Spanish razée war galleon, Viscount," said Van Gelder. "It's the *Holy Christ*."

"Order her to give way. They have no cause to stop us."

"She's demanding we surrender."

"But we are allies with the Spanish," said Van der Hagen.

The *Holy Christ* approached, and a Spaniard called through a speaking trumpet. "Surrender your ship, German witch, and face justice!"

"He can't. It's illegal," Van der Hagen protested.

"Have you not heard of the Spanish Inquisition?" van Gelder said to Aurora.

"Like in that painting of the men in red outfits torturing little girls?"

"That's the one."

Van der Hagen patted his face with a handkerchief. "Can we escape?"

"Not without taking heavy damage and possible casualties."

"Don't risk the girls over me," Aurora said. "Tell them I'll surrender."

The Spanish ship fired a warning shot and the Spaniard yelled at his crew, cursing.

"What's he saying?" Van der Hagen said. "I can't make it out."

"Something about the other ship. What other ship?" Aurora said.

Twelve cannonballs screamed overhead, smashing into the *Holy Christ*.

Aurora held her ears and turned around.

"The French warship again," said van Gelder.

Cheval Marin lit up, charging from behind a small island. She fired her secondary guns, igniting the air with smoke and a thunderous clatter.

"*Abschied.*" Aurora went inside.

"Full sail," van Gelder ordered. "Let's get out of here."

Explosions of water crashed around *Holy Christ* as she turned to fire. The Spaniard was jumping up and down on the deck, shouting. The French ship fired again.

Aurora went inside to the grand stateroom to hunker down with Persephone and Katrina as *De Heilige Graal* fled from the skirmish.

Full Moon Bay

Puerto Rico was surrounded by inviting azure water. Palm trees swayed and the landscape swelled with lush bushes and hibiscus flowers. Helena and Dodo gave each other impressed looks as *Fama* rowed up a twisting waterway to a private estate. A group of people waited at a stone pier with marble pillars, casting flower petals before a man riding tall on a white horse.

Helena assumed it was Don Medina. He appeared to be in his late forties, with silvering dark hair. He dressed in black breeches with matching long boots, a pristine white silk shirt and leather vest with gold embroidery. An entourage of noblemen and guards followed.

"*Attraktiver mann*," said Dodo.

"*Ja*." Helena's face warmed, just looking at him.

The ship docked and Helena was assisted down the gangway by Rivero.

A nearby estuary teemed with wildlife. Helena's jaw dropped at the sight of bright pink birds with long legs and curled necks. She wanted to break free from the crowd to go examine the amazing creatures.

Don Medina dismounted.

"This is not necessary," Helena said, as a child threw bright red flower petals.

"Is this for us, or does everyone get the petal treatment?" Dodo asked her.

"These are the people of Full Moon Bay," explained Don Medina. "This is the welcome I come home to every time."

"This is for you?" Helena said.

"Of course. Who did you think it was for? Welcome to my home, Helena Braunschmidt. I am Don Tomás Domingo Romero Medina. You are my guests, and under my protection—you and your painter friend."

Don Medina kissed Helena's hand and guided her to a whitewashed stone villa at the top of the hill. The entrance was marked by sweeping stone steps and ornamental bushes in terracotta pots.

An astonished Helena was shown to her chamber by slaves. The room was neatly appointed, with a four-poster bed, table, chairs, a scenic view, and vases of freshly cut flowers in every corner. She thanked the slaves, but her politeness was wasted, as they did not interact. She stuck her head out the door. Dodo's room was right across from hers. He gave orders to his new slaves.

Helena ventured down the hall, where Dodo was having slaves set up a painting area in the courtyard.

"Is this satisfactory?" Don Medina came up behind her.

"It's beautiful."

"But something bothers you?"

"Yes. I'm not used to having slaves."

"If they bother you, tell them to leave." He motioned to them. "Get out."

"That's not what I meant," said Helena.

"I'll leave you to get settled," said Don Medina. "I'll have some dresses brought to your room. Dinner is at six on the terrace; I hope you'll join me."

"Thank you. Six of the clock."

He exited.

Helena's belly fluttered as she strode down a hallway lined with oil paintings of ship battles and landscapes. The walls were textured with stucco and the ceiling beams fashioned into decorative trusses. By the time she returned to her room, an assortment of gowns was hanging in the wardrobe. She poured water from a pitcher into a basin to wash.

Afterwards, she looked through the dresses to find something plain, then decided on a black and red one with gold trim. A female slave assisted her. At dinner, she ventured out of her room and met Dodo.

"You look beautiful." Dodo inspected the fabric with great interest. "I have to paint this."

Helena brushed him off. "I see you have new clothes, too."

Dodo was dressed in black and gold. "Spanish fabric is so alluring, don't you think?"

They followed torches to a terrace surrounded by white marble pillars and a trellis with robust grapevines. A supper of roasted pork, chorizo, and shrimp marinated in garlic with olive oil had been laid out on silver platters. For dessert, there was almond cake with mango, pineapple, and coconut slices.

Don Medina welcomed them, bidding them to sit. He caught Helena's hand to kiss it. "You look truly beautiful."

"Thank you." Helena smiled almost bashfully. "It's so lovely and tranquil here."

"I will show you the gardens after we dine." Don Medina's eyes kept intruding upon her.

Dodo sat down and sipped some wine. "How long have you lived here?"

"All my life. This is my family estate."

"You live here with your family?" Helena asked.

"Not anymore." Don Medina sipped his wine. "My wife died in childbirth; my daughter, less than a year later. She was a sickly thing."

"I'm sorry."

"My own father died two years ago, and I inherited all this." He began to eat.

Helena relished the sweet air. "How long are we staying?"

"*Mi Luna*, this place was meant for you. You can stay as long as you like."

"You mean, forever?"

"If you wish." He smiled. "You just said you'd like to."

"I did, I do, but I must find *De Heilige Graal*."

"If you let me help you, I can find her for you."

"You'll do that?"

"Consider it done."

"When found, I will move on to our colony."

"If that's what you wish. In the meantime, be my guest and enjoy all my home has to offer."

After supper, they strolled through the gardens. A fountain babbled and water lilies floated on a pond. Helena put her nose to a bright red flower on the trellis. A subtle perfume. Don Medina picked it and slid it behind her ear.

"Lovely. We call this *flor de maga*." He stroked her brown hair.

Helena shied away and continued to explore. She caught sight of a small lizard on a tree branch and extended her arm. It climbed on.

"Uh, do they bite?" Dodo asked.

"She's not afraid of anything, is she?" Don Medina remarked.

"Not at all."

Later that evening, Helena and Dodo sat on the window bench in Helena's room.

"Do you like him?" Helena ate a slice of mango, offering the remnants to the lizard.

Dodo shrugged. "I don't know yet."

"Oh, look!" Helena pointed out a shooting star.

"A seascape," Dodo exclaimed. "I must paint a seascape."

"With a shooting star?"

"Maybe."

Helena went to bed. At first, she had a hard time falling asleep, unaccustomed to the absence of vicious waves rocking her to sleep. She looked to the far side of the room, half expecting Gretsch to be at his table, stealthily peering at her. Her thoughts then turned to her dog, Ares. He would love to cuddle beside her in such a large bed. She'd wake in the middle of the night sometimes and reach down for her furry companion, then realize he was not there. Helena wiped a tear away. At least Ares was with Oskar. She hoped both of them were safe.

The following morning, Helena's slave helped her acquire a plain linen skirt, old leather boots, a peasant blouse and an apron. Perfect for exploring the estuary. After packing a satchel with her notebook, a quill and a pot of ink, she swiped a stick of graphite from Dodo's supplies.

She trekked into the stable to saddle a horse, then rode down the hill.

The flock of pink birds waded, feeding on fish, while iridescent dragonflies skimmed the water's surface. Bright green parrots nestled within clusters of almond trees. Helena sighed happily, not knowing where to begin. She followed various water channels, pausing to sketch the unique creatures she found there.

After hours of exploration, she returned to the villa. After freshening up, she changed into a garnet red gown with frilled cuffs.

As she entered the courtyard, Dodo was putting the final touches to a landscape painting while sipping a drink.

"What's that?" asked Helena.

"*Sangaree*. A recipe from Martinique, made from Madeira wine, sugar cane, lemon and spices." He took another mouthful. "*Wunderbar!*"

It wasn't long before he passed out on a chaise longue.

Helena sat down to review her notes on animals. Hearing a clank, she investigated and found, just over the hedge, Don Medina practicing his sparring with a dummy clad in armor. His bare chest glistened with perspiration, and he spotted her as he changed swords. He waved her over.

Helena slipped through the path in the hedge.

"Come to spar with me, *mi luna?*"

"Not *Countess?*"

"You seem to prefer it." He continued waving a sword.

"I was getting used to it."

She inspected various sword styles, choosing a thin metal one.

"What type is this?"

"A rapier, *señorita.*"

"Intriguing. Spar with me," she challenged.

"I don't want you to get hurt," he said. "Take my wooden one."

"You are trying to get me to hold your wood."

Don Medina seized a wooden sword and stood with his legs apart.

"Is that a Spanish stance?" Helena asked. "Well, this is a German stance."

She held a wood sword with both hands and spun it around, attacking. Wood cracked against wood.

"Something wrong?" Helena queried.

"I was not expecting you to be so fast." He seemed impressed. "Now *I* don't want to get hurt."

"I'll be careful with your wood."

Don Medina demonstrated a basic forward thrust move. Helena parried and faked a right jab. He blocked. She went for his groin, and he overprotected. She slipped her sword past his and stopped at his neck.

"Ha!" She smiled. "I killed you in ten seconds!"

"You cheated."

They shared an amorous look before returning to a combat stance.

"There's no such thing in war. Besides, you didn't say *go*."

"Again?" he offered.

"Ready, set, go!"

They cracked swords again, and their eyes locked. Helena demonstrated a fake forward thrust. Don Medina parried. She faked a jab to her left. He parried again. Helena manoeuvred past his defense and again stopped at his neck. "Ha, you are mine!"

"From the moment I first saw you, *mi luna*."

Helena patted her face with her sleeve.

"Where did you learn to fight?" he asked.

"Ten years living on the front lines in Transylvania and Prussia." She unlaced her top to show the scar over her heart. "By the time I was a year old, I had this."

"Impressive. How did you get that?"

"I don't remember." She pointed downwards, by his groin. "Tell me, why is it so curved?"

"I beg your pardon?"

Helena indicated the sword. "That one. That one there."

"A cutlass. That's for fighting in close quarters on ship," Don Medina said. "You see, under all that rigging, you don't want it too long."

"Isn't that a matter of preference?"

She put down the wooden sword and went for the cutlass.

"Careful with that."

"I will be. And it's for slicing, I see."

"That's enough for today." He snapped his fingers and pointed. Slaves cleaned up the swords.

"Perhaps later, you can challenge me with your wooden sword again?"

"I am at your disposal night and day. But I must leave soon. I must go in search of your ship. There have been sightings in Bocas del Dragón."

"I'm coming with you."

"Have you not had enough of sea battles? I would be honored if you were to wait here for my return. Here you will be safe and comfortable."

Helena nodded. "Besides, I don't think Dodo can travel anytime soon." She kissed his cheek. "Thank you, Don Medina."

"Anything for you, Countess."

"I did tell you, I'm not the countess."

"You are a countess to me." He kissed her mouth.

She reacted awkwardly at first, and then tackled him, tearing down his breeches. He raised her skirt and mounted her from behind. He penetrated her hard and fast. When he stopped after only a minute, Helena waited to see if there was anything more, but no.

"Forgive me. I couldn't help myself," he said. "You are so beautiful, my countess."

"When do you pull out? I mean, leave?"

"Tomorrow I leave for San Juan."

"Then we have all night, don't we?"

The light of the full moon beamed through the windows of Helena's room. Silver platters with remnants of food and empty wine bottles sat on the table. Blankets were twisted and scattered all over the bed as Helena, with her backside in the air, was being penetrated by Don Medina. They both moaned loudly, not caring who heard them.

Eventually they exchanged positions. Helena pushed him down, climbing on top. She straddled him, facing the window. His hands held her hips as she gyrated until her thighs quivered and spasms of pleasure came.

Helena fell back on the bed and Don Medina was upon her. His manhood brushed her thigh, then plunged into her, pumping hard and fast. They kissed passionately and Helena gently bit his lip. They undulated until finishing.

Helena reached for a half-full wine bottle and took a throatful. She handed it over, and he took a mouthful.

They stared at the moonlight.

"No wonder it's called Full Moon Bay," said Helena.

"I could stay here forever. I have everything I want right here," said Don Medina.

"How about tomorrow and the next day?"

"I have always wanted a son."

"A son? Mijo? Little Miguel?"

"Domingo-Romero, after my father. A strong son. A son born from your womb."

"Mine? That's a bit fast."

"Life is fast. Bear me a son?"

"You never know about these things. You may end up with a daughter."

He gave her such a menacing stare that for the first time, she was uncomfortable around him.

"You could give me the most handsome, strong, intelligent son."

"We can certainly try."

Don Medina spread her thighs and delved into her again. The bottle dropped to the floor and rolled. The liquid gushed onto the marble floor.

Life's Mingled Yarn

May 1690

The imposing though incomplete citadel of Fort Charles guarded the entrance to Port Royal's harbor, where the fish docks and turtle pens bustled. The sun reflected pristinely on the water's surface as ships sailed in and out. Smoke from bake houses whorled through the air as merchants opened their shops.

A week had passed since the pirate siege, and townsfolk were cleaning up. During the chaos, Rosie Burghill had stayed hidden within the walls of the Wild Orchid Palace, the former home of the Dutchess of Albemarle. When things settled, she ventured to the Swiftsure to find her friend Atia, but the tavern was deserted. The only person she found was the strumpet Sierra Lee, who had cowered in one of the broom closets. Bleedin Art's men, Scarcliff and Blackmoor, arrived to assess the damage and hired the two women on the spot to start repairs and clean up so they could reopen.

Soon after, she received a note from Atia, who had been ushered away by her Capitaine. She wasn't sure when she'd return but promised to write. With the note came a separate message for Bleedin Art, which Rosie had delivered to a servant at Valentine Mansion.

It was odd, suddenly being made a bar wench, but Rosie cheerfully pushed the cart along towards the King's Landing.

Sierra Lee joined her, and they continued.

"Are you quite well?" Rosie asked.

"Aye." Sierra Lee massaged her abdomen.

They continued to push and pull, only to get the cart stuck in the mud. Rosie slipped and fell on her behind, while Sierra Lee doubled over.

"You with child or something?" asked Rosie.

"Nay. Just ill is all."

Selina Spotswood approached them. "Give them a hand, will you?" she told her servants.

Soon the cart was back on solid ground.

"Thanks, Selina," said Sierra Lee. "We gotta go. We got Violante Hayze to look after. Bleedin Art wants to capitalize on the new strumpet heroine."

"She's in some awful pain. You can hear her screams all night," said Rosie.

"I saw them take the poor little wretch away," said Selina. "Her collarbone was sticking right out. We shan't see the likes of her again. Lady Beeston says Captain White thinks otherwise. Well, MacAskill's the bone-setter, and he's likely to die as well. Poor Violante."

"She's a bitch," Rosie said.

They all laughed.

"I know she is. Give her a pat on the shoulder from me." Selina went on, with the servants following.

Rosie and Sierra Lee continued to pull the cart.

"I didn't know you knew her," said Rosie.

"Aye. They're not all bad at Beeston's. I've known Selina since I first came here. She's me mate, and she's a wench. Don't let her delicate appearance fool you."

"She's a Spotswood?"

"Aye, a cousin. She comes from a rich family, but she still had to wench when she came here. Notice she doesn't like Violante much. Selina had to leave Nevis. She disgraced her family."

"What did she do?"

"She had an affair with her cousin's husband—Captain Longstaff," Sierra Lee said, her voice lowered.

"With Longstaff?" Rosie pondered. "Who hasn't had an affair with Longstaff."

"And apparently she still has feelings for—it."

They both chuckled.

"So, she's jealous of Violante. A woman of wealth, jealous of a strumpet," said Rosie. "Life's certainly a mingled yarn."

"And of course, Violante is not too keen on Selina."

"Selina could do so much better. Why don't we have a horse?" Rosie said. "Or is that a donkey? Maybe you can ask Selina to rent us a horse."

"Bleedin Art said he'll get us a horse as soon as he's out of prison. All his horses got killed in the attack."

"Prison? He's not in prison no more. He's on *Guernsey,* up the harbor a way, as the prisons are full."

"But if he's under house arrest, shouldn't he be at home?" Sierra Lee wondered.

They rolled the cart up to King's Landing. Repairs and salvage operations were taking place everywhere. Fort James stood opposite the clock tower, where a broken sign indicated *The King's Grand C-ock.* Beneath, the town crier and his drummer readied for the morning news. The drummer pounded away until the town crier covered his ears. With one last beat from the drummer, the crier cleared his throat. Townspeople gathered.

"And now for the morning news," the crier bellowed. "Brought to you by Snuff It! The very best in tobacco imports this side of Cuba." He paused. "Acting Governor Dewar and Justice Llewellyn have been arrested for corruption, along with our senior navy officials, but Acting Governor Captain Council Chairman President White assures you all that our leadership is in complete control."

At that moment, a fire erupted on a nearby ship and a dock hand fell screaming into the sea. The town crier shielded his head from flying debris. "The situation is entirely in hand. In May, our heroic English troops conquered Port Royal—the other Port Royal, in Nova Scotia."

"Oh, *that* Port Royal," someone heckled. "Well, who cares about them?"

"Any Port Royal is a good Port Royal, as long as it's English," said the town crier.

"Bloody well right," the drummer said.

"The Act of Grace law is in effect over all English territory. This forgives followers of King James so long as they stop following him…White wrote that himself, did he?" the town crier said quietly to the drummer, who nodded.

Rosie and Sierra Lee continued up to Thames Street.

"Is there not a law that forbids the same man from being both governor and council president?" a bystander questioned.

The town crier looked as though he were about to answer. "Meanwhile, in the Bahamas, Colonel Cadwallader Jones has been declared a traitor for proclaiming himself King and Supreme Ruler of New Gwynedd. Your government assures you that law and order will be restored. Colonel Jones will be brought to justice and the Welsh shall never again return to the Bahamas.

"In other news, many fishermen have gone missing off south Jamaica. Some fishermen claim the feared Samaná Bay kraken has returned. Acting Governor Captain Council Chairman President White assures you that the beast poses no threat." The crier paused for a breath. "And finally, an Indian raid in Lake Maracaibo has destroyed the German settlement of Little Venice. Spanish officials say the small port was completely destroyed and there are no known survivors."

Sierra Lee and Rosie rolled by a great Tudor-style inn on the waterfront, the Catt and Fiddle, on the front of which hung a sign offering the premises for sale or lease. They pushed on to the busy King's Warehouses, where goods were being unloaded.

Men aboard the *Lady Sarah* lowered crates to the pier, while Humphrey Freeman supervised. He was tall, gray and wore a permanent scowl. With him was silver-haired John Morris, dictating the supply inventory in a raspy voice.

"Stubbs, you carrion," Freeman growled. "Why must you always dock too close to the goddamn lane!"

Captain Thomas Stubbs, with a leathery face and a patch over his left eye, peered over the rail of the quarterdeck. "She'll be out of the way in a few hours. Besides, it's for fast getaways."

"Make a fast getaway to Smith's Landing next time. We have a shipment of goods coming in from China. I want this spot clear before it gets here," Freeman barked.

"When's this junk due to arrive?"

"Not immediately," Freeman said.

Stubbs swung down to the wharf.

"Mr. Morris, you old seadog. Are ya well?" Stubbs asked.

Morris gave an inaudible answer and raised his hands.

"Glad to hear it," Stubbs said. "Gentlemen, I've returned home with goods and spices to keep your businesses happy, but I see all is not well in our fair city."

"Indeed not, Captain Stubbs. We recently found ourselves in a hostage situation," said Freeman. "We lost many a friend and foe. Some formidable ones, too. We should talk."

"I'll dock at Smith's Landing."

"Next time, I said. Unload where she is. We'll store it all here until things get sorted out. Welcome home, Captain Stubbs."

"Aye, Mr. Freeman."

As Stubbs moved on, Freeman noticed Sierra Lee but ignored her.

"Good day, sir," Sierra Lee began.

"Uh, good day, ladies. Miss Burghill," replied Freeman.

"Mr. Freeman," Sierra Lee said.

"What is it you want?" Freeman frowned.

"We're just passing through on our way to the Swiftsure. I'm a wench there now."

"You are? Well, good for you." His face saddened and he returned to work, yelling at dock workers.

Rosie and Sierra Lee pushed on to the next block.

"I serviced Mr. Freeman regularly when I was a strumpet," said Sierra Lee.

"You did?" Rosie's eyes grew large.

"I'll miss him some; he's kind. He's got a strong cock for an old man."

Rosie cringed, and her left eye spasmed.

"All those years of maintaining wood has served him well. I've also serviced Captain Stubbs from time to time, but not as often, as he's happily married, and Cherry Banks was his favorite anyways. Who knows why."

"Captain Stubbs used to be an officer for John Coxon when he was a privateer," Rosie said. "My father used to put up their bond. He used to tell me that John Coxon and Stubbs liked to practice sword-fighting with Cherry."

"Well, we know what kind of swordplay."

"What about Mr. Morris? Did you service him?" Rosie asked.

"Nay, he likes the cheap slags on Lime Street."

"Ew!" Rosie recoiled and they rolled on to the next block. "That German captain, Dietrich, likes you."

"He's me patient, not me customer. Art's got me nursing him back to health. Let's just say he's not up to standard yet. Soon, though. He's startin' to have a maypole in the morning. That's a sign of improvement, MacAskill says."

"He likes you all the same."

"Why do you say that?"

"He stares at you. He likes you, trust me."

A pirate passed by and grabbed Sierra Lee's breast.

Sierra Lee clutched herself.

"Bastard!" Rosie said.

"Just keep going," Sierra Lee said. "I really miss Atia sometimes." She began to limp. "I'm in need of Dr. Strangewayes's Miracle Plug."

"What's that?"

"A pessary of poppy extract and belladonna shoved right up yer backside. Makes nothing hurt below the waist. Crisp's men did me in, in me lady parts."

"What did they do?" Rosie's eyebrows peaked.

"They rough-handled me in all the tight spaces. You seem very interested."

"Of course not. What else did they do?"

Sierra Lee and Rosie pushed the cart by the Old Forge. Lady Anne Beeston stood barking orders at her slaves as they unloaded barrels of water. Her auburn hair was curled into the latest fashion, and she stood there in a shimmering red satin gown.

Selina was there, overseeing the cart of fish products.

Rosie and Sierra Lee gave her a wink as they passed by.

"Selina did good gettin' in with Lady Beeston," said Sierra Lee.

"I heard a rumor that Beesty Bill is winning his trial," said Rosie. "What do you think will happen if he comes back?"

"More of this, I suppose."

"Lady Beeston's been running the family business now for so long in her husband's stead, I can't remember a time before," said Rosie. "I overheard meetings; Violante's Big Dick often spoke highly of Beesty Bill. Lady Beeston is respected and feared because everyone in the city knows he was framed, and his trial in England is more to do with political parties competing for dominance than it is about the charges of fraud. Everyone's expecting Beesty Bill to return, and when he does, there will be blood." Rosie took a deep breath.

"You seem to know a lot, girl. Do you know where we go next?"

"Just one more stop. There's the Market Square, off Honey Lane, for all the fancy imports and fresh bread. They have salmon from Ireland, and kippers."

They rolled the cart down the alley towards the Wherry Bridge and to the loading bay of a three-story building, the Swiftsure Tavern.

The past ten months had been a bit of blur for Dr. Sander Strangewayes. It started with a hurricane, a change of government, his assignment to provide disaster relief for Nevis, his plantation in the Jamaican Blue Mountains getting blown up, being mandated aboard *Blessed William* under Captain Kidd, being nominated by the French to be the new governor of Jamaica and returning home to Port Royal in the middle of a pirate siege, only to immediately suffer severe angina.

When he regained consciousness at the infirmary at Fort Carlisle, his large marmalade cat, Boots, was sitting on his tender chest. "Uh, hello, old chum." He struggled to breathe. "Long time no see." At first it was a shock that he was still alive. He mulled over the events of the past few months, convinced that his recounting might have left out a few details, though confident they would eventually surface.

As his strength returned, he was inundated with requests from people asking him how to set bones and how to stitch this and that—obviously injuries from the pirate siege. He also learned that Dr. Marcus MacAskill, the acting chief surgeon during his absence, had also been wounded. Doctors were dwindling in the wickedest city on earth, and he determined that reaching age sixty-one would indeed be an achievement.

Strangewayes unearthed a small box of coca-leaf powder and a silver spoon from his medical bag. He snorted through his crooked nose, shuddered, and began to perspire. He then tended to Violante Hayze, who was lying in bed. Her recently born son, little Richard, slept in a cradle next to her.

Violante had broken her collarbone firing a blunderbuss at a pirate during the siege. The collarbone protruded through the skin and was difficult to reset. There were over thirty stitches, gunpowder burns, and bits of shrapnel embedded in her marred flesh.

Strangewayes leaned over her, unaware his sweat was dripping onto her face.

She cursed under her breath.

"Did you say something?" Strangewayes said. "No? Hold still."

After cleansing all the wounds with gin, he administered some laudanum.

"Oh, dear, you are sweating a lot." The doctor dabbed her forehead with cotton. He packed his medical bag and paused on a small brown bottle. "Do you want me to leave an extra one?"

"Yes please, Doc."

"Promise not to take too much?"

She groaned in the affirmative and he left it on the night table.

Strangewayes went next door to the parlor, where silver-haired Mrs. Abigail Beazley napped on a chaise longue.

The front door slammed downstairs and female laughter resonated up the stairs. Sierra Lee and Rosie Burghill returned from their supply run.

"Good news, Mrs. Beazley, the day shift is here," said the doctor.

Mrs. Beazley rolled onto her side. "Thank goodness."

"Dr. Heath is not much of a bonesetter, but I must admit, despite the terrible stitching, it does seem to be healing nicely."

Violante's bell rang, which sent her baby into a crying fit.

"Oh, she wants something." Strangewayes examined his pocket watch. "Look at the time. Rosie and Sierra Lee are here to look after you, Violante. I think little Richard needs a changing, too."

"Sorry we're late," Rosie said. "It's busy out there."

"I must be off to tend to other patients," Strangewayes continued. "I'll leave Vie in your capable hands."

The baby cried louder.

"We'll be right there, Little Bastard—I mean, little Richard," Sierra Lee yelled.

Strangewayes assisted Mrs. Beazley to her feet. "Come along, Abbey, dear, I'll drop you at home."

"I'll come with you. I'm puzzled by MacAskill's infection."

"You'll get no argument from me."

They went to the infirmary at Fort Carlisle by carriage and were met by Port Royal officials Captain White, Colonel Beckford and Commissioner Snead.

"Good day, gentlemen. Are we all here to check on the status of the city's chief surgeon?" Strangewayes said.

"It is a nasty infection," said White. "Obviously, we missed something in the good doctor's wounds."

Strangewayes continued through to a room where many wounded lay.

Red Legs Greaves sat with his head in a bandage, a straggly ginger beard hanging off his face. Red Legs was a comrade from the doctor's adventures aboard the *Blessed William*. The crew had later mutinied and renamed the ship *Sainte Rose*, leaving Captain Kidd stranded in Nevis.

"Doc, did we do it? Did we take Port Royal?" Red Legs asked groggily.

"Well, not exactly."

"Red Legs Greaves, you are a prisoner in Port Royal," White said. "In due time you will be moved to Marshallsea prison to await trial."

"I thought he was pardoned by the Act of Grace law," Strangewayes said.

"That was for pirates who left the city. You two never left. You're both under arrest for piracy and treason," Beckford explained. "As soon as Mr. Greaves is better, both of you can spend the next twenty years in prison together."

"I of course, may plead insanity, and it's a defence I'm willing to prove," said Strangewayes.

"Oh, you've proved it," Beckford said.

"I'm not sending you to prison, Sander; we have plans for you," said White.

Mrs. Beazley took bottles of leeches and maggots to Dr. MacAskill.

"I'll be right with you, Mrs. Beazley," said Strangewayes.

"When you're finished with Dr. MacAskill and your other patients, you'll report to the King's House," White said.

"For a fair trial, or just sentencing?"

"Would you like a trial?" Beckford offered.

"You need a chief surgeon at a time like this," Strangewayes said.

"The Samaná Bay kraken would be less problematic," White remarked. "Don't you worry, Sander. I'll have it all tried, sentenced, and executed by this evening's end. Just make sure you're at the King's House on time."

"Incidentally, who have you chosen as chief surgeon?"

"Dr. Heath."

"Heath? The shaky hand of God himself?" Strangewayes shook his head and went behind a screen to where MacAskill lay, his abdomen swelling purple and blue with pus seeping from a large surgical wound. "Good news, Marcus. I have two of your favorite remedies, maggots and leeches. Now, I hear Dr. Heath performed your surgery. I do hope he didn't rely on Jesus to close."

Strangewayes took a closer look at the wound. "Oh dear, he did."

"Are you cleaning it with the rum?" Beckford asked.

"Hell no. The rum is for us," Strangewayes said. "The gin's for cleaning. Now, Marcus, Heath said he removed the shot and cleaned the wound. Do you remember who shot you?"

"Does that matter?" Beckford asked.

"I want to find out what kind of gun it was. We may be looking for several more rounds." Strangewayes referenced a book. "Now, which one was it? No, that's for the autopsy. Okay, Marcus, I'm here to cut you up—aren't you lucky!"

"Came all the way from Nevis for me, did ya?"

"That, and Captain Kidd was difficult to get along with." Strangewayes cut away the remainder of MacAskill's shirt to see that the stitches had broken on his swollen abdomen. "Unfortunately, further surgery is necessary. Mrs. Beazley will assist."

"You're going to let a *woman* assist you?" Snead scoffed. "That's preposterous!"

"Are you up to the challenge, Snead?" MacAskill barked.

"Perhaps just this once, as it's an emergency," Snead said. "After all, I heard we have Bizy Gale on the gun battery."

"In times of war, everyone pitches in, Commissioner," said White.

Mrs. Beazley and Dr. Strangewayes set up a large magnifying glass with adjustable lenses.

The doctor altered the settings to focus in on extra-fine details. "Courtesy of our friends the Braunschmidts of Hanover. We import their telescopes and microscopes. Very impressive." Strangewayes finished cleaning the surgical tools. "Right. Any last words?"

Mrs. Beazley wiped down MacAskill's belly with gin, and he yelped.

"You have to tell me if you have no intention of leaving me alive," MacAskill uttered.

"Dr. MacAskill, sir, I assure you, if you wake up at all, you'll wake up a man, I promise." He handed over a vial. "If that's the bronze liquid, drink it. I'm color blind."

MacAskill sucked it back and then coughed it back up. "What was that?"

"Oops, wrong one."

"You quack!"

"There are two kinds of doctors. One who wants to cure the sick and injured, and one who wants the title. I, sir, am a doctor." Strangewayes nodded to Mrs. Beazley, who produced a bottle of dwale.

"Are you gonna give me opium tablets for the pain?" asked MacAskill.

"I've got something called *dwale*; you won't feel a thing!" Strangewayes poured the bottle down MacAskill's throat.

When Captain Arthur Valentine awoke in the Lime Street lockup chained to two strumpets, a man in a corset and a donkey, he wasn't sure if he was awake or dreaming. Then the stench crept into his nostrils.

"Right, clear out, you lot!" The jailor banged the bars with a wood truncheon. "Arthur Valentine, you've been released by Acting Governor White."

Art clambered from the cell. "Nice sleepin' with you ladies." He tipped his hat.

Arrested after the pirate siege, he had been charged with conspiracy, consorting with pirates and treason against the Crown. All prerequisites to live in Port Royal.

He was to be transferred to Marshallsea prison, but it was full. So, he was released under the condition of house arrest. He negotiated with Captain White to be under ship arrest aboard *Guernsey*.

Before resigning to his ship, he ventured to his mansion for a badly needed bath. Hoping to avoid a confrontation with his wife, he snuck through the servant entrance. Art pulled the servant's cord, and a white-haired maid charged down the hall.

"Sir?"

"Ready me a bath."

"Yes, sir."

Art retreated into the sanctuary of his Inferno Room. He set his leather pouch on his desk, and half a dozen scrolls escaped onto the floor. Poems he'd written in his cell for his revered redhead. He was disappointed, to say the least, when he heard of Atia being taken away from Port Royal on the Capitaine's ship.

"That French bastard!" Art said under his breath and returned the scrolls to his bag.

An envelope sat on his desk with his name on it, inscribed with the childlike handwriting of Rosie Burghill. He opened it and found a folded parchment.

My Bleeding Heart, sorry I didn't get to say goodbye in person. No idea where I'm goin'. Find out when I get there. Will let you know. Whiskey kisses, A.

A ridiculous grin crept across his face as he put the note in his pouch. "That's my girl."

Servants arrived, pouring buckets of hot water into his copper tub.

Art went behind a screen to peel away his soiled clothes. He tossed his jacket and silk shirt to the floor, revealing a dozen scars across his back, various tattoos on his arms and a pair of crossed cutlasses on his chest. After unlacing his boots, he removed his trousers.

"Anything else, sir?" a servant asked.

"Bring me a Sir Cloudesley." Art kicked his ruined clothes across the floor. "And you can burn these."

"Yes, sir."

He waited until the door clicked before venturing out. A clean towel and a cake of soap waited on a chair next to his tub. He slipped into the hot water and sank deeply. Within minutes he was delivered a drink of beer and spiced brandy. He savored the flavor, a drink named after Sir Cloudesley Shovell, who once battled Barbary corsairs.

His peace was disturbed by the stomping of feet growing closer to the Inferno Room. Mrs. Katheryne Valentine threw open the door and stared daggers at him.

"Do you mind? It's me private time," Art said.

"You've embarrassed me for the last time. Do you know how this makes us look? Mother is furious," Mrs. V snarled.

"Oh, I upset Granny, did I?" Art rolled his eyes. "Oh, dear."

At that moment, Granny's bell rang.

"For whom the bell tolls," Art chided.

"You make me sick. Your failed deals, your stupid mates, and your pathetic infatuation with that red-haired slut wench! I don't want to see you in this house."

"I'll do ya better than that; I'll give you a divorce."

"A divorce?" Mrs. V laughed icily. "Don't make me laugh."

"You forget your place," Art said.

"My place is picking up after you, as always. I'll run the properties the way I want to from now on."

"After all I've done for you. Marrying you when no one else would, and writing you songs."

Her face turned crimson. "Songs! Songs?" She went over to his desk and grabbed several pages. "Oh, like 'Crow's Nest Kathy!' 'Ships that Go Bump in the Night.' 'Bend Down so I Can Get Over You!'"

"That's me favorite." Art grinned. "They show genuine affection and artistic flair."

"I can't even begin with this one." She flapped another piece of paper. "For your redhead, I suppose. I've never even heard of this position! For someone who despises the Earl of Rochester, you write just like him."

Art mimed an arrow through the chest. "Is that it?"

"I'll have my own protection from now on. Inform your thugs to stay away from the house. We're finished. I'll have to sell the Salutacon and the Swiftsure. I'm not losing the Feathers!"

"You won't have to sell nothin'."

"Oh, you have another hare-brained scheme, of course. Are you and your mates going to swindle the Vatican?"

"As it is, I've been charged to hunt pirates."

"Pirate hunting with a commission? Who, Laurens?"

"Cadwallader Jones and Pierre le Grande, to start."

"Cadwallader, your old partner. I warned you about him."

"Aye, that you did," Art admitted.

"Sounds dangerous." His wife sounded pleased.

"I might never return."

"The pirate hunter who brings down Laurens de Graaf will go down in history with fame and fortune—or just go down."

"I'll save Laurens for last; that'll drive the price up a bit."

"Update the will before you leave. When do you leave?"

"After my bath, if you're nice enough."

"I'll have some of the private stock brought out to make your voyage more comfortable." She closed the door on her way out.

Art sank back into the tub, taking another mouthful of beer and brandy. "Already taken care of." He scanned the room. Most of his stuff was packed and would be couriered to *Guernsey* presently.

He scrubbed himself clean and dried off before going to a wooden wardrobe that housed new custom-tailored clothes and shiny new footwear. Art selected a suit of Persian red with embroidered gold accents. His leggings were black, the matching shoes embellished with gold buckles. The final touch was a silk sash around his waist. Next, he combed his oily locks, adding some pomade and gathering it at the back and tying it with a ribbon. *Now, that's ship of the line*, he thought and topped his head with a black tri-cornered hat.

He took out a fresh sheet of parchment and wrote a list he intended to drop off at Strangewayes Apothecary. Then, with his pouch on his shoulder, he collected his best ivory walking cane and departed the room with a spring in his step.

He passed his future ex-wife on the way out and paused. "We had some good times in this house. Not at the same time, but good times they were, nonetheless."

"You know where you can stick your farewell sonnet," she chided.

Art gave her a cold smile and exited. He paused at the wrought-iron gate to the property and inhaled deeply, savoring freedom.

After dropping off an order at Strangewayes Apothecary, he went to the Merchant Exchange, a cluster of buildings at the center of town, where you could buy anything from anywhere in the world. He went to the dressmaker at Annabelle's and purchased an assortment of dresses, silk nightwear, a parasol, and other fancy accoutrements to be delivered to the ship.

Next, he crossed over to the Salutacon, an inn, tavern, and private dock, near the Wherry Bridge. The corvette *Stingray*, formerly *Stachelrochen*, was under refit in the harbor, next to his new home, *Guernsey,* a larger, pretty merchantman with red and gold trim, docked in front of his establishment.

Art followed the gangway up to the main deck.

Crewmen were preparing for luncheon, readying tables and chairs and setting the sails horizontally to block the sun. On the captain's private deck, Art sat in the shaded area. A servant brought him bread, cheese, cured meat and fruit. Having plenty of time before a meeting at the King's House, he covered his eyes with his hat.

The Tying of New Threads

Dr. Strangewayes arrived at the slightly charred King's House around six. Captain White and Beckford were kind enough to collect him from the infirmary. Strangewayes had quickly discovered pieces of shrapnel lodged throughout MacAskill's belly, which turned the surgery into an all-day ordeal.

They were directed to the study, as the dining hall was under construction. Hammering and sawing vibrated the walls. Strangewayes took a seat at a table and discreetly took a pinch of coca-leaf powder while everyone's attention was at the door.

"Where's Valentine?" Snead asked.

"He'll be here," said White.

"All the same, I sent an attaché to get him," Beckford said. "Incidentally, he has properties that remain undamaged. Why does he stay on his ship? House arrest should be house arrest."

Captain Stubbs and Freeman entered, followed by Dr. Heath and Skean, who was pale and shaking in his clean clerical robe.

"You don't like the sea much, do you?" White said to Skean.

"Maritime? What's merry about it?"

Everyone sat, Skean next to Strangewayes.

"My god, man, what happened to you?" Strangewayes asked.

"Mr. Skean swam all the way from Santa Catalina," White said.

"How'd you survive?" Captain Stubbs said.

"I was picked up by some old fishermen."

"Lucky break," said Freeman.

"Not luck," said Skean. "Justice Goblet asked them to follow *HMS Relentless* in case such an incident should happen. Which it did."

"I'm still missing something," Strangewayes said.

"Captain Longstaff threw him overboard, Doctor," White explained.

"What a dick," Strangewayes remarked.

"*Former* Justice Goblet," White corrected. "He became unraveled in our recent hostage crisis."

"I'm sorry to say Justice Goblet died from the ordeal," added Beckford.

"I am aware," Skean said.

Bleedin Art entered the room. "Longstaff made ya walk the plank, did he?"

"To tell you the truth, Captain Valentine, I thought *walk the plank* was a figure of speech," said Skean.

"Dick must like you, or he'd have had you keelhauled," Art said. "I suppose that takes care of the murder charge."

"We still have Captain Longstaff on corruption. And you too, Art," White said.

"We're all glad to see you well," Stubbs told Skean.

"Brother Skean is from the Secret Service," Beckford said. "Ministry of Intelligence, level three?"

"So, you're a Whig?" Freeman growled. "A Whig spy? If I was Longstaff, I might have thrown ya over myself."

"Justice Goblet was my superior. I was sent here to uncover corruption in the slave industry. We uncovered Bleedin Art's shady practices with Barbados and the ties to Crisp with Curaçao and Tobago—and the smuggling ring of Dr. Strangewayes," Skean explained. "The level of corruption in the slave industry is costing the Royal Africa Company an estimated twenty million pounds a year."

Art grinned sardonically.

"What we recently discovered is that the Earl of Inchiquin, soon to be governor of Jamaica, signed a contract with the Fuggers in Germany to take control of your banking project in Ligania," Skean continued. "The Fuggers have signed a deal with a landowner from the Barbary Coast called Baron de Klauwen. One to replace all the slave trade in the Caribbean."

"Where is this enterprise?" Morris asked. "I've never heard of it."

"We don't know the location, but Baron de Klauwen's flagship has landed at Tobago, and the Earl of Inchiquin is due here in October. So, we can only assume construction has begun."

"If what you're saying is true, they'll need us out of the way if their plan is to succeed," White said.

"We should just report him to the Royal Africa Company," Beckford said.

"Then he reports *us* to the Royal Africa Company," said White.

"The Earl of Inchiquin plans to kill all of you," Skean said.

"All of us?" Beckford blanched. "Me?"

"All of you, but most of all Lady Beeston."

"Why her?" Beckford insisted. "She's not in the slave business; she's in the pig business."

"There is a bitter rivalry between the Earl of Inchiquin and Admiral Beeston. All those pig farms they're buying are all around your new bank in Ligania. The Beestons are planning an indentured servant's prison on Jamaica to sell out of Port Royal. A simple case of conflicting interests."

"Who will do the shipping?" Freeman asked. "The Dutch? Not likely; they'll be killing Curaçao and Tobago."

"Pierre le Grande out of Hispaniola, Samuel Seele, Black Caesar, and Cadwallader Jones," White deduced.

"We know Baron de Klauwen's contact is Don Medina in Puerto Rico," said Skean. "The don is distributing slaves between San Juan and Santo Domingo. I suspect Governor Carlitos of San Juan, but we have no proof."

"How did you tie the earl and the baron into this?" White said.

"By accident. I stumbled upon an insurance claim through the city records. Baron de Klauwen's claiming compensation for four hundred slaves without receipts," Skean said.

"Not unheard of; I lost four hundred slaves last year," Art said.

"Partly due to a hurricane," said White.

"In part? The bloody hurricane sunk my ships!" Art protested.

"Well, those caravels were said to be as old as Columbus," White added.

"Baron de Klauwen is claiming four hundred *a month* lost at sea," said Skean.

Both White and Beckford raised their eyebrows. "A month?"

"Could be disease. They keep them in a terrible state on the Barbary Coast," said Art. "Slaves are on the ship for two years or more, stacked like fish. Most are dead before they arrive."

"Seems terribly wasteful," said Beckford.

"Keeps the economy going," Art said.

"The Earl of Inchiquin has signed orders by the king to have all of you hanged as soon as he arrives, for the state the city is in—and the economy, as you say," Skean said.

"Very well, Mr. Skean," White said. "You have our attention. What do you propose we do?"

"I suggest you strike first: clean up the city, clean up corruption and tie up loose ends before he gets here. Cadwallader Jones is a wanted criminal in the Bahamas. Laurens de Graaf is the most wanted pirate in the Caribbean, next to Roc Braziliano. Bring in some famous names. Demonstrate law and order, and he'll have nothing to execute you for. Their plans have gone tits-up. What was supposed to be a military operation by the French ended with pirates being greedy."

"Commodore Valentine is temporarily pardoned," said White.

"Temporarily pardoned?" Beckford scoffed. "We've been far too lenient with him. Talbot should be commodore of this mission."

"Talbot's searching the Jamaica Channel for Laurens de Graaf. Valentine is the only choice."

"If it were my decision, you'd be indentured right now and digging lime," Beckford said.

"Becky grows balls, does he." Art crossed his arms. "You've been Port Royal's policeman for a while now, Colonel. Let's not forget yer place in the order around here."

"Your place is in prison, Captain Valentine. Or worse. I'll send you home to your wife."

"Have *HMS Guernsey* ready to sail presently," White barked. "Along with the *Stackel-rock-cher-friytz*."

"*Stachelrochen*," Beckford corrected.

"*Stingray!*" Art said. "And she won't be ready for weeks."

"She looks fine to me; finish her refit at sea." White slammed his ledger closed. "You're leaving as soon as provisions are loaded. Captain Stubbs will command *Guernsey*, and Dietrich, *Stingray*."

"Do we know where Cadwallader is?" asked Beckford.

"Cadwallader recently captured a Spanish treasure galleon out of Havana. A straggler from the annual fleet on its way home to Spain, loaded with Incan gold and silver plate," White said. "Cadwallader's hiding it in the southern Bahamas. Capture the Bahamas first and arrest Cadwallader Jones. Then track down and destroy this slaving enterprise before it starts."

"There is to be nothing left when the Earl of Inchiquin gets here," said Skean.

"Aye." White reopened the ledger. "Mr. Freeman will go as first officer to Stubbs."

"I gathered as much," Freeman snarled. "Morris outranks me."

"My knees hurt," Morris mumbled.

"I'm growing lemon trees," Freeman moaned.

"Those trees died last year," Beckford pointed out.

"What more is there to say?" White said. "Dr. Strangewayes will serve as ship's doctor."

"Lucky for MacAskill, I was able to track down all those nasty bits of debris left by Dr. Heath," said Strangewayes. "MacAskill wasn't shot; he was hit by a fragment of grenade that exploded inside his belly. Something the new chief surgeon of Port Royal missed."

"Well, that proves it, Sander; you're the best man for the job," White said. "You will report to *Guernsey* immediately."

"I have a heart condition."

"I have here a signed order by three city officials, including Captain White, to have you executed for treason. How's your heart condition doing now?" asked Beckford.

"I can have a certain small box of plant crystals delivered to *Guernsey* within the hour," White said, enticingly.

"Excellent. Let's shove off, Art."

"Commodore Valentine, bring me Cadwallader Jones, and I'll not only make sure you're pardoned but give you the biggest parade this city has seen since Morgan returned from Panama with the clap," White said.

The gargantuan wrought-iron gate of the governor's mansion was open, its gravel pathway lined with fiery torches. Costumed partygoers passed through the stone arches of the main entrance, which led to the ballroom. Kegs filled with signature ale from the Swiftsure Tavern sat beside silver trays brimming with fruit, meat pies, and various cheeses from the Cheshire Cheese Tavern. Playing music were a guitarist and flautist called Duality; the ensemble had been known as Trinity until their fiddler was killed in the recent pirate siege.

Although sacked only days ago, the grand ballroom had been restored to its full splendor. Former Acting Lieutenant Governor Dorcas Dewar was supervising its immediate repair, coordinating his efforts from his prison cell. He and former Chief Judge Lord Lawrence Llewellyn had looked at dozens of fabric swatches to determine the new look.

Though under house arrest, they were meant to be in solitary confinement. Therefore, the ballroom's restoration had been divided between the two of them. A long, narrow piece of fabric marked the center of the room. Each side had its own sitting area with red and gold Persian rugs, damask sofas and various Italian tapestries hanging on the walls. It wasn't much, but it was better than the oceanside retreat in Ligania where they had sent the children, along with Llewellyn's wife, Lyla.

From his side of the room, Dewar flipped through the gazette *Modern Codpiece,* occasionally turning it upside down, trying to determine which to order. There was Red Bull, a velvet-lined piece with silver studs. Black Stallion, a strictly leather piece with an exaggerated tip. And Dewar's current favourite, the Cape Horn, ribbed, with gold stitching and crystals.

"Oh, I like this one—The Padded Job." Dewar turned the magazine around and waved at Llewellyn, about twenty feet away.

"That's a good one." Llewellyn slipped on a plague doctor's mask. "Do they have anything in marigold?"

"I'll check." Dewar flicked through the rest of the gazette.

A naked servant girl emerged from the hallway with a deck of cards stuck to her body. She navigated her way through a crowd of masks—some mimicking birds, cats, bats, dogs. Others wore beaked plague doctor masks or harlequin disguises.

"Ah, excellent! Time for One and Thirty!" Dewar clapped.

The servant girl stopped in front of Llewellyn. "Stick or have it?"

"Um, have it." He remained seated and nudged a card off her thigh with his plague doctor's beak. His mask landed in the crevice between her legs. "Ah, I think I've discovered what these masks are for! Ingenious!"

Snead entered the hall, staring with disapproval.

"Shall I see what he wants?" the servant girl asked.

"It can't be that important," Llewellyn said. "Does he want to stick or have it?"

The servant girl went over to Dewar's side of the room. "Do you want to stick or have it?"

"There you are." Snead proceeded towards Dewar. "Lord Llewellyn, please join us. Lord Dewar, sir, I have an urgent appeal for help from our contacts in Hanover."

"That's all very well, Mr. Snead, but you're not practicing social distancing. I'll have it." Dewar plucked a card off the girl's left nipple and went to stand beside the center line. "See, this is my side." He then pointed. "And that's his."

"Social distancing was for the yellow fever outbreak," Snead said. "You're in solitary confinement. Or, supposed to be."

"I'm being very solitary; I'll have you know." Dewar stuck his nose in the air.

"Well, I need to speak with both of you, right now."

"We don't want to break Whitie's rules," Dewar mocked.

"I need to see you." Snead waved at Llewellyn but was ignored.

"What is he talking about?" Llewellyn asked the servant girl. "And does he stick or have it?"

"Just get over here!" Snead shouted.

"I'm being solitary!"

"It's solitary *confinement*, and you broke it! Please come here!"

Llewellyn ventured closer to Dewar's side of the room. He adjusted his mask. "I've discovered what this is for; it fits perfectly between—"

"I told you, it's for a yellow fever outbreak," Dewar said. "You put it on, and you can't get sick."

"It's an erotic symbol, isn't it?" Snead said.

"Exactly!" Llewellyn brightened up. "You could dip it in honey, and it'll slide right in!"

Snead waved. "Get closer, please."

Llewellyn stood right beside the line dividing the room.

"Come along, I'll tell Beckford it's my fault."

"I'm upholding the law." Llewellyn posed with his hands on his hips. "Now, what kind of a judge would I be if I broke the law?"

Snead took out a handful of gold coins and tossed them on a sofa. Dewar and Llewellyn instinctively dove for them.

Snead dragged over a mobile silk screen. "Now, I received a message hidden in the Hanover billing from Sophie."

"Ah, yes, Sophie. Which one was she?" Dewar looked around.

"Sophie of Hanover," Snead said.

"You remember, the porcelain girl in the painting," Llewellyn reminded.

Snead sighed. "No. The Duchess of Hanover, Sophie!"

Llewellyn pointed at a painting on the wall behind them.

Snead looked. The painting was engraved with the name *Sophie of Hanover*. "Oh, right."

"She sent it as a gift," Llewellyn explained. "It's covering a hole."

"I say, nice bubbies," Dewar remarked. "Didn't you say she's soon to be single?"

"Well, her husband's in a coma, apparently," Snead said.

"Yes, I've heard of it," Llewellyn said. "Somewhere in Africa. No man ever comes back from there."

"Indeed. Well, Sophie sent us a letter." Snead brought out a parchment.

Llewellyn skimmed it. "I'm fascinated. Look, it's even in English, so we can read it if we want to."

Snead looked. *"Thank you for the Port Royal smoked oysters.* Do we have smoked oysters?"

Dewar and Llewellyn both shrugged.

"No, we must have sent her Chocolata snails. I made note of all the inconsistencies and errors in her letter, and I came up with this. It's a code." He removed another page. "She needs us to send a ship, or ships, to St. Eustatius."

"We just bought a bunch of Dutch ships from St. Eustatius for the move; why does she need another one?" Llewellyn deliberated.

"Not just any ship, but a privateer."

"Don't they have privateers in St. Eustatius?"

"I wondered the same thing," Snead said. "Why, out of everyone in the world, would she pick you for help? So, I did some digging. She thinks you rescued two German noblewomen a while back. The same two German women who survived a botched kidnapping you financed on the Braunschmidts."

"They make great sausages," said Dewar.

"Now, Sophie wants you to do it again. She's asking you to send Cormac O'Malley to St. Eustatius to ensure safe passage for her people fleeing the Holy Roman Empire."

"This is getting complicated," Llewellyn said.

"It would be different if she was single," said Dewar.

"Soon to be. How old's the painting?" Llewellyn observed it once again. "I mean, check the date; girls are always flogging old paintings of themselves."

"She's in her sixties," Snead said. "The painting is thirty years old."

"I'm right again," Llewellyn said. "But you know, you could marry younger if you got a divorce," he told Dewar.

"True. But I'm sure Margaret will be back any time now."

"She's been gone ten months. Don't let one rotten pear spoil your appetite; pluck another from the tree." Llewellyn gave him a thumbs-up.

"Well, a good idea is a good idea." Dewar nodded.

Snead cleared his throat. "Back to Sophie. She's not only asking for your help, but she's also doing it in a way to avoid detection from her business partners, notably Van der Hagen Shipping. She wants us to pick these people up when they reach the island. See? It must be done in a way that does not upset our normal shipping."

Dewar thought for a moment. "Which is what?"

"When we invested in the castle, we leased five ships. Big East India ships built by the Van der Hagen shipyards, to carry over the pieces of Calenberg Castle. Their stopping point is St. Eustatius. Now, look who invested in Van der Hagen shipyards: Crisp of Barbados. That means he was involved with Van der Hagen."

"Well, Crisp died in the pirate siege," Llewellyn said.

"And we win again." Dewar clapped.

"Not yet," said Snead. "Crisp's estate has been awarded to a Baron de Klauwen from the Barbary Coast. He's moving his slave operation here, and he has the backing of the Fuggers."

"Those dirty Fuggers!" Dewar scoffed.

"The same dirty Fuggers who finance the Whigs?" Llewellyn's eyes bulged. "Oh, we can't allow that. I quote the Goddess Hepatitis: he who hesitates to beat thine enemies is surely to finish last."

"You made that up," Snead said.

"He did, but he's right," Dewar said. "I'll do it. Order Cormac O'Malley to St. Eustatius at once."

"He's dead," Snead reminded.

Dewar's shoulders dropped. "O'Malley or the saint?"

"O'Malley. His sons were here just last week," Llewellyn said. "Remember the filthy Irish rabble? All red and black, like a deck of cards."

"The red-haired wench had a nice set," Dewar remarked.

"That's them. They smelled up the place, just like that French Capitaine. The last time he bathed was when long mustaches were in style."

"Still can't get the smell out. Might have to burn it all down and build a new governor's mansion," said Dewar.

"The O'Malleys are back in Hope Bay," Snead said. "I'm sure they'd do it. They're the ones who took the last Germans to Aragua, and they just lost everything."

"They're hardly privateers," Llewellyn said. "Won't Sophie be disappointed when we send her slow-minded Irish cave dwellers?"

"The redhead sister is with the French Capitaine, last headed for Tortuga. You've hired him before," Snead said. "Tom Jones is docked at the Swiftsure. We can send him to deliver the message to both the O'Malleys in Hope Bay and the French Capitaine."

"Excellent!" Llewellyn clapped.

"This operation needs a name," Dewar pondered.

"You mean like, Operation Send a Welshman to Find a Bunch of Irish Cave Dwellers and a French Capitaine to go Fetch a German Duchess's Ship?"

"Too wordy. How about Operation Go-Getter," Dewar said.

"Very clever."

"I must say, that is catchy," Snead agreed.

"That's why I'm governor." Dewar fluffed up his doublet. "Solitary or not."

The following morning, Dr. Strangewayes pulled up in a carriage at the Belford house. He grabbed a wicker cat case from the back, and a tin of catmint. When he ascended the stairs, he found his cat Boots curled up peaceably in a chair. "There you are, old chum." Boots purred as he received a chin scratch. "I'll see you when I return."

Strangewayes pulled a bell cord.

Ellsebeyth "Bizy" Gale opened the door. Her long, dark hair was pinned up, while a scar ran down the middle of her forehead to the bridge of her nose. "Good day, Doctor." Her eyes appeared red from tears.

"Good day, dear. Are you ready to go?"

"Yes."

"Oh, here, I forgot to give Esmerelda this, the first time I went away." He handed over the case and catmint.

"Are you going away again?" she surmised, setting the cat supplies inside.

"Indeed."

"They're not sending you to prison?"

"No, I'm being sent on a ship with Bleedin Art."

"Oh, that might be worse."

Boots went inside to investigate the catmint.

"Are you able to continue to look after Boots?" Strangewayes asked.

"Oh, yes."

"We get to keep Boots!" Jamie, Bizy's seven-year-old son, raced down the stairs.

"Careful!" fifteen-year-old Isabella said.

"I want to stay here with Boots." Jamie sprinkled catmint on the floor.

"I'd better stay too; dogboy will get into trouble," Isabella said. "We already had a service for Nanna Bell."

"Well, Dr. Strangewayes was unable to attend, so I'll be back in a few hours." Bizy collected a bouquet of hibiscus flowers from a vase by the front door.

Bizy and Strangewayes headed to the carriage.

"I'm sure I can have you home within the hour," Strangewayes said.

"If I come home early and catch them up to no good, then I have housekeepers for a week." Bizy climbed up.

"Frankly, I'm still in shock that I wasn't hanged." The doctor gathered the reins, and they took off towards the sandy spit to the Palisadoes, a tiny village with a cemetery by the water.

"Beckford spent many a sleepless night trying to add up evidence and witnesses, and I must admit, his adding up is adding up. As it is, White used the Act of Grace law and pardoned me, on the condition I go pirate-hunting with Valentine."

"They're charging Art to go after Laurens?" Bizy said. "That's like sending a boarhound to take down a lion."

"Oh, heavens no. Art in *Guernsey* versus Laurens and the French fleet; that's a recipe for disaster. No, we're sailing for the Bahamas to arrest the self-appointed king of New Gwynedd."

They approached High Street and turned, passing by *Guernsey* being loaded in a hurry.

"Yes, it's all very hush-hush. We're sailing straight up through the Jamaica Channel, through the windward passage," Strangewayes said. "White is convinced the French are rallying to Hispaniola and will be too busy mounting a land defence against the Spanish. Art plans to fly a French flag and sail right past Tortuga, then straight up by Crooked Island to Long Island. Then we'll have Cadwallader cornered and surrounded."

"Brilliant. So, you'll sail out today?" Bizy said.

"Sorry dear, that's top secret. Very hush-hush, remember."

They arrived at the cemetery, where the land was being eroded by the sea; sections were flooded. They ventured to an area of slightly higher ground.

"It does have that lovely, deathly bog smell," Strangewayes said.

"I'm glad we buried her up here." Bizy's nose wrinkled.

They stood before the gravestone: *Esmeralda Belford 1641-1690.*

Bizy placed the hibiscus flowers on the grave.

Esmeralda Belford, Strangewayes thought. *Widow of the pirate Rowdy Belford. Daughter of Annabelle and the carpenter Peter Bartaboa. Landed in Port Royal since it was the Cagway, back in 1655. Killed during a pirate siege. An arrow through the chest. Such a senseless tragedy.*

"She was fourteen when I first met her. Seems we've lost a piece of history." Strangewayes wiped his eyes. "Seems I loved her more than I let on."

"We both did." Bizy gasped for air and hugged him.

Next to the graveyard stood Barre's Tavern, connected to an inn and mercantile. Bleedin Art was having crates loaded on his carriage by his two men, Scarcliff and Blackmoor.

Scarcliff tripped over a rock, and the crate jarred.

"Stop pissing about," Art reprimanded. "We gotta get this stuff on board!"

"Commodore, you're looking particularly dapper today," Strangewayes began. "Being discharged from Port Royal seems to agree with you."

"Indeed, it does, Doctor."

Art approached the graveyard and removed his hat. "Miss Gale, I can't tell you how sorry I am for your loss. Easy was a beautiful gal. Those were terrible events. I take it very personal when someone under my protection is killed. I want you to know that I'm going to bring in every one of them bastards for what they did." He unpinned the flower on his breast pocket and placed it among the others.

"Commodore." Bizy nodded.

After a minute's silence, Art replaced his hat. "Glad to find you before Colonel Beckford did, Doctor. He wants you chained in the hold until we leave. He's afraid you'll flap your gob, as they say."

"Me? Never."

"Perhaps you should come with me, all the same."

"Loading extra provisions?"

"This is private stock, not meant for ordinary human consumption. We don't want it left behind."

"Now, that would be irresponsible."

"Perhaps Blackmoor could drive you home, Miss Gale?" Art offered. "I've got to get the good doctor on board. Duty calls."

"I can drive myself back," Bizy said.

"Fret not, Bizy, my dear. You'll be safe with my men until I return," Art said.

Scarcliff and Blackmoor watched a pretty girl as she passed by, turning their heads. Blackmoor tripped on a loose floorboard and hauled Scarcliff down with him.

"I have no doubt, Commodore," Bizy said.

"Anchors away, Doctor, anchors away!" Art started back to his carriage.

Strangewayes climbed into the carriage beside Art.

"She'll be well looked after," Art said.

"Of that I have no doubt," replied the doctor. "Anchors away, Commodore."

They arrived at the Salutacon Landing, where *Guernsey* sat. Strangewayes was escorted on board while Art stretched, almost hitting Scarcliff with his walking stick.

"You're in charge of security while I'm gone," Art began. "If MacAskill lives, he's got the responsibility of the taverns and brothels. You keep all those under our protection from harm and you'll get a sizeable reward when I return. I have full confidence in you."

"I can look after the brothels, too," Scarcliff said.

"The hell you can."

A wagon being driven by Sierra Lee pulled up next to *Stingray*, to deliver Dietrich.

"I want to thank you; you were very helpful," Dietrich said.

"Helpful? Aye, I was that." She waved to Scarcliff.

"I hope to meet you again if I should return here. One day you should see Aragua."

She smiled at him. He kissed her, but she pulled away, unnerved. He apologized and limped towards his ship. Sierra Lee tried to say something but instead watched him leave, then drove off.

Dietrich paused to pet the horses before getting aboard.

"He'd better not be teaching my horse German," Scarcliff said.

"*Nein*! This is all wrong," Dietrich said.

"Vat's all wrong?" Art asked.

"The rigging. The sails!"

"This is called a Bermuda rig," Art explained. "Maneuverable and adjustable. She'll have plenty of speed with all that foresail. She'll turn better. Around here, that's the difference that's gonna save your life. Yer happy with her armament, I hope? Reconfigured for cannons that are small and light, to give her more speed. Here in the Caribbean, yer gonna need to carry a bigger stick."

They inspected the deck towards the aft and all the shiny new cannons being loaded from the carts.

"She's been fitted with eight one-pound swivel guns, for close action. Fore and aft have four of the very latest eight-pounders," Art said. "Long range and accurate, with a real nasty punch. Anyone gets in front or behind will regret it."

They continued to the main deck.

"Next, we have port and starboard, fitted with six-pound British sackers. We made 'em bronze, since you're of the House of Braunschmidt, after all. They can smash through any hull, I tell ya. And, then yer four-pound minions are very accurate and lightweight, so you won't bitch at me for being too slow."

Dietrich began to look impressed.

"You'll be able to sink a ship twice yer size without sacrificing speed or agility. We also added four sweeps. I figured ya can get more speed out of her with twenty oar slots between the cannon ports for, forty sweeps." Art led them up to the quarterdeck and hugged a swivel gun.

"Commodore Valentine, I have to say, she's fit," Dietrich said.

"She's seaworthy now, but is her captain and crew?" asked Art.

"We are ready to sail, Commodore Valentine. At your service."

"Yaw, das is good," Art teased. "Ready the towlines. You'll lead us out."

"Departure stations!" Dietrich ordered.

Art went ashore and sauntered towards *Guernsey*. Crewmen were preparing the ship for sail. Morris waved his hands and mumbled, while Freeman barked the orders. Art strolled up the gangway as the rest of the crew boarded.

On the waterfront, a crowd gathered, cheering.

"Hell of a day, eh, Morris?" Art said.

Morris continued to complain, gesturing with his hands.

"What'd he say?" Art asked Freeman.

"He says it sure is."

Art went to the quarterdeck, where Bach repeated orders from Stubbs.

"You do remember the way to the Bahamas, Captain Stubbs?" Art said.

"Somewhere between Cuba and England, apparently, sir."

"Very well. Take her out, Captain Stubbs."

"Right. Shove off!"

"Ya know, this ship and crew are a tad too old to be taking on pirates at close quarters," Morris said.

"That's what we have *Stingray* for, Morris." Art waved to the crowd. "We'll be back with our city's honor restored, folks."

Guernsey was towed by the smaller *Stingray* as she rowed out of the harbor. Art and his officers gathered to watch Port Royal slip away.

The Elixir of Life

Rain pelted a man carrying a flag up a grassy hill. The wind nearly blew him over as he clawed his way up the dilapidated stonework of a crumbling castle, Fort Roche. The whole island could be seen from the tower, including the coast of Hispaniola to the Cayenne Harbor. At the top of the tower flew a tattered French flag, beaten by the elements. The man took down the current flag and replaced it with a Spanish one.

Atia la Roche sat on a stool behind the counter of the tavern and poured herself a shot of whiskey. She stared at it for a moment, then decided it would save time to just drink straight out of the bottle. Two deceased men decayed next to the front door. No one could be bothered to take them outside during the storm.

Atia's husband, Jean-Paul la Roche, or simply the Capitaine, glanced at a handful of cards while the four unconscious men he played with snored heavily. Things were quiet in Tortuga inside the *Élixir de vie*.

The broad-billed parrot, Minuit, squawked.

"No, no, you are wrong!" la Roche slurred.

"No, no, you are wrong," Minuit replied.

"You don't know what you're talking about," la Roche continued.

"You don't know what you're talking about," Minuit said.

La Roche pointed. "No, *you* don't know what you're talking about."

Minuit flapped his wings. "No, *you* don't know what you're talking about."

"Who's winning?" Atia asked between mouthfuls of whiskey.

"We'll settle this another time, uh?" la Roche said.

"Another time," Minuit replied.

A peasant burst through the door, stumbling and out of breath. "The Spanish have taken Tortuga!"

La Roche cursed in French, throwing down his cards. He led those who remained conscious outside.

Drunken peasants and buccaneers staggered up the hill into the ruins of the fort walls to the dilapidated tower. They climbed to the top, where a Spanish flag fluttered. La Roche cut it down and ripped it up. "Fuck you, uh!"

La Roche and the crowd returned to the tavern.

"Not exactly *Sérénité*, my love," Atia said.

"Really." He pointed to a freshly painted sign above the door that read: *Sérénité*.

"Wishful drinking," said Atia.

La Roche kissed her lips, his breath thick with rum. "This is where they look last for us. We would be followed to *Sérénité*."

They went back inside. Atia went to the bar for another drink, while a semi-conscious Dashiell Dupris, 'de Kreep,' stirred and tried to light his pipe.

"Get me one, too," la Roche said. "Besides, this is where Laurens will pay you the bounty for Slasher Al. You want to get paid, don't you?"

"Did I miss something?" asked de Kreep.

"The Spanish took Tortuga," Atia said.

"Again?" De Kreep ran his fingers through his dark, curly hair before trying to light his pipe again.

La Roche helped and they got it lit. They laughed, as if achieving greatness.

"Liberated once again," la Roche said.

"Hell of a battle." Atia returned with drinks. "Too bad ya missed it."

"I am no good for you," la Roche said.

"Neither's whiskey. But tonight, I shall endure." She downed a shot. "But not with this treacle rum of yours. There must be more whiskey somewhere. And where's Miles?" Atia glanced around.

"Upstairs at the inn," said de Kreep. "He won't come down."

"Been here before, has he?"

A pirate with a scar across his whole face sat with his four mates, inspecting Atia. Zoe, the barmaid, served them, getting groped and prodded in the process.

"Oh, they look friendly," Atia spoke dryly. "Who are they?"

"Pirates." La Roche drank more rum.

"Nooo," she exaggerated. "Not in Tortuga."

"Reed." La Roche indicated. "The one with the happy smile. I don't know the other one. Hired by Laurens de Graaf."

"Hired? Did they bring my bounty?" asked Atia.

La Roche shook his head. "He rapes women."

Atia's eyes widened. "Which one?"

"All of them," de Kreep said.

John Coxon arrived, grimy, unshaven, wearing a weathered leather vest.

Atia took a drink, unimpressed. She was about to leave when Reed tried to molest her. Instinctively, she slapped him. Reed went for his sword. La Roche knocked Atia out of the way, while Coxon and de Kreep drew their blades.

Atia shook herself and drew her stilettos.

Coxon parried Reed's blade.

Drunkards stumbled and laughed.

"Apologize to the lady. We're under parley," Coxon said.

"Apologize to a bloody strumpet?" Reed spat.

"She's no common strumpet. She's the wench who killed Slasher Al."

"That's right. And yer friend touches me again, he can join him," said Atia.

"We was never properly introduced. John Coxon, miss. I knew yer father. Too bad the Capitaine here got to ya first. Don't mind us, dear, you go on."

"Don't mind a bit." Atia departed.

Reed grinned at her.

As the door closed, arguing commenced.

"Where was I? Where were you?" were the last words she heard from la Roche.

Atia headed outside into the rain and trekked up an exterior staircase to the second floor. She ventured down a short hallway and knocked gently on the door at the end.

Gladstone opened the door quickly and pulled her inside. After fixing a chair beneath the doorknob, he collapsed on the bed.

"Are you all right?" Atia squeezed the water from her hair.

"Those are the worst of the worst out there," Gladstone said.

"So I heard. Are you hiding from anyone in particular?"

"Hiding? Who's hiding?" Gladstone puffed out his cheeks.

"You're doing well." She checked a bottle of Strangewayes Calming Formula on the counter.

"I took it all."

She picked it up. "It says three to four drops, maximum."

Gladstone massaged his face. "We've got to get out of here."

"I know." Atia went over to the window. Pirate ships were still arriving in the harbor. Longboats brought ominous figues ashore who then made their way up the road. "I'll send Zoe up with some food. She likes you, yer the only one who's ever thanked her without a catch."

"I just want to go home to *Sérénité*."

"Me too," Atia said. "When Laurens de Graaf gets here, I'll get the bounty for Slasher Al. That'll be more than enough to pay for passage."

"Passage where?" Gladstone said nervously.

She checked the window again. Pirates converged below, their guns and cutlasses shimmered in the rain under their large hats. "Anywhere but here, Miles."

Laurens de Graaf slid on a raincoat and secured a hat before venturing to the quarterdeck of *Cometa*. He checked his pocket for a pouch of Strangewayes Brand Love Barriers, this was Tortuga afterall. The navigator, Nigel, fought to turn the tiller against the wind and rain.

"Ten degrees to port." Laurens scanned the Cayenne Harbor with his telescope. "Keep your eyes out for *Toro*."

A huge wave battered the sails, and they all grabbed the lifelines.

Laurens indicated a ship in port. "There's *La Lune*. Dead ahead. At least he's here on time, for once."

"Maybe he brought this redhead everyone's been on about." Nigel smirked.

"She's due to collect for Slasher Al. I for one would like to shake her hand and buy her a drink. And if she's as pretty as they say, I'll shake her backside too." Laurens shifted focus to the other ships. There was *Hornet*, with black and white stripes, and *Dragonfly* in green with swirling patterns. "Ready to land."

Cometa and her escorts rowed in and anchored.

Laurens's biographer and friend, Ravenau de Lussan, swung over from *Dragonfly*.

"You took long enough," Laurens said to Ravenau.

"You were too fast for me, Sieur. I lost you off Jamaica."

"No, you lost Yaguara off Jamaica. I had time to circle Cayman Brac Island, twice," Laurens said.

"What's that?" Nigel looked overhead. "Bird coming in."

"That's the Capitaine's bird, Minuit." Laurens took out a whistle and blew.

A large, iridescent black parrot landed on a rail. Minuit exchanged greetings with Laurens's parrot, Henry V.

Laurens checked Minuit's leg bracelet to find a roll of parchment there. He read: "*The capture of Port Royal did not go well. So, I bite you?* What's he mean by that? Surely, he means bite me."

Minuit bit Laurens's hand before flying away.

Ravenau aimed his pistol. "It attacked you."

"Don't shoot the messenger," said Laurens. "Besides, he's on account."

Minuit defecated on the deck before heading to the tavern.

"Now, that is personal," Laurens said.

Cometa landed at the Cayenne dock.

Laurens secured his raincoat. "Secure the fort and meet me at the *Élixir de vie* in thirty."

"Oui, Sieur," Ravenau replied.

"This shitty rain is ruining my hair anyway," Laurens said.

Atia stood by the open window, staring out at the harbor. The air was muggy, charged with rain and thick black clouds. More ships and pirates arrived. A black figure swooped in, landing on the windowsill. "*Bonjour*, Mademoiselle."

Atia's heart leapt. "Bloody hell, bird!" She patted his damp head. "Come on in."

He flew over to the bed and roosted next to Gladstone, who was in and out of consciousness. She fed Minuit some cashews and checked the window again. A group trod along the path to the tavern, led by a man in a raincoat. A large medallion the size of a shackle hung from his neck. "Is that Laurens?"

Gladstone rose to peer out. "Laurens de Graaf himself. Voted most popular pirate ten years running."

She closed the window and made damn sure her stilettos were ready. "I think he owes me money."

"The Capitaine said we're going to keep it in his chest," Gladstone said.

"We are, are we?" Atia's mouth slacked.

"Aye, he said he's gonna hold it for you."

"He can hold his own; no way is he taking mine. You gonna be okay?"

Gladstone groaned. "Absolutely. I've gone straight to the blinding headache part. Minuit will nurse me back to health. You be careful."

"I will." She descended the stairs. Raucous laughter and the singing of drunken pirates came from the tavern. She paused, peering around the corner. Atia's hands fixed around her stilettos.

"We got unfinished business, wench!" Reed accosted her again.

She plunged the weapons into his throat and yanked them out without so much as flinching. The pirate dropped to the ground, dying.

A pair of eyes were upon her. Laurens de Graaf lowered his blunderbuss and pushed his wet blond locks out of his eyes. He winked. "Hey doll, wanna take a ride on my *Cometa*?" He looked down at her handiwork. "Looks like he had it coming."

"He did that. One of your men?"

"Not anymore. But, like I said, looks like he had it coming. You must be Atia."

"You must be Laurens de Graaf." She wiped her stilettos on her dress and put them back in her holster.

"Sorry about the dress. I've got some nice ones on board that might suit you. I came to square up with your Capitaine."

"He's in the tavern with John Coxon, catching up. It's me yer supposed to be squaring up with." She unrolled a piece of skin with a rose tattoo.

"Slasher Al, huh? You'll have to tell me all about it. I have your bounty on my ship." He opened the door, and they entered the tavern.

La Roche and de Kreep were playing cards with Coxon.

"There he is. Seems fine to me," Atia remarked. "Now, about me bounty."

Laurens winked at her. "You are a bounty."

La Roche, having just won a hand, exclaimed, "Ah, better than sex!"

Atia rolled her eyes. "He's going to be a while. How about I ride on your comet while we wait?"

"Your bounty awaits, doll, this way." He removed his raincoat and draped it over her. They took the footpath down to the ship. *Cometa's* white lines blended with the churning waves. At Laurens's approach, men rushed to their stations.

"She's a beauty," said Atia.

"She's a Spanish guardacosta schooner, built in Biscay," Laurens boasted. "She arrived in 1680, named after the great comet. She was new and sent here to hunt pirates. I took her a week after she arrived. So pretty I didn't even change the name. Pretty as the comet was, and so are you."

They boarded.

"Sail the ship around the island a few times, Nigel."

"Oui, Sieur."

Atia was guided to the captain's cabin. Her mouth hung open at the sight of polished mahogany walls, a canopied bed, mounted swords and shields, Italian tapestries, glowing brass wall sconces and a copper tub in the far corner. "It's like a museum."

"Of course, this is my home." He took the raincoat from her and hung it by the wardrobe. "Join me for a drink?"

"Aye."

"What's your poison?"

"Whiskey."

"Nice. I'll have one too." He stripped down naked and hung his wet things. His physique was muscular, his skin quite smooth, even with scars and tattoos. His manhood swayed provocatively as he moved.

From the wardrobe he took out a silk robe, letting her take a look before putting it on. He handed her a spare.

She took it and peeled off her wet layers. Atia set the piece of skin that bore the name Mary Rose on Laurens's desk.

Laurens poured them whiskey and looked more carefully at it.

"That's Slasher Al's, all right. Sixty thousand gold pieces to you, doll, well done. So how did you do him?" He took out a velvet pouch, put the trophy inside and handed it back. "You can keep it."

"I strung him up with hooks, put a scold's bridle on his head and fed all his small parts to the rats."

"Creative." Laurens took a mouthful of whiskey. "You could rival Montbars the Executioner."

"It was personal. He killed me sister."

"My condolences. But this in retribution for the murder of Bartolomeo el Portuguese, one of the founders of the Brethren of the Coast."

Atia sipped the whiskey.

"Wanna take a look?" Laurens waved her over behind the desk.

A fluttering in her belly began at the sight of a chest of gold. "Wow."

"Wow indeed."

"Where should I put it?"

"Anywhere you want."

"Let me think about it. Right now, my mission is whiskey and sex." She groped his balls.

"Far be it from me to interfere with such a well-thought-out plan." He tongued her nipples through the silk robe.

Moisture trickled between her legs, and their mouths met. He navigated her to the window seat, and she straddled him. Her robe went awry, and Laurens buried his face between her breasts, lapping at the jutting nipples. Grasping his erect manhood, she slid him inside.

The weather outside rocked the ship to and fro. Which only enhanced their undulations. Atia's back arched as she gyrated, contracting with pleasure. Laurens slid fingers into the cleft of her buttocks before squeezing her cheeks until he groaned joyously.

The rest of the night was a mixture of whiskey, delicious food, periodic sleep, and testing out various sexual positions.

At dawn, light streamed through the balcony doors, illuminating a small garden. A violinist entered and began to play. Next, a slave came in and started filling the copper tub full of hot water.

"Do you want to get dirtier before we get cleaned up?" Laurens asked.

Atia winked, and they succumbed to pleasure as the music played.

Atia's legs constricted around his powerful backside, and she raised her hips. He thrust her back down again and then flipped their positions. She bounced upon him, thighs trembling. They both hollered, wanting everyone on the ship to hear every sordid detail. Laurens cupped her breasts and tweaked her nipples until they were hard stones. An explosion came from within her, and Laurens gasped, climaxing.

Afterwards they lay there, strength waning, smoking Cuban cigars.

They ventured to the tub.

"Smells familiar." Atia drank in the herbal fragrance. "From Strangewayes Apothecary?"

"Only the best."

The water was perfect, just hot enough.

"He's wrong again, the Capitaine. He's been wrong a lot."

"About what?" Laurens said.

"About everything. He was wrong about you."

"How?"

"He described you as a *connard* with a small dick."

Laurens laughed.

"Yer not like any pirate I've met before," Atia said.

"Of course not. I'm Laurens de Graaf. I make pirating look good."

After they cleaned up, they put on fresh clothes. Laurens handed her a spare gown. "I like to be prepared."

"Also, you may like this." He fished out a tin of ointment—Strangewayes Special Ladies Cream.

Atia took it gratefully. "Have many women aboard?"

"I've had many women everywhere."

She indicated a box of Strangewayes Brand Love Barrier on a side table. "What's that exactly?"

"Nothin' you'd want between us, doll." He winked. "Those are for momentary lapses of reason."

Slaves brought in breakfast, setting it up on the cabin deck.

"Hope you like smoked salmon from the Gitche Gumee."

"I haven't had smoked salmon in ages."

There was also coffee, coconuts, mangoes, and honeyed yams.

"So, is the Capitaine not your true love?" Laurens faked a French accent.

Atia couldn't speak for a minute. "Umm."

"If you must think about it, then he's not. Trust me. You can only pretend for so long."

"He swept me off my feet and into the broom cupboard. I thought he was the one. There is another I was getting to know well in Port Royal. I find myself missin' him."

"Well, you're a young beauty; you'll have no shortage to choose from. If you feel good about yourself with that person, then that's what counts. It's the laughter and quiet moments that make everything worthwhile."

"Do you have a true love?" Atia pondered. "Are you married?"

"I was married. I'm recently divorced," Laurens said.

"Were you in love?"

"We were when we were young. Petra is her name. She lives in the Azores."

"What happened, then?"

"I was never there. I was always at sea. She began to love the income and the properties more than me." Laurens sipped coffee. "Every time I returned home, she was less interested in me and had a new addition to my will for me to sign. So, last Christmas or two ago, I sent her tulips and divorce papers."

"So, now there's no true love for Laurens de Graaf? Voted most popular pirate ten years in a row."

He looked away and lit his pipe.

"There is someone. Who?"

"There's one. The one I love more than life itself."

"And where is she?"

"I don't know. I lost her. My Marie-Anne."

Laurens removed a silver locket from his pocket and opened it. A hand-painted portrait of a woman with long, chestnut hair stared straight ahead, a slightly careworn look to her.

"I think I might've seen her during the pirate siege. When I was going to meet Strangewayes, I saw her being carried aboard a ship. There was a little girl with her."

A flicker of hope ignited in his eye.

"I'm sure she was alive and got out of Port Royal."

"I hope you're right." Laurens looked out his window.

More dangerous adversaries approached.

Atia drank coffee and finished breakfast.

"Slasher Al's ship, *Bloody Mary*, isn't here. I sent her on to Port de Paix with Picard and the rest of the wounded. By rights, she's yours," Laurens said. "Al owned the ship himself. Picard may want it when he recovers, but no one's going to argue if I give it to you."

"You gonna teach me to sail?"

"That's what crews are for. I'll teach you to fly, doll."

"Who do all the pirate ships belong to?"

"The fastest ships in the Caribbean are all here. There's *Dorado*, over there. A galiot belonging to John Coxon." Laurens pointed out the long galiot, while other ships arrived from all directions. "Over there is *Hero*. Until recently, it belonged to Lady Beeston in Port Royal."

"Lady Beeston's *Blessing*."

The rolling green hills looked like a turtle's shell. On the northeastern side, a dilapidated mansion came into view, nestled within trees.

"That house over there was the governor's house. Governor T. Watts ruled this island with his corrupt entourage, Dewar and Llewellyn," Laurens said. "Since then, Tortuga has belonged to the Spanish, then the French, then the Dutch, French, Spanish." Laurens counted his fingers. "The English, Spanish, and now we're back to French."

Cometa sailed down the coast.

"I was surprised to see Dutch shops in Tortuga."

"Try the Dutch Bakery. Every time we invade Tortuga, we try not to damage the bakery."

Another dilapidated house came into view with a long walkway leading to a private dock, partially sunk into the sea.

"That's the old Valentine manor," Laurens said. "Where ol' Bleedin Art himself married into the Crosshatch Shipping Dynasty."

"Art lived there, you say. And married there?"

"You know Art?"

"I do. I've met his wife, and that house suits her."

They manoeuvred around a point, and a smoky city came into view across the water.

"That's Port de Paix."

"Ah, where my ship is." Atia smiled.

A fleet of ships floated in from the west, like gold flakes under the sun. Laurens trained his telescope on them. "It's time to put in, doll."

"Aye, aye. Ya wore me out some, Sieur Comet."

They went up to the main deck.

"Ready cannons, Nigel."

"Cannons ready."

"Who is it?" Atia asked.

"It's *Surreptitious*, *Serpentine* and *Servillian*. And that means Sammy the fucking Seal."

"And *Toro*, too," said Nigel.

"Le Grande?"

"No, Montbars."

"He's as bad as Sammy the fucking Seal."

"Are they going to attack us?" Atia asked.

"Probably not. But tempers are high, and they can. Once we're on land we're protected by parley. Still, you better stay close to me until we're away from here. Leave with me tomorrow?"

"To where?"

"To my house in Cape François. A day's sail." He gave her a lustful wink. "A whole day's sail, if we want."

"We're supposed to be going home to *Sérénité*."

"I know him better than you do," Laurens said earnestly. "He's not taking you to *Sérénité*. Not right now. There's too much to do here first. War is on, and there's no running from it."

"Gladstone wants to come, too."

"Sure. The more the merrier."

"Now, if you find yourself with child, I'll always be there for you. Remember, the name's Arthur Valentine, 1244 York Street, Port Royal, Jamaica."

"I take it back," Atia said. "You're exactly like other pirates."

"Yeah, but I'm better dressed." He winked.

Atia burst out laughing, and *Cometa* drifted into the harbor.

The rain continued as Laurens de Graaf and Atia reached *Élixir de vie*. Pirates filled the tavern, drinking and arguing. La Roche and de Kreep raided the bar, while Coxon dozed with his feet on a table. Silent Sam grinned maniacally, sporting a decorative suit and pearl-tipped walking stick. Montbars the Executioner glared at everyone with his beady dark eyes. Emanuel Wynne, Nathanial 'Grubby' Grubing, and Jan Erasmus Reyning shared a table, waiting for the meeting to begin.

Laurens entered, wearing his best blue and black suit, fringed with gold. The bronze Spanish medallion inlaid into a shackle hung around his neck. Ravenau, Nigel, Atia and Arsenault flanked him.

The pirates erupted in cursing and yelling.

Laurens waved. "Thank you all! It's good to be back in Tortuga!" He pointed his fingers like imaginary pistols. "*Parlez vous*, all. Thanks for coming."

"Where's our payment, Laurens?" Montbars growled.

"Where's Jamaica, Monty?" Laurens put his hand to his ear.

"In English hands," Wynne said. "In Whig hands!"

"Where was Laurens de Graaf while Port Royal was under siege?" Coxon demanded.

"Keeping the English ships busy so you lot could get the job done—which you did not."

"It seems to me that the battle fell under poor leadership," said Wynne.

"Some of us kept our side of the bargain," Grubing barked.

Silent Sam cleared his throat and licked his fingers to push his hair to one side. "I was in Port Royal waiting for you lot. Doing my part for a better world, only to be left to my own devices. And that, ladies, and gentlemen, is something no one wants!"

"Your own devices," Laurens said, his group sitting down at a table. "You weren't even invited, Seele. Le Grande had no business hiring. That was done by me, Governor de Cussy and Chevalier Du Casse, no one else. This was a military operation, not a bloody pirate raid. There was an agreement not to kill civilians, and that rule was broken. All deals are off."

They erupted in angry shouts again.

"Since when does war come with a no-kill policy?" Sam questioned. "That kind of defeats the purpose of war. Therefore, you're not winning the war for the French, Larry."

"You're too nice, it seems," added Wynne.

"And what of Slasher Al?" Sam said. "I mean, he had a nice name, was a snappy dresser, and he was also under contract, but he's not here. Why not?"

"Slasher Al broke the pirate code and killed those under protection of the Brethren of the Coast," Laurens said. "He got what was coming to him."

More roaring.

"There is no longer a Brethren of the Coast," Montbars said. "It's over."

"Who's collecting the bounty on Slasher Al?" asked Grubing.

"There's a thirty thousand bounty by me, doubled by the late Bartolomeo el Portuguese. Makes sixty thousand, to the redhead over here on the right. Paid in full." He winked at Atia.

"What about the rest of us?" Grubing said. "When do we get paid?"

"The agreement was not kept; Jamaica did not fall. There will be no payment by Saint-Domingue," Laurens explained. "Our intelligence tells us that half of you are working for Crisp of Barbados. We were betrayed by Pierre le Grande, weren't we, Sammy?"

"My intelligence suggests you were outsmarted by the Marquis de Toledo, a sixteen-year-old girl," Sam chided.

All the pirates laughed.

"A little girl!" Sam waved his hands. "Ya got beaten by a little girl!"

Pirates pointed and laughed.

"Laugh if you will," Laurens said. "The Spanish Armada is poised to capture Hispaniola. They're meeting at Santo Domingo. Yes, the Marquis de Toledo has successfully diverted my forces to Jamaica. That little bitch was a decoy of her own accord."

"Bloody duped by an adolescent girl," Coxon said. "Leave that out of the book."

"She had help from Captain White, and our own forces were divided," said Ravenau.

"Coxon, you failed to meet your objectives. Now I find out hostages were tortured and killed in the streets. People on our side were killed. Its total failure falls on you."

Tempers boiled and weapons were raised.

"The Jamaica offensive is canceled," Laurens said. "Recall all ships and buccaneers. There will be no compensation for the failure at Port Royal."

"Then I say it's time for new leadership," Coxon said.

Laurens nodded. "I agree."

"You do?" several pirates, including la Roche, said simultaneously.

"Yes. Captain Castle died at Port Royal. That's a shilling, by the way," Laurens said to Ravenau. "Castle would have been the natural choice, being the son of Bart Portuguese. I'm not letting this betrayal by le Grande go unanswered. All the pirates belonging to the Brethren of the Coast will have to account for what took place and vote."

"Vote for a new leader?" Sam said.

"Vote on its very existence. The Brethren of the Coast is not divided in two, the English and the French, but many," Laurens continued. "The English civil war has contaminated the brotherhood. War between us is inevitable, but first we must regroup, cover our losses, and get paid."

"Paid?" Grubing exclaimed. "You said we ain't getting paid."

"We're here to offer a new contract," said Laurens. "We intend to capture all of Hispaniola."

"The silliest thing I've ever heard," Sam said.

"I like it," Montbars said thoughtfully. "Santo Domingo. That means Monte Cristi, the lemon fields and Samaná. All of it?"

"All of it," Laurens said.

A silence fell over the room, followed by a wave of cheers.

"We take Santo Domingo and every Spanish town on the island," Laurens said. "And you keep the spoils of every Spaniard we find."

"Our ships are spread too thin, anyway," Wynne added.

"Hispaniola is the target. Where is Du Casse? Why is he not here himself?" Coxon asked.

"Chevalier Du Casse is in France, facing trial," said Ravenau. "The Spanish intend to strike Saint-Domingue."

"I intercepted a sloop out of Port Royal and Cuba. The English, Spanish, and Dutch are poised for a major offensive in the Caribbean. You'll all be under Whig law unless we put aside our differences and join the fight," said Laurens. "I also have a report from the Leeward Islands that the English have a new fleet and captured the islands. Le Grande lost St. Kitts. There's nothing left of the Leeward Islands. He's responsible for that mess, too. I say we declare le Grande an enemy, a Whig ally."

"What do you offer, Laurens?" said Wynne.

"Help us win a united Saint-Domingue. Governor de Cussy is hungry to take the island. The Spanish Armada is closing, and this battle will shape the Caribbean forever. This is what we all have been fighting for. A free and democratic Saint-Domingue."

"Democratic until King Louis says otherwise," said Coxon.

"Or, join us and enjoy the spoils of war and land titles for all," said Laurens.

"Like the old days," said Montbars.

"This is the type of war that makes men rich," said Wynne. "We capture the island, just like Jamaica in '55."

"Except, you wasn't at Jamaica in '55," said Montbars.

The pirates laughed.

"Leave here empty-handed or come with me and get rich," said Laurens. "It's on to Saint-Domingue. Vive la Saint-Domingue!"

They all cheered, "Saint-Domingue!"
Singing and dancing commenced.

Jean-Paul la Roche pushed his way through the crowd of drunken pirates. Outside, a sobering rain cascaded over him. His head throbbed, and he contemplated how badly things had gone since he rescued Atia from Port Royal. He lit a pre-rolled cigarette from a torch on the wall and staggered along the path to Cayenne Harbor.

His career had taken him on infamous raids with top buccaneers and privateers under the aliases El Capitaine, le Sage, La Salle and Gator Gar. La Roche had pirated with the Henry Morgan, l'Olonnais and Grammont. But once his privateering license expired and opportunities evaporated, he resorted to illegal pirating, as there was little profit in merchant shipping and he didn't believe in running slaves. The mission to capture Jamaica failed. War still raged, and wherever he went it would find him.

La Roche inhaled the damp night air; it made his chest ache. Any dream of retiring to *Sérénité* with Atia dissipated in the rain. Her time in Port Royal had changed her, and his time away from her had only aged him.

He continued down a lantern lit path and passed by cottages and stables. Footsteps sloshed behind him; he drew his cutlass.

Two men stepped from the shadows.

"You want to play, oui?" la Roche asked.

"Capitaine? I served with you at Panama. I am Reyning."

"Oui, Reyning. I remember. Henry Morgan hired you."

"We have business with Carlitos of San Juan."

"So do I," la Roche said.

Rivero stepped into the light.

"We didn't come here to fight," said Reyning. "You worked for Governor Carlitos in the past."

"Oui, in the past. I do not trust him or the son of Jorge Rivero," said la Roche. "What do you want of me?"

"We remember you as an honest man," said Reyning. "We need you to capture a ship."

"What ship?"

"A Dutch ship," said Reyning. "She's carrying German nobles—a countess, in fact. She has broken the law and stolen from her own government and the church."

"She's also known to be a witch," added Rivero.

"A witch?" La Roche scowled. "Fuck off!"

"The court in Hanover has charged her with witchcraft. She's a wanted criminal, anyway."

"Even still, there are legalities," said Reyning. "There is no Dutch warrant, and the Vatican haven't admitted they're looking for it."

"I am bound by treaty. There is no legal way for us to seize the ship under a Spanish flag," said Rivero. "Therefore, I ask you, my friend, to capture her under a pirate flag and deliver her to us secretly."

"I'm needed here in Hispaniola," said la Roche.

"Have you not heard? Laurens plans to demote you. Of course, he doesn't want to do it now, in front of the buccaneers," said Reyning. "He plans to leave you stranded at Monte Cristi and let the Spanish kill you for him. I heard this from my wench in Cayman Brac."

"I don't believe you."

"No? He spent the last day and a night penetrating your woman on his ship."

"No, he didn't. She would never."

"My wench recently found herself carrying a bastard belonging to Laurens and is not happy with him, to say the least," said Reyning. "We have a reasonable offer for you."

"What can you offer me?"

"Your freedom," said Rivero. "Carlitos is offering you a full pardon. The last major bounty on your head will be no more, and you can finally retire—with fifty percent of the booty."

"But time is critical," Reyning put in. "You must leave now; the ship is imminent. I can arrange for a pirate crew of one hundred men, grenades and muskets on Crab Island. Quality wheel-lock guns and all the men you need. What do you say?"

"What's to stop me taking this ship for myself?" said la Roche.

"By all means, take it for yourself. Carlitos just wants the witch. And remember who gave you this opportunity, my friend," said Rivero. "But don't throw away a chance at a full pardon."

"No. I don't work for Spanish. I'm going to be too busy kicking you out of Hispaniola."

"Sorry we could not reach an agreement, Capitaine."

"Then we bid you good tidings," said Reyning.

"What makes you think I will let you leave the island alive?"

"Are we not under protection of parley, Capitaine?"

"Oui. Adieu."

The men departed.

La Roche slid the cutlass back into its baldric. His spirit sank even lower when Laurens and Atia came out of the tavern together laughing.

Giddiness filled Atia as she left the tavern. Her first pirate meeting, and soon to have her own ship! Her da and uncle would have been proud. Neither the rain nor la Roche's scowling face could dampen her mood.

"Hey love, there ya are," Atia began. "We were looking for you. I'm catching a ride on Laurens's comet."

"I hear you already did."

"With yer blessing, remember? I've been waiting for you now for a long time. I'm tired of waiting."

"Going where?" la Roche said.

"To Cape François with Miles."

"What about *Sérénité*?"

"Oh, are we going? Aye. That does change things. I'll get my chest, Larry."

"We can't go right now," la Roche said. "I must secure our future first. I must stay here."

"I see. Then I'll wait for you in Cape François," Atia said.

"Fine, then, you wait for me in Cape François. I am duty-bound to defend Saint-Domingue."

"Oh, about that." Laurens patted la Roche's shoulder. "I'm sending you to Monte Cristi. I need someone I can trust to watch over Montbars and Wynne and the like. I need the Capitaine."

"Do you?" la Roche said.

"Yes, I do. You'll take de Kreep and his men. Arsenault comes with me. I'll need him to protect the coast."

"Arsenault will protect the coast?" la Roche spoke bitterly. "I see. Then I bid you both adieu."

"Will you come for me in Cape François?" Atia asked.

"Of course," he said, unconvincingly. "As always." He turned and went into the tavern.

"Goodbye, then," Atia remarked.

"Pay no mind to him, doll," Laurens said. "Ravenau already escorted Gladstone aboard, and I'll meet you at the ship shortly. I have more business to take care of first."

Atia stepped towards the ship but then noticed Laurens sneaking off down a path with a cloaked figure. She snuck off into the darkness to investigate, hiding behind a large wooden pillar that marked the entrance to a stable.

Laurens kissed the figure and slid down the hood. Atia recognized her from the siege on Port Royal. Cléo was an exotic dancer, kept as a pet by Silent Sam.

"Where are you going? I must have you. I've waited for you for ages."

"I can't." Cléo turned her head.

"Yes, you can, and you will."

Laurens opened his trousers, and he took her on a bale of hay. The act didn't take long, and Cléo seemed eager for it to be over. When he finished, he buttoned his trousers and Cléo covered herself in the cloak.

"Please don't send me back," she said. "You said you wanted me here with you."

"This is the last time," Laurens said. "After this one, you'll have the house in Cape François, with a thousand slaves."

"You know I don't want slaves. I just want all this to be over."

"You'll be fine."

"They will know."

"Never. I'll have men always close by. War is war, Cléo dear. I will need you with me, by my side, when we throw the Spanish out for good. But right now, I need to know who he has and where, or this island will be lost. I intend to die rather than lose Saint-Domingue. Do it for me?" Laurens smiled.

"I tried that concoction you gave me to smell bad, but the bastard liked it. I need something with more permanent effects."

"I'll send you along with a Sam-repellant. You can you use it as you see fit." Laurens shrugged. "Like I said. It's war."

"And when the war is over, I get to retire to Cape François?"

"To live, and garden, and clean to your heart's content if you wish, or, as my wife."

Cléo kissed him again. "I will go with Silent Sam one last time."

"I knew you would. I promised to buy your freedom, and I will."

They kissed again.

Atia shook her head. *What a pig. A pig in a sharp suit*, she thought and backtracked to the ship. When she got there, Gladstone was waiting on deck.

"All ready to go?"

"I am." Atia reached up her sleeve. "Here, I found a spare."

Gladstone took the bottle of Strangewayes Bliss Formula and slipped it in his pocket. "Thanks. Where'd you find it?"

"Lifted it from Laurens's personal store."

That's when Zoe the barmaid boarded.

"Are you coming too?" Gladstone asked.

"Oui, I'm going back to Cape François." She winked, pouting her lips.

"Told you." Atia elbowed him. "She wants you. Are you ready to cast off?"

"Yes. I'm ready for a new adventure."

Laurens leapt aboard, posing heroically with his hands on his hips. He winked at Atia. "Ready to cast off, doll?"

"Oink, oink." Atia winked back.

"Right you are, my little piggy." Laurens put his fingers in the air like imaginary pistols and bounded up the stairs.

Gladstone ogled Zoe as she went below deck. "I could give her a tip." He sighed, turning to Atia. "So, what do you think of the famous Laurens de Graaf?"

"Pigs, the lotta ya!" Atia pushed past him, going below. "Oink, bloody, oink."

Cape François

Miles Gladstone sat in the cook room aboard *Cometa*, eating braised mutton. He stared at Zoe, the barmaid from Tortuga, as beads of perspiration slid down into her cleavage. He indulged in visions of licking treacle off her bare skin and exhaled deeply.

"I best check and see how Atia's doing," Gladstone said.

"Atia's fine. She's playing games with Laurens," came Zoe's thick French accent.

"What kind of games?"

"Just silly games." Zoe brushed up against him on her way to the water barrel. "She asked me to keep an eye on you."

"On me? Oh, I'm, I'm doing fine. Just happy to be away from Tortuga."

"Is this your first time to ze cape?" she asked.

"It is. I've been to Tortuga a few times before, but never have I been on the island. Just missing Port Royal is all."

"Did you grow up there?"

"Aye. How about you? What brings you?"

"Laurens lets me stay at ze cape when Tortuga gets dangerous. I would say right now is dangerous, yes."

"I agree wholeheartedly." Gladstone laughed.

"Married, are you?" Zoe brushed by him again.

"Me? No. Well, almost. I wanted to, but she was killed."

"How?"

"When we were attacked on a plantation in the Blue Mountains."

"So sorry. Is there anyone special now?"

Gladstone shook his head as she thrust her bosom forward.

"I like you," said Zoe.

"Really? Did Laurens tell you to like me?"

"Oui, but of course. He paid me six doubloons to like you." Zoe groped between his thighs. "Zat is a lot of liking."

"Well, then, like me all you want."

Later, as *Cometa* neared Cape François, Gladstone emerged from the forecastle, refreshed and stretching, to find Atia on deck, while Laurens commanded on the quarterdeck.

"I'm glad you came," Atia said.

"Oh, so am I, dear Atia, so am I!"

A huge estate came into view as the ship neared the dock.

Zoe kissed Gladstone's cheek. "Come to my room tonight. Servant's quarters."

"He makes you stay in the servant's quarters?"

"Zit's not as bad as zit sounds."

"I wouldn't miss it if it was a stable. Hey, that's an idea." Gladstone grinned. "When was the last time you did it in a stable?"

"Ze last time I was in Cape François."

"You didn't have to be that honest. But I'll see you tonight."

Zoe kissed him, sliding her hand between his legs before she left.

"I see you're getting on with Zoe?" Laurens remarked.

"Aye, I like her."

They took the gangway down to the dock and followed a stone path. Emerald-green grass lay like a carpet, bordered by neatly cropped beds of white and pink bougainvillea. "This way," Laurens said. "I like to call this island Cape Laurens, or Messina for short." They passed a bungalow. "This is my apothecary, stocked with all your favourite Strangewayes Brand items, legal and not so legal. Just remember, nothing's illegal in Cape François."

They continued along into the heart of the garden. A stone water fountain in the shape of a clamshell burbled pleasantly. Red flame trees lined the property, next to gravel paths that formed a labyrinth pattern. Dazzling beds of hibiscus, desert rose, flamingo flowers and birds of paradise nestled like jewels next to a whitewashed mansion.

"Wow." Gladstone's mouth gaped. "You even have your own giant clam. You just need a naked goddess to go with it."

"You want me to get in the clam?" Atia offered.

"You'd play the part well," said Gladstone.

"He means the painting," said Laurens. "Don't you know the *Birth of Venus*?"

A black man with neatly tied hair, dressed in a deep plum suit with gold stitching, waved.

"You were at the card game." Atia went for her stilettos.

"Now, that's gratitude for you," Theodore Binge replied.

"Aye, relax. He won you for our side," Gladstone said.

"Did he?" Atia relaxed. "Sorry, mate, my memory of that night is a bit foggy."

"Then you belong with Miles. His memory of every night is foggy," Binge said. "How did you make out with our German girls?"

"Mission accomplished. Atia's brothers made the final delivery to Aragua. Oh, I think I owe you another set of thank-you kisses."

"You can keep the kisses in trust for now. So, what are you up to?" Binge scrutinized Gladstone's outfit. "Still trying to be a travel writer?"

"Well, you know, a pirate siege here and a pirate siege there, it's all kind of samey after a while."

"I'll leave you with Mr. Binge while I check in," Laurens said. "You're all expected for dinner tonight. Seven of the clock. I'd like Gerty to make it."

"Hey, I been trying for six months," Binge said.

"Order her some more tulips," Laurens suggested.

"I've given up on tulips. That stock's never coming back up."

Laurens went to meet with his staff inside.

Gladstone was unable to speak for several minutes, taking it all in. "You've been living here all this time?"

"Can you think of a better place?" Binge said. "We ran into trouble on Cayman Brac."

"You were there when Bartolomeo bought it?" Gladstone asked. "The wives are well, I hope."

"A fool's hope, sorry to say, mate." Binge frowned. "Henrietta was taken from us by Ginger that night. Gerty's married to melancholia now. Her sister and her were close."

"Aye. Inseparable. My condolences."

"Is she here with ya?" Atia asked.

"She's got our bungalow on the hill, behind the house, to herself," Binge said. "And she's got Madeira wine to get her through the day."

"She and her sister were there that night, too," Atia said.

"They participated in your rescue," Gladstone said.

"That they did," Binge said.

"I'd like to thank her meself."

"If you can find any common ground, be my guest." Binge extended his arm. "She's as lively as the guest of honor at a wake."

"Common ground is what we got," said Atia.

"Tell ya what, I'll let you invite her to dinner."

Atia strolled through the garden. It reminded her of Strangewayes's plantation in the Blue Mountains. A paradise on earth. She found shade beneath a cluster of lemon trees.

Laurens returned with a man wearing a French chapeau. "Change of plan. Seems I'm going to have to leave right away, doll."

"What's wrong?" Atia asked.

"Just trouble with the war. I'd like it if you both stayed here as my guests."

"I'm thinking the servant's quarters seem nice," Gladstone said.

"Things are getting out of control, well, everywhere. So, stay at the palace as my guests, with Bernanos here, my Captain at Arms."

Bernanos bowed. "At your service, madam."

"He knows I'm a wench, right?"

"De Graaf says you are to be treated as Venus herself while you are here," Bernanos said.

"Okay, I'll stay a while and keep Miles company. However, yer not gonna leave without paying up for Slasher Al, are ya?"

"I wouldn't dream of it. Your chest is in the vault. Bernanos will let you in whenever you wish," Laurens said.

"Atia, I'm glad I finally got to meet you in person. Perhaps when I return, we can pick up where we left off." He winked.

"At least I'll remember the weekend I rode on yer *Cometa*."

Laurens kissed her hand and departed.

They followed Binge up to the house. It stood three levels tall, turrets at each end, with round, coned roofs. Pillars accented a wraparound veranda, and there were over a dozen rectangular windows with gold-leaf casings. Exterior staircases led up to balconies at various levels. They climbed the steps up to the main doors and crossed a white marble floor.

"It's a gallery!" Atia said.

"Indeed, Laurens has an impressive collection," said Bernanos. "This way, madam."

Atia followed.

A massive crystal chandelier hung next to a curved staircase. A recessed ceiling was decorated with a *trompe l'oeil* of blue sky and white clouds, with wrought-iron scroll patterns. Highly polished mahogany panels adorned the walls, alongside works of art.

"His art collection includes *The Girl with a Pearl Earring* by Johannes Vermeer; *Medusa* by Michelangelo Merisi da Caravaggio; and *Danaë* by Rembrandt Harmenszoon van Rijn," said Bernanos.

Atia, wandering open-mouthed, crashed into him. "Sorry, it's a lot to take in."

Her room was furnished with a curtained four-poster bed, red and gold damask wallpaper, a wardrobe, fireplace, writing desk, and green satin curtains.

"Thank you," said Atia.

"If you need anything, don't hesitate to ask." Bernanos kissed her hand and went to show Gladstone his quarters.

As evening approached, Atia ventured all over the upstairs. It had eight bedrooms, a library and a washing room with a large copper tub. Downstairs, there was a dining room, lounge, library, study and smoking room with paintings of nude women sprawling on the walls. She found a staircase leading down to a kitchen, adjacent an oversized pantry, and servants' quarters at the end of a long hallway.

Angry voices filtered through the walls, one of them belonging to Laurens. Atia followed it down a corridor hidden in shadow, which opened into a large room with a banquet table and fireplace.

Laurens, Binge, Ravenau, Bernanos and Arsenault were having a heated debate over a map spread on the table.

"Tell me you jest," Laurens said. "The goddamn fool."

Nigel rushed into the meeting from a door at the other end of the room. Evening sunshine burst through. "What's happening?"

"Governor De Cussy is on the move with every man we got from Petit Goâve and Port de Paix," Laurens said.

"Going where?"

"Where do you think?" Binge added.

"By land." Nigel's face sagged.

"You got it," Laurens said. "I told him to wait. Why do the French even make plans?"

"It says here, in the letter to King Louis, that he complains the island is weak, and I quote, 'I have destroyed privateering because the court so willed it,'" Bernanos said.

"That's right," Laurens said. "We have no ships. None to protect the island, and Du Cussy mounts a land war. We have nothing protecting our backs. The Spanish Armada has at least a dozen war galleons, and the English still have Port Royal."

"The English have a new Leeward fleet." Bernanos showed him a letter. "They stopped at Newport. A whole new fleet of ships of the line."

"We lost our Leeward fleet," Laurens said. "We have three ships of the line left running up and down to the Windward Islands."

"Where are the men hired to take Port Royal?" Bernanos asked.

"Pirates for defence? That may have worked in '55, but I'm not letting one of them smelly bastards in my town," said Laurens. "I sent them to Monte Cristi to keep them busy for a while. I have a mind to let the Spanish wipe them out, but now I need them."

"What about la Roche?" Arsenault asked.

"He can get us three, maybe four good ships," Binge said.

Bernanos laughed. "That can't hold off the Spanish Armada."

"No, but it'll be enough to stop them entering Cape François. Capitaine's been getting sloppy," Laurens said. "I sent him to Monte Cristi, too."

Gladstone came up behind Atia. She jumped and gestured to him to remain quiet.

"After Port Royal, do you think you can trust Coxon or la Roche?" Ravenau asked.

"Coxon, no. But we need la Roche for now. I'm sending Arsenault to get him," Laurens said. "His woman is here; he'll come back and act as admiral of the fleet while I follow Governor De Cussy."

"Where is Governor De Cussy?" Ravenau said.

"They marched out of Petit Goâve three days ago," said Bernanos.

"Marched?" Nigel questioned.

"That's right, marched," Laurens said. "With banners and flags, like he's Julius fucking Caesar. I'm going to have to leave tonight. Make sure the redhead stays; I need Capitaine here," he told Bernanos.

"A thousand daggers went through my heart when I saw that beautiful girl," Bernanos sighed.

"You can have her for a night when we take the island. She's a sweet ride, a bit wild. And she may have baggage. I may have planted a seed."

Atia and Gladstone shared an awkward moment.

"Oink, oink." Atia glared.

"Nigel, *Cometa* stays here in the Cape. Theodore, go on with that party tonight. I want everyone to think I'm still here," Laurens said. "Have Slasher Al's *Bloody Mary* brought over from Port de Paix. Add it to the Capitaine's fleet. Oh, I promised her to the redhead. Now she'll have to stay; her ship will be here. It's up to you two to hold the fort until I return."

"Aye, we'll hold," Bernanos agreed. "Is Ravenau going with you?"

"Into a war, no thanks," said Ravenau.

"No, he's going to Paris to write my book." Laurens turned to Ravenau. "Leave tonight after the party. I've got you on a tobacco ship."

Laurens and his men dispersed.

Atia signalled Gladstone that it was time to leave.

Binge stepped towards Laurens.

"What's up?" Laurens said.

"I think the girl and Miles might have overheard our conversation."

"Then it's real important she doesn't go anywhere."

"I think she'll like it here," Binge said.

"I'll leave that up to you, then."

Atia and Gladstone ascended the stairs back to the first floor. The pair slipped into the library and closed the door. Each grabbed a book and pretended to read on the window bench. Gladstone glanced up periodically. Several minutes passed before a knock came at the door.

"Come in," Atia said.

Binge entered. "Good, Miles is here too. I trust yer almost ready."

"We're going to celebrate Laurens's return without Laurens?" Atia said.

"Am I not enough for you?"

"I have no fancy dress," Atia said.

"We're stoppin' by my place before we go. I'm sure Gerty has a spare."

"Lead the way." Atia and Gladstone followed.

They followed Binge through the elaborate garden. They passed the apothecary and continued along a path bordered by bright, fragrant roses to a stone house. Inside, Gertrude Binge, in a black dress, sat at the window, which overlooked the water.

"Get comfortable; I just gotta get changed. Gerty, you remember Miles and Atia." Binge went to the adjacent room.

"Miles Gladstone and who?" said Gertrude.

"Atia," Atia said.

Gertrude rose. "The Irish girl from the card game. I remember. And Miles, my goodness, I can't believe it. I miss coming into your apothecary."

"Everyone does; it's called withdrawment," Binge said from the other room.

"It was such a pleasant shop."

"It was always a pleasure, Miss Binge," Gladstone said.

"I wanted to thank you for what you did," Atia said. "And I'm sorry you lost your sister. I'm truly sorry."

"Thank you. Did your sister make it out okay?"

Atia shook her head.

"Oh, I didn't know. I'm so sorry."

"Me too," Atia said.

"Say, why don't you come with us," Gladstone spoke chirpily. "We're going for a drink at the tavern."

"I just got paid. I'll buy," Atia said.

"Gerty isn't into the kind of drinking we're into." Binge emerged in a shiny black suit with purple and green stitching. His hair was neatly tied back with a gold ribbon.

"No, I'll come. I'll just get ready." Life sparked in Gertrude's eyes. "Come, I have a dress that might suit you." She led Atia away.

The Mermaid Tavern overlooked the waterfront. It had a white stone patio with a water fountain, topiaries, and a fully stocked bar. Musicians provided the entertainment.

Atia, in a sky-blue dress with white trim and ruffled sleeves, sat next to Gertrude, who wore a similar dress but in deep plum. The two women drank whiskey and reminisced about their sisters.

Meanwhile, Gladstone and Binge chatted about the old pirate days over a bottle of rum.

Atia volunteered to get the next round of drinks. Skillfully, she slid some liquid from a Strangewayes tincture into Binge's mug before delivering it to the table.

Zoe joined them and soon got Gladstone to his feet in an intoxicated dance.

Servants lit the torches, and the grounds of the estate glowed. In the distance, Laurens rode a horse out of the main gate, accompanied by a handful of men. Later, Arsenault led two war-piraguas out of the harbor.

Atia tried to place a song the band was playing. "What song is it?"

"I know it." Binge raised his hand. "I know it."

"I heard it at the Swiftsure," said Atia.

"Tom Jones!" Gladstone said, watching the harbor.

"Jonesy!" Atia leapt to her feet and rushed along a wooden walkway to the dock. She threw herself into his arms. "I've missed you!"

"I didn't know you still cared," Jones said.

"Of course, I do, Jonesy. What brings you here?"

They walked to the tavern arm in arm.

"I came here to find you and the Capitaine. I know yer brothers don't like me much, but we got a job to do," said Jones.

"What kind of job?" Gladstone asked.

"Firstly, we gotta find yer brothers," he told Atia. "There's more Happybergs, or Calliebergs, or Germanbergs, or whatever type of berg they are."

"More like Natalia and Catharina. Are they related?"

"Aye. There's more of them coming, and we've got to get to them before someone else does."

"Where's this all coming from?" Binge asked. "Who's your source?"

"A German noble contacted Lord Dewar and asked for help."

"Dewar?" everyone said.

"That's what I thought. She's better off asking Nostradamus. But we gotta get going. The ships have already reached the Caribbean."

"How do we contact the O'Malleys?" Gladstone said.

"They're in Hope Bay by now."

"Why didn't Dewar hire Bleedin Art?" Atia questioned. "He always hires Art."

"I think they had a falling out, lass. Besides, Bleedin Art's on his way to the Bahamas."

"The Bahamas? What for?" Binge said.

"Pirate hunting. He's to bring in my brother, Cadwallader. The self-appointed King of New Gwynedd and renowned crack-brain. I never liked that side of the family much. They're as inbred as the Hapsburgs."

"So, which is it? Do we go see the O'Malleys or wait here for the Capitaine?" Gladstone asked.

"Atia could come with me to get her brothers," Jones suggested. "If the Capitaine's coming back here, one of us should wait for him."

Atia shook her head. "Neither."

"No?" Gladstone said.

"We go to the Bahamas to get Art."

"Bleedin Art?" everyone said.

"Aye, Art. If he's pirate hunting, he's better equipped than me brothers anyway. Leave them out of it. I lost enough family. We'll go to Bleedin Art. Who's with me?"

"I think we outta stay right here and wait for the Capitaine," Binge said.

"Capitaine's gone away with his friends, Montbars and John Cox, or whoever. I'm going to see Art," Atia asserted.

"I'm sorry, girl. I can't let ya leave the island just yet," Binge said anxiously. "Not until Laurens is far...far away. You gotta understand secrecy."

"I won't tell anyone," Atia said.

Alarm bells sounded.

"That was quick," Atia added.

"Sorry. No one leaves tonight," Binge reiterated.

"This being in charge thing is new for you, isn't it?" Gladstone said.

Binge looked up at the sky for a moment. "I must have forgotten something. How am I looking?" He checked his outfit.

"What?" Gladstone gave a slight head shake.

"Exactly." Binge straightened his collar.

"Exactly what?" Gladstone said.

"Exactly." Binge nodded. "Oh shit, someone gave me something."

"That would be me," Atia confessed, a mischievous grin formed on her face. "I slipped you something a little while ago. I want some answers, Mr. Binge."

Binge guffawed, clapping his hands. "See, she goes straight for the apothecary! And here I thought you were getting something for Miles."

"Is he all right? Gertrude asked.

"I feel like I'm gonna die!" Binge exclaimed.

"It's just a Strangewayes concoction," said Gladstone. "You'll be fine in twelve hours."

Binge puffed out his cheeks.

An explosion came across the water and lights appeared on the horizon.

"Jesus Christ!" Jones exclaimed.

"Really?" Binge said. "Where?"

Bernanos ran towards them.

"What the hell is it?" Atia asked. "I didn't cause this, did I?"

"It's a Spanish war galleon," said Bernanos.

"Man the forts!" Binge said.

"I did," Bernanos said. "That's my job."

"That's a relief." Binge's hands trembled. "We're all gonna die!"

"Her cannons can't reach us," Bernanos assured.

A cannonball smashed into the palace, obliterating what was once the dining room.

"I hope ya don't mind, but I'm into running hysterically away. Bye." Binge took Gertrude's hand, and they ran.

"The war galleon can't get into the bay, but our ships are trapped," said Bernanos. "Jones, I put your *Cymru* back with the fish barge, along with *Cometa*."

"Cheers," Jones said.

"Laurens gave you *Bloody Mary*, right?" Gladstone asked Atia.

"Aye. How far is it to get my ship?"

Bernanos signalled a guard. "Get a carriage ready. It's in Port de Paix. Go with Monsieur Binge, take the carriage down this road to Baie de l'acul, where there's an old Indian temple. There's a boat there. We use it for smuggling."

Cannons blasted at the ships on the horizon.

"I'm not leaving without my bounty," Atia said.

"Right, the treasure," Gladstone remembered.

"I'll have *Cymru* follow us when the coast is clear," Jones said. "We'll take your chest with us. How much can there be?"

Atia's treasure chest was brought out by four slaves and loaded onto a carriage.

Jones ogled the treasure chest. "We're going to carry that on the boat?"

"I got a bad back," Gladstone said.

"I'm not leaving it; I earned every bit of it." Atia turned to Bernanos. "Thank you, but why are you helping me? Aren't you going to get into trouble from Laurens?"

"Even Laurens didn't see a war galleon coming tonight. Everyone must go. Besides, when this is over, I'm hoping you remember me and come back."

"Don't wait too long," she said under her breath and hopped aboard.

Binge and Gertrude secured a few clothes and weapons before climbing onto the driver's bench.

"Let's make sure I got all the important things. I got the green satin suit, the buckle shoes and the tuxedo. Am I missing anything?" Binge snapped his fingers. "Gertrude!"

"Here." Gertrude took the reins.

Gladstone, Zoe, and Jones also climbed aboard, and the carriage took off.

"Watch out for the big spider," Binge said.

"Quiet," Gertrude said.

They drove through a giant spider web.

Gertrude screamed as a spider scuttled across her face.

Binge smacked it, crushing it on her cheek.

"Are those eggs hatching?" Gladstone remarked.

Gertrude's face went ghost white as the carriage sped up.

"Uh, you might wanna slow down," Binge said.

"I think those are eggs," Gladstone said again.

The carriage barely made the corner.

"Can I drive?" Gladstone said. "I'll drive."

"Fuck, I'll drive." Zoe climbed onto the driver's bench.

By morning they had reached the boathouse, which was surrounded by a swamp with a ruined temple behind it. It took all six of them to navigate the chest onto the boat.

"No one carries a chest like this anymore," said Jones. "You're not Henry fuckin' Morgan!"

"Besides." Gladstone stumbled. "This is outdated currency. No one pays in coins anymore."

"Watch what yer doing," Jones barked, narrowly avoiding having the chest land on his foot as they lowered it.

"Oh, my back," Gladstone groaned as his toe clipped the edge of the trunk.

They took turns rowing up the Haitian coast to Port de Paix.

"You doing okay, Gerty?" Binge asked.

Gertrude huffed, avoiding him, rowing in silence.

"Well, at least you're out of the house," Binge continued.

"Where are we, Jones?" Gladstone asked.

"Uh, I've never come this way."

"Just around zee point," Zoe said.

At dusk they arrived at the landing. The port was busy with people rushing around, readying their vessels for departure. Thunderous booms sounded in the distance.

Atia looked for the ship named *Bloody Mary*. "Shit, there's so many. Look for one with a big round window at the back."

"Laurens has a private dock." Zoe pointed. "Just a bit further."

Bloody Mary came into view. The mosaic glass window with lead casing at the aft cabin was lit.

"Zat's her," said Zoe.

"Wow, that is a nice window," said Jones.

They ceased rowing and glided the rest of the way.

The men aboard were conversing in French.

"What are they saying?" said Gladstone.

"The ship has been chosen to fight against the Spanish," Binge said. "She is now the property of the king of France."

"Like hell she is," Atia said.

"Quiet all." Jones signalled them.

The French called orders and moved on to the next vessel.

"Let's get aboard," Jones said.

The figurehead, a once-proud goddess, now had both arms broken and multiple wounds carved into her breasts.

"This is Slasher Al's boat, sure enough." Gladstone cringed.

"What did you do to Al, Atia?" Zoe asked.

"Everything."

"Everything?" Binge raised an eyebrow.

"Aye. Some cutting, sawing, peeling, squeezing and whole lot of oozing."

"I quite understand, thank you," Gertrude said.

"Go on," Binge said. "I like this part."

Their boat hit the pier.

"Oops," Gladstone said. "Let's get the chest up first."

"Tie the boat so she can't slip free; then we lift it out," Jones said.

They tied down the boat and everyone grabbed a side of the trunk and they heaved it up.

Dock workers arrived.

Atia's group tried to look occupied.

Zoe translated into Gladstone's ear, while Binge attempted to speak with the dock workers.

"Get these ships out of the way and clear this dock," said a French officer.

"The trunk is coming or going?" the dock worker said.

"Oui," Gladstone said.

Zoe spoke in French to the officer, telling him, as she translated, "this chest goes onto this ship into the forward weapons storage for the big gun."

"Good thinking," Binge said.

The dock workers transported it aboard.

Zoe thanked them.

The French officer asked her what they were doing, and she replied, "Binge runs an inn, and they've been ordered to stock the ship with provisions by emergency order."

The officer nodded.

Atia's party boarded.

"She's doing well," Atia said.

"I'll say," Gladstone replied.

They came face to face with a muscular man who stood over six feet tall. His dark eyes challenged them. "What are you doing?"

"It's my ship, and I'm taking her." Atia went for her stilettos.

The man reached for his sword and then stopped. "Tom?"

Jones stepped forward. "John."

"Sure as hell is you. Haven't seen you in ages."

"I take it you two know each other," Gladstone said.

"This is my cousin, John Grymes," Jones introduced.

"What are ya doing here?" Grymes asked.

"We're taking the ship. This is my goddaughter, Atia."

"Cormac's little girl. Not so little. You say it's your ship?"

"Laurens gave it to me," said Atia. "I killed Slasher Al."

"You killed Slasher Al?" Grymes towered over her. "That's what they're saying, all right. But I got to hear it from Laurens."

"Laurens is gone to war. The military is coming to take me ship," said Atia.

"So, how did you end up here, Johnny?" Jones asked.

"I was hired by Laurens to look after the ship until she's ready to go back to sea."

"Is she ready to go back to sea?" Jones pressed.

"Aye. I don't see why not. We don't have a full crew, only a few of my mates."

Decorated French naval officers arrived by the wagonful.

"Time to go, maties," Atia ordered.

Zoe and Gertrude pretended to solicit the officers, giving the men enough time to cut the mooring lines. They were interrupted by an explosion further down the dock. The French officers and dock workers ran to see what happened.

"Shove off!" Grymes ordered his five men, who took the ship out of the slip.

"Oars," Grymes said. "Let's get out of here."

Jones ran up to the quarterdeck to take the wheel.

A French guard aimed his musket right at Gertrude's back. Binge dove between them, knocking her down.

"Don't return fire," said Grymes. "Everyone stay down and row."

Atia and Gertrude rushed over to Binge. He lay on the deck, whimpering.

"Theo?" Gertrude turned him over.

A hole smoked in his coat, beneath his arm. "My best suit, why, oh why!"

"You're so lucky," Gladstone said.

"Lucky? You can't fix that! Oh, pure gold stitching. It can't be replaced."

"You saved my life. Again." Gertrude helped him up.

"Like I said, some things can't be replaced."

"We're clear," Grymes said. "We can go to full sail."

"We sail for the Bahamas, to Bleedin Art," said Atia.

"Make it so, Mr. Grymes," Jones said.

"Aye."

"Hang on," Gladstone said. "Technically, she's a pirate ship. Shouldn't we vote for our leader?"

"I own her," Atia said. "She's my ship."

"Works for me," Binge said.

"I'm square with that," Grymes agreed.

"Set course northwest for the Bahamas," Jones said.

"And Mr. Grymes," Atia added. "Cut loose the figurehead. She's been in pain long enough." Grymes and a couple of his men broke it, and it splashed into the sea.

"And I rename this ship *Whiskey Kisses*." Atia climbed to the quarterdeck. "Steady as she goes."

"Steady as she goes, Captain," Jones said.

"It's the only order I know," Atia admitted.

"Aye, we'll work on that, Captain." Jones smiled at his goddaughter.

The New Kingdom of Gwynedd

Guernsey dropped anchor in Lovely Bay, just off Crooked Island in the Bahamas. Bleedin Art basked in the sun on deck. Surrounded by shimmering white sand and lush green palm trees, he sighed as he sipped his brandy. The only thing missing was his revered redhead. And his parrot Cupid, but he had been killed in the recent pirate raid on Port Royal.

Art hadn't stepped foot on Crooked Island in five years. Their last dealings were four months ago, when his men Scarcliff and the late Jag'd Jayne visited to form an alliance. *How can one safely govern home unless he purchases a great alliance with rats, cockroaches and Cadwallader Jones*, Art thought.

Nearby sat the Bermuda sloop *Cunodagos* and the Bermuda sloop of war, *Y Ddraig Goch*, guarding the entrance to the bay. Three of *Guernsey's* longboats were rowing out, in different directions. Crazy Cadwallader Jones was watching from somewhere.

Dr. Strangewayes ventured on deck, medical bag in hand.

"What kind of concoctions has the good doctor brought with him?" Art asked.

The doctor took out a couple of vials, which he mixed. "Commodore, I could put everyone on this island into a coma, but for you, something simple and palatable." The formula fizzed.

"You want me to drink that?" Art asked.

"Well, if you prefer it rectally…" Strangewayes said.

"We'll have to test it on Bach. Bach!" Art called.

Strangewayes laughed as he split the formula into two shot glasses. "I never prescribe anything I'm not willing to take myself. Here you are."

"Bottoms up." Art drank and cringed. "MacAskill told me never to drink one of your concoctions."

"Ah, but MacAskill never cured your rheumatic knees, did he?" Strangewayes drank.

"How long does it take?"

"Not long." Strangewayes shuddered. "Oh, there it goes. That's better."

They both perked up, smiling.

"What the hell?" Art hunched over. "I feel sick, very sick."

"Not to worry, it's perfectly normal."

"This is normal?" Art's mouth seemed paralyzed, along with the rest of his body.

"Oh, dear, did I get it right?" Strangewayes pondered.

"Dat's butter." Art showed less eye and more teeth.

"Aye, now sit back and rest a bit."

"Aye, breast a rit."

"How's the knees?" asked the doctor.

"What knees?" Art melted into his seat.

"Good."

They sat back, watching the birds and the clouds roll by, sipping wine. Crewmen put down lines to catch some fish while Art temporarily blacked out. He was woken by Stubbs leaning over him.

"We've been invited ashore, at sundown," Stubbs said.

"I see Cadwallader Jones fixed us accommodations," Art said, glancing over at the makeshift cages along the shore. "He's so damn predictable, you can set a clock to him. I'm going to write a song about this venture. Predictable Cadwallader Jones, as sure as sinking stones."

"He's got swords and guns stashed in the bushes behind the logs on the beach," Freeman said.

"Yup. Predictable. We don't want to be early," Art mused. "Have a bit of trouble lowering my yacht. The show starts at sundown."

Later that evening, they got the thumbs-up from the lookout in the crow's nest.

Art's group was lowered in a longboat, very slowly.

"Don't be late, Captain Stubbs," Art said.

"I'll be there before the second course, sir."

"Any last-minute advice for Mr. Bach, Commodore?" Freeman asked.

"Mr. Bach, don't eat the food and don't touch the locals. In fact, don't eat or touch anything while yer here. That's not an order; that's sage advice."

"I will obey, Commodore."

The sun sat low on the horizon as the longboat rowed in. It rounded a bend. Colonel Cadwallader Jones, wearing a crown of gold and human bones, sat on a captain's chair fashioned into a sort of large ribcage made of femurs and other skeletal remains. He sheltered beneath an old boat house attached to the remnants of a Spanish galleon. Everything was tied together haphazardly with rope and vines. A beechwood sign over an archway indicated the New Kingdom of Gwynedd.

"Permission to enter the, what's it say?" Art began.

"The New Kingdom of Gwynedd," Morris and Freeman read aloud.

"The New Kingdom of Gwynedd," Art continued.

"I bid you welcome, Captain Valentine," Cadwallader said.

Art's boat came ashore. He and his men climbed out, dragging the longboat up the beach. Another boat rowed in with Rob Slaughter and his cutthroats, their clothes makeshift, wearing strings of teeth around their necks. The townspeople gathered, equally dirty and unkempt, decorated in jewels and various gruesome tokens.

"May I introduce my daughter, the Duchess of Gwynedd, and the future Queen Frances."

Seren Slaughter stood in a linen dress, a white-gold tiara on her head, melded with the skeletal remains of a turtle. A small child slept in her arms, wrapped in pigskin.

"Charmed." Art bowed and tipped his hat.

"My niece, Lady Jane Niece and esquires Little Robber and Benny Hornigold."

A scantily clad juvenile stood naked, her body covered in soot. She grinned, showing missing teeth. The rest of the clan looked pretty much the same. Art's face hurt from grinning.

"And you know my son, the Duke of America," Cadwallader continued.

Rob Slaughter joined him. "You owe me for damage done to my ship at the hands of yer men."

"Robbie, Captain Valentine is here to pledge allegiance to the New Kingdom of Gwynedd. Is that not so, Captain Valentine?" Cadwallader said. "I've been waiting on you to join our enterprise. Be you and Governor Dewar prepared to swear allegiance and declare Jamaica New Lower Gwynedd?"

"Do I get a nice title?" Art asked.

"Aye, ye shall be Valentine, Baron of New Lower Gwynedd when you've proven yourself worthy. By yer account, does Port Royal intend to help Spanish conquer Saint-Domingue?"

"Well, they did hit us mighty hard. It'd be irresponsible to let it go unpunished. But we in Port Royal have no interest in taking the island for ourselves."

"Port Royal is small." Cadwallader gnawed on a bone that looked suspiciously human. "The French will lose Saint-Domingue. You can have a seat at the round table and a fleet of ships."

"Mmm, it's tempting, but, sorry to say, Colonel, yer under arrest for treason, piracy and conspiracy, no offense," said Art.

Cadwallader and his people laughed.

"I thought you had potential." Cadwallader whistled.

Nothing happened. Cadwallader and Rob Slaughter looked to the bushes on the beach. One man fell forward, dead.

"You underestimate the Kingdom of Gwynedd," said Cadwallader.

"But, my liege, your pawns are taken, and your rook and knights are in check by my man of war." Art tipped his hat. "Your bishop's exposed along with yer queen, no offense."

"*Guernsey*, a man of war?" Cadwallader laughed.

Lights flashed at sea and cannons fired. *Stingray* came into view, glowing with lantern light. Art grinned to himself in the knowledge that the puppets situated throughout the ship gave the illusion that they were far better prepared than in fact they were.

Lights came from *Cunodagos* and *Y Ddraig Goch* in the harbor. A signal indicated they were secure. Stubbs and twenty men sprang from the water with short swords and took Cadwallader's family prisoner at blade-point.

Cadwallader and Rob Slaughter peered through their telescopes at the ships.

"Not my *Cunodagos*!" Cadwallader said.

"Not my *Y Ddraig Goch*," Rob Slaughter said.

"Captain Stubbs. Take your men back to the ship, along with Colonel Cadwallader and his sons," Art said.

"*King* Cadwallader to you!"

"King of the hold perhaps," Art said. "We'll keep the rest of them together here while we interrogate the prisoners."

"You have made an enemy of the New Kingdom of Gwynedd!" Cadwallader yelled.

The townspeople shouted Welsh curses.

"Predictable," Art said.

Another longboat landed, carrying Morris and a squad of men. They searched the realm and made note of the people. Dietrich landed on the beach to join them.

"Tell Dietrich what you found," Art said to Morris.

"What I found makes no fuckin' sense. I indeed found prisoners. All dead."

"What prisoners?" Dietrich said.

"Cadwallader had prisoners. Lots of them. People taken from all over Florida, throughout the Keys and the islands," said Art. "But no one's seen or heard from them for over a year."

"That's not what the locals on Long Island said," Morris grumbled.

Art crossed his arms. "Oh?"

"Oh, sodding right. The people around here are terrified of Cadwallader and his dog Black Caesar," said Morris. "They led us to a mass grave where they said the prisoners were dead upon arrival. Cadwallader dressed slaves in their place and made them paint their faces to prove they were alive. They're all dead, too, still wearing the clothes of nobles, some dressed as animals."

"Why would he make them dress up?" Dietrich asked.

"Because he's completely barking mad," Art said. "Why does he call himself king of New Gwynedd? Because he's barking."

"I'll testify to that," Morris said. "All up the islands the bodies of men, women and children are on display in gibbets and on spikes. He's not discriminating; English, Spanish, native, and black—he doesn't seem to have any preference for who he kills. The locals on the southern island say he's stealing people and selling them on the black market."

"Then I've got him for fraud, too. I don't see many slaves," Art said. "Where's he keeping them? The farms?"

"What farms?" Morris said. "You said he stole all the farms up here. Every farm I found was dead. Rumor has it he just shipped a bunch to Samaná Bay."

"Samaná Bay?" Art rubbed his chin. "Yet, legally he made more money in cow and pig farming than Lady Beeston. If there's no farms, where's it all comin' from? I got him for tax evasion too. Find out what they got going on in Samaná Bay."

"Something else. A parrot, I think." Morris was about to speak again.

"What'd he say?" Art asked.

"He has to go powder his dick?" Freeman said.

Morris returned, carrying a rusty cage with a bald, festering parrot slumped over inside, and handed it over to Art.

"Are you going deaf, Freeman?" Art asked.

"It's dead," Freeman said. "No, it's moving."

"I figured, seeing as how you like birds, I thought you'd want it," Morris said.

"You thought right, Mr. Morris." Art took the cage. "On the morrow, you and Bach are going over every book and receipt Cadwallader has."

"Why me?"

"Captain Dietrich oversees security for the harbor and the island. Mr. Freeman, see to it that Cadwallader and his son are in the spiked collars, with leg and arm restraints. They will attempt an escape tonight."

"Aye."

Art returned to *Guernsey*. The grand cabin was being transformed into a dining room when he arrived. He took the rusted cage to where his bed stood behind a curtain. He unpacked a bird perch, a box of seed and a platform that attached to a hook on the ceiling.

Dr. Strangewayes came in.

"I have a patient here for you, Doc," Art said.

"Not of the venereal sort, I hope." Strangewayes scanned the room. "Where?"

Art showed him the cage as he snipped the bars with a cutter.

"What am I supposed to do with that, cook it?"

The bird looked up at them.

"I'd say it's alive."

"Can you save it?" Art asked.

"I'm not Jesus Christ, but if you're willing to hand over my special snuff box, then I can work miracles." Strangewayes examined the bird. "Who knows how long that thing has been caged, or even when it's last had food or drink? Keep it in a towel in a box. Give him some seeds and water. We'll see if he survives till morning."

"I think it's a *she*."

"Very well, she," Strangewayes said. "What makes you think so?"

"A Valentine knows these things." Art opened the cage and the bird trembled. "Cadwallader likes to see the pain he causes. Something I'm obliged to return in kind."

"I could whip him up something terrifying," Strangewayes offered.

"Something lethal?"

"Of course."

"Good idea, but I must keep him alive for the time being."

They fixed up a soft box by the window, next to the perch.

"Many people around here are in as bad a condition as the bird, here," the doctor said. "You'll be a local hero for dismantling the New Kingdom of Gwynedd."

"I will, will I?" Art said. "You differ from MacAskill. He'd have killed the bird by now. He'd say it's better for it."

"The correct term is *euthanasia*. When there's no hope of a better life, he'll kill the patient to end the suffering."

"That's MacAskill for you. You see potential in the bird?"

"Yes, I do," Strangewayes said. "Nature has a way of healing that modern medicine can't compete with. For example, the bird is still alive."

"Obviously."

"Exactly. In some cases, MacAskill would be right. A quick death is better, but I'll bet that this bird will fly again, given proper care."

"Cadwallader's people show signs of nasty infection," Art said. "Examine the lot and determine what they got."

"Do I have to? The bird is going to need constant reassurance."

"I wouldn't want to see them all euthanized," Art said.

Freeman and Morris entered.

"Is it still alive?" Morris asked.

"It's alive, Morris," Freeman replied.

"Don't let him stuff his face," said Morris.

"She," Art corrected.

"Mr. Morris does make a good point," Strangewayes said. "Perhaps limit what she has to eat or drink for now."

Bach arrived. "Commodore?"

"Finally, someone gets it right. Come in, Bach."

"Captain Stubbs sent me to tell you another ship is coming in. A sloop."

"A sloop?" Art said doubtfully. "Whatever shall we do?"

"It's *Bloody Mary*," Bach said.

"*Bloody Mary*?" Art exclaimed. "Slasher Al's old boat? This is a popular spot. I'm going to have to charge rates. On deck please, gentlemen."

Art tucked in the bird before following.

"*Bloody Mary* was last seen in Port Royal," Freeman said. "In the hands of French pirates."

"Aye, but she sailed out with a pardon under the Act of Grace law. Most of Slasher Al's men were killed. Who's in command of the bloody thing?"

Stubbs watched the approaching ship. "It's her, but there's a nameplate on the bow. *Whiskey Kisses*."

"*Whiskey Kisses*?" A smile formed on Art's face.

"That's what it says," Morris said. "Don't Art have a lousy song called 'Whiskey Kisses'?"

"What'd he say?" Art asked.

"He said that's the song you wrote for your favorite wench," Freeman translated.

Art peered through his telescope. A mane of red hair filled the lens. His heartbeat increased. "Well, blow me down, she thinks she's Henry fucking Morgan. It's a fancy-dress ball, tonight, lads. Welcome *Whiskey Kisses* alongside and show her officers to the table."

Whiskey Kisses tied to the side of *Guernsey*.

"Who is it?" Stubbs asked.

"That, Captain, is the daughter of Cormac the pikey," Art said. "And Alban Jones, captain of *Cymru*."

"Getting the young lady acquainted with her ship is all," Jones said. "My ship's not far behind. Guess that makes us both commodores."

"Permission to come aboard?" Atia asked.

A happy chill crept up his spine. "Come aboard, my lovely." He took her hand in his, giving it a prolonged kiss. "Welcome to Lovely Bay. I'll need to search your ship, you understand."

"Aye. Some of my men are from these parts; may they go ashore?" Atia asked.

"Be my guest. I'm expecting you and your officers to dinner."

"Aye, I'm starving," Gladstone said.

"Mr. Gladstone of Strangewayes Apothecary?" Art said.

"Evening, Commodore Valentine." Gladstone nodded.

"The good doctor is with us on board," Art said.

"He is?" Atia's mouth dropped.

"Miles, my old chum, good to see you." Strangewayes approached.

Atia rushed to Strangewayes, embracing him. "I thought you were dead."

"I thought I was, too. Miles, I can't believe it. You look a hundred percent." Strangewayes gave him a hearty handshake.

"Not a hundred percent, Doc. I lost all the best parts."

"I'm afraid we're also out of provisions," said Atia.

"Captain Stubbs, assist Mr. Grymes in stocking her stores," Art said.

"May we also come aboard?" Binge and Gertrude emerged.

"This is a surprise," Art said. "Theodore Binge, you're taking a chance."

"Um, parley?" Binge offered.

"I'd be inclined to sit on the commodore's lap and free up a chair for my crew, should there not be room for all of us," Atia said.

"I have no objection," Art agreed. "Indeed. Where are my manners. Mrs. Binge, I always enjoyed your presence; I hope you're well."

"I am, thank you," Gertrude said.

"You are my guests, and dinner's getting cold." Art extended his elbow and Atia took it, leading the group inside.

"I see your knees don't bother you tonight," Atia said.

"My knees don't bother me in Lovely Bay. The Bahamas have a way of making things lighter."

"You can go ashore, Mr. Grymes," Atia said.

"Aye."

"She's even giving orders; a girl after me own heart," Art mused. "We'll be watching. Mr. Grymes, you go on ashore."

"What have ya got goin' on here, Art?" Atia straightened his collar. "Have ya invented a new way to fish?"

"It's *Commodore*, pretty pikey. In a manner of speaking. I'm installing a new boom. One strong enough to withstand the weight of our new diving bell."

"A diving bell? Someone goes in that and then down into the water?"

"You are astute," said Art.

"It's lowered down to the bottom, where some unlucky bastard can breathe for hours while we bring up sunken treasure," said Freeman.

"There's sunken treasure here?" Atia said.

"You are keen to learn the ways of the sea. Cadwallader sunk a treasure ship around these parts. She's down there somewhere. The sea holds many riches, but this spot should pay off nicely. Who knows, you may want to partner up?"

Atia gave him a look. "Partner?"

"We'll speak of it over dinner."

They all filed into the grand cabin, where servants set plates and brought in extra chairs.

"I wasn't expecting company, or I'd have cleared the deck," Art said. "Come and meet someone." Atia followed him to the bed chamber, where he pulled back a curtain.

"Who have ya got stashed in here?" Atia asked.

"One of Cadwallader's subjects."

Atia watched the parrot napping in a box. "The poor thing."

"She's in Dr. Strangewayes's care, but I don't yet have a name for her."

"I like *Freyja*," Atia said. "After the Norse goddess of love, sex and gold."

"Freyja couldn't be more suitable." Art gave Freyja a light pat on the head. "Where is Cadwallader's treasure, Freyja?"

They returned to the table.

"Mrs. Binge," Freeman began, "my apologies for earlier. I was not expecting to see your husband again so soon."

"Mr. Freeman and Mr. Morris, hello," Gertrude said.

"Where's your Capitaine?" Art asked. "Is he not touring the Bahamas?"

"Well, you know him. Here one day, gone the next, uh?" Atia imitated. "So, you're here pirate hunting? Am I a wanted pirate for you to pursue?"

"Wanted? Absolutely, but not for piracy." Art met her eyes. "You and yer party fall under the Act of Grace. Although I'm sure I have an outstanding warrant for Mr. Binge."

"Uh, remember that time you won that hand and took Coggshall for that pretty old frigate?" Binge said.

"What are you saying, Binge?"

"Lucky timing for those two kings to show up like that, wasn't it?"

"Are you saying you handed me those kings that night?"

"Indeed."

"I always thought so."

"You're welcome."

"You just wanted to see your boss lose. I'll give ya a two-week head start. You and the missus. I see you only got one. My condolences. What brings you lot here?"

"As it is, Commodore, I've come with a proposal for you." Atia gently knocked his leg with hers.

"Now you really got my full attention."

"Can we talk privately?"

"We are talking privately."

"I'm going to rescue some German nobles, like the ones we did before," Atia said.

"Germans? Where? Bach?" Art goaded.

"Truly," Atia said. "Jonesy was in Port Royal."

"She's right," Jones said. "Dewar and Llewellyn found out about a Dutch ship bringing some German nobles."

"I never made a profit on that enterprise," said Art.

"Yer the one who had them kidnapped. But this one's carrying the treasure of Hanover." Atia ate a piece of salted pork.

"A treasure ship," Art said. "Why didn't ya say so?"

"Aye, a treasure ship, then," Atia said. "They expect me to hire the Capitaine to capture it and free the hostages. I thought of you instead."

"Aren't you a sweetheart," Art said. "Sorry, my love, and I do mean it. Yer not a pirate and you're not taking a treasure ship. Yer being fooled, the lot of you."

"You've rescued Germans before," Gladstone said. "We saved Natalia and Catharina."

"I'm charged with pirate hunting in the Bahamas, and this is where I'm obliged to stay," Art said. "No offense meant to you and yer stout crew, Captain Jones. But it's a fool's errand, a suicide mission, if you take it on. Frankly, Mr. Binge, I'm surprised you have anything to do with it."

"We're not cut out for this war," Binge said. "We're just catching a ride."

"At least you have some sense."

"You underestimate us," Atia said.

"Not at all. I'm sure you, Alban, Miles, and Grymes, plus a handful of men, and a French wench, will be plenty to handle a treasure ship on your own."

"Don't mock me." Atia distanced herself.

"Nay, I'd never mock you. My worry is genuine." Art took her hand in his. "Your German treasure ship is folly."

"It's a Dutch ship."

"I ask you to stay here with me, under my protection, and work for me," Art said.

"I don't want to hunt pirates or rescue hostages. I just want a home," Gertrude added.

"Mrs. Binge, to you I offer my protection and passage."

"Thank you, Commodore Valentine."

"If I may impose on your hospitality, the wife and I are thinking of retiring to the far side of Florida. But our ride isn't taking us all the way," Binge said.

"Yer welcome to commandeer one of Cadwallader's boats," Art said.

"Much obliged," Binge said.

"I'll call us even. This war was bound to cause casualties at home among family and friends on both sides." Art raised his glass. "A toast to Easy Belford and the others we lost."

"Aye. We all lost loved ones in this war," Gladstone lamented. "For what? Decent people forced into difficult decisions by terrible circumstances, or by stupid idiots. Maybe it's time for us to put aside our differences and stand up for what's right."

"You can stand up all you want. Every time someone stands up for what's right around here, they lose their heads," Binge said. "You all can have it all, do it all, and spend it all. All we want is to *leave* it all. You know what I mean?"

"Mr. Morris and Captain Dietrich seems to think Cadwallader is involved in kidnapping free locals from the islands and selling them into slavery," said Art.

"Black Caesar, too. The people of New Providence say he's a giant. Ten feet tall," Stubbs said. "A monstrous black pirate who takes them from their homes and sells them to Cadwallader. They're never seen again."

"We saw Black Caesar in Port Royal just a few weeks ago. The big African pirate with the Barbary galley. Kabaka is what his men call him. Crisp called him Mandingo," said Freeman.

"Kabaka to the Maroons, and Mandingo to Barbados and Tobago," Art said. "Black Caesar to the people of the Bahamas."

"They're all one and the same?" Gertrude asked.

"And he's not ten feet tall; he's barely eight," Art said.

"I wouldn't argue the difference," Freeman growled.

"The bigger they are, the harder they fall," Morris said.

"Let me know how that works out, Morris," Freeman said.

"Black Caesar may have been nobility back in Africa but he's a thug now and is next on my list." Art put his hand on Atia's thigh. "He was running slaves and hostages for Cadwallader, and he's up here somewhere. I'll reward you if you help me find him. You and yer mates can join my crew as a scout ship. Yer first job. What say you?"

"I'm tempted to help ya rid the Caribbean of monsters who take innocent people from their homes and sell them into a life of pain and suffering," Atia replied.

"Just men, Atia, not monsters," said Art. "We each have our own story to tell."

"What's Black Caesar's story?" asked Gertrude.

"He's just a boy, barely eighteen, like my pretty Red. Hardly a monster. Crisp bought him straight from the Barbary Coast. He's said to be the son of a king of a tribe of giants. They're all wiped out now. He's the last one. Worth an absolute fortune on the market."

"He's still a slave?" Gertrude said.

"He escaped Tobago, killed the crew of a ship and got away to the Bahamas, only to be recaptured, twice. The trouble with him is that he stands out in a crowd. He's got nowhere to hide," Art said. "They tortured him for a few years and turned him into the pirate he is today."

"He's a monster, just like Slasher Al," Atia said.

"No man is all bad. Except maybe Cadwallader," Jones said.

"The sea can turn men to monsters, sure as greed," Freeman added. "Cadwallader wants more and more. He doesn't know when he has enough."

Jones and Binge shared a chuckle.

"What's funny?" Atia asked.

"They're laughing because Humpy owns more of Jamaica than anyone else, even the king," said Morris.

"Beckford's got as much," Freeman said.

"Not yet, he don't," said Morris.

"Soon, mind you," added Art.

"Are you in the slave trade, Mr. Freeman?" Atia wondered.

"No, girly, I'm in the building business. I was awarded land by keeping our ships and harbor in prime condition."

The men at the table burst out laughing.

"And I inherited a bit."

"A bit? Half of Jamaica." Art grinned widely. "He inherited it from his late wife, who acquired it from her late husband, Port Royal's most famous and celebrated privateer, l'Olonnais."

"I've heard of him," said Atia.

"Of course, you have," said Art.

"Fear is most effective," said Freeman. "More than greed. You make a man afraid, and he's capable of anything."

"I like the real monsters," Morris muttered. "You know, the ones with giant tentacles."

"Did he just say giant testicles?" Gertrude spoke quietly to Binge.

"He's describing Black Caesar, I think?" said Jones.

"No, he's talking about sea monsters, now," Freeman said. "Giant ones."

"I've seen my share of them," Stubbs said. "The sea holds the biggest monsters of all. As huge as an island."

"Not around here, surely?" Gertrude said.

"Aye, around here," Art said. "They call this area the Devil's Sea. Some call it, the Dragon's Sea." His eyes gave an oddly menacing look.

"The Bermuda Triangle is what I heard," Morris added. "Shapes in the sky that come down and sink ships."

"Who calls it that, Morris?" Art frowned. "Pythagoras perhaps?"

"Navigators call it that." Freeman waved his hand. "The area forms a triangle on a map. You can only see the triangle on a map, Morris. Even then, it depends on who drew the map."

"My first time out on a ship in the Caribbean Sea, I saw my captain taken off the deck by a sea monster," Stubbs explained.

Gertrude gave a nervous laugh.

"I jest not, Mrs. Binge," Stubbs said. "He disappeared off the poop deck one night. He was talking one minute; the next, I heard a splash. The deck was covered in water, and he was gone."

"Gone?" Bach questioned.

"Maybe he married a mermaid?" Atia suggested.

"Or, he partook of a Strangewayes brand elixir?" Gladstone said. "I've seen weird things happen. Happened to me a number of times."

"No, 'twas the Samaná Bay kraken," Stubbs asserted. "It was out for a feed."

"The kraken?" Binge scoffed. "Don't listen to them, Gerty. It's just myth. I've never seen any such thing, and I've been in the Caribbean for years."

"Maybe you haven't seen it all, Mr. Binge," Art said.

"The kraken?" Strangewayes said. "It's real. I've seen it."

"I'm not the least bit surprised," Binge remarked.

"I don't believe in the monster," Bach said.

"Believe what you want, Mr. Bach. I've seen it," Art said.

"Me too," Freeman said.

"And me," Morris added.

"Both of you have seen it?" Bach tilted his head and gazed into their eyes.

"There's a real big one in the Mona Passage, I hear," Strangewayes said.

Morris took a drink and wiped his chin. "The kraken's no myth. I've seen 'em both."

"Both?" Binge and Gertrude said.

Everyone leaned in.

"It lives deep down in Samaná Bay. Black it is, and a mile long," said Morris.

"This isn't Caesar we're talking about," Freeman growled.

"Not a fucking word. Not a word." Morris pointed at Freeman. "The kraken comes out in the months of July and August to feed on the humpback whales as they gather to mate. She can imitate their calls."

"*She?*" Gertrude said.

"Aye, it's a she," Art said.

"When she circles your boat, she creates a whirlpool; you don't dare put your oars in the water. She'll turn a bright red and green or even purple when she attacks. She's as big as a ship of the line and can pull you into the sea. She feasts on the crew when she pleases."

"My bird Cupid had the ability to warn us when it was near," Art said.

"How'd he do that?" Binge asked.

"He'd fly away."

"How do you get away from the kraken?" Atia asked.

"You deploy your sails to the fullest and run." Art's shoulder brushed against hers. "You dare not make a noise on deck in her presence."

Atia took a mouthful of wine. "You said there's two?"

"Aye. The other prowls the waters down in the Darien. He's a creature you'll never mistake. First you think he's an island, until he follows you," Morris continued. "A moving island, if you can imagine! When he strikes, the ocean lights up with flashes of red and silver. His tentacles can reach the top of the tallest mast to snatch a man off a yardarm. Imagine being dragged down into a hideous beak of death. The screams fade quickly into the snapping maw of the beast as he tears a man to pieces."

Gladstone looked quite pale as he swallowed. "Delicious supper, that was."

Gertrude stared at the glass tilted to her lips, not yet drinking.

"I didn't catch a word. What did he say?" Bach asked.

"The sea holds many wonders and monsters even the best fiction cannot match," Art said.

Freeman and Morris both nodded.

"You never told me that before," Freeman said to Morris.

"Maybe he did, and you missed it," Art said.

"If I told every sea monster tale I had, I would become a bore. Anyway, it's said by the Indians, the two met off south Jamaica a year ago in a giant tangle of tentacles and lightning that was seen through the whole Caribbean," Morris said. "Remember that storm we had that lasted a full week? No one ever knew if the creatures did battle or were there to mate. Then there were sightings of a new one, big as a brig, that began to surface off Port Royal, Jamaica."

"Port Royal?" Bach said.

"Thinking of moving, Mr. Bach?" Art chided.

"Where did you say you were going, Mrs. Binge?" Bach said.

"I've sailed the Pacific, and it goes on forever," Stubbs said. "There's an island guarded by giant stone heads. And we heard stories of a great red island beyond the Pacific, where there's giant rabbits as big as houses, deadly black snakes, and a creature that howls at night with a growl so loud it shakes the trees. I saw something I thought to be the sail of a boat. It turned out to be a fin. The fin of a shark that surpassed our own foresails. In the South Pacific, there be monsters aplenty."

"I prefer water where I can see the bottom and a quiet sunset, thank you," Strangewayes said.

"On that, we always agreed," Gladstone added.

"What is your decision, Atia? Jones?" Art said.

"We still have Jonesy's ship, and I can find me brothers. I'm going after the Germans," Atia said.

"Then, enjoy the hospitality of my ship before you go."

"Do ya have a tub on board?" Atia asked eagerly.

"Of course," said Art.

It was near midnight when servants were filling a copper tub in the captain's cabin. Atia emerged from the privy. Gladstone and Jones reminisced with Art about the buccaneer days.

"Your hospitality knows no bounds." Atia tested the half-full tub. "Miles, you were around in those days—how'd Freeman inherit all that l'Olonnais had?"

"Capitaine never told you the story?" Jones said.

"L'Olonnais was eaten by cannibals, is what I heard. Capitaine was the only one who made it out."

"Capitaine was just a boy called Frenchie in those days. Then Capitaine Nau showed up on the Cagway," said Jones. It's what we used to call Port Royal, before the royals returned. Jean-David Nau was his real name; l'Olonnais is what he was known as to his men. *Les flibustiers*. The roughest, toughest, meanest—"

"Fastest," said Gladstone.

"The fastest buccaneers around," Jones continued. "They're named after their flyboats, specialized war canoes. L'Olonnais made his home port the Cagway, and from there he and his men plundered the seas around Jamaica, taking Spanish ships at will. The Cagway became Port Royal and the place to sell and trade plundered goods. Freeman wasn't a privateer like l'Olonnais; he owned and ran the docks, including the warehouses on the inner harbor."

"His family's part Jew," Gladstone added.

"Figures," said Jones. "Anyway, Freeman fancied l'Olonnais's wife. She was the daughter of our first head carpenter."

"I thought that was Bartaboa," said Gladstone.

"Before Bartaboa. Anyway, this young girl came to the Cagway to live with her father, and he's dead before she arrives. She's got nowhere to live. Freeman was the carpenter on *Torrington,* and he was brought over to finish the work. He was sweet on her and let her stay at the house she was supposed to live in. The house at the point."

"The Catt and Fiddle, it's called now," offered Art.

"When Tortuga was bombed by the Spanish, l'Olonnais moved to Jamaica and became the Cagway's most prolific privateer," Jones said. "They signed him as Captain Noy. His real name was Nau, but who can spell French anyway?"

"I thought Henry Morgan was Port Royal's privateer," said Atia.

"Henry wasn't legally privateering, per se," explained Gladstone. "In those days, he was more of a seller of goods. A broker if you will. His family had connections in Barbados and London. Jews, I think."

"L'Olonnais moved into town and took Cecelia as his wife, the woman Freeman fancied," said Jones. "He also took the house at the point. For the next ten years, he's Port Royal's top pirate, raiding the Spanish and bringing in plunder to make the city what it was. The pirate capital of the world."

"All the while, Freeman was giving Nau's wife his wood, if ya know what I mean," said Gladstone.

"Then Henry had his own buccaneers, your Capitaine being one of them. The French *les flibustiers* and the English filibusters ruled the Caribbean as the Brethren of the Coast. But, after taking on Cuba, both sides decided there wasn't enough of the spoils to go around," Jones said. "Henry led his men down to Puerto Bello and sacked the city, while l'Olonnais and *les flibustiers* went on to raid the Mosquito Coast. They hit Nicaragua, all the way down to Costa Rica.

"But it went badly for them. There were storms and Spanish. They lost the flagship and were stuck with longboats. Crammed in there like cattle. They ran out of food. Then storms and Indians drove them down into the Darien. Where no civilized man wants to go. Frenchie led an expedition, then went looking for him after Puerto Bello, and he went missing, too. Months passed, then Frenchie turned up with his Indian friend Yaguara, and his son, Dashiell. He's got this tale of l'Olonnais being eaten. Hacked to pieces, along with all his men."

"Explains why Frenchie remains a bit twitchy after that," Art added.

"Who wouldn't be," said Jones, and all the men nodded. "Nau was declared legally dead. Over the course of a decade more than half of Jamaica was awarded to Nau by Governor Ed D'Oyley. I miss Ed."

"Those were fun days," said Gladstone.

"There was never a dull moment with D'Oyley." Jones smiled. "He granted the privateers all the land they could handle, so most retired as planters."

"Cecelia inherited all the land in Jamaica her husband was granted," said Gladstone. "With l'Olonnais out of the way, Freeman moved right in and married her. Then, a year later, she was dead."

"And it all went to Freeman," mused Atia.

"Aye, but here's the best part," said Gladstone. "We found out years later that Freeman was hired to resupply *les flibustiers*. But when they asked for help, Freeman sent the supplies down to Henry Morgan, who was already on his way back from Puerto Bello."

"So, Freeman, in fact, left all those men to die. And just happened to inherit half of Jamaica in the process?" said Atia.

"Exactly."

"So, what the hell's he doing here?" Atia said.

"Well, he's gotta pay taxes on all that land don't he," Art replied.

Art resigned himself to a comfortable chair in the gallery next to the captain's cabin. Fragments of Atia's singing could be heard through the open window, lulling Art to sleep. The sound of shifting water intersected with his dream, and then he heard whispers.

"Lower deck. We go in the lower deck, they said," the first voice whispered.

"I'm just having a peek," whispered the second.

"We gotta break out Cadwallader. We gotta be quick."

Atia's sweet voice chimed a Gaelic lullaby.

"Oh, mighty god in heaven!" came the first whisperer.

Standard ship sounds continued as voices from the shore carried through the night air.

There came a thud, as if something had hit wood.

Art was soon woken by Stubbs.

"What is it?" Art uttered. "Are they making their attempt?"

"Not quite," Stubbs replied.

They approached the window, seeing two small shadows just outside where Atia was.

"Not on my deck, ya little vermin!" Art scowled and signaled men to approach from all sides, while he entered through his cabin.

Atia dove under the water when Art burst into the room and there was a commotion at the window.

"What the hell is going on?" Atia demanded.

"The little bastards! Caught ya red-handed. Okay, not quite red, but filthy-handed." Art stood at the window as the boys were apprehended.

"What were they doing?"

"What do you think they were doing?"

"Oh." Atia pondered a moment. "Oh!"

Jones and Freeman entered.

"What happened?" Freeman barked.

"Are you okay, Atia?" Jones asked.

All the men gawked at her.

"Sorry, love," Jones said. "She's all right. Sorry to intrude."

Atia covered up. "Honestly, have ya not seen a woman before?"

"We got prisoners on deck." Art led the procession out.

Stubbs unveiled a skeleton key. "They were here to break out Cadwallader."

"Who's watching Cadwallader?" Art asked.

"Cadwallader's covered. Who's this?" Freeman said.

"Little spies," Art said.

"Little Robbie and Benny Hornigold," Jones said. "Can't blame the boys for trying."

"They're spies," Art said. "Execute them both."

"We'll have none of that." Atia arrived, dressed in a robe. "They're just boys."

"They got caught with their dicks in their hands," Jones said. "Send 'em home to their mothers, Art."

"No one tells me what to do on my ship. Strip 'em," Art said.

"Don't hurt them, Art, please," Atia said.

"Bring fish blood."

Minutes later, they stripped the boys down and poured fish blood all over them.

"I'll get you when I'm King of Gwynedd," Little Robber said.

"I'll talk, I'll talk." Benny Hornigold surrendered.

"Better swim fast, boys. There's lots of sharks out tonight. Okay, throw 'em over," said Art.

Stubbs and other men threw the boys over, with a splash.

Freeman held the boys' clothes at arm's length. "What about these?"

"Phew!" Art cringed. "Over it goes." He turned around and Atia was gone. He returned to his cabin.

Atia was drying her hair with a cloth. "Lucky you came along when you did. I'd have a hell of a time explaining the mess left outside the window."

"Aye, well, Jones is right, ya can't blame the little bastards. Who can resist Venus?" Art said.

"I've been called that a few times this week. Thanks for the bath. You realize it's big enough for two?"

"Is it? Is that incentive for you to stay?"

"I'm kinda hell-bent on me mission."

"Then you at least need to look the part." Art guided her to a large wardrobe and opened it to reveal an assortment of dresses. He handed her a satin nightdress. "You'd look stunning in this."

"Would I?" Atia let her robe slide off and slid the dress over her head.

Art's throat went dry. The fabric clung to every curve in all the best places.

"You were expecting to run into me?" she said.

"Always, my whiskey kisses girl." He grinned widely. "I was hoping to find you somewhere in the Caribbean."

"You scoundrel."

"Me?" Art made a gesture of innocence. "I seem to recall you have a penchant for scoundrels?"

"That's a scandalous lie," said Atia. "All right, for a select few."

"Am I on this exclusive list?"

"What do you think?"

"You could tease a man to death, you know that?"

"It's all part of me charm."

"Is there anything else you want before you leave?"

"A good night's sleep. I ain't exactly slept since Tortuga."

"What the hell were you doing in Tortuga?"

"Taking in the Elixir of Life."

Art laughed. "You are welcome to the best bed in Lovely Bay."

Atia sank into the bed in the corner, while Art draped himself into the comfortable chair in the gallery next to the captain's cabin. Next he knew, morning light shone in the window. Atia was already in a dark blue dress, pinning up her hair, letting a few ringlets frame her face.

"Why can't I wake up to you every morning?" He stretched and yawned.

"Who knows what the future holds?"

Once presentable, they ventured to the quarterdeck for breakfast. Sails were rigged as sun blocks, shading an assortment of fish and fruit. Art went to the rail to examine a diver's head dome with various tubes sticking out of it. Close by, *Whiskey Kisses* was being readied for departure.

"Now, what have you got there?" Atia asked.

"This here's a diving helmet." He tried to fit it over her head. "A man wears it like this."

Atia pushed it away. "Like ya said, it's for a man."

Art set the gear aside. "You really don't like small spaces."

"I don't like small anything."

"Yer Achilles' heel, my dear, your weakness."

"We all have weaknesses, Art. I can see why yer all fighting over Gwynedd Bay. It's beautiful here."

"It's *Lovely* Bay, and it'll always be Lovely Bay."

"Ever bring your wife here?"

"Never. It wouldn't be lovely. This remains mine. It's where I'd go to get away while we were retaking Tortuga from the Spanish, in, whatever year it was."

"Ya don't remember?"

"We retook Tortuga so many times I lost count." Art gave a huge grin and took a drink. "I was sent here in my *Falmouth* to Lovely Bay to wait out the Spanish Armada. Took weeks for them to get their ships organized off Santiago de Cuba, and I fell in love with this place. See, you do belong here."

Atia raised her glass and drank.

"I had quite a feast in mind for this morning but found myself short on a few things. It's not on your ship, is it?"

Atia's face colored. "I had to make sure Mr. Binge had enough provisions to get by. After all, he served on my ship. He deserves no less."

"Your ship, love, not mine. Who's going to pay me?"

"I'm sure we can arrange compensation." Atia's foot slid between his legs. "How much will you get for Cadwallader?"

"I don't know how much he's worth yet. The governor of New Providence wants him for crimes committed here. If I take him back to Port Royal right away, that goes against the free market."

"Why are you in the slave business? You got a parrot that you treat like it's yer own baby. You don't seem like the slaver type."

"Hey, I don't believe in slavery; I'm just out to make an honest living. It wasn't always about slavery, ya know," he replied. "Okay, it was. Even in the old pirate days we took folks everywhere we went and made them slaves."

"That's why I won't work for you. I was a slave."

"I know. Free and clear with the law, but now you've made enemies in the Brethren of the Coast. You oughta stay with me, under my protection. I'll let ya sail around the Bahamas with a real crew, dipping yer toes in the water. I don't want to see anything bad to happen to me whiskey kisses girl."

"You make it sound like a marriage proposal," she teased.

"I'd never get over it if you were to lose the face of a goddess and the hands-down nicest tits I've ever seen."

"Spoken like a true poet."

"I'll let ya poke Cadwallader with a stick, anywhere you like." Art paused. "Yer falling in with a bad sort. Even your Capitaine should know better. What the hell is he doing, leaving you unguarded in times like this? Laurens has lost. The moment he hired the likes of Coxon, Seele and Montbars."

Atia rose and kissed his cheek. "I'll see ya again, Arthur Valentine, we must be off."

Art caught her hand. "Don't be following your friend Binge up to the Florida Keys, neither. Black Caesar's up there, and he's looking for blood."

"I was thinking of stopping by Hope Bay. See the brothers, maybe do some fishing."

"If I'm in the area I'll stop by. Until then, I'll wait here a few weeks in case you choose to return." Art kissed her hand.

"Take care of Freyja," Atia said.

His mouth met hers, not wanting to let her go.

Atia pulled away and headed out.

Art caught Bach's attention. "Follow her."

"Me?"

"Aye, take some men and follow her."

"But I'm sailing master," Bach said.

Art indicated the bay. "Well, we're not sailing at present! Just follow her; make sure she stays out of trouble."

Art stood at the rail while Atia, Gladstone and Binge passed barrels and boxes of food such as dried meat, fruit and bread.

Grymes helped load it, periodically scratching his groin.

"It's not the local stew, is it?" Gertrude almost gagged. "It stinks."

"Don't worry, love, this stuff is from *Guernsey*." Binge began to eat.

Atia gave them a few bottles of rum. "Here ya be. Worry not, it's from Art's private stock. "He won't mind when he sees what I traded for it." She glanced up, knowing she was being watched.

Art rolled his eyes, a smile forming.

"You can sail this okay with just the two of you?" Atia asked.

"Darling, I can make this thing glide," Binge said.

"I'm sorry to leave you, Atia," Gertrude said. "I'm just not pirate material."

"She understands," Binge said.

"I picked a few favorites from the Feathers crate for you too, Mrs. Binge," said Atia.

"See?" Binge said. "She understands."

"I hope it's not goodbye forever, Mr. Binge," said Atia. "Although this could be considered desertion."

"You take care of yourself, little red pikey." Binge winked. "And take care of her," he said to Gladstone. "Don't let her out of your sight."

"Bleedin Art may yet toss me off into the sea," Gladstone remarked. "I'll see you at *Sérénité* sometime."

"There'll be a place set at the table for both of you," said Atia.

Gertrude gave Atia and Gladstone a quick hug but stopped short of Grymes who feverishly scratched his groin. She hopped in the boat to take the tiller while Binge pushed off. They sailed out to sea while the others waved from the beach.

"Our hearty crew is gettin' pretty slim," Gladstone said.

"I'm not deterred." Atia boarded her ship.

"No, you never are." Gladstone followed.

"She never is." Art went into his captain's cabin and spent the rest of the day in seclusion, occasionally glimpsing *Whiskey Kisses* as she shrank smaller and smaller on the horizon.

Barbarossa I

The last few years felt like a dream to Fatima now. A life that belonged to someone else. She'd been conditioned since birth to accept that her place was to serve and that her slave life was of no consequence. Until the pirate siege in Port Royal, where her life intersected with Caesar's. A pirate named Le Grande sold her to "Kabaka" as a translator.

Also known as Black Caesar, he stood seven and half feet tall, a fiercely muscular eighteen-year-old African king, stolen from his home. Tortured for years in the Barbary Coast, he became a feared killer in the region. His ship *Barbarossa I* was a Mediterranean war galley with a red hull trimmed in black and gold. Two hundred slaves, mostly African, but also white and native, rowed hard to Key Largo.

Caesar's command deck was the tallest point at the aft, sheltered by a canvas and Barbary banners. Statues of Romulus and Remus held the deck above the rest of the ship.

Fatima's position was on the deck below the command platform. Her tattered clothes had been replaced by a linen dress topped with a crimson satin kaftan, with a gold sash belt. The robe was short-sleeved and revealed a branding scar that indicated *RAC*. The Royal African Company. She could feel his eyes upon her at times. When she reciprocated, he looked away.

Caesar's crew were Barbary Janissaries and two officers: the raïs, in a red turban, and the agha, in a white turban. Both disliked Fatima; they viewed her as Caesar's pet. This couldn't have been further from the truth.

Fatima was not only a translator but skilled at medicine. Although her medical training was limited, she had picked up the basics during her time with Dr. Sander Strangewayes in Port Royal. The doctor had been kind to her, but he was buffoonish and scattered. Lately, Fatima's small size sometimes made her unnoticeable.

She glanced down at the rowing slaves. Among them was Ekene, a man she had met at Strangewayes's Plantation. Although they'd been romantically involved, she wasn't sure if she loved him. Things were changing, and she saw her life in a whole new way. Ekene met her gaze, but her attention turned to the maze of coral reefs that *Barbarossa I* was navigating.

It was sunset when they reached Manatee Bay. The ship glided up an estuary where caimans snapped their small, sharp jaws along the bank. The ship reached a Spanish ruin overgrown with weeds. A dilapidated dock sat just beyond.

Caesar had one of his regular arguments with the raïs and the agha while the ship struggled through the weeds. A group of Janissaries and slaves ventured into the wilderness, guided by lantern light.

Later that night, a scream erupted, and light streaked through the foliage. A boat returned with wounded. A Janissary reported to the agha.

"He says an alligator gar took off a Janissary's head and pulled the body into the water," said Fatima. "Another man lost his arm trying to save him." She inspected the wound. "His arm was twisted off."

"Help him," said Caesar.

Fatima did her best, but the wound was fatal. Her patient died within minutes. "He lost too much blood."

"She should go next," said the agha. "She's lighter than the rest of us."

"Send two boats of slaves to search for a place to land," replied Caesar.

The agha gathered men. Ekene was chosen.

Fatima took a deep breath as the narrow rowboats were lowered.

"You know him?" Caesar asked.

"Yes, from Jamaica."

"Don't look at him so much. It distracts him from his work."

"Pardon me, but I can't see him at all." She walked away, failing to ask permission as she went to the privy at the head of the ship. It was the only place she could truly be alone for a few precious minutes. Upon her return, the raïs gave her a dirty look.

"Insolent," Caesar snapped. "Go to your quarters and stay there."

Fatima ventured inside Caesar's cabin, where she had a private recess with a cot, mirror, and a chest of clothes. She also had access to a wash basin and the cabin's window.

Fatima opened the window. Lanterns moved through the swampy jungle, but she could see nothing. She felt the sting as something latched onto her arm. A massive snake coiled around her, and she screamed.

Caesar burst into the cabin. "Anaconda." He drew a blade and stabbed the serpent's head. When it was dead, he unraveled her.

Fatima collapsed into his arms, catching her breath.

Then a vibration hit the ship, and the agha yelled. It was Ekene who bounded to the cabin door, out of breath. "I found the way, Caesar."

As dawn broke, *Barbarossa I* pulled up to an area with solid land and a path. Makeshift ramps were erected, reaching the ruined stonework.

Fatima sat on her cot, checking her wound. It was a deep puncture, and the site was bruised. She dusted the bite with sulfur powder, cringing.

Ekene ventured inside the cabin, asking, "Are you sick?" He felt her clammy forehead.

"A little."

"Was it poisonous?"

"I don't know. I don't think so." Fatima wrapped the wound in cotton. "I think I'd be sicker if it was poisonous."

Fatima rose to look out the open window. Her nose wrinkled. "Can you smell that?"

Ekene sniffed. "It's like rotting fish."

Caesar and the agha were trekking across swampy jungle.

"I can't find anyone, Caesar," a Janissary called. "They're all gone."

Caesar and his men continued the search, to no avail.

"Indian raid," said a Janissary. "The hostages are all dead. Those that survived the attack were left chained in cells. They starved to death."

Fatima left the cabin.

"Where do you think you're going?" Ekene asked.

"To see for myself."

Fatima charged down the gangway, going headfirst into giant leaves. She encountered the bodies of two Spanish children, a boy and a girl. Their fingernails had been torn off in their desperate attempt to escape.

Caesar roared, unable to contain his anger and grief.

Fatima discovered a pile of dead women—"wives," as Caesar called them—at least two dozen, bound in chains, stabbed or bludgeoned. Half-dazed, Fatima wandered back towards the ship.

The agha blocked her way. "Caesar's wrong to keep you. I should kill you. You're weak—a menace."

"Take her to the ship," Caesar boomed at the raïs. "If anyone touches her, they die. She is worth more than you. Remember that."

The raïs complied, ordering some slaves to carry her.

"We should not have come this way," said the agha.

"We had to come back for the hostages," said Caesar.

"The hostages have been dead for weeks. We must see our benefactor."

"Our benefactor is dead," said the raïs.

"He has a successor," replied the agha.

"There is not enough food on board to reach Tobago," argued the raïs. "We must stop, maybe twice."

"We will raid to get the food we need," said the agha.

"I will speak with Cadwallader Jones," said Caesar.

They returned to the ship.

Fatima felt very ill, so Caesar allowed her to sleep. Even with the bickering of Caesar and his officers, she was able to rest. When she woke, she was drenched from perspiration. She rose to check the window Caesar slept, his bed not more than a few feet from hers. The moonlight guided *Barbarossa I* back out of the estuary, away from Key Largo.

Binge and Gertrude sailed their skip towards the island of Cuba. Palm trees baked beneath the midday sun and mountains lay ahead. Just a few days out of Lovely Bay, the coastline Binge was looking for came into view.

"Not much further." Binge wiped his brow. "I tell ya, I'm not cut out for this sailing shit anymore."

"There's a ship coming fast," Gertrude said.

Binge recognized it as Caesar's *Barbarossa 1*.

Gertrude raised an eyebrow. "Are they friendly?"

Binge swiftly hoisted another jib. "Head straight for the coast. Gotta try for that island, just gotta try!"

"Not friendly, then."

"You don't want to know who that is, and I don't wanna tell you, so don't ask."

"It's Black Caesar, then?"

"I told ya not to ask!"

A gust of wind came up.

"Oh, please, oh, thank you God, give us some wind!" Binge pleaded. "I'll be good, I will. Not like last time, I'll follow through this time, I swear it!"

The wind grew in intensity and the skip picked up speed.

Binge raised another sail.

The added wind stirred the waves against *Barbarossa 1*, slowing her down just enough for the skip to reach the coast. Gertrude spotted a river through the trees that led inland. She turned the tiller. Once behind the trees, the river opened into a lake.

"Oh, shit, look for a place to hide!" Binge said.

Lateen sails approached; a drumbeat sounded alongside splashing oars.

Binge spotted a small lagoon through the bushes and trees. He grabbed an axe to cut down as many lines as possible and brought down the sails. The shoreline came quickly.

"Drop the anchor," Gertrude said.

"Great idea," Binge said. "Where is it?"

They crashed into trees and vines. Wood snapped and the bottom of the boat scraped.

"Shush!" Gertrude hissed.

"Don't tell me to shush," Binge said. "I am shushing!"

They sat quietly nestled within the flora and fauna for hours. Brightly colored birds chirped, circling above them on the wind. Lizards hung from a branch just above their heads.

"They're going away," Gertrude said.

"He keeps searching in the wrong place. He'll figure it out or give up."

"You used to do this sort of thing for a living?"

"You can understand why I chose a change in occupation," Binge said.

Gertrude climbed the mast to look out.

"Don't get us seen," he said.

"They're still going the other way." Gertrude slid back and stared at Binge.

"How you holdin' up?"

She ventured over to him, unlacing the front of her dress. Kissing him, she fumbled with his trouser buttons. "Fuck me, now!" She braced herself against the hull.

"Nothing for six months and it's 'fuck me now'?"

She tackled him, pulling him inside. They undulated, panting and moaning. Gertrude's hips gyrated and her thighs quivered. Binge shook, releasing a long sigh. She smiled, licking her lips.

"I may have been a tad overexcited," he panted.

"Mmm, it's okay."

He went to pull out, but she gripped him.

"Stay inside me."

They remained pinned against each other, kissing.

A shadow caught Binge's eye, forcing him to pull away. Out of the trees several figures appeared: natives with tribal tattoos and piercings.

"Okay, new deal, God," Binge began.

"Who are you and what do you want?" Gertrude secured her dress.

"We're not tasty," Binge said. "Not right now, anyway."

A silver-haired mixed native named Yaguara, carrying an atlatl, came forward.

Binge eyed the newcomer. "If you're who I think you are, the code word's *La Lune de Miel*. If not, uh, hi there."

"*La Lune de Miel*," said Yaguara.

"Gerty, this is Yaguara," Binge said. "I know him."

"Do you know everyone in the West Indies?" Gertrude asked.

"Just about."

"Nice to meet you, Yaguara," said Gertrude.

"Theodore Binge and his woman pick a strange time to mate," Yaguara remarked. "They're coming back this way. Come with us."

Caesar's voice boomed in the distance, and the lateen sails returned. Binge and Gertrude abandoned the skip and followed Yaguara into the bushes to a path.

Binge glanced back. *Barbarossa I* was now fully visible.

They paused in a clearing that overlooked the lake, remaining under the cover of bushes. For hours they waited, until Caesar inspected the abandoned skip and returned to his ship.

"Not too bright, is he?" said Binge.

"Black Caesar is very smart—and dangerous. His weaknesses are inexperience and impulsiveness," said Yaguara. "What was the Capitaine like at his age?"

"It's hard to remember. We were drunk all the time."

"Your woman, Gertrude, is beautiful. Is Binge a monogamist, or can Yaguara mate with her too?"

Gertrude gave Yaguara a coy smile.

"Well, not at a time like this. How did you find us? Where is the Capitaine?"

"Yaguara quit Capitaine. Yaguara wouldn't be caught dead siding with Montbars and Sammy the fucking Seal. Doesn't matter who's on whose side anymore. The New World has gone to shit. Besides, Yaguara didn't find Binge; Yaguara is following Fatima and Ekene."

"The two kids that worked for Strangewayes?" said Binge.

"Exactly. Black Caesar has them."

Gertrude checked through a telescope. "You're right. I see her. The young girl Burghill used to parade around. She looks like a doll next to Caesar."

"Strangewayes and I helped her escape slavery," said Binge.

"Pretty poor escape, if you ask Yaguara."

"Obviously things didn't work out as planned," Binge replied.

"What were you going to do?" Gertrude said. "Help them escape from Black Caesar?"

"Yaguara hasn't yet got close enough to attempt a rescue."

Gertrude's eye lingered at the telescope. "What does Black Caesar want with us? We have nothing."

"Hostages," said Yaguara. "When the economy is slow around here, the going commodity is people."

"I'd be a hostage. You'd be a concubine," Binge said to Gertrude.

"How big is he?"

"Black Caesar is huge," said Yaguara.

"You had your fill, sweetheart," Binge remarked.

"I jest." Gertrude smiled. "Come on, everyone else does."

"Being captured by Black Caesar would mean certain death for Mr. and Mrs. Binge," Yaguara added.

"Yes, I gathered that, thank you," Gertrude said.

The warriors conversed with Yaguara.

"What is it?" Gertrude asked.

"Black Caesar is leaving. His ship is turned out."

They ventured up a rock to watch *Barbarossa I* row back out of the estuary.

"Yaguara must follow Fatima and Ekene. What will Binge do?" Yaguara asked. "Can you find your way?"

"Where are we?"

"Cuba."

"Where in Cuba?" Binge said.

Yaguara pointed to a distant peak. "That way is a road that will take you south to the Santiago port or up to Puerto del Príncipe."

"I know where we are now. How are you for a long, scenic walk?" Binge asked Gertrude.

"Lead on, Mr. Binge. I hope you find your friends, Mr. Jaguar," Gertrude said.

Yaguara and his warriors ran off into the bush.

Binge and Gertrude set out on a hike.

"How far is it to Santiago de Cuba?" Gertrude asked.

"Oh, we're not going there. There's a nice little town up the island a day or so away, and from there we travel in style," Binge said. "We'll be home to the Gardens of the Queen in three days if we hurry."

"What's the hurry?" She winked.

Binge extended his hand, and she took it. He hadn't seen her this lively since they left Port Royal. Being on the run had rejuvenated her and rekindled the love between them, which he had thought was lost. They followed a path into the hills towards a new life.

A whip cracked and slaves cleared the benches, while others rushed in to take their place at the oars. Exhausted slaves were led below, while the galley continued without slowing. *Barbarossa I* reached north of the Windward Passage. Caesar and his officers monitored the horizon with their telescopes.

Fatima found her way behind one of the capstans under the benches, where the slaves rowed.

Ekene followed a long line and was about to go below deck when Fatima caught his arm, pulling him to a secluded area. She fondled the bulge between his legs and caught his mouth with hers, before licking the sweat from his chest.

"Here?" said Ekene.

"They won't look for you till after the rest break."

"I need a rest break."

"Rest later." Fatima raised her dress, wanting him inside her. He mounted her. Both tried to be quiet, but he released a grunt: half pleasure, half pain. Quickly, he finished, and Fatima released a slightly disappointed sigh.

Angry footsteps bounded down the stairs.

Ekene slid through a nearby hatch, while Fatima navigated up a hatch under the command deck. She had almost reached a door when a huge hand pulled her back.

"Where were you?" Caesar demanded.

"In the privy," she said.

"No, you weren't. You were with him. Do not see him again. If he enters you, I'll cut off his cock and make you wear it around your neck. You are worth much more as a virgin."

"If you must know, Caesar, it's a bit late for that."

"Shut up, stupid girl." He paused. "I know. Do not get with child. I own you, not him. Don't test me. I'll kill him, I will."

"And you want me?" Fatima challenged.

Caesar's fist clenched, ready to strike. "Just don't see him again."

Voices erupted on the deck and Caesar rushed away.

Fatima followed.

"Spanish galleons," said the agha. "Many of them."

A line of Spanish ships, looking like flakes of gold, were traveling along the horizon from Hispaniola, to disappear behind Cuba.

"I've never seen so many ships before," exclaimed Fatima. "Is it the Spanish Armada?"

"It must be," said Caesar. "The galleons are razeé for fighting. The treasure fleet doesn't go this way."

"They are in striking range," said the agha.

"We have the colors of a slave galley," said the raïs.

"Fatima, come with us," ordered Caesar.

Fatima followed Caesar and his officers into the captain's cabin. They reviewed the ship's logbook, trying to find a description of the armada. Hours later, the raïs took command on deck, while the agha called for a meal break and shift change.

When it got dark, Caesar and Fatima lit lanterns and finished reviewing the log entries. She helped him with words he didn't know and was impressed by how quickly he learned.

They leaned over a map.

"They're coming from here," he pointed. "Down to here. They must be going to Guantanamo Bay."

Fatima's fingers brushed his as she indicated lower down. "Or here, Santiago de Cuba."

He frowned, but she knew he was impressed. She gave an involuntary yawn.

Caesar closed the logbook. "Go to sleep, Fatima. Tomorrow will be a busy day." He left the room.

Fatima retired to her area, pulling the curtain across for privacy. The next morning, she washed and replaced the bandage on her arm before venturing on deck. Bright orange light beamed down, nearly blinding her. Caesar and his officers were speaking to the crew of a pirate ship about a raid. The pirates soon continued their journey.

"Full speed to Monte Cristi," Caesar ordered.

The agha cracked the whip at the rowing slaves, while the raïs shouted for them to row at full speed.

Caesar took his position at the command deck, while Fatima occupied her spot on the deck below.

Soon an inlet with a jagged rock face came into view. Hundreds of pirate ships of all shapes and sizes were anchored or resting on the beach of Manzanillo Bay. Around a rocky point sat Monte Cristi.

Monte Cristi

Cymru followed *Whiskey Kisses* behind a rocky point. Just beyond, pirate ships gathered: dozens of boats and canoes. Smoke billowed through the trees, where the tip of a bell tower projected.

Aboard *Whiskey Kisses*, Gladstone and Zoe stood watch in the crow's nest. Zoe's hand was down his trousers, and he gripped the edge of the basket, trying not to fall out.

Minuit swooped in, landing behind them.

A startled Zoe retracted her hand, grazing his manhood.

"Ouch." Gladstone nursed his wounded parts.

Zoe realized. "Sorry."

"Bonjour," said Minuit.

"No, we weren't," said Gladstone.

"Weren't what?" Atia climbed up the rigging to them and landed in the basket.

Minuit hopped onto her shoulder.

"Nothing," Gladstone insisted as his erection brushed her leg and he shied away into a corner.

"Did I interrupt something?" Atia said.

"We're just looking out. See, another big one coming," said Gladstone. "A ship, a galley."

Grymes climbed the mast behind them. "Don't be seen."

"It's Black Caesar," said Atia.

"We don't got the men for a quick escape. Come to think on it, we don't got the men for much of anything. Sit quiet," said Grymes. "We want to find your Capitaine without being seen."

Minuit flew away.

"Don't shit on that boat, bird," said Atia. "Maybe I shouldn't have let him out."

"If we're spotted, we're finished," Gladstone said.

"He won't see us," Jones assured. "We're just like every other pirate ship here."

"This was Slasher Al's boat," Gladstone reminded. "He hates Slasher Al."

"Oh, you're right! Let me have a look." Atia took the telescope from Grymes. The oars were rowing at top speed, while Black Caesar and Fatima stood on deck.

"I see Fatima." Gladstone looked through his telescope.

"So do I; she's tiny next to him," said Atia.

"Poor girl must be terrified, being that close to that beast."

"Terrified?" Atia said. "She looks like she wants to swing from that thing. If she stands any closer, she could wear it around her neck."

"Aye, you got a point. I wonder if Ekene is with her?"

"She's doing what she has to do to survive," Jones said. "The pirate ships are gathering in Manzanillo Bay and around the point to Monte Cristi Bay."

Barbarossa 1 went out of view.

Atia handed back the telescope to Grymes.

"At least we know Fatima's all right." Gladstone tried to sound optimistic as they climbed down to the deck.

Minuit landed by Atia on the rail. She extended her arm and he climbed on. "It's too dangerous for you out here."

"*Ma chérie,*" Minuit said.

She caressed his head and put him back in his cage with a handful of cashews. "Good lad."

A group of buccaneers scaled the side of the ship.

Gladstone screamed, but Zoe had the sense to cover his mouth.

"Arsenault," said Zoe.

The buccaneer landed on deck.

"Scared us half to death!" Jones collapsed.

"Half? I'm about two-thirds, meself," Gladstone said.

"I was trying to get your attention," Arsenault said to Grymes. "I try whistle, I try bird call. You never looked my way. How did you not see me?"

"Sorry." Grymes scratched his crotch. "We was a wee bit preoccupied."

"We thought it was the bird." Gladstone rubbed his groin.

"Mandingo is here, too," Atia said.

"I know," said Arsenault. "Silent Sam, Montbars and Coxon all have hundreds of men."

"Where's the Capitaine?" Atia asked.

"I lost the Capitaine in the Mona Passage. He turned north suddenly, and I saw a canoe. I thought he stopped for a message. Looked back and he was gone. I figured he came here."

"Without telling you?" Atia said. "No."

"What's happening here, do you know?" Jones asked.

"*Les flibustiers* are engaged in combat with the Spanish. Silent Sam and Montbars have Monte Cristi surrounded. They already destroyed its defences," Arsenault said. "They tried to get in a few times but didn't succeed. They don't want to bring the ships in closer, in case the Spanish Armada comes."

"We just saw the Spanish Armada heading the other way," said Gladstone.

"Aye, we couldn't go south for Hope Bay," Jones said. "Nor could we go back to the Cape."

"Now there's nothing stopping the pirates from getting in," Gladstone said. "We know these types—Silent Sam and Montbars. They kill people. The Capitaine should be here."

"I'm going ashore to find the Capitaine, if he's here or not," Arsenault said.

"This is where he said he was going," Atia said.

"Something's not right. I can find out what," said Arsenault.

"We saw Fatima," Gladstone said. "We can get her back."

"We find the Capitaine first," said Arsenault.

"Hang on. We don't know if the Capitaine is even here," argued Gladstone. "We can't just leave Fatima with these ruthless murderers."

"What do you propose, lad?" Jones said. "Go up to Black Caesar and ask for her?"

"Atia's got money. Lots of it. We'll buy her back."

"No," Atia said. "We're not contributing to slavery. We'll steal her back."

"You risk much for one slave girl." Zoe beamed at him.

"She's my friend," Gladstone said. "I'd do the same for you."

Zoe kissed his cheek and squeezed between his legs.

"First, we must blend in with the other pirates," Arsenault said. "We'll take the back way into Monte Cristi so as not to be seen by canoe. Leave your ship here."

"Montbars and Sam have it out for you," Jones told Atia. "You should keep yourself hidden."

"Nice try, Jonesy," said Atia. "Miles is right. I'm going to get Fatima back."

By nightfall, the iron gate to Monte Cristi had fallen, and pirates flooded the city. Townspeople ran screaming for their lives. Silent Sam skipped inside, singing, while Montbars and Wynne led pirate gangs into buildings, smashing windows and torching shops.

"Time to put Monty back in Monte Cristi," Sam declared.

Later that night, in the town square, Sam had a makeshift stage around the town fountain. Men, women and children were corralled to be an audience. Pirates stripped members of the clergy and borrowed their clothes, letting the men of God walk around naked.

Sam shook a rattle made from a coconut husk and danced around the fountain. "Come gather round, *señors* and *señoritas,* drop your gazpachos and tortillas, Monte Cristi, Monte Cristi. The unluckiest town you ever did see, Monte Cristi, Monte Cristi. Death has come for thee.

"Silent Sam's the name, death is the game, and once you've met Sammy yer never the same. The Devil has come, and he's brought some mates, with poison and pestilence, mark the date. Monte Cristi, Monte Cristi. He's hungry, you see, and very thirsty, Monte Cristi, Monte Cristi.

"Sacked to the ground and washed to the sea. You cannot run, you cannot flee, Monte Cristi, Monte Cristi. The milk's gone sour, the maids all cower, we might just have to devour all Monte Cristi!"

Sam bowed. "Monty, separate boys from girls. With scissors if you must."

Pirates rounded people up. Those who resisted were killed or dragged away to be tortured to death.

"There's lots for all to see and do, for retribution has come for you, Monte Cristi," Sam continued. "Over here we have a fun game. What's this one, Monty?"

"It's Piggyback, Sammy."

Pirates made clergy ride on each other's backs while being jabbed by red-hot pokers.

"And here's a game I like to call Test Yer Faith," Sam said.

They forced a priest in a burlap sack to walk across a fire pit.

"Come on, Father. It's not like roasting in hell. Let's go." Sam clapped.

When the priest reached a side, they stabbed him with swords, forcing him backwards.

"Which way, which way?" Sam said. "Oh, he's going up in flames."

The priest flailed, burning to death.

"He made a believer out of me!" Sam exclaimed.

They dragged out the mayor and town officials, forcing them to their knees.

"Tonight, Monty will treat us to one more," Sam said. "I'll expect to see payment by dawn. Or we play another round."

"We have no money," the mayor said. "There is no treasure here!"

"Wrong answer again. Soooo, Monty's going to treat us to his eye-poppin' specialty, which I call Devout Beyond Sight."

They brought out the magistrate with a rope band attached to his head. The rope had many knots and wooden pins.

"Let the people join in. This be a demonstration of the superior judicial department of Monte Cristi," said Sam.

Montbars made townspeople push a pin on the wheel, tightening the rope.

"Monte Cristi, where's your enthusiasm?" Sam said.

Montbars and two pirates used blades and fire to force people to push.

"Do you confess your sins, Magistrate?" Sam leaned in.

The magistrate screamed as the ropes tightened, cracking his skull.

"Do you hear what I hear?" Sam put his hand to his ear. "That's a confession if I ever heard one."

Eventually the magistrate's eyes popped out of his head.

"Now we see eye to eye."

Pirates tied the mayor to a post, then brought out a section of mast.

"This one's called God's Decision," Sam said.

Men spun the mast on its axis and let it fall. It dropped beside the mayor, just missing him.

"God likes you tonight, Mayor."

"We have nothing," the mayor sobbed.

"You better have something by dawn, or you're going to feel unimaginable pain," Sam replied.

"You can torture me all you want. We have nothing," the mayor asserted.

"Search every house and every street, because when dawn comes, your maker you will meet." Sam danced away singing the Monte Cristi song.

Whiskey Kisses entered Manzanillo Bay at dawn on the outskirts of Monte Cristi. They arrived at a villa under siege. Smoke swirled through the air, and pistol shots echoed from bushes and behind houses.

"This is gonna be another bloody Church Street, ain't it?" said Atia.

"Silent Sam likes to play cruel games," replied Gladstone.

Grymes readied a large hammer and wheel-lock pistol and led the group ashore.

The pirate John Coxon and his men were pinned behind bales of hay. Coxon's clothes were drenched in blood. They moved towards the pirate group, taking cover behind large barrels.

"If the Capitaine's here, he wouldn't be part of this," said Gladstone.

"If he's part of this, I'll kill him meself," Atia said.

"Your Capitaine is not here," Coxon said. "He was duped as well."

Gladstone tended Coxon's wounds.

"What do ya mean by that?" Atia pressed.

"Will I live?" Coxon uttered weakly.

"Uh, we'll know just as soon as we can," Gladstone said.

"Where is the Capitaine?" Arsenault asked Coxon.

"Who knows. Not here. Like I said, duped. They lured him somewhere."

"And all these people?" Atia demanded.

"Death, slavery, whatever the pirates have in store," Coxon said. "It's outta my hands. I'm out. Sam's men didn't attack with us. They waited till we were beat before advancing. One more thing: he's got a black spot on Miss Red."

"On me?" said Atia. "What's that?"

"He's put it out to all pirates to take you down."

"Just for killing Slasher Al?"

"The price of being famous. Don't get famous. Get out. You got paid. You got more than most pirates end up with. Clear out now. Call it beginner's luck."

"He makes a valid point," Gladstone said. "The Capitaine's not here; we can get Fatima and go."

"Retreat," Coxon told his men. "Get *les flibustiers* away."

"The order's given," said one of Coxon's men. "Pull back."

"You're leaving?" Arsenault said.

"I'll not go out like this. A black spot on Silent Sam," Coxon said. "I'll put up a thousand in gold."

"A thousand, you say?" Atia perked up. "Is that dead or alive?"

"Take my advice and sail away with what ya got. Get me to my ship, lads."

"Let's help him to his ship," Atia offered.

"You shouldn't be moved," Gladstone said.

"Why not?" Coxon said.

"The doc says that sometimes. Aye, let's get you to your ship, then." Gladstone went to raise Coxon beneath his arms.

Coxon screamed and blood oozed.

"Oh, that's why not," Gladstone said.

They carried him to the rowboat; *Dorado* sat in the bay nearby.

Arsenault intercepted them.

"I must go," Arsenault told Atia.

"What about the people here?" she said.

"How do we take on that many men? I must find out what happened to the Capitaine."

"Will you come back?"

"I will do everything I can to come back to help you. Stay with Jones, and don't go with the pirates. If you can, go back to Hope Bay with your brothers and wait there."

"What if I find the Capitaine before you do?"

"Then get word to Tortuga or Cape François." Arsenault kissed her cheek before running to his boat.

"Take care of yourself," Atia said.

After seeing Coxon off, *les flibustiers* started to leave.

"Can we rescue Fatima?" Atia asked Grymes. "Is it possible?"

"And what of Monte Cristi?" Gladstone added. "We can't just leave all these people to die."

"Aye, I can." Grymes readied a rowboat.

Atia and Gladstone climbed aboard, and they all began paddling. Two *flibustiers* flagged them down on the way back to *Whiskey Kisses*. "Coxon wants you," one said.

"I'm sure it's you he's talking to," Gladstone said to Atia.

They detoured to *Dorado* and were shown to the captain's cabin. Coxon lay in bed, nursing a bottle of rum.

"Captain Coxon?" Gladstone began.

"I called you back here because things have changed. Captain Allison of *Sainte Andrew* sent me some promising news. The ship they're all looking for, *De Heilige Graal*, is headed for the big lake in Maracaibo."

"*De Hilly* what?"

"It's Dutch for *The Holy Grail*." Coxon clutched his wounds. "Someone's got to go down there, but it ain't me."

"Is Lake Maracaibo far?" Atia asked.

Gladstone thought a moment. "Um, yes."

"Once in Maracaibo, she can't get out quick. She's practically gift-wrapped," Coxon said. But I'm going home. Allison says the countess has a decoy. The decoy ship is in San Juan. Miguel Rivero caught her. Like I said, gift-wrapped."

"We'll go," Atia volunteered. "Give me some men and we'll go get *The Holy Grail*. I'll split what's in the hold."

"The Capitaine," Gladstone said. "We need an experienced captain."

"It's too good to pass up." Coxon passed out, and his men escorted Atia and Gladstone to their rowboat.

"How soon do we get under way?" Atia asked.

"We don't got much food on *Whiskey Kisses*," said Gladstone.

"But Art just stocked us up."

"We got enough to reach San Juan, but not Maracaibo. Let's go see Jones," said Gladstone.

The last of the Spanish garrison surrendered at dawn in Monte Cristi. Silent Sam led the parade of officials and landowners onto a rocky beach below the famous cliff. From above they heard the cries of women and children being herded to the edge by Montbars.

"Everyone, wave to Monty!" Sam gestured to Montbars. "Payment was not received, so this morning we're going to play Leap of Faith. Who goes first?"

Montbars used his knife to point to different hostages, while Sam judged the mayor's reaction.

"That one, Monty." Sam pointed to one of the women.

Montbars snatched her from the group. The woman pleaded but was thrown off the cliff, screaming. Her body broke on the beach below.

Montbars singled out another crying woman, and Sam agreed with a thumbs-up. The same fate was delivered, and the mayor screamed.

"The little girl in curls," Sam indicated.

Montbars tossed the child to her death.

Sam sensed that the townspeople were finally breaking.

"How about this small boy in the embroidered vest?" Montbars said.

The mayor threw himself before Silent Sam.

"Oh, no, not little Pablo, no, not little Pablo!" Sam mocked.

The boy's mother attacked Montbars, clawing and spitting.

"I'll give you everything you want," said the mayor.

"I know you will. We're just going to have lots of fun along the way," Sam said. "Come on down, Monty. Lock up little Pablo and the rest of the hostages in the church. Mayor Manuel is going to take us for a walk."

An ominous orange cloud formed above Monte Cristi. In the harbor, *La Lune* dropped anchor. Men rowed ashore.

Sam retracted his telescope before heading down the steps of the bell tower. He entered the church, where townspeople were praying and weeping. The mayor waited on his knees.

Montbars returned with pirates from pillaging the town.

"Nothing. Not a thing of proper value," Montbars said.

Pirates argued over what to do about the hostages.

Sam leant into Montbars. "Gather any stragglers and lock them in here."

Reyning arrived.

"Well, what do you know, it's Reyning," said Sam. "Try not to be too inconspicuous."

Sam and Montbars joined Reyning behind an archway.

"I had to come. There's no time to lose," Reyning began. "The German countess, the witch. She's been captured by the pirate Rivero and is in Puerto Rico. The ship is on its way to San Juan."

"Fortune smiles on us," said Sam. "All we got here is hostages. There's more booty in it if we sell off the church bells."

"Can you convince your men to move on San Juan?"

"Let's see. Dutch here says San Juan is ripe for pluckin', men," Sam called.

"San Juan—now, there's a city worth taking," said Wynne.

"It's been a long time since we had a Spanish capital," said Montbars.

The pirates chanted, "San Juan, San Juan."

"That was easy enough." Sam mimed wiping his hands.

Fatima ventured on deck of *Barbarossa I* amid gunfire. Janissaries fired shots at Spanish ships in the haze beyond the docks leading to the town of Monte Cristi. Pirates were already in the city and taking the spoils by the time Caesar was able to capture the docks. He ordered Janissaries into Monte Cristi to find out what was happening when a small Dutch ship approached. At nightfall, Caesar went aboard the Dutch vessel to meet her captain.

Fatima wondered what they spoke about and who the Dutch captain was. She recognized the ship from the siege at Port Royal. After Caesar returned to *Barbarossa I*, a janissary returned from the city to make a report.

"They're killing the hostages, there's nothing here," said the janissary. "They are going on to San Juan."

"The hostages were the only thing of value here," Caesar huffed. "San Juan is a capital. It will take proper planning to invade a capital."

"There is a treasure ship with a German noble already there."

"I know. Prepare to leave."

"To San Juan?" the agha asked.

"Yes, to San Juan," said Caesar.

"We don't have the food to get to San Juan," said the agha.

"I received a message from our new benefactor, Baron de Klauwen," said Caesar.

"Where is this Baron de Klauwen?" asked the raïs. "He was supposed to send provisions from Tobago."

"Tobago was attacked. Baron de Klauwen relocated. The prize will be in San Juan. It's the decoy they're all chasing," Caesar explained. "Our benefactor wants us to take part in the raid and capture San Juan until *De Heilige Graal* is in our hands. Then we're to deliver it to Samaná Bay, where our benefactor will grant our freedom and make us all very rich men. Bring up the cables; we go now."

Aboard *Whiskey Kisses*, Jones discussed the food situation with Grymes and Gladstone. Atia kept scanning the harbor with a telescope, hoping to see a familiar ship.

"We could transfer some stores," Jones said.

"It still wouldn't be enough," Grymes argued.

Atia paused on a ship with yellow sails. "*La Lune* is here!"

"What?" Jones replied.

"See for yourself." She passed the telescope to Gladstone. *La Lune* sat at the far end of the bay.

"We gotta contact him," Atia said.

"I'll get the lamp," Gladstone volunteered.

"That's no good," Jones said. "What if it's not him?"

"I'll row over and see," Atia said.

"I'll go with you," Grymes volunteered.

"I'll be quick. I'll disguise myself. You get the ship ready to go."

"I still don't like it," Jones said.

"If it's the Capitaine, we can get Fatima back before Mandingo leaves," Atia insisted. "We might be able to save these people, too."

"Fine, but be quick," Jones replied. "We'll get the ships ready to go. Be careful and come straight back, whether it's him or not."

Atia heaved the oars until her arms burned. When she finally came alongside, she tied off the rowboat and climbed up the stern mooring line to the side window of the captain's cabin. She raised herself to see a figure in a familiar vest and wide-brimmed hat, fitting on belts. She climbed through the window.

"Where the hell have ya been, my handsome stranger?" Atia began.

Silent Sam turned around. "It is sight at first love, no?"

Atia went for her blades, but Montbars hit her upside the head, taking her stilettoes.

"Oh, she's quick with those jabbers." Sam grinned.

"She might have got ya," Montbars said. "I got her first."

Atia groaned, squinting through her left eye.

"I owe you one. This one's coming with us. She's worth more than you know," Sam said.

"I'll bet she's not," Montbars replied.

"There's no betting on account, it's in the code."

"Women aren't allowed on board. It's also in the code."

"Mansvelt wrote that rule, and they didn't call him the flamin' Dutchman for nothin'."

La Lune's cables were cut, and the ship went to full sail, exiting the bay. Atia thought she heard screams from the distant town before she lost consciousness.

Gladstone watched helplessly from *Whiskey Kisses* as an enormous fire mushroomed out of control in the town's center. "My god, that can't be real." Screams echoed on the wind, screams of men, women and children burning alive. "My god, it is."

Zoe arrived on deck. "Where's Atia?"

"She didn't come back," said Grymes.

"They killed all those people, and we've lost Fatima and Atia." Gladstone massaged his temples.

Zoe put her arm around him.

"Welcome to war. It's not the Capitaine," Grymes said. "She walked right into a trap."

Gladstone leaned over the rail to call to *Cymru*. "They got her, Tom! It's not the Capitaine."

"I knew it!" Jones threw his arms in the air. "You'll never catch her, in the shape *Kisses* is in. I'll get after her; try to follow me."

"Aye, we'll get her back," Gladstone said.

"I'm in command, mates," Grymes announced. "We're goin' after Red."

Cymru cut her lines, aiming for *La Lune* as she entered open sea. The crew of *Whiskey Kisses* scrambled. Gladstone teared up as they sailed out of the bay, while smoke and flames consumed Monte Cristi.

Manikins and Murder

The full moon illuminated Port Royal as Violante Hayze stood on the top-floor balcony of the Swiftsure Tavern. She pulled her robe tightly around her. The ships that lined the inner harbor were dark and quiet. Gingerly she stood, wavering from the pain in her shoulder. Violante winced as she sat on a padded chair, just comfortable enough to light her clay pipe. She took a puff, exhaling smoke rings.

Below, a door opened, and Sierra Lee snuck off to the wharf next to the Wherry Bridge. A cloaked figure approached from Honey Lane.

Selina carried with her two bottles of alcohol.

"Shit, that better be you," Sierra Lee said. "We should have a signal."

"You mean like this?" Selina whistled.

"We gotta be quiet. Violante will kill me if she finds out."

"Lady B won't be too thrilled, neither. This is her private stock of apricot eaux-de-vie. Someone's going to get beaten over it. As long as it's not me."

Sierra Lee took out two small bottles. "This is the last of the Strangewayes Brand Laudanum Plus, and Laudanum Plus with Vigor."

"They're both full. You know what Violante would do?" Selina gave a wounded wave. "Uh, mine, gimme!"

They both laughed.

Violante's lip curled into a snarl.

"This doesn't make me a wench, does it?" Selina teased.

"Yer too high society for us wenches," Sierra Lee said. "Be off with ya."

Selina went back the same way she came.

Sierra Lee went back inside the Swiftsure.

Violante finished her smoke, determined to give Sierra Lee a piece of her mind. She descended the stairs to the tavern.

"Oh, no, you don't!" Sierra Lee snapped.

"I'll just want a wee drink," a man slurred.

"Two words: press gang. Come on, out with ya, or yer going to war!"

Drunken footsteps clambered to the door. "Fuck off," he growled.

The door slammed shut.

Violante had nearly reached the landing when she heard more footsteps.

Sierra Lee screamed. "What the hell!"

Violante approached cautiously.

A cutthroat had Sierra Lee by the arm, while another took out a long, sharp blade. A cloaked figure emerged, bottle in hand, and raised it to the head of the cutthroat. There was a crash, and the cutthroat fell.

Sierra Lee managed to wriggle free, while Selina took the second bottle of apricot brandy and clobbered the other cutthroat. After the initial shock, he came back fighting mad.

Sierra Lee clasped her knife.

"Do 'em both," the first cutthroat said.

"The monk said only the blonde. Don't touch the brunette, no matter what," the other replied.

"We got no choice now, do we?"

The cutthroats advanced, twisting their blades.

Violante casually strolled out from behind the bar with a blunderbuss under her arm.

Sierra Lee and Selina moved off to the side.

"What's this?" the second cutthroat said.

"The brunette!" said the other.

"Be gone, or I'll shoot." Violante aimed the weapon.

"She can't even fire that thing," the second cutthroat said. "Look at her arm."

Sierra Lee took the gun from Violante. "I'll shoot the fuckin' thing."

The cutthroats charged, swinging blades.

Sierra Lee pivoted with the gun under her arm, cocking it. It fired. A tremendous blast sent both men soaring across the tavern. Sierra Lee was thrown backwards, crashing into Violante.

The concussion threw Selina against the wall, blanketing her in burning dust.

"Holy shit, that's a huge gun," said Sierra Lee.

"What?" Selina yelled.

"Better make sure they're dead," said Sierra Lee.

Both women checked the men, who had been torn to ribbons.

Violante whimpered and drew her knees to her chest.

"Oh, we better get the doc," Selina said.

"There is no doc. How about old Mrs. Beazley?" Sierra Lee replied.

"No," Violante gasped. "Just give me my medicine."

Selina handed back one of the bottles of Strangewayes's formula.

Violante sucked back a dropper.

"Sorry. We got lots of slaves with bad infections," Selina said. "The city's all but out of this stuff, and Lady B won't take off the shackles to let them heal."

Violante was trying a third full dropper when Sierra Lee snatched it from her.

"What the fuck are you talking about, Spotswood?" Violante snapped.

"You can't have that much. Remember Katie? You'll get sick or die."

"Good. Just cut it off." Violante sniffed. "Just kill me."

"Let the potion kick in. How long should it take?" Selina asked Sierra Lee.

"It says to make sure you're lying down first, with your head on a pillow."

"Feeling better?" Selina asked.

Violante threw up on the floor.

Sierra Lee got a mug from the bar and filled it from a water barrel. She forced some down Violante's throat.

"Lady B's going to have me flogged to death," Selina said.

"No, she won't." Violante took small sips. "Sierra Lee's going to pay her back. Through installments. I'll speak with Lady Beeston. I'll say it was a mistake. She don't want trouble, with Art away. We'll get her sorted out when *Lamb* comes in; he's bound to have replacement bottles."

"You'll do that?" Selina asked.

"Aye, just help me up."

Each took a side, and soon Violante limped over to the cutthroats.

"They were after me, not you," said Sierra Lee. "He said the *monk*."

There came the clanking of armor and footsteps. Three city guards burst through the entrance, followed by Beckford.

"Over here," Violante called.

"A shot was reported. What happened here? Who are these men?" Beckford asked.

"They came here to kill me," Sierra Lee said.

"And they told you that?" Beckford stared down his nose at her. "I'd say a couple of whores and a couple of drunks couldn't agree on payment. And you, young lady," he addressed Selina, "you should not be in this establishment at this hour. You should know better than to consort with this sort, Miss Spotswood."

"I came running when I heard the screams, all the way from Honey Lane," Selina argued. "They were going to kill Sierra Lee. I heard them say it."

"Did they?" Beckford said.

"They did," Violante confirmed. "They also mentioned a monk."

"A monk. What else?"

"They took a vow of silence after that, Colonel Beckford," Violante said. "They wasn't after me this time. They wanted her; we all heard it."

"I want sworn testimony from the three of you." Beckford turned to his guards. "Escort Miss Spotswood to Beeston Manor. Miss Hayze, you should invest in security. Perhaps a pimp. Sierra Lee can come with me for protection tonight."

"All the same, I'm duty-bound to attend Miss Hayze," Sierra Lee replied.

"We're under Bleedin Art's protection, Colonel," Violante said.

"I see that's working out for you. Best lock up tight. I'll have the undertaker stop by to collect them." Beckford indicated the corpses. "I bid you goodnight." He and the guards escorted Selina out.

Sierra Lee bolted the door. "I'll clean up down here." She wiped her neck and found traces of blood on her hand.

Violante slowly headed upstairs. "Yeah, you will. And don't ever cross me again, Sierra Lee."

Along the waterfront, press gangs rounded up drunkards, while guards escorted Selina Spotswood home to Lady Beeston. Dread trickled down her throat, souring her stomach. The lady of the house had been less than enthusiastic about Selina coming to stay in Port Royal in the first place. It had been arranged by her uncle Spotswood in London with Bill Beeston. Her scandalous affair with Longstaff had caused such an uproar, she was banished from the Spotswood family in Nevis.

The guards marched her along Thames Street and turned down Bird's Alley until they reached the main gates of the next block. As they passed through the grand archway, nausea sat at the back of Selina's throat. She liked living there, and she liked Jane. Even Lady Beeston herself could be charming and humorous, though the constant nagging about marriage grated on Selina's nerves.

The gatekeeper emerged in a night robe.

"This young lady lost her way," the guard said. "She's had trouble and is expected to give testimony."

Lady Anne Beeston, carrying a lantern, marched across an upper balcony and came down the stairs. "What is this? What's going on?"

"There's been some trouble," the guard said.

"Trouble? What has she done?" Lady Beeston demanded.

"She's not a suspect; she's a possible witness."

"*Victim*," Selina interjected. "We were attacked."

"We'll determine that," the guard said. "She's to give testimony."

"Not now. It's the middle of the night," said Lady Beeston.

"No, my lady, on the morrow."

"Be off with you, then." Lady Beeston ushered Selina inside the gate, letting the gatekeeper lock up.

"We were attacked," Selina said.

"Attacked by whom? Where were you?"

"Sierra Lee was attacked by cutthroats. They said they were working for a monk."

"A monk?"

"I don't know." Selina shook her head.

"What were you doing out in the first place?" Lady Beeston asked.

"There was a mixup. Violante said she'd explain."

"She doesn't have to. You're off consorting with whores."

"They're wenches, not whores," Selina said.

"They're whores. And you're no better. I took you in when no one wanted you because of your filthy slut ways. You are no better now than the day you arrived. Do you want to go live with the whores and strumpets?"

"No, my lady."

"Go to your room. We'll speak no more of this right now. I'll want to know everything that happened. We'll write your testimony later, together."

"Yes, Lady Beeston."

Lady Beeston left with her bottles to head back upstairs.

Selina went to her room and lit a lantern. Blood stained her neck, and her dress was a disaster. She smiled to herself.

"Have a bath and get cleaned up," Lady Beeston's voice penetrated the door. "Don't dirty the bed. I'll be back to fetch you early. We'll speak then. You disappoint me, Selina."

"I'll see you on the morrow, my lady." Selina looked at her reflection. "I don't need a bath. I'm a wench."

Selina was up at sunrise, after very little sleep. She readied herself quickly, knowing Lady Beeston would collect her soon.

When they left, the clouds above were scattered and golden. *HMS Relentless*, a towering man of war, sat at the north dock, while a group of women raised a banner chanting, "Free Big Dick, free Big Dick!" Lady Beeston, who had arranged the gathering, continued to solicit people assembled for the morning news.

Selina stood quietly beside Jane, yawning.

"What were you up to last night?" asked Jane. "Did you get into trouble?"

"We were attacked by cutthroats; we fought for our lives."

"Impressive." Jane smiled. "You have a wild side."

They shared a chuckle.

"Your mother is very upset with me."

"She'll get over it," Jane assured. "She's easily distracted when Big Dick's in town. Besides, she has her politics. She'll forgive you, you'll see. Just be quiet as a monk for a few weeks and she'll forget all about it."

"The monk!" Selina realized. "Of course."

Captain White's official carriage skidded to a stop on Thames Street, while Beckford and his militiamen approached from Lime.

"Lady Beeston, what are you doing?" White asked.

"Captain White, why have you not sent *HMS Relentless* to destroy Laurens de Graaf?"

"I agree," a shopkeeper said. "I'm tired of tiptoeing through the tulips. We go after Laurens de Graaf and finish him, once and for all."

"We need all our captains," Lady Beeston asserted.

"What yer doing is illegal," White said.

"This is not a protest; it's a demonstration," Lady Beeston said. "This city was attacked. We need real protection. We want Big Dick freed."

"Do you?" Beckford spoke from behind her.

"Yes. You released Valentine on more serious charges. I tell you, the city needs to show strength above all. The French hit us hard. We have a man of war, Big Dick."

"As it is, we have decided to pardon Captain Longstaff, for the most part," Beckford said. "As you said, there was no murder."

Selina saw Sierra Lee and Rosie heading up Thames Street. "I'll be right back," she told Jane and disappeared through the crowd. On Waterman's Wharf, Selina caught up with them as they loaded barrels on the cart. She stumbled over herself and practically crashed into them.

Selina caught her breath. "It's Skean, the monk."

"Of course," Rosie replied. "He was dressed as a monk the first time I saw him."

"Aye, you're right. The bloody bastard," said Sierra Lee.

"That doesn't explain why he wants Sierra Lee dead and not Violante," Rosie continued. "Both saw that white-haired fellow. So, what does Sierra Lee have that Violante doesn't?"

"Or is it the other way around?" Selina said.

"Maybe 'cause she's famous now, too high-profile?" Sierra Lee said. "Maybe he can't kill her."

Later that morning at Fort Carlisle, Lady Beeston stood in anticipation of Big Dick's release. A guard vanished down a long corridor of locked doors. White and Beckford waited beside her. She felt Beckford's eyes burrowing into her.

Snead arrived, attempting to sneak past them unnoticed.

"Just in time, Snead," White said.

"For what?"

"To pardon Longstaff."

Snead frowned. "Why are we doing that?"

"I need every ship out there right now," White insisted.

"That will leave the city defenseless."

"No, it won't," Lady Beeston interjected. "There are six merchantmen in the harbor and one of those Van der Hagen East Indiaman ships in Ligania. All perfectly capable of mounting a defensive line."

"You've thought this through," Snead said.

"Oh, she's thought of everything," White agreed.

Longstaff emerged, followed by the guard.

"Captain Longstaff, we're here to release you," said Lady Beeston.

"Lady Beeston." Longstaff kissed her hand. "Captain White, I thought you'd let them make an example of me."

"I need to send someone away, and I thought of you, Dick. I have here a letter of marque, signed by myself and Colonel Beckford." White removed a scroll from his pocket.

"We want revenge on Laurens de Graaf and his French pirates and buccaneers," said Lady Beeston.

"I charge you to take down Laurens de Graaf—if you're going to clear your name," said White. "And we want the Capitaine."

"You made an arrangement with the Capitaine," said Longstaff.

"Guards, leave us," said White.

"Our obligation to him was fulfilled as he sailed out," Lady Beeston said.

"Let us cut through the fat, shall we?" White continued. "Officially, we're sending you to bring in Laurens's buccaneers. Unofficially, it's a Van der Hagen East Indiaman. She took on a passenger that made everyone very angry."

"*De Heilige Graal*. The Countess Aurora of Calenberg, if I'm not mistaken," said Longstaff. "She was last seen off Margarita."

"Very good, Dick, but she's in the Bay of Maracaibo," Lady Beeston said.

"They're going to Little Venice," Longstaff said.

"Little Venice is completely destroyed. There is no way into Aragua from there," Snead added. "The Indians have the entire lake coast and several islands. It's foolish for them to go in."

"She'll figure that out in short time. *De Heilige Graal* will have quit Maracaibo by the time I get there. It's figuring out where she'll go from there. I shall leave immediately," Longstaff said.

"Indeed, Captain Longstaff. Godspeed," White said.

White and Snead went to discuss how to word the documents to make it legal.

Lady Beeston escorted Longstaff to a private office, under the jealous eye of Beckford.

"My husband will return soon, Dick." Lady Beeston shut the door. "He'll be back with the full might of the law and with a real navy. It'll be yours to command as admiral of the fleet. I even had a new suit made for you. I think you'll find it enhances your image."

"Does my image interest you, my lady?"

"Of course, it does. I have considerable investment in you and *Relentless*. We need a larger-than-life hero. We're going to win this war, mark my words. If you'll marry Jane and give me a grandson, we will rule Jamaica forever."

Sierra Lee knocked on the door to the parlor of the Swiftsure Tavern. She entered to find Violante trying to slide on a robe. Sierra Lee tried to help, but Violante covered up with a blanket instead.

"I have to go see Beckford," said Sierra Lee.

"To give testimony," Violante replied.

"Among other things."

"What other things?"

"You know, things."

"No, I don't know. What?" Violante pressed. "Are you whoring on the side?"

"Not by choice; just Beckford. He was my regular before, and he won't let me stop."

"Did you say no? Never mind. How often?"

"Just about every day." Sierra Lee shrugged.

"Every day on your lunch break you gotta go see Beckford." Violante shook her head.

"It's my problem."

"You're protected by Bleedin Art. Beckford is not allowed to be fucking Art's wenches."

"Not fuckin' per se; he makes me suck it off."

"Go to the tavern and bring up two of those green peppers from Mexico. Fuck it, bring up five."

"Jalapeños?"

"Aye, Mace Scarcliff likes the spicy Mexican drink with the peppers," said Violante.

"They're too hot for me."

"Do you remember last year? Jag'd Jayne got his wood polished by Lilly right after she had some of those."

Sierra Lee smirked. "Aye. He was screaming."

"That he was." Violante smiled.

"But, they're too hot for me. I couldn't—"

"Fine. Go on sucking his cock, but if he pays you, the house gets half."

Sierra Lee pondered it, and a fiendish grin formed on her face.

When she arrived at Fort Carlisle, guards brought her to Beckford's office. He pretended to be interrupted.

"Leave us," Beckford said.

The militia guards left, closing the door.

"Lady Beeston has a lot of faith in Big Dick. They seem to have quite a relationship." He noticed her watery eyes and tears running down her cheeks. "I say, are you well? You're crying."

"Aye, sir. I think I ate something off. Me tummy hurts to no end, and with the fright of last night, I'm in just a terrible state."

"Yes, I'm sure you are. Are you ready to give testimony?"

"I am, sir. I'll try." Sierra Lee dictated her side of the story, and he took notes.

"This is your sworn statement of events?" said Beckford.

"It is, sir," said Sierra Lee. "The men spoke of a monk."

"That's right. You said it here. They referred to a monk."

"If you remember, last year, the white-haired fellow with pink eyes stabbed Violante—he was dressed as a monk. Then the man we know as Skean was also dressed as a monk when he first arrived here."

Beckford pondered it; his eyes revealed that she was correct.

"Does that mean something?" she asked.

"No, it doesn't. Speak of this with no one until we have all the facts."

"Aye, I won't, sir. May I take my leave?"

"You're in a hurry to go?"

"I'm a belly of fire, sir, and I have my duties," she said.

Beckford unbuttoned his trousers. "Yes, you do." He took her by the hair and forced her down.

She resisted, but he pushed his member into her face. With her mouth afire, she took it in. He gave a satisfied exhale, then after a few more seconds he squirmed, withdrawing, his eyes wide with panic.

"Something wrong, sir?" she asked.

"Ahhhh!" he yelped.

"Sorry, sir, what?"

"Ahhhh! What did you do? What did you do to me?" He waved his hand, trying to get a breeze going over his manhood.

"Oh, that must be the medicine," Sierra Lee spoke pleasantly. "Violante gave me some medicine. Burns a bit for a few minutes at first."

"Ahhhh! A few minutes? Ahhhh!"

A knock came at the door. "Colonel Beckford are you there?" the voice of Lady Beeston called.

"Ahhhh!" Beckford continued.

"That must be Selina with her sworn testimony. Shall I let them in?" Sierra Lee offered.

"No. Be gone with you. Ahhhh! Now!"

She went for the front door, and he toppled towards her. "Not that way, you fool! Out the back."

"I can hear you," Lady Beeston said.

Sierra Lee went out the back door. Despite a burning mouth, she was enjoying the moment too much to leave. She peered back through a space in the door jam.

Beckford poured water into a basin and put it on his chair. He crouched behind his desk, bathing his burning member.

Lady Beeston, with Selina at her side, stood in the doorway.

"Wait here a moment," Lady Beeston told Selina and went inside. "Colonel, as you're aware, I'm very busy. Here's Selina's sworn statement." She removed a scroll from a satin pouch. "I trust you'll bring these pirates to justice for the attack on this wench."

"Yahhhh!" he roared, gyrating behind his desk.

"What?" Lady Beeston stared at him.

"Aye, I'll get right on it. Thanks for stopping by."

"That's it?"

"It's adequate, I'll read it later."

Lady Beeston turned to leave, then turned back. "One more thing."

He fell against his desk, gripping below.

"Until my husband returns, it's not in our best interest to have any social contact. I'd appreciate it if you'd only visit on business matters and only in appropriate company," Lady Beeston said. "Good day, sir."

"Whatever you say, Lady Beeston."

She returned to the doorway, as if expecting him to say something else.

Beckford put the basin on his desk and began vigorously washing, grunting.

"Oh, for god's sake, Beckford, get ahold of yourself!" Lady Beeston shut the door behind her.

Sierra Lee smirked all the way back to the Swiftsure Tavern. When she returned, Violante was nursing her baby in the sitting room.

"Well?"

"Beckford's gonna need time to cool off, methinks."

"Remember, you're a wench, not a whore."

Outside, a mail runner docked at the causeway. A monk disembarked with a case in his hand. He rushed through the crowd into the heart of the city.

"What is it?" Violante asked.

"Another monk. I just don't trust their sort," said Sierra Lee.

"That reminds me. There's a couple of special dress forms at Howatt's Hats. I want you and Rosie to go pick them up."

"You mean like manikins?"

"Not quite; these are specially made. It'll help us look better protected than we are. Scarcliff and Blackmoor are no match for what we got coming. They're guarding no less than six properties."

"Aye," Sierra Lee agreed.

"We want to look intimidating."

Longstaff admired himself in the oval mirror of the Admiral's Room at the Catt and Fiddle. He had never looked better. The white vest, worn with a Prussian blue suit, fitted perfectly, and the pouch holding his manhood in place accentuated its size. His cock, like his man of war, *HMS Relentless*, was legendary. He had wealth and fame. Wherever he went, women wanted him. No port was safe from his ten-inch purple-headed man of war.

Longstaff had had many women in Port Royal. Anne Beeston, Violante Hayze, the wives of government officials, such as Margaret Dewar and Lyla Llewellyn, and hundreds of nameless wenches and strumpets.

Lady Anne Beeston ventured inside from the patio, where a crowd below cheered, "Big Dick, Big Dick!" She approached him. "Positively heroic. And observe." She opened four trouser buttons, and his manhood sprang out. Lady Beeston gripped it until it hardened.

"I thought you said we were in a hurry," Longstaff said.

She fastened his trousers back up, leaving it protruding. "We are. Yes, positively heroic."

"Somewhat frustrating. I'll want to see you after."

"I'm sure that can be arranged." Lady Beeston tugged on his member, guiding him along. They ventured outside to the patio where Jane and Prudence Pinhorn double-glanced at his swaying maypole. Longstaff waved to the crowd below.

"Go on and look, Jane. That's the father of your future children there," said Lady Beeston.

Jane gave her mother an uneasy stare.

"Meet me at the Forge afterwards," Lady Beeston panted in Longstaff's ear. "I want you inside me."

"I must tend my ship first and prepare to leave." He watched her chest heave, knowing she wanted him right there, in front of everyone.

Afterwards, Longstaff went onboard *Relentless* for a few hours. The men knew their duties; there was no need to linger on deck. His future was at stake, and he knew what had to be done. Inside his cabin, he gathered a few items from his desk and put them in a small box. When the sun headed to the west, he ventured out.

"I'm going ashore for a while, Jim," he told Fishhook.

"Aye, sir."

Longstaff took a wherryman's carriage up Thames Street to the Swiftsure Tavern. He went upstairs to Violante's chamber, where she showed him his son, who lay asleep in a crib.

"I never wanted any of this to happen to you," said Longstaff.

"Aye, but it did." She stared at her son. "Surely buggered up now, eh? I can hardly even lift my own baby."

"I'm coming back for both of you."

"Right," she said doubtfully. "Are you really? I can't wait. Where shall we go, Nevis?"

"Boston."

"Boston?"

"I've already bought land. You and Richard are coming with me when I return from this mission. We're relocating to Boston for a new beginning. The three of us."

"You're jesting." Violante turned her back to face the window.

"No, I'm not. I love you. You're still the most beautiful woman I ever met." He took her in his arms, and his member brushed against her.

"No," she said.

Longstaff opened the four trouser buttons and his manhood hung out.

Violante stared at it longingly. "You're the only man who ever took me there. But that was then, and I have a new life now."

"I must have you."

"After the pain settles down a bit." She pushed him away.

Longstaff raised her dress. She squirmed as he drove his full length into her. He carried her in his arms to the bed. He stared into her lovely, tearful brown eyes. She moaned loudly. He withdrew, mistaking it for pain.

Violante's hand slid down and guided him back inside her. He thrust and they undulated together, her insides milking his cock. Her face glowed and her thighs quivered until she groaned with pleasure. Then came his turn as he finished, forcing it in her as far as it could go. Both of them grunted, and each jolt gave her both pain and pleasure. They stayed together for what seemed like an hour before he got up to leave.

Longstaff rummaged through his breast pocket for the box. "I have a commission in Boston, and I want you to be my wife."

Her eyes narrowed as he placed a ring on her finger. "You mean it?"

"I'll come back for you."

"I'm nothing but a cripple now."

He revealed a small pouch, inside which was a brown chunk the size of a doubloon. "This is pure opium. Better than anything Strangewayes has. This will take away all the pain."

Her face warmed. "Oh, Richard, thank you."

"I'm sure you know how to smoke it."

"I do."

He moved to the door. "I'll always love you, Violante."

"You make me want to believe, Richard," was her reply.

He blew her a kiss and closed the door on his way out.

Longstaff continued to the Old Forge, where Lady Beeston waited in a private office. She sat naked on a chaise longue sipping apricot eaux-de-vie. At his approach she slid her fingers down between her thighs to caress her swollen pink femininity. Eagerly she performed the four-button trick and Longstaff's manhood protruded.

At first it wouldn't harden, and Lady Beeston was forced to lick and nibble at it. "I've been looking forward to this all day, and now it's like an eel." She gave it a few light smacks and tormented his balls with her long fingernails. When he finally stood at attention and was about to enter her, Skean emerged from a private side door. "Oh, bravo!"

The couple scrambled to cover up.

Longstaff charged at the short man, who held out a cross for protection.

"Twice in one afternoon? Bully to you, Dick," said Skean.

"What the hell are you doing here?" Lady Beeston demanded.

"He's a Whig spy," said Longstaff.

"I know who he is. My wenches keep me well informed. What are you doing in here?" Lady Beeston spoke shrilly.

"What am I doing here?" Skean mused. "What is the future governor's wife doing in here with her future son-in-law?"

"What do you want?" Longstaff said.

"The same things you want. Only, our enemies grow stronger and nearer. We cannot allow your indiscretions to go on any further. The Earl of Inchiquin will be here in weeks. He and his supporters have a grand design not seen since Oliver Cromwell's time. All your hope for the future of Jamaica and your own lives are at stake. We'll not let you jeopardize our plans. All loose ends will be tied. That means you, too."

"I should have keelhauled you," said Longstaff.

"That's right, you should have, but, as it is, you'll be better Christians from here on out, or you'll both be even more exposed."

It was evening at Beeston Manor and the wall sconces were lit, illuminating Jane's study. Selina and Jane sat opposite over a game of chess, pondering.

"You're quiet," said Jane.

"Sorry." Selina moved her knight.

"You made an illegal move."

Selina slid the piece back.

"Your head is not in the game," Jane said. "Why are you so quiet?"

"So, when's the big day?"

"What day?"

"When you and Captain Longstaff get married."

"Longstaff's a dullard."

"What?" Selina perked up. "He is?"

"I'm not marrying that dick," Jane asserted.

Selina sprang to life. "But your mother said."

"My mother said. My mother says a lot of things." Jane listened for Lady Beeston before continuing. "I don't understand what the fuss is all about. He's just a dick."

"I didn't know your mother knew him so intimately." Selina laughed.

"She wants me to marry him so she can have him for herself."

"She'd do that to her own daughter?" Selina moved a piece on the board. "And they called *me* immoral and tossed me out of Nevis."

"Your bishop is exposed." Jane made a move, snagging a piece off the board. "What's the attraction?"

"It's huge."

"It hurts."

"Only at first." Selina smiled to herself, reflecting. "Wait? How do you know it hurts?"

"My mother has a casting of it. I tried it a few times. It hurts, and he's a bed swerver, so, no thank you."

"He's a bed shaker, too."

"Besides. I have a boy at school who fancies me," said Jane. "His cock may not be news on King's Landing, but it suits me just fine. So what if he hasn't got a war ship and property. That's not what I want, and I don't want Big Dick. You can have him."

"I can?"

"Of course." Jane smiled. "Him and all his tropical and venereal diseases. When my father returns, that will be the end of my mother's love affair with Big Dick, and he'll be yours."

"You mock me."

"A little. You can do better."

"I'm in love." Selina moved her bishop.

"Well, it's still a mistake." Jane took the bishop and trapped Selina's king.

"You are certain your father will win his trial?"

"He's already won; it's a certainty now. No one knows it, but he's in with King William. This time next year he'll be knighted and on his way home as governor of Jamaica."

"You know so much of what goes on. Like your mother."

"But, unlike Mother, I know when not to go around squawking to everyone."

They were sharing a laugh when Lady Beeston appeared at the doorway.

"Selina, come here," Lady Beeston said. "I need you to do something."

"We're in the middle of a game," Jane said.

"Your game can wait."

Selina went over. "Yes, my lady."

They exited by the side door.

"I need you to go pick us up some more spirits," Lady Beeston began before her voice went low. "Selina, we have real trouble."

"What sort of trouble?"

"Big trouble. The monk you're all on about—it's him, it's Skean. He's a spy."

"I knew it!" Selina exclaimed. "I'll go tell Sierra Lee."

"Not yet." Lady Beeston handed over a letter. "You have to get this note to Captain Longstaff."

"To Richard, Captain Longstaff?"

"He'll be at Fort Charles. You must go now. If he's not there, wait for him. I don't care how long it takes."

"I will."

"The carriage is ready."

Selina fetched her cloak and went to the carriage. The driver opened the door without speaking before taking the reins. On Lime Street, they passed the Wild Orchid Palace. The figure of Rosie Burghill stalked a window on the top floor. The carriage turned down Fisher's Row, near the turtle pens, eventually halting between the Chocolata Hole and Fort Charles.

Selina got out and went to the quiet fort, where the gate was open. The tower was still under construction and scaffolding ran all the way to the top. She had never been in the fort before, despite the tower being prominent from many parts of the city. She grew dizzy looking straight up at it.

From a dark archway, Longstaff emerged.

"Richard!" she cried. "Captain Longstaff, you startled me."

Longstaff approached. "Captain Longstaff? It hasn't been that long."

"It has been for me."

"I didn't mean to scare you."

Selina handed him the letter. "She gave me this to give to you. She said it's very important."

"Did you read it?"

"No sir."

"Enough with the *sir*. What have they been doing to you?" Longstaff read the note. "I see."

"The man who wants to kill Sierra Lee is Skean," said Selina.

"I'm aware of this. This is nothing to worry about. Lady Beeston is concerned over nothing. Seems as though she underestimates me. I have taken care of this."

"She'll be relieved. Now I better go warn Sierra Lee," Selina replied.

"She's safe. Skean can't get to her; I've seen to it."

"You think of everything."

"I think of you. I think about you constantly."

Selina's heart raced. "You do?"

"You have no idea how much I've missed you."

"But you're going to marry Jane after your divorce is final."

"You know about that?" Longstaff leant into her.

"Everyone knows about that."

"It's all in Lady Beeston's mind. I have no interest or desire for plain Jane."

"Truly?" Selina pressed.

"Truly. How soon does Lady Beeston expect you back with my reply?"

"She said nothing of my return. She said to wait all night if I must."

"Good." Longstaff kissed her hand. "Then I have you to myself."

"If you want." Her lips curled into a smile.

"I never should have left you. I should have divorced and taken you away with me. But war was coming, and I'm a man of action, as you know."

"I know. I hoped and prayed that you loved me."

"I never stopped loving you." He took her in his arms. They kissed passionately. His hands slid up and down her body, gripping her tight.

"Have you ever been up the tower before?" Longstaff asked.

"Never."

Longstaff tucked the note away and took her arm. "Let me show you."

He led her up the spiral stairs. Selina's stomach fluttered from desire and nervousness. She wiped her clammy hands on her dress. Halfway up, she paused. Dizzy.

"Don't be afraid. I'll take care of you." He raised her chin with his finger and bent down to kiss her.

They proceeded to the top, where scaffolding and wood planks awaited further construction. The entire city was visible from here. Streetlamps glowed and multicolored glass lanterns marked the various taverns. Ligania twinkled across the harbor.

Selina's fear melted into awe.

Longstaff grabbed her arm, pulling her to him. "Careful. Not too close to the edge."

His scent was intoxicating, as was the warmth of his body.

"Oh god, I want it." Selina groped between his legs.

Their mouths met again and she fumbled with his trousers, so he showed her the four-button trick, and it popped open.

"I won't tell Lady Beeston if you don't," Longstaff said.

His hand slid between her thighs; his fingers delved into her depths. She massaged his already erect manhood. Then she knelt, pleasing him orally until he was ready to burst. He lifted her up until her bottom rested on the tower's barrier. She guided him inside her. He gripped her tightly and thrust in.

Selina eventually let go of the stonework to claw his back as she quivered. She felt him pulsate inside her, finishing. After he groaned, he pushed her backwards. Before Selina even realized it, she was falling. She expelled a brief scream before hitting her head on the stone steps. All went black.

Sierra Lee finished wiping down the tables and sweeping the floor of the Swiftsure Tavern. She snuffed out the main lights. An eerie silence made her look around. After adjusting her oil lamp, she flashed it around. Everything was still, except for the flickering shadow of the lamp.

Sierra Lee finished closing and climbed the staircase. She passed by Violante's chamber before heading to her own. A pungent stench seeped into the hallway. "That's some stinky shit. You trying to smoke us out?"

She opened the door to her room, unable to shake the sense that something was wrong. After turning off the oil lamp, Sierra Lee passed one of the dress forms by her window. It was like a manikin, but life-sized, with a head, torso and arms created from wool and fabric. Sierra Lee slipped behind a curtain, where her wash basin sat on a table. She drew a loaded pistol from the holster on her thigh.

She heard a floorboard creak and then the sound of fabric ripping. Sierra Lee peered from behind the curtain to see a figure at her window, brandishing a knife. She fired, and the figure dropped, groaning.

"Violante, come quick!" Sierra Lee hollered. "Come on, you lazy whore, yer not that crippled," she added under her breath.

Rosie's footsteps thumped up the stairs.

"I got him. I got the bastard." Sierra Lee adjusted the oil lamp. It was the monk, Skean.

Rosie entered the room, her face flushed with tears.

"What is it?" Sierra Lee asked.

"Selina's dead." Rosie blew her nose into a handkerchief. "Longstaff killed her."

Sierra Lee couldn't speak for a moment. "What?"

"I followed them. He threw her off the tower at Fort Charles."

Sierra Lee made fists with both hands. "That son of a bitch! Make sure monk here don't get away." She went into Violante's room. "Vie!"

The baby cried, and she picked him up and stood over Violante, who was unconscious. "Wake up." No response.

The thumping of a body being beaten by a blunt object sounded from the other room.

"Rosie, get in here," Sierra Lee called.

"Now?"

"Yes, now."

There was one more heavy whack.

Sierra Lee set the baby back in its crib and tried to lift Violante.

Rosie arrived. "The monk didn't make it."

"You killed him?"

"Nay, you killed him. I just made his transition a lot more painful. So, what's wrong with her?"

"Help me get her up. She won't waken."

They hauled Violante to her feet and moved her around the room. Still no response.

"She's not coming around," Rosie said.

"We should get a doctor."

"We don't got a doctor."

"Mrs. Beazley, then, go get her," said Sierra Lee.

They rested Violante in a chair.

Sierra Lee continued trying, unsuccessfully, to revive Violante as Rosie left. She searched around and found a remnant of a smoked dark substance. Sniffing it, she found it pungent and nasty.

Pre-dawn light penetrated the room. Sierra Lee checked the window, hoping to see Rosie return with Mrs. Beazley.

In the harbor, *Relentless* was drifting out.

"Curse you to hell, Big Dick."

The Wrong Side of Moonlight

De Heilige Graal sailed through Lake Maracaibo towards the ruins of Little Venice. Storm clouds gathered like a curtain behind the trees. Forks of lightning stabbed the earth, and thunder rolled in.

Aurora was escorted by Van der Hagen to the quarterdeck, where van Gelder and de Britt scoped out a way inland.

"The weather is foul. It's prone to lightning strikes here. All decks on fire alert," ordered van Gelder. "Close-reef."

"Will you be able to look for survivors today?" Aurora pressed.

"Not in this."

"They say this is a normal occurrence down here," Van der Hagen said. "The most intense lightning in the world."

"I'm surprised the colony lasted this long," van Gelder said. "Who'd want to live in a place with storms like this?"

"Natalia would," replied Aurora.

Van Gelder indicated the mountains in the distance. "There's Aragua. The only way in is via Caracas. Pagans are very unpopular in Caracas. Witchcraft is taken very seriously here."

"Here? As opposed to where? Anyway, who says I'm pagan?" Aurora protested. "I went to a few parties; girls got naked, some blood spilled—it can happen to anyone."

Lighting struck again, followed by horrific thunder.

"Inside, shall we?" Van der Hagen extended his hand.

Aurora reluctantly went in.

In the grand cabin that night, the women watched the lightning show during supper.

"On the morrow I'll send longboats in and find a way into Little Venice. After the storm." Van Gelder drank wine.

"I am going too," Aurora said.

"Absolutely not," van Gelder said. "It's very dangerous. The natives control the area now, not the Spanish."

"I must see for myself."

"You're the Countess of Calenberg, not Joan of Arc. I'll go ashore and search for survivors."

"Let Captain van Gelder secure the place first. Then we'll let you go ashore," said Van der Hagen.

"What a waste of time," Aurora huffed.

"This time, you must do as we say," Van der Hagen said. "You're staying aboard, and that's final."

When the time came, Aurora covered her head in an itchy mosquito net, while crewmen rowed towards the stone causeway. The wreckage of several boats marked their path. Van Gelder remained close to Aurora, gun at the ready, while de Britt led another longboat of men. They slid through a swamp and around a sunken sloop, its mast and rigging intertwined with weeds hanging off the causeway wall.

De Britt leapt off his boat first, with some other men, to secure the area.

Aurora moved to get out, but van Gelder stopped her.

De Britt finally signalled, and they went ashore.

The once finely crafted houses with stained-glass windows lay in ruins. Weeds grew over everything, including the decomposing bodies of men, women and children. One body, with soiled light blond hair, still wore the remnants of an exquisite Romanian gown.

"There's no way to identify them all," said van Gelder. "A merchant sailor made some identifications at the time."

Aurora's eyes prickled with tears. "This was Catharina."

"You're sure?"

"Yes, I'm sure."

"Have you seen enough?" van Gelder said.

Aurora insisted on continuing the search through Little Venice. All she found was charred and mutilated bodies. All afternoon, Aurora trudged among the ruins, her eyes puffy from tears.

A local fisherman arrived and spoke with de Britt, who reported to van Gelder.

"It's time to go," de Britt said.

"What is it?" van Gelder asked.

"Indians are coming. They thought we were a warship coming to take revenge, so they left in a hurry. Now that they've figured out that we're no army, they're coming back fast."

"Return to the boats," van Gelder called to his men.

"The fisherman said a group of people were in the hills on an excursion when the attack happened," said de Britt. "They were captured by revolutionaries when they returned and taken deep into the jungle. One of them was a woman."

"Natalia's alive, out there somewhere." Aurora pointed to the hills.

"She may be. But there's no way we can help her. Not from here," van Gelder said. "There's no way into Aragua, not anymore. When you reach Aragua itself, you can begin a search, but I'm afraid there is nothing else we can do here."

Aurora nodded pensively, boarding the longboat. As they pulled up alongside *De Heilige Graal*, a crewman suddenly slumped forward, an arrow through his neck. Van Gelder quickly ushered Aurora up the ladder to the deck.

De Britt and his men fired guns in retaliation as dozens of canoes approached. The longboats brought the ship to motion while the crew shot muskets for cover fire.

Van der Hagen gave orders from the poop deck, and the cannon slots opened on both sides, blasting the canoes.

Van Gelder checked the wind direction. "Perhaps just enough. Get all crewmen aboard. Sail her out. Rudder hard over. Turn her to broad beam reach and sail her out."

The navigator spun the wheel.

"Hard over!" de Britt ordered.

Aurora rushed inside to her cabin.

When *De Heilige Graal* sailed past the fortress walls of Maracaibo City, the Indian canoes ceased their pursuit.

By nightfall, the city lights were mere specks on the horizon. Aurora sat alone in the aft gallery. She could hear Van der Hagen and van Gelder discussing casualties in the next room. Three men dead and two injured. Their voices lowered. Minutes later, Van Gelder popped his head in the doorway.

"How are you holding up, Countess?"

She gave a weak smile.

"There's a passage to Aragua at Puerto Cabello. We'll try there next." He left abruptly, not saying another word.

Later, Aurora wandered to the grand cabin hoping to find left out food. The moon rose outside the starboard window, yet it wasn't enough to light the way, so she adjusted an oil lamp. She knew Van der Hagen had stashed a few bottles of Oranjeboom lager, she had only to find the right cupboard. Careful not to make a noise, she unlatched several doors until she found them.

"For Catherina." She drank it back, cringing as tears ran down her face. A map sat on the table before her. She ran her finger over the coastline, following the route from Maracaibo to Puerto Cabello.

The voices of Katrina and Persephone drew near. She turned down the lamp. Van der Hagen's voice also chimed in, trying to calm them.

"Viscount, when are we heading for Puerto Cabello?" Aurora asked.

"Oh, I didn't see you there. We're on our way now, Countess," said Van der Hagen. "We'll get you there as soon as we can. Now, get some sleep. All of you." He continued to his chamber.

Aurora returned to her cabin. As she sat on the bed, feeling uneasy, she realized the moon was rising on the other side of the ship. They were not sailing for Puerto Cabello. The ship was sailing north, into the Caribbean Sea.

In the Eyes of the Beholder

Helena woke with a sense of foreboding, though she had no memory of what she had been dreaming. As the sun began to rise, she set out to explore a trail carved in the thick brush of Full Moon Bay. A cascade of bright green leaves framed a hidden waterfall. She followed it to a creek connecting to the ocean. A lizard ran up a tree in front of her. She approached it with her spyglass in one hand and her drawing materials in the other, when the small animal jumped and ran across a pile of rocks. She carefully followed, trying not to scare it away.

An eagle swooped down, just catching her hair before snatching the creature. Helena ducked, dropping her things. Something splashed into the water. The lizard had fallen, wounded and was struggling on the surface. She climbed down rocks to reach it, twisting her knee. "*Scheisse!*"

After regaining her balance, she waded into the water to retrieve the lizard. Its thigh was ripped open. "You and me both." A caiman splashed nearby.

I've had enough exploring for one day, she decided. Starting back, she felt something warm trickling down her leg. Her knee was bleeding. With the lizard cradled against her, she limped back to Don Medina's estate.

When she reached the gate, Dodo was calling her.

"I'm here. I went exploring."

"There you are." Dodo approached. "Don't go running off by yourself."

"Did you want to come with me?"

"No. Are you limping?"

"I had a battle with the local wildlife." She showed him the lizard, who latched on to the tip of her finger.

Dodo released a blood-curdling shriek, waving his fingers in the air.

Slaves came running.

"Let go!" Helena pried the creature off. "It's fine," she told the servants.

"Kill it," Dodo said. "Shoot it!"

"No, nobody shoots anything," Helena spoke firmly. "Everything is fine."

"Is it poisonous?" Dodo hid behind his easel.

"I hope not."

A slave girl informed her that the lizard was not dangerous.

"Help me inside," Helena said. "The thing is wounded, too."

Dodo followed at a safe distance.

Once inside, she placed the lizard in a jar while she cleaned up. She squeezed blood from her finger and then washed off her leg. After her knee was bound in cotton, she searched through her tools. A clock and a broken telescope lay on the table. She set them aside and grabbed some cotton bandages before opening the lizard's jar.

"What are you doing?" Dodo asked.

"I'm going to try to help this thing."

"Help it? It tried to eat you!"

"Oh, please, it's harmless. The girl said so."

Helena got to work, using a magnifying glass. She fashioned a tiny cotton bandage. After a few tries she managed to tie it onto the creature's leg. Next, she dumped out a vase and put rocks inside before depositing her patient. "You'll live or die, I suppose."

Scattered on the far side of the desk were pastel sketches of a kiln and glassier.

"There are my pastels." Dodo collected them. "You could ask, one day. I might even let you have them." He inspected the designs more closely. "A new kiln?"

"The don has an old bakehouse they don't use anymore, it's just for storage," said Helena. "I'm turning it into something I can use."

"What about Aragua? They're all waiting for us."

Helena went to her wash basin. "I might just stay. Ares can play in the yard right here. Aurora will send for you, and you can join her. I like Puerto Rico."

"With all this excitement, I need a drink." Dodo departed.

Helena put her tools away in the drawer of a desk she commandeered as a workstation. She covered her glass pieces with a chamois before joining Dodo in the courtyard, where several easels stood with canvases perched upon them. One was a landscape sketched in charcoal.

"It's a full moon tonight." Dodo stretched out on the chaise longue with a *sangaree* in his hand. "I have some time to waste before I paint."

Helena limped to a table decked out with fruit and bread.

"How's the knee?" Dodo swirled the dark liquid in the glass.

"Fine." Helena took a sprig of grapes and sat down in a padded wood chair.

"You're still posing, right?"

"Tonight?" Helena shook her head. "No, I'm not up to it."

The afternoon passed in a warm, relaxed haze and soon slaves set up the table for dinner. The blue sky ignited into pink and gold as the sunset illuminated the garden. The outdoor torches were lit, and the moon began to rise across the bay.

"See, this is why it's called Full Moon Bay." Dodo grabbed his brush. "You must pose!"

Helena stood and marched inside.

"You're leaving?" Dodo called after her.

She returned with a telescope and tripod.

"Beautiful idea!" Dodo waved his brush. "You can look through with some hip and thigh showing."

Helena set up beside him.

"You're too close."

"No, no me. You're painting that." Helena indicated the giant, glowing moon.

"The moon all by itself? What a waste! This could make you the next *Mona Lisa*."

Helena posed briefly, her hands clasped, giving a faint smile.

"Very nice," said Dodo.

She moved the telescope closer. "Now look through."

He did. "Oh, *wunderbar!*"

"Now, paint it."

"Just that?"

"*Ja*, that."

"Very well, but I'm keeping my trees."

"Just the moon."

"My painting, my trees." Dodo began to paint.

Helena gazed through the lens at the magnificent orb above. "I could certainly stay here."

Fama docked at the waterside of La Fortaleza, the executive mansion in San Juan, and Don Medina and Rivero disembarked. Guards escorted them up a winding stone path to a wrought-iron gate. Inside, they passed two circular towers on their way to an observatory, where an eight-foot telescope was aimed at the ocean.

"Why can't I have ships like that?" Governor Carlitos said.

"Don Medina sent for the *Holy Christ*," an aide said.

"A galleon?" Carlitos scoffed. "Outdated and lumbering. Fuck the *Holy Christ*."

Cardinal Grimaldi cleared his throat.

"I mean, as a ship, she's past her prime," Carlitos retracted. "But look at those guns. I'd very much like to acquire those for my El Morro."

"More obtainable than you think, Governor Carlitos," said the cardinal. "The Brandenburgs are not financially stable. I recommend keeping the German ships close for now. Who knows what possibilities might arise?"

Don Medina and Rivero admired a painting of Helena, posing in the nude.

"She is beautiful," Rivero said.

"She is. I owe you," said Don Medina.

They shared a smile.

"Captain Rivero," the cardinal acknowledged, "have you seen the Brandenburg fleet?"

"In 1680, I served the armada in battle against the buccaneers of Laurens de Graaf. We were joined by the Brandenburg fleet."

"A very famous battle it was—in the Yucatan." Carlitos scratched beneath his wide ruff collar. "The armada is poised to repeat the battle at Hispaniola."

Don Medina frowned. "Except, we lost in 1680."

"It was a tie," Rivero affirmed. "Both sides drew very heavy losses, and Laurens himself was wounded and expected to die."

"Except he didn't, and the buccaneers continue to ravage the Spanish Main," Don Medina tutted. "The deciding victory will be at Hispaniola."

"Too bad. I'd have preferred to see it happen here, with my new fortress, El Morro," said Carlitos. "No buccaneer raid would stand a chance."

Don Medina continued to admire the painting. "I have the countess; she is a guest at my estate."

"You have the decoy. Helena is nothing but a handmaiden." The cardinal waved to a monk, who brought out another painting. This one depicted a woman in fancy dress holding a bird.

"I've met the real Countess Aurora of Calenberg. You see the face is different. The eyes, the nose; the body, however, is that of the decoy."

"To further the disguise?" Carlitos asked.

"No, simply because the countess is self-conscious. She wants to see herself as being like the handmaiden."

Don Medina stared at the portrait of Helena. "The handmaiden is the decoy. And this is the handmaiden, you're sure of it?"

"Very sure," said the cardinal. "This was being sent as a gift to the acting governor of Jamaica. You have the decoy."

Don Medina gritted his teeth.

"The decoy is also wanted," Carlitos said. "There is a bounty. Bring her to me so that we may collect."

"She's to be tried as a witch back in Hanover. But she cannot go to trial," the cardinal added. "It's important she does not fall into the hands of the Germans. You must find the real countess first. The decoy and the painter must be killed, and their bodies never found."

"*De Heilige Graal* was sighted in Maracaibo," Carlitos said. "You, Rivero, are charged with sorting this out. Dispose of the decoy and find the real countess, pronto."

"The decoy is my responsibility," said Don Medina. "I'll deal with her. Rivero should go now."

"Yes sir, I shall collect my men at once."

"Make sure that painting is destroyed." Cardinal Grimaldi said, indicating Helena. "You can see her Venus mound; how disgusting."

Don Medina took the painting, careful not to damage it on the way out.

Off Puerto Rico sat the Brandenburg fleet, their great warships decorated with elaborate gilded carvings and yellow-tinted sails. The white, red and black Brandenburg flag was draped at the aft and atop the mainmast.

Einhorn, the last warship in line, was a slightly smaller design with a unicorn figurehead. It followed the grand flagship, *Kurprinz Von Brandenburg,* north of the Virgin Islands near San Juan.

Baron Maximillian von Gretsch stood next to Bohn on a swift ketch that pulled up alongside *Einhorn*. Gretsch paid the fisherman captain before climbing the ladder to his ship. Once aboard, Gretsch and Bohn were greeted by Captain Fuchs and the officers before entering the baron's cabin.

"Impressive ship," said Bohn. "You're in with the owner?"

"I am the owner," replied Gretsch.

"I should have known."

"Captain Bohn, welcome aboard my ship, *Einhorn*."

Bohn inspected the lavish quarters, from the intricately carved pillars to the smooth, polished rails.

Gretsch excused himself to his corner bed, where he cleaned up and put on a fresh black and white uniform that displayed his medallions.

Trays of food were brought in, and Bohn helped himself.

"I have a cabin for you," said Gretsch.

"Thank you, Baron, for your hospitality," Bohn said. "At least we know they don't have *De Heilige Graal* or the countess. I know you'll want to stop me, but I'm going to file an official protest on the taking of my ship and killing of my officer."

"Very well. I'll go ashore with the German delegates. Fuchs knows you. You'll have no trouble getting on board. Just don't forget the passcode."

"Which is?"

"He hasn't given it to you yet," Gretsch replied.

A messenger knocked at the door.

"What is it?" Gretsch asked.

"Prinz Maximilian is here in San Juan. He demands Baron Gretsch report to the executive mansion."

Crewmen from *Einhorn* rowed Gretsch and Bohn ashore. Bohn set off to the town, while Gretsch carried on towards La Fortaleza. A Brandenburg yacht also arrived nearby. Maximilian, in royal blue, and Count Molke, in shimmering red, were escorted by two ship captains and officials.

"Baron Gretsch, you failed to find *De Heilige Graal* or the countess," Maximilian began. "And lost Helena Braunschmidt. I don't know what Mother sees in you."

"Prinz Maximilian." Gretsch bowed. "I am at your service, my Prinz, as I am your mother's. I serve Calenberg. I had Helena but lost her. She's quite resilient."

Carlitos and his entourage entered, and Cardinal Grimaldi limped in as well.

"Welcome, our German guests." Carlitos smiled. "Prinz Maximilian, I am honored."

The main hall came alive with music. They sampled refreshments; then Carlitos led Maximilian to his table to speak privately, while Gretsch waited on the balcony. He examined the ships in the harbor. *Where is she?* he wondered. *Where do they have her?*

"Baron Gretsch," an officer called. Gretsch reported to the governor's table.

"I was told in St. Eustatius that you had both the countess and the ship in your possession. Now we only find a Dutch cargo ship," Maximilian snarled. "Where is Helena?"

"Our own Don Medina knows of her whereabouts," Carlitos bit his nails. "He is on his way now to apprehend her. And I have good news. *De Heilige Graal* has been seen. I have my fastest ships on the way right now. We'll have her shortly. In the meantime, the Brandenburg Navy can take their ease on Puerto Rico."

Some officers seemed happy to hear this, but Maximilian and Count Molke grew angry.

"We did not come here for rest. We, too, have fast ships. I'll send my own to collect her," said Maximilian. "Baron Gretsch will make up for this loss."

"I shall go to retrieve the handmaiden," said Gretsch.

"Leave now," Maximilian ordered. "And bring me Helena."

"She's under my charge, until Sophie says otherwise."

"I say otherwise, Baron Gretsch," Maximilian barked. "You'll go where I tell you or you'll go to your death."

Helena fitted a metal ring on the end of a telescope and snapped it into place. She smiled at her lizard as it climbed down the wall to see her. Its leg had healed nicely, and it climbed up her arm.

"Good morning, Lizard," Helena said.

She set the telescope next to other navigational equipment and a shiny brass astronomical compendium. Each instrument had been repaired and restored by her over the past two months, since her arrival in Full Moon Bay.

Dodo arrived with breakfast on a tray. "Sorry I'm late. It's hard to find good help around here."

"You're not late. You're just in time. I'm the one who's late."

"Late for what?"

"You know, late," Helena said.

"Is this a game? I don't get it."

Helena patted her belly.

"Oh, *that* late." Dodo caught on. "Still, that doesn't mean anything."

"No, it doesn't, but it could."

Dodo's face upturned as he cut mango slices.

The lizard ran out, snagging a mosquito.

Dodo shrieked, leaping onto the bed.

Helena rolled her eyes. "You don't like him."

"Well, he attacked me."

"He did, did he? He's harmless, I told you. And I meant our host, Don Medina. You disapprove of my relationship with him." Helena swiped a slice of mango.

"I didn't say that. He's wealthy."

"Yes, you did, the other night, and the night before last."

"That was due to *sangaree*; that doesn't count."

"Sure, it does."

"I just don't trust him. No one else has been on our side; why should he be?"

"That's it—you're jealous. You want him for yourself." Helena laughed as Dodo fidgeted with his sleeves.

"Come along, I need a model." Dodo regained his composure.

Helena followed him out of the room and into the courtyard, where a chair and easel were set up. Finished paintings sat in the shade to dry. Helena was striking a pose when Spanish soldiers arrived. She recognized Silvestre, clad in black with gold stripes, a pearl-handled sword hanging from the belt around his waist.

"Oh, hello. We're guests of Don Medina," Helena said.

"Of course you are, *señorita*." Silvestre bowed. "I saw his ship come around the point. He will be here shortly."

"He is?" Her face ignited, and she let her hair down.

Dodo gestured towards a new painting of Helena in Spanish attire, holding a rose.

"Beautiful." Silvestre flushed.

"She wanted to surprise him," said Dodo.

Helena went into the hall to observe herself in the mirror. She checked her hair and pushed up her breasts, and then patted her belly. "Oh, yes, I am."

Dodo caught up with her. "You look stunning."

The clop of hooves approached. She rushed to her chamber window, overlooking the estate and the harbor. Just up the coast, a German long galiot anchored. A figure clad in black disembarked, but she couldn't make out who.

Don Medina's carriage was almost there. She ran excitedly to the front gate to meet him, gliding down the steps and rushing to him with open arms. "Don Medina, I've missed you. I have a surprise for you."

Don Medina disembarked. "Indeed. So have I."

At first, Helena wasn't even aware of the blade that pierced her abdomen. First came a burning cold, then searing pain. She stared into his expressionless eyes.

Don Medina yanked out the blade.

Helena collapsed, her body trembling as she clutched her belly. She folded onto her side, bringing her knees up to her chest as she gasped, her chest heaving with sobs.

Dodo suddenly realized what had happened and leapt off the stairs into the garden and darted away.

"Your painter friend is quite the coward," Don Medina said, and then, turning to his men, "Track him down. He won't get far."

"Why?" Helena gasped. "Why?"

Silvestre and his men were surprised.

Helena writhed, her blood pooling on the ground.

"Sir, I protest," said Silvestre. "She was unarmed."

"All is well, Captain Soler," said Don Medina. "I have the matter in hand."

"What has she done?" Silvestre insisted. "Arrest her or finish her off. I won't stand for torturing a woman."

"What's the hurry? Let her bleed."

"Why?" Helena uttered.

"You think I'm going to have a simple handmaiden carry my son? You're nothing but a servant. The body will be sent back to Germany as proof." Don Medina hovered over her.

Helena couldn't move.

Don Medina raised his blade as if to stab her again.

A shot fired.

Don Medina was grazed.

Gretsch charged through the garden.

Silvestre and his men aimed their guns in defense.

"No," Don Medina said. "He is mine."

Don Medina took up a dueling stance with his rapier, while Gretsch drew his sword, much larger and heavier. Both brandished daggers as well as they traded jabs. Don Medina's superior skill and speed bestowed a wound in Gretsch's left shoulder, then another in the hip.

"If you serve the House of Hanover, Baron Gretsch, then you must surrender and face justice," said Don Medina.

Gretsch counter-attacked, the weight of his steel knocking Don Medina off-balance, but the don pushed back with both blades. Each strike wounded Gretsch, and his strength appeared to be waning as he made eye contact with Helena.

Gretsch faked a jab.

Don Medina stabbed him in the middle.

Gretsch pulled the don closer. The blade went deeper. Gretsch prevented the don from withdrawing his blade. There was a brief delay—just enough for Gretsch to smash the butt of his blade against Don Medina's head.

The don fell, his head hemorrhaging.

Gretsch staggered to Helena.

Silvestre readied his sword.

"No, I beg you," Gretsch said. "Don't kill her. Not her. Take me and let her live. She's a citizen of Calenberg."

Silvestre looked at Helena again before addressing his officer. "Go get a doctor."

Gretsch toppled over, reaching for her. Their fingers almost touched as Helena passed out.

Steady as She Goes

Aurora woke with tears streaming down her face. Her chest heaved and she sobbed. A faint knock came at the door.

"Countess?" Katrina came in. "Whatever is the matter?"

"Something happened to her. My Helena."

Katrina sat on the bed. "There, there, you had a bad dream."

Aurora buried her head against her.

De Heilige Graal's alarm bells and whistles chimed.

Katrina walked Aurora to the gallery, where the morning light poured in. Tiny gold flakes seemed to sit on the horizon while Aruba came into view.

Van Gelder was already on deck. "Break out the arms. Prepare for close-quarters combat!" he shouted. "Take her westerly with the wind and get her up to full speed."

"Surely you can get away at this distance?" asked Van der Hagen.

"She'll be on us in a few short hours. We'll have to hold them off any way we can. Once we're up to speed, I'll turn and take a shot. She'll be forced to change her course when facing a full broadside."

By evening, *Cheval Marin* had caught up with them. The crew were beginning to have minor accidents, crashing into each other. Aurora could only imagine how exhausted everyone was as she was on her third bottle of brandy.

"They're signaling!" de Britt said. "They're ordering us to surrender and prepare to be boarded."

"Never!" said Van der Hagen. "Do whatever you have to. We cannot fall into the hands of the French. Clear?"

"Clear," said van Gelder.

Aurora massaged her temples as Van der Hagen approached. "Will they catch us?"

"They might. Just in case, we need to hide you," said Van der Hagen.

"Hide me? I'm not getting into a box, if that's what you have in mind."

Van der Hagen guided her down to the grand cabin, where Katrina and Persephone huddled in the corner.

"Persephone says we're in danger," Katrina said.

"Danger? Well, no, well, maybe a little. Persephone says?" Van der Hagen questioned.

"She's a French frigate that has the wind," Persephone spoke brightly.

"Yeah, yeah, Persephone is right," Van der Hagen said. "We can't outrun the frigate."

"What should we do?" Katrina asked.

"Hide, all of you," Aurora said. "It's me they want."

"You can escape on a longboat by yourself," Katrina offered.

"We won't let them have you," said Persephone.

"If they board, they'll search the ship," Van der Hagen said.

"If they board, I'll give myself up," Aurora said.

"Do that, and we all die," Van der Hagen said. "Pirates don't keep prisoners anymore. Only nobility are worth anything."

"We have to make them think they've got the wrong ship," Persephone insisted.

"I'm afraid we played that hand," Aurora said.

"Then we should disguise you," Katrina said.

"I know," Persephone exclaimed. "How would you like to be a cabin boy?"

"A what?" Aurora frowned.

Orange light streamed through the grand cabin as the women sorted through a pile of common clothes. *De Heilige Graal* continued its escape, turning starboard, as in the distance *Cheval Marin* followed relentlessly.

"I can hide her bosom, but what about her big round bottom?" Katrina remarked.

"What big round bottom?" Aurora protested. "I'm big-boned."

"She's big all over," Persephone added. "We need something stiffer for bracing."

Cheval Marin now filled the entire window frame.

"Why aren't we sinking them?" Katrina asked.

"I told you, she's a frigate; they're too fast," Persephone said.

Katrina tried to work with Aurora's hair. "We should cut your hair."

"No, no and no!" Aurora said. "Leave the hair."

"We don't have time," Persephone said. "Tuck it into her shirt. They're going to catch us. Hurry up!"

"If they board, you girls stay behind me," Van der Hagen said. "You understand?"

"Yes, Father," both Persephone and Katrina said.

The ship ceased rocking.

Katrina and Persephone finished disguising Aurora, who now wore breeches, stockings, and a puffy gray shirt with a brown vest. Her hair was tied and tucked into her collar, while a kerchief covered the top of her head.

"Do I look as silly as I feel?" Aurora asked.

"You look like a cabin boy," Persephone said. "Well, sort of."

"She looks like a mad troll," Katrina remarked. "A fat, mad troll."

"Fat? Again, with the fat!" Aurora gritted her teeth.

"Girls, get your coats and scarves ready, just in case," said Van der Hagen.

Under the twinkling stars, Aurora and Van der Hagen joined van Gelder and de Britt at the wheelhouse. A lantern lit up a chart.

"Viscount, we've had a stroke of luck," van Gelder said. "On this chart, there's a reef ahead. *Cheval Marin* will have to go around the reef the other way. We will fire a broadside to ensure she does; then, once clear of the reef, unless the wind changes dramatically, we can get *De Heilige Graal* up to full speed. *Cheval Marin* will have to change course. If she follows to intercept, she'll go straight in, and wreck. Mr. de Britt, you're concerned about the reef."

"With all the evasive maneuvers, I cannot be certain we won't hit the reef ourselves."

"We have to risk it," said van Gelder.

"As you see fit, Captain," Van der Hagen said.

"Prepare to fire," de Britt said.

"We don't have enough time to reload the cannons, so we only get one shot at this," van Gelder said.

"They will be able to shoot back," de Britt said.

"And we should be up to full speed by the time they do," van Gelder replied.

As sunrise neared, *De Heilige Graal* turned hard to starboard, leaning. In the grand cabin, the women held on to whatever they could. Cannon fire reverberated through the ship.

Cheval Marin made a hard turn to port and dropped her anchor. Cheers erupted from *De Heilige Graal's* crew. The celebration was cut short by a broadside. Cannonballs splashed into the water, soaking the ship.

The moon was a giant golden orb by the time *Cheval Marin* appeared. The ship only a tiny flicker on the horizon. Aurora ventured on deck, where she was met by van Gelder and de Britt.

"We're well away now, Countess," said van Gelder. "Feel free to stretch your legs."

"I'm impressed. I hope I'm not disturbing you," she replied.

"Not at all, Countess."

"I was wondering if I could have a moment of your time, Captain."

"We're still on alert tonight, Countess," van Gelder said. "You'll need to stay inside, and no smoking."

"So much for luxury."

"Go on, sir. I can handle things up here," de Britt said.

Van Gelder excused himself and escorted Aurora inside.

"If the danger has passed, I'll be glad to change into ladies' clothes again," said Aurora.

They entered the dark captain's cabin. Van Gelder adjusted an oil lamp and the room glowed.

"You'll have to excuse me, I'm all wet." Van Gelder cleaned up at a wash basin.

"Aren't we all."

"I'll just change back here. Have a seat."

Aurora tried to untie her belts, but the knots were awkward.

"I have a night shirt you can have," Van Gelder said.

"Perhaps you could help me with these?"

He returned, shirtless, and fumbled with belt strings around her waist. "These are too tight; I should cut them."

"But the girls put so much work into it."

One of the knots gave and he loosened the belt, his hands on her hips. "How's that?"

"Yes, fine."

He went to reach for a shirt.

Aurora intentionally stumbled, grabbing at his manhood. "Oh, silly me." She rubbed him eagerly.

"Something on your mind?"

"Yes. I'm a countess, and I want it."

"I see." He latched the cabin door.

Aurora was already unfastening her trousers. They kissed and fondled each other. His cock was hard in her hand. Aurora's trousers were stuck, so he tore them. Once disrobed, he kissed her thighs, then lapped between her legs. She worked on getting her top open.

"I feel safe around you," she panted. "You won't let anything happen to me, will you?"

"Never."

As her breasts flopped out, his tongue glided upwards to her nipples.

"Take me."

He mounted her against the cabinet beside his bed and they undulated.

"Don't come inside me," she said.

"No, no. I won't," he gasped, thrusting so vigorously that the cabinet broke.

They moved to the desk, where Aurora thrust her legs in the air. "I blame the brandy. Fuck me!"

They writhed faster and harder. Aurora was close to climaxing when she saw shadows go by the window. The glass shattered and pirates flooded into the room.

Aurora shrieked.

Van Gelder reached for his weapon, but a pirate knocked him on the head with the butt of a sword.

Aurora leapt for the door, haphazardly tying her clothes back on.

Pirates pushed and prodded, blades drawn.

Screams came from Katrina and Persephone in the grand cabin.

Van Gelder came to, and pirates forced him and Aurora into the hallway. He managed to break free and ran for the sword hanging on his wall. The pirate with the cutlass shot him in the back.

"Nicholas!" Blood spatter ran down Aurora's face. She checked him, but he was dead.

They were all dragged on deck.

Van Gelder's body was dropped next to de Britt's.

Pirates kept Katrina at knifepoint, while Persephone was dragged kicking and screaming to the ship's rail.

Van der Hagen was forced to his knees, a sword aimed at his eye.

"Yer not the countess, but you're mine now." A pirate threw Holly to the ground.

"Stop that," said a pirate. "Let's all be friends, uh?"

Van der Hagen pulled Katrina to him.

"Papa!" Katrina said.

"Calm, dear," said Van der Hagen.

"See?" The pirate grinned. "Listen to him. All slaves below, and take the prisoners inside."

"This one stays with me, Barns." A pirate grabbed Katrina and played with her long, dark hair.

"No more dark-haired beauties, Ding Dong. She's going with the rest of them," Barns insisted. "You're going back to *Rascal*. You'll tow us to Guadeloupe."

Ding Dong and Barns stared each other down. Then Ding Dong pushed Katrina back to her father. Men dragged slaves, including Holly, away.

Persephone latched onto them. "She's mine, you bastard!"

"Look after your sister, Persephone." Holly was dragged downstairs.

Persephone collapsed to the deck, sobbing.

Aurora finished covering up with what was left of her shirt.

Barns pushed van Gelder's body down the steps to the main deck.

"The ship is ours," declared Ding Dong.

Persephone ventured forth, but Van der Hagen and others reached out to stop her.

"No! What are you doing?" Van der Hagen hissed.

"Go back!" Katrina waved.

Persephone tried not to look scared. "How do you do, sir? I'm Persephone Leanne Van der Hagen. I'm technically the owner of this vessel. I'm sure we can come to some sort of agreement."

"*You* own the ship? Well, that's fascinating, dear," Barns snorted. "You're not the German witch, though, are you?"

"A German witch?" Persephone continued. "Sorry, there's no witches here. No Germans, either. See, we were on our way to the magistrate's wedding on Curaçao."

"No Hanover treasure, I suppose?"

"No, sir."

"Your daughter?" Barns eyed Van der Hagen.

"I beg you," Van der Hagen pleaded.

"Over the side with her, Ding Dong," said Barns.

Ding Dong picked her up.

Katrina screamed, clawing at the air, but Ding Dong threw Persephone over.

"Persephone!" Van der Hagen reached down as she splashed into the sea.

Ding Dong caught Katrina in his arms next.

Persephone came up, treading water. She swam as hard as she could, but her dress slowed her, pulling her down. She panicked.

"Please sir, I beg you, you can have anything," Van der Hagen said.

"I'm the one you're looking for," said Aurora.

"I know you are, and this is for lying to me." Barns slammed the blunt end of his sword into Van der Hagen's head. He fell, blood streaming down his face. "Lying is not acceptable. You must be punished." He put a knife to Katrina's throat. "I'll cut this one and bring up the other."

"Please, you don't need to do this," Aurora said.

Below, Persephone tried to climb up the ladder, but pirates pushed her back down.

"Please don't hurt my girls," Van der Hagen said. "I'll do anything you ask."

"Where is the Hanover treasure?" Barns asked.

"On another ship."

"Wrong answer," said Barns.

"It's true," Aurora added.

"We'll search every corner of this ship," Barns said. "Full sail for Guadeloupe."

Crewmen and pirates ran to their stations.

"Bring her up," Aurora said.

"Help me, please," Persephone called.

Barns strolled to the starboard side, with Katrina and Van der Hagen following, pleading.

"Will you bring up my daughter, please?" Van der Hagen said. "I'll do what you say."

"I don't have the Hanover treasure," Barns said.

"Please bring her up," Van der Hagen said.

"You can have all our gold," Aurora said. "I can get you a huge ransom."

Barns motioned to his men, and pirates dragged Van der Hagen and Katrina away.

"No, don't do this," Van der Hagen protested.

"Persephone!" called Katrina.

In the water, Persephone clawed at the ship, screaming. She choked on water, scrambling to grab hold as the ship slipped away. "No! Please, no!" A wave pulled her under, and she bobbed back up. "Help me! Please!"

Rascal, with ropes attached, dragged *De Heilige Graal* behind. Pirates moved all prisoners to the lower decks, and the sails caught the wind.

"Raise the French flag," Barns ordered.

Aurora watched helplessly as Persephone struggled. Still clawing, still panicking, until eventually she disappeared below the sea's surface.

Battle of the Two Bills

Deep in the Caribbean Sea, *Amity* raced with the wind, heading southwest towards two ships. Lieutenant William Kidd stood on deck, peering through a telescope. He smiled and passed the instrument to Gilbert. *De Heilige Graal* and *Rascal* sailed north, off the port bow.

On the deck below, Tewsteps oversaw the loading of the cannons.

"East Indiaman, right where he said she'd be," Gilbert said.

"Aye, pay up, the lotta ya," Kidd said.

Gilbert handed over a coin. "'Tis frowned upon on ship."

"Laws never apply to those who write them." Kidd put the coin in his pocket.

"*Rascal* with her, coming out," said Gilbert.

"Double for finding them in open sea."

Gilbert indicated his empty pockets.

"Then ya have to earn it. We're taking *Rascal* back, too," said Kidd.

De Heilige Graal turned slowly to line up a shot.

Being faster, *Rascal* was ready.

"They're shooting," said Gilbert.

Rascal fired shots at *Amity.* The first just missed, and the second came after a short delay.

"She's revealed herself. *Rascal* is undermanned," said Kidd.

"They have barely enough to work the oars, says I."

"Aye, Gilbert. Let's get her."

The helmsman turned the wheel, and *Amity* moved towards *Rascal.*

"Hard over," Kidd said.

Amity turned portside as *De Heilige Graal* fired, missing.

Wind stalled *Amity's* speed.

"Hard to starboard, damn it!" Kidd hollered.

"She's becalmed!" cried Tewsteps.

The helmsman spun the wheel hard over, while men pulled the lines. *Amity* leaned, picking up speed.

De Heilige Graal fired a dozen scorching shots, obliterating the water just behind *Amity*. Kidd and Gilbert searched with their telescopes to find *Rascal*, but she was already rowing away against the wind.

"*Rascal's* leaving," said Gilbert.

"Go after her," said Kidd.

"*De Heilige Graal* will have another shot on us, now."

"Argh! Full on *De Heilige Graal*."

Amity gave chase.

Kidd and his crew readied their weapons as they closed in on the larger ship.

"Keep us from her guns," Kidd said.

"Wind change, nine knots, south, southwest!" replied Gilbert.

"Slow her down," Kidd insisted.

"Prepare to fire!"

"Thirty degrees starboard," Kidd continued.

"Thirty degrees starboard, aye," replied Tewsteps.

The helmsman spun the wheel. *Amity* turned to starboard.

"Fire," yelled Kidd.

Amity's chain shots tore through the sails of *De Heilige Graal*. Lines, rigging and men were cut to pieces in the masts.

"Ship ahoy!" Gilbert said.

Another ship caught Kidd's eye. "My winnings here to any man who can identify that warship yonder."

"'Tis *Cheval Marin*," said Gilbert. "The game's afoot. Now pay up."

"How do you know?"

"She's got a seahorse, all shimmering gold, there at the bow. That's *Cheval Marin,* says I. Means *Émerillon* and *Hazardeux* are close by."

"So, if ya knew all that, why didn't ya fill us in back there with ship ahoy?" Kidd asked.

"Wanted to see if you'd bet," Gilbert said.

"Sly, Gilbert, real sly," said Kidd. "We take *De Heilige Grail* now, or she'll never come again. Full speed ahead. Run her down."

Amity closed in on *De Heilige Graal,* while *Cheval Marin* also closed in.

"Ready to fire chain shot," said Tewsteps.

"Fire!" Kidd ordered.

Men torched the cannons. More chain-link balls spewed through *De Heilige Graal's* rigging. The top part of the mizzenmast broke, toppling over.

"She's turning to starboard," said Gilbert.

"More speed," Kidd said.

"They're ready to fire, Captain Kidd," Gilbert said.

"Thirty degrees port! Double quick!"

Amity turned, remaining behind *De Heilige Graal* as she leveled out.

De Heilige Graal fired. Cannonballs screamed towards *Amity*, soaring by.

Kidd stuck out his tongue. "Missed me, Billy!"

"Fuck you, Billy!" Barns shouted, watching helplessly as *Amity* turned at them again.

Men scrambled aboard *De Heilige Graal.*

"Ship ahoy!" a pirate called.

Cheval Marin approached.

A signal mirror was used to communicate between *De Heilige Graal* and *Cheval Marin.*

"You don't stand a chance, now," Barns chimed.

The wind changed. Kidd and his men felt it. In seconds, a gust propelled the ship forward. *De Heilige Graal* lost its momentum.

"We have her," said Gilbert.

Kidd and his men readied their weapons.

"Men, prepare to board," said Kidd.

"*Cheval Marin* will be on us," Gilbert said. "We can't take 'em both."

"We have the wind, now." Kidd bobbed his head. "Not a problem."

"Load the port batteries with round-shot," said Gilbert. "We may need to defend ourselves."

"Port batteries!" Tewsteps said. "Unload chains and prepare to reload with rounds!"

"Stay on course; take her aft," Kidd said.

Gilbert turned the wheel while crewmen rolled the cannons forward into firing position.

"Portside ready!" Tewsteps called.

Kidd trained his telescope ahead. "Don't take your eyes off the prize."

By nightfall, *Amity* zigzagged closer to *De Heilige Graal,* while *Cheval Marin* drew closer.

Kidd felt his chance slipping away again as *De Heilige Graal* moved faster.

"She's up to gaining speed," said Gilbert. "We're losing her again."

"Bloody Barns. I've had about enough of this shit." Kidd spat at the sea. "Take out her sails. Thirty degrees to starboard."

"Thirty degrees starboard."

Gilbert spun the wheel, and the ship leaned to port.

"Stop her cold; aim for the mainmast, Tewsteps," said Kidd. "All abreast."

"Port batteries prepare to fire," said Tewsteps.

They waited for the ship to level. Kidd raised his sword, and the port side came back up.

"Fire," Kidd ordered.

"No, wait," said Tewsteps.

Amity fired her cannons. Boom! Fiery cannonballs screamed straight at *De Heilige Graal.*

"Oh, shit." Kidd realized they'd overstepped the mark.

The pirates aboard the East Indiaman dove for cover as the shots blew holes in the ship. Windows exploded, debris flew and down came the cabin walls. Body parts and fires were scattered on deck.

"Argh!" Kidd reached for Tewsteps's throat and then clenched his fists. "What have ya done?"

"Just try and take me, Billy!" Barns hollered.

"Take her before the frigate gets here," Kidd said to Gilbert. "Go straight at her!"

Gilbert spun the wheel, and *Amity* came closer to *De Heilige Graal.*

"Tewsteps, take control," Kidd said.

"Boarding party!"

Kidd led pirates up the bow, where they deployed grappling hooks.

"Gunners to the ready!" Kidd said. "With me!"

They swung over into a shroud of smoke.

Kidd ran to the forecastle.

"Aft guns, fire!" Barns ordered.

De Heilige Graal's rear cannons fired. One of the three cannonballs smashed into *Amity*.

Barns and his pirates fired their guns.

Tewsteps instinctively fired back. Someone fell on deck.

"Hold your fire!" Kidd yelled.

"Back away, Billy, or I kill everyone," Barns said.

"Surrender, the lot of ya," Kidd demanded.

Barns and his remaining pirates dashed inside. Tewsteps managed to shoot one dead. The body landed next to a writhing cabin boy with a smoking backside.

"Put out the goddamn fires," Kidd screamed. "Somebody!"

Men rushed down the stairs to the gun deck.

The cabin boy tried to get up, but Kidd pushed him back down with his heel.

"They have hostages, but we have the ship," said Kidd. "Mr. Tew, put out the goddamn fires. We've got to hold off *Cheval Marin*."

"We have the ship. Stand down!" Gilbert said. "All hands on fire control!"

Slaves doused the flames, while *Amity's* crew passed buckets of water, edging forward with sand in front of them.

"Call Dr. Sober up here," Kidd said. "We need to tend the wounded."

Tewsteps dragged himself up the stairs to the main deck, gasping for fresh air.

"Bag the dead later, Tommy," said Kidd. "Make the ship battle-ready and leave the cabin boy."

"All fires out," said Tewsteps hoarsely. "Ship secure. Slaves below with Dutch crew out, pumping water."

"About bloody time. Barns has hostages inside," Kidd said. Gilbert joined them.

"How many dead?" Kidd asked.

"English casualties: nine dead, twenty-seven injured," said Gilbert. "Dutch crew casualties uncertain; at least fifty to sixty dead."

"Where's the countess?"

"They must have her inside," said Gilbert. "*Cheval Marin* will be on us within the hour."

The cabin boy crawled on his side. Kidd stood over him.

"The cabin boy doesn't have time for sitting, anyway, do ya, lad? Are ya Dutch?" Kidd asked. "Do ya speak English?"

There was no reply, only a groan. "Hold on, lad, you're still burning." Kidd wiped away blood and took out his knife. "This is gonna hurt."

He cut across the wound and dug his fingers into a hole on the upper left buttock. There was a scream as he fumbled with the wound. The shrapnel was stuck, but there was something else in the wound. He bent right down and pulled out a piece of smoldering fabric with his teeth and fingers. Kidd spat it out and tried the shrapnel again. This time it came out. He dropped the sizzling lead ball.

"Well, I got the lead out, but you sure as hell ain't a cabin boy."

"Thank you." She exhaled with relief.

"Yer the countess, ain't ya? Bleeding buggering hell."

Dr. Sober arrived on deck.

"Over here, Doc; I have a patient for you." Kidd sniffed the air. "Spill something on yourself this morning, Doctor?"

Dr. Sober coughed guiltily before examining the woman. "Nobody told me I was to be kidnapped by His Majesty's navy and thrown into a bloody war. Did you remove it?"

"Aye."

Dr. Sober pulled out more dirty fabric from the wound. He tried to turn her over, but she resisted. "Sorry, lad, I have to look."

The woman was turned, and the doctor pinned her down with his knee as he pulled down her breeches. He wiped away blood and his eyes bulged. "My god, it's gone, completely gone!"

The woman pulled the breeches back up to cover her femininity.

"You did graduate from this school of yers, didn't ya Doctor?" Kidd asked. "Congratulations, Mr. Tew, you shot the prize."

"Her wounds must be cleaned and dressed properly, or it'll fester, and she'll die," the doctor said.

"Captain Gilbert, take the doctor and the young countess to the infirmary in Charlietown, with my compliments to Governor Codrington," Kidd said. "I'll follow presently. Just do me a favor—give *Cheval Marin* a shot or two."

Kidd's men carried the countess on a makeshift hangmat to *Amity*.

Tewsteps shouted orders.

"You don't have the men for this, methinks, Kidd," Gilbert said.

"*Cheval Marin* don't know that, Gilbert. Tell Codrington to find his best bottle. He's opening it when I arrive. Godspeed, Captain Gilbert." Kidd puffed out his chest and swung over to *De Heilige Graal*.

Amity sailed away easterly, while *Cheval Marin* sailed towards them from the south.

The English flag was hoisted. With guns in his hands, Kidd went to the quarterdeck. "Hostages or not, I rename this ship the *Holy Grail* in the name of King William. Ready for battle."

Regarding the Incident at Fort Charles

South of Puerto Rico, miles from anywhere, the man of war *HMS Relentless* bounded through the waves beneath a blanket of stars and rolling clouds. James Fishhook, first officer to Captain Longstaff, read a book by lantern light while sipping a glass of port in the officer's quarters. He had just turned a page when Mr. Cook entered.

"She's maintaining speed; it's commendable," said Fishhook.

"Lucky wind, but then, Big Dick always had lucky wind," Cook said.

"You wanted to speak to me in private?" Fishhook lowered his book. "Something I can help you with, Mr. Cook?"

"Sir, it's my duty to inform you of a possible murder involving the captain, which took place in Port Royal."

"I heard. A strumpet fell from the tower at Fort Charles. I've known Dick a long time. He's notorious for mishandling women, but murder? She probably fell. Who reported it?"

"Jim, I saw the body. The young lady was your friend, Miss Spotswood from Nevis."

Fishhook spilled his drink before setting it down. His head lowered.

"It was reported to me by two men, one an officer, the other a midshipman, that Dick threw her to her death after being intimate," Cook continued. "I intend to give testimony that men under my watch did witness our captain bring the young lady to the top of the tower from which she fell. And, that it is my belief he intentionally dispatched her."

"I can't believe it." Fishhook's voice cracked. "You need proof before you can make an accusation like that. Do these men intend to testify?"

"They reported it to me as an act of murder. I had no choice but to enter it into the log. I know she was friends with your wife. You were also close with her."

"Aye, very close."

"Indeed, you had feelings for Miss Spotswood?"

"I suppose I had. I loved her, and now you say she was murdered by a man who led us through hell and saved our lives—yours and mine—on more than one occasion. Dick's my best friend." Fishhook's hands fidgeted, exhaling heavily.

"Jim, he murdered a girl. I can't abide that. Not even from Dick."

"When do you plan on making these accusations?"

"I will notify the local magistrate wherever we make landfall. Back in Port Royal, perhaps."

"Let's hope," remarked Fishhook.

"Do I have your support?"

"If an officer makes a legitimate charge against our captain for something like murder of an innocent girl, then we must report it."

"I know. Give me a moment with my grief," said Fishhook. "We'll continue this conversation when we make landfall. Make sure the men say nothing of this, to no one, not while we're at sea. Thank you, Mr. Cook."

"Aye." Cook departed.

Fishhook bit his lip hard and pounded his fist against the wall. "Selina."

Unable to sleep or sit still, Fishhook crept out on deck. The air was cool against his skin, and he took deep breaths of salty air. Below on the quarterdeck, Cook issued orders to Rogers and Kyle for the watch change. Rogers flipped the hourglass, and thunder rumbled from afar.

Fishhook took out his telescope and scanned ahead. There was more rumbling, and seconds later, Longstaff came out, sliding on his jacket. Lights flickered on the horizon.

"A ship battle, dead ahead," said Fishhook, keeping his distance from the captain.

"Maintain course and speed," said Longstaff. "Let's check it out."

Near dawn, all eyes watched intently as the ships in the distance grew larger, smoking heavily.

"*Cheval Marin* and a Dutch East Indiaman under English colors—Gentlemen, I give you *The Holy Grail,*" said Longstaff.

"Two smaller ships, a sloop, and a small galley to the east, leaving in a hurry," said Cook.

"*Cheval Marin* will have the prize before we get there. Burn oil, throw black smoke, drag weight, make her think *Relentless* is not up to the challenge. She'll disengage and come after us."

Soon, black smoke billowed from *Relentless*, and she turned at half-sail, lumbering. The officers on deck rejoiced as the plan worked. *Cheval Marin* moved away from *De Heilige Graal* and gave chase.

"I'm certain *Cheval Marin* is on an intercept course, Captain," said Fishhook flatly.

"Thought you'd be more pleased, Jim," said Longstaff. "That's your ship out there."

Rogers spoke with a crewman, looking confused.

"A question, Mr. Rogers?" said Cook.

"Aye, sir. I'm at a loss as to why the captain was certain the French would deviate?"

"*Relentless* was French-built. We took her in nearby waters a few years ago," explained Cook. "The French want to take the ship at all costs to reclaim her. If *Cheval Marin* thinks we're undermanned and running away, she'll make the mistake of coming after us."

"Right you are, Mr. Cook," Longstaff spoke from the deck above. "Prepare to attack."

Relentless turned swiftly, charging at the French ship under full sail. A strong crosswind on the aft quarter aided the attack, and they gained distance before *Cheval Marin* realized what was happening. *Relentless* turned hard to port, firing a broadside. Cannonballs streaked through the sky, soaring over the French vessel.

Cheval Marin fired her secondary guns and a broadside. Two of the shots hit *Relentless,* causing minor damage. A splinter cut Longstaff's cheek, infuriating him.

The French ship kept turning to line up a shot with her port side. She slowed, turning into the wind. *Relentless* was faster. The French couldn't turn in time, and *Relentless* crashed into *Cheval Marin*, locking on with grappling hooks.

Men immediately crossed the bowsprits, while others swung across from the forecastle.

Fishhook led the first wave of nearly fifty men aboard *Cheval Marin*, while Rodney led twenty marines with muskets as the second wave.

Longstaff, with a cutlass in his right hand and a pistol in the other, charged, ready to do battle with the French captain.

They arrived on the French ship under fire. Fishhook raised his sword, charging up the stairs to the quarterdeck. Shots were exchanged.

"Fire!" ordered Rodney.

English marines fired their muskets, killing most of the French officers. The French captain and his crew attacked ferociously to recapture the quarterdeck.

"Take the quarterdeck!" ordered Longstaff.

"Bayonets!" said Rodney.

The main deck was seized. Longstaff and the French captain met for a final showdown. Their swords clashed and jabbed. Longstaff knocked the French captain off-balance and took the opportunity to run him through the ribs. The French captain dropped dead on deck.

"The ship is ours!" declared Fishhook.

"The ship is yours, Jim," said Longstaff. "Captain Fishhook, take charge."

"Aye, sir."

"Mr. Cook, you're my new first officer," said Longstaff. "Come with me. We still have *De Heilige Graal* to contend with. Three cheers for Captain Fishhook, men!"

The men cheered three times: "Huzzah, huzzah, huzzah!"

"What name you the ship, Captain?"

"*Sea Horse* is a fine name," said Fishhook.

The men chanted, "*Sea Horse, Sea Horse.*"

Longstaff, Cook and others returned to *HMS Relentless*, leaving Fishhook aboard his new vessel. He ventured to the poop deck. Overwhelmed, he kept his face covered as a tear streamed down his cheek. His dream of having his own ship came true, but at what cost? He always pictured that Selina would be with there with him when he made captain.

Aboard *De Heilige Graal*, Lieutenant William Kidd observed the approaching *HMS Relentless* and *Cheval Marin* through his telescope. An officer ran up the stairs to meet him. "Barns wants to parley."

"Does he, now?" Kidd replied. "He don't know what I know."

Kidd ventured down to an entranceway that billowed with smoke. Barns stood just inside, holding a knife to a girl's throat.

"Are ya done yet, Billy, or do ya need a bit longer?" Kidd said.

"I have the ship, Billy, not you," said Barns. "I'll kill them all, starting with this lovely creature here, if you don't get off my deck!"

"Yer deck? Have a look out there, Barns, that's *Relentless* with one of yer pretty frigates. Those are English flags waving. You know Big Dick, don't ya?"

Barns went to the gallery to see for himself.

"You got nowhere to go," Kidd said. "I have the countess."

"Bullshit."

"Bullshit?" Kidd laughed. "Where'd ya lose the cabin boy, Billy?"

"The cabin boy?" Barns pulled the girl's hair. "Fuck! But I got more where that came from."

"Give yerself up."

"I'm getting out of here," said Barns. "This girl and her family are coming with me. Lower the longboats. We'll leave and you can hold off Big Dick."

"The boats are right there, waiting. Be my guest, Billy," said Kidd.

Sailing master Cook watched *De Heilige Graal* through his telescope. "You won't believe this," Cook said to Longstaff. "Kidd has the ship, and Barns has hostages."

"What's Kidd doing?" Longstaff said.

"He's allowing Barns to escape with hostages to longboats."

"He knows better than to trust Barns. This is Kidd we're talking about." Longstaff folded his arms. "Rodney, your best shots up front."

Rodney and his marines took up positions on the forecastle of *Relentless* with their bayonets.

As they drew closer, Barns could clearly be seen with Lord Van der Hagen and his daughter Katrina, being forced down to the longboats.

"Now, Rodney," said Longstaff.

Rodney's marines fired, killing several pirates. Barns was hit in the arm and lost his grip on Katrina, who ran back to her father. They both dove for cover.

Aboard *Relentless*, men readied their weapons before launching grappling hooks.

"Mr. Cook, with me," Longstaff said. "Boarding party to *De Heilige Graal*. Take control of the ship and find the countess. With me, men."

Longstaff swung over.

Marines took aim and fired again.

"Mr. Rogers, take the poop deck," said Cook before swinging over.

Longstaff and his men found themselves cut off, surrounded by pirates. Rodney's marines fired again, picking off the pirates one by one.

Barns tried to escape.

"Where are ya going, Billy?" Kidd goaded, capturing him at knifepoint.

"We have *De Heilige Graal*!" called Cook.

Kidd presented Barns to Longstaff.

"Well, who'd have thought I'd see you again like this, Barns?" began Longstaff.

"Dick."

"I'm going to leave ya somewhere very far from anything this time, Billy," Kidd said.

"Where is the countess, Captain Kidd?" Longstaff asked.

"She's perfectly fine. Well, not perfectly; she was wounded. Captain Gilbert aboard *HMS Amity* is presently taking her to the infirmary on Nevis."

"Governor Codrington will be pleased." Longstaff gritted his teeth. "Take me to Viscount Van der Hagen."

Kidd led Longstaff, Cook and the officers inside, where they found Van der Hagen consoling a bloodied and bruised Katrina.

"Viscount Van der Hagen, and your lovely daughter, Katrina." Longstaff opened his jacket. "I'm afraid your ship is in ruins, sir. Let me show you both to my ship, where you'll be my guests. You're safe, dear," he told Katrina.

"This is my flagship, and she's seaworthy," replied Van der Hagen. "Thank you for your hospitality, but we're remaining on board."

"I must insist. I'm forced to impound your ship and deliver it to Governor Codrington in Nevis while we sort this all out."

"We will remain on my ship," Van der Hagen asserted.

"If your daughter doesn't mind choking on smoke, by all means, stay aboard."

An officer spoke with Cook, who then relayed the information. "Captain, we just received word that a French fleet is off Puerto Rico, heading for San Juan."

"The Capitaine and his buccaneers?" Longstaff said.

"No, sir. Ships of the line."

"Viscount, I bid you farewell. My dear." Longstaff bowed to Katrina. "Captain Kidd, I must return to *HMS Relentless* and proceed to San Juan. Proceed to Nevis."

"I'll need men," said Kidd. "They're a tad short on this ship."

"Too short. The viscount hasn't a single officer left," said Longstaff. "Mr. Cook and some men will be left in your charge. When you reach Nevis, have Barns and the rest of the prisoners interned. Go over every inch of this ship and don't let anyone out of your sight until you've searched everyone and everything. And keep the countess safe. Don't let anything happen to her."

"Aye, sir. Am I to remain on *Relentless*?" Cook asked.

"Collect your log and report back here, on the double. You'll serve Captain Kidd as first officer. You'll have enough men with you."

"That'll leave you quite undermanned as well, Captain Longstaff," said Kidd.

"We'll make do. Godspeed, Captain Kidd."

Longstaff and Cook returned to *Relentless*.

Cook collected his personal effects and gathered the men he needed, including Rogers and Kyle.

By evening they were sailing aboard *De Heilige Graal*. Rogers kept watch on deck while Cook inspected the ship for damage and took inventory.

"There's a brig out there," said Rogers. "She seems to be waiting."

"Could be a smuggler," replied Cook. "Dutch colors. Keep an eye on her; could be pirates. Be on the lookout for *HMS Rascal,* too; she's a red galiot. We know she was taken by pirates."

"Something else is strange."

"What's that, Mr. Rogers?"

"*Relentless*. She has a red light at her stern."

Cook aimed his telescope. *Relentless* sailed away in the distance. There was in fact a red light glowing in the captain's cabin. "Well, I'll be. And she's not turning around."

"What does it mean?" asked Rogers.

"I think it's a signal, but to who?" Cook pondered this while he and Kidd checked on Van der Hagen and his daughter.

"Damage control is done. We'll have these windows sealed up shortly. I'm Captain Kidd, and I'll treat you well." Kidd received no reply and returned to the quarterdeck, with Cook following. "Ungrateful bloody Dutch barbarians!"

"They've been through a lot," Cook said.

"They have, have they? Try having yer crew mutiny on ya—now, that's a rough day. Are we ready to sail yet, Mr. Cook?"

"Aye, Captain Kidd. Set sail for Nevis."

"Where the remainder of my prize awaits. They can't deny me now. This ship is my prize, and so is the countess. If that doesn't warrant a commission, nothin' will."

"This ship?" Cook questioned.

"Hell no. *HMS Assistance* recently lost her captain. God rest his soul; it's only right I be the logical replacement."

The sails unfurled.

"She's under full sail now, barely five knots," Rogers said.

"We can do better," said Cook.

"Aye, do better, Mr. Cook," Kidd pressed. "Get her up to speed."

By the time they reached west of the Aves Islands, *De Heilige Graal* was up to speed, heading northwest.

Inside the captain's cabin, supper was set up. Cook stood at the portside window, watching a brig lumbering in the darkness.

Kyle was busy eating stew when Rogers entered and sat down at the table.

"Captain Kidd?" Cook asked.

"On his way. He's finishing up the gun deck inspection," said Rogers. "I stopped in to check on the Dutch owners, but they won't be joining us."

"How is she?" asked Kyle.

"Thirty-six cannons operational. I'd say that's impressive," Rogers said. "We're already up to seven knots."

"I meant the girl, the pretty Dutch girl," Kyle added.

"Stay away from them. This is their ship, and everything we do will be scrutinized," said Cook. "This is not Captain Kidd's prize ship. This is a rescue mission, simply an errand."

"Hope ya didn't wait on my account." Kidd emerged in the doorway. "You didn't even wait, ya no good fancy-boy prats! It may be an errand, Mr. Cook, but you and yer silver-spoon-licking adolescents better show proper respect, or yer not eating again till we reach Nevis."

"Aye, sir," said Cook.

They each apologized, talking over each other. Eventually all was forgiven, and they returned to supper.

"Is the brig still shadowing us, Mr. Cook?" Kidd asked.

"Aye. Damn suspicious," Cook said.

"So, how is it Big Dick came to choose you to be my first officer?" Kidd asked. "What made you his choice? Luck of the draw, perhaps. You served with Dick a long time; I saw you in 1680 under the comet."

"I wasn't on board in 1680," said Rogers. "Can you tell us what happened?"

"1680 was a mean year of sea battles, which saw the annihilation of the Spanish Armada at the hands of Laurens de Graaf's buccaneers. Privateers aplenty. English, Dutch, Spanish corsairs, German mercenaries, and even the Brandenburg fleet, all brought to fight the buccaneers of Hispaniola." Kidd paused for a mouthful of wine.

"All the while the great comet filled the sky. No one knew if it meant the death of us all, and, one by one, in every battle Laurens came out victorious. The admiral of the armada up and died on the deck of his ship in the Yucatán. Mr. Cook and I saw battle together twice that year, off Roatán, and not too far from here, off San Juan and the Mona Passage."

"Aye. *Relentless* and Captain Longstaff were both put out of action in that fight. We limped into Port Royal with half the men we left with," said Cook. "And a few personal tragedies along the way as well."

"Maybe this is Dick's way of thanking you for your loyal service," Kidd remarked and then continued his story.

Cook's attention was elsewhere. A creeping sensation pricked the back of neck. As if a flood of cold water filled his limbs, he gasped. His logbook—it had been sitting open in the officer's quarters at the incident at Fort Charles, with the names of the two witnesses, Mr. Rogers and Mr. Kyle. He could still see the faint red light glowing from *Relentless* as they sailed off.

"Are ya listening, Mr. Cook?" Kidd queried. "Food not to your liking?"

Cook staggered to his feet to look out the gallery window.

"Mr. Cook?" Kidd asked.

The brig was closer on a parallel course.

"The brig—it's not a Dutch smuggler," Cook said. "I've seen that ship before. It's *La Lune de Miel*."

Kidd choked on his supper. "As in Capitaine le Sage?"

"The red light, Mr. Rogers, means no quarter," Cook said.

"You didn't by any chance have a falling out with Big Dick, did you, Mr. Cook?" Kidd gave a nervous laugh.

"Uh," Cook couldn't get words out.

"Oh, ya fuckin' did," Kidd exclaimed. "Oh Christ, what have we got going here?"

"We, uh, saw Captain Longstaff murder a girl," Kyle said.

"'Tis true, and she was related to the Spotswoods," Cook said.

"Why the fuck does this always happen to me?" Kidd hit the table with his fist. "Call battle stations!"

The officers scrambled out the door, collecting their hats and coats along the way.

"What the fuck did I ever do to yew, God!" Kidd looked skywards.

La Lune edged closer.

"Bloody goddamn fuckin' nut sucker, this always bleeding happens to me!" Kidd waved his fists.

Cook ran up to the poop deck. Deep colors played along the horizon as the pirate brig closed in. *HMS Relentless* was only a speck now, heading north. "You've finally shown your true colors, Dick," said Cook.

Around midnight aboard *La Lune*, Silent Sam doused a parrot in soot, attempting to make him look like the Capitaine's broad-billed parrot. The bird made a coughing sound. "Bring up the barrels," Sam ordered. With him was Fish and Chips, and Master Half-Lovely, formerly Master Lovely until the left side of his face melted from a powder burn.

"*Surreptitious* is behind her," said Montbars.

Sam peered through his telescope. "There's my baby, right on time. Full sail and full speed. Twenty degrees to starboard."

The helmsman turned the wheel, and men pulled lines.

"Look friendly, men. We're happy Dutch traders, remember. Everyone look friendly." Sam paused on Half-Lovely. "Not you. You look aft. Just keep a lookout to aft. The rest of you, smile and look happy. Happy, happy, happy!"

The pirates laid low, smiling, looking happy.

"A signal," said Half-Lovely.

"Saw it with yer good eye, did ya? Look that way!" Sam pointed. "Monty?"

"They're asking for identification," Montbars said.

"We're Dutch. What does he want to see, blond pubes? Tell him we're carrying Strangewayes Brand Coca-Leaf, and what's he gonna do about it? Tell him that."

Montbars shook his head.

"I'll tell him that," said Sam.

Montbars used a signal lamp at *De Heilige Graal*.

The men sniggered.

"Shh!" Sam hushed, fitting a wig on his head. "We're a Dutch trading ship." Sam readied a whip and flogged Spike. "Make it look real."

"Feels real to me," Spike said.

"They know something's up," said Montbars.

Sam grinned. "But they don't know what."

"I see movement on the gun deck," Montbars said. "They're loading cannons."

"Too late for them, anyway. Give 'em hell!"

La Lune turned, sailing straight at *De Heilige Graal*, with *Surreptitious* following close behind.

Sam ordered chanting and a drumbeat before taking the wheel. Like the Capitaine, he now had silver hair and a wide-brimmed hat.

Montbars loaded a cannon at the bow.

"Raise our true colors, Mr. Half-Lovely!" said Sam.

"So, that's yer flag or the Capitaine's?"

"Capitaine's! Stay in character. And stay ahead of her. One broadside from her and we're holier than thou."

The black flag was raised.

Bird Island

Captain Kidd stood on the top deck of *De Heilige Graal*, while the crew paced. *La Lune* drew menacingly near.

"Muskets to the ready," said Rogers.

"I am le pirate Capitaine!" a pirate declared with a fake French accent through a speaking trumpet. "Surrender or die, *Anglais* pig!"

Cook and Rogers shared a perplexed look.

"That's not the Capitaine; it's Silent Sam," said Cook.

"Silent Sam?" Kidd scoffed. "Sammy the fucking Seal? He owes me money."

On *La Lune*, Montbars rotated the swivel cannon, angling it higher, taking careful aim.

"You shall not take this ship, Seele," Cook called. "You're nothing but a no-good pirate."

"Aye, don't hold back, Mr. Cook," Kidd said.

Montbars fired a cannon. The cannonball slammed into Cook. His body flew off the deck, split in two. The head and right arm seemed to hover for a moment before dropping into the sea.

"Cook?" Kidd swallowed hard, searching for remnants. "I'm not bloody losing this ship to Sammy the fucking Seal. Let him have it!"

"Fire at will," said Rogers.

A handful of crew manned the cannons, firing one, then running to the next. Other men fired muskets. *Surreptitious* arrived at the aft, while *La Lune* slammed into the starboard side. Pirates boarded *De Heilige Graal* from both ships. They were outnumbered and surrounded.

Kidd ran out of shots and tossed his last gun. He retreated down to the cabins as pirates swarmed the quarterdeck.

Mr. Rogers was shot in the chest and fell down the stairs.

Kidd rushed to the grand cabin, where Mr. Kyle's hands trembled, clutching a pistol. Kidd was nearly shot upon entry. "They're coming," Kidd said. "Seele's pirates have the ship."

Kyle moved to protect Katrina, while Van der Hagen staggered to his feet.

"They won't take my Katrina." Van der Hagen readied his sword. "I'll die first."

Barns was there, silently waiting. The door burst open. Silent Sam, Montbars and others sauntered in. They noticed Katrina.

"Have no fear, Sammy's here. I bring treats and joy for all, my dear. I accept your surrender, by the way. Is that Captain Kidd?" Sam gave an exaggerated sniff. "Aye, laddie, smells like Captain Kidd."

"Sam Seele. You haven't changed a bit," Kidd said. "Still a bottom feeder scrounging for leftovers from Big Dick. And where's the ten doubloons ya owe me since Campeche?"

"Me and Big Dick go hand in hand, so to speak." Sam grinned. "He's soon to be admiral of the West Indies fleet, and he's gonna make me captain of a warship. A man o'war."

"A man o'shit. You'll never command nothin' more than a pirate brig; you're a hull-sucking barnacle. You'll be buggered by Dick in the gibbet while it's still swinging." Kidd spat. "Your body lice have a better chance of gettin' a commission than yew do!"

"If you're begging for your life, Kidd, yer doing a terrible job. As it is, Dick's no longer involved in this venture. Tell me where the countess and gold are, or watch Monty play with the little girl here."

"You'll have to go through us first." Mr. Kyle blocked them, alongside Van der Hagen.

"Don't look at me, lads. Chivalry's dead," said Kidd.

Fish and Chips knocked down Van der Hagen, while Montbars stabbed Kyle. Montbars then raised a knife to Katrina. "Beauty is in the eyes of the beholder."

"They took her to Charlestown," Van der Hagen uttered weakly.

"Is that true?" said Sam.

"They took her to a *doctor* in Charlestown," said Van der Hagen. "She was wounded. Now, please let my daughter go."

"He's telling the truth, Seele," Barns said. "They took her to Nevis."

"Look what I have to deal with. Now I must go to Charlestown and get her. That means delays and hassles. You lot cause me nothing but problems." Sam shook his head. "You head straight for Crab Island," he told Montbars. "We'll catch up. This thing must get moving if we're gonna make it in time. Continue repairs on the way. Bring the hostages for now—well, the ones that are worth something."

"What about Kidd?" Montbars asked.

Sam pointed to the deck. "Look Kidd, a penny—go get it!"

"Maroon him," said Barns. "We'll be passing Aves Islands shortly. Bird Island is especially nice."

"Bird Island, eh? You like birds, Kidd?" Sam chided. "I'm assuming Bird Island has birds."

"Not always. Bird Island is only above the sea for four or five hours a day," said Barns.

"That's fascinating." A maniacal grin spread across Sam's face. "I'd like to see Bird Island. Monty, can we swing by Bird Island?"

At sundown, *De Heilige Graal* and *La Lune* dropped anchor off a shallow, barren island. A longboat was lowered. Barns and Sam, alongside a dozen men, escorted Kidd.

"So, this is the famous spot where Big Dick won his prize, *Relentless*," Sam said. "So, which one's Bird Island?"

Barns indicated a small mound protruding from the water.

"Can he swim to one of those other islands? I mean, they're close and there might be food on one of them."

"Not a chance," Barns said. "The current here will have him out in the middle of the Caribbean, and there is nothing he can do about it."

"It's not too late to work out a deal," said Kidd.

"Nay. Stranding a man on a desert island is one of the all-time favorite pirate tortures. It's like watching your second cousin give birth to your twins; it's like seeing your first-born son kill his first kitty cat." Sam gave a satisfied exhale. "It's a special moment. I only wish I could wait a while. We wanted to place bets on how long you can swim, but, to tell ya the truth, I don't give a shit. I hate Scots. I'd like ta eradicate the lot a ya," he said, doing his best Scottish accent. "Over he goes, Mr. Barns."

"We'll leave ya one shot, as per the code, Billy."

The longboat returned to *De Heilige Graal*.

"I'll get the lot a ya, ya kelp-sucking plague sores! I'll hunt ya down and chop ya to bits like the lubberworted, saddle-goosed bunch of low-life scum that yeh are!" Kidd yelled. "Bugger ye all to hell!"

HMS Assistance docked at Charleston in Nevis. Next to it sat *HMS Amity*. The dock glowed beneath lantern light as Gilbert, Dr. Sober and Tewsteps escorted the countess Aurora to a wherryman's carriage. They crossed beyond the city wall, up the street to the infirmary, where English officers escorted them inside. Wounded men lay on cots, some badly burned. Tewsteps nodded to Gilbert, indicating a man wrapped in bandages. Fokman, *Rascal's* pilot, lay asleep.

They took Aurora to the next room, where she lay on her stomach, partially covered with a blanket.

Dr. Sober and Gilbert cleaned the wound, while Tewsteps checked on Fokman, returning shortly.

"How's Fokman?" asked Gilbert.

"Not well," said Tewsteps. "How's she?"

"Better," said Dr. Sober. "Let's give it another rinse."

"No," Aurora protested. "Have you nothing for pain?"

Gilbert put a bone between her teeth. "Last one."

Dr. Sober poured a bottle of liquid on the wound, and it bubbled. She shook violently. Gilbert took the bone out and wiped her sweat and tears with a handkerchief.

"We'll let you rest a bit, dear," said the doctor.

"Undertaker!" Aurora huffed.

Gilbert and Dr. Sober went into the hallway, each taking a lantern, leaving the room dark.

"Tell me, Mr. Gilbert, does she look like a witch to you?" asked the doctor.

"Not my place to say, says I. Captain Kidd will take charge upon his arrival. I be getting back to *De Heilige Graal*."

"Well, take a good look at her. You'll remember her for the rest of your life if you hand her over to them."

"Who's *them*, Doc?" Gilbert asked.

"Whigs. The Whigs want her. She cannot fall into the hands of Longstaff or Codrington. You've got to get her out of here. Tell Kidd they want her out of the way so she can never marry into the Stewarts. That would give the Jacobites a legitimate heir."

"Yer splitting me head, Doc; take it up with Kidd," replied Gilbert.

"By then it'll be too late."

Tewsteps rushed by the open door.

"Where you going, Tommy?" asked Gilbert.

Tewsteps paused, mid-stride. "*De Heilige Graal* changed course. She's heading east for Guadeloupe or Dominica."

Gilbert wondered what Kidd had got himself into now. "Can you manage from here, Doc? Keep her here until we get back. Come on, Tommy."

Dr. Sober gave a noncommittal shrug.

When Gilbert and Tewsteps arrived at the dock, Governor Codrington and General Thornhill waited next to a carriage.

"I say, Kidd?" Governor Codrington called.

"'Tis Gilbert, sir. The countess be at the infirmary. Captain Kidd commands *De Heilige Graal* out there, now fighting the French. We're on our way to assist."

"I wonder what happened," said Thornhill.

"Kidd left in charge, that's what happened." Codrington's eyes narrowed. "You can't trust pirates."

Gilbert and Tewsteps boarded *HMS Amity*, while Governor Codrington and Thornhill remained, speaking with marines and officers.

"Have two marines guard the doors to the infirmary," ordered Thornhill.

There was a flash and a boom to the north. Gunfire erupted. An explosion came from the docks just up the island.

"What's this?" Codrington huffed. "Surely not the French?"

Aides and guards scrambled. Lady Codrington stuck her head out of the carriage. "What is it?"

"I don't know. Perhaps you should stay inside," said Codrington.

"The island is under attack," said Thornhill.

"I don't see any ships," said Codrington.

"It could be an Indian attack or freebooters from St. Kitts, in retaliation," said Thornhill.

A huge explosion from the docks nearby blew them back a step.

"Goddamn Indians," said Codrington.

Explosions came from *Assistance* and *Amity*. Gilbert and Tewsteps helped to get the fires under control. Broken glass scattered on the deck. Gilbert broke away from the heat and went to the rail for several deep breaths.

"Gilbert, what's happening?" asked Thornhill. "What the hell is going on?"

"Bottle bombs, sir. They attacked and fled."

"Search the area. They can't be far, bloody Indians. Maybe Kidd turned French on us," Thornhill speculated.

"If Kidd turned French and stole it all for himself, he'll hang, with only himself to blame," said Codrington. "His harebrained schemes are for the birds."

Meanwhile, on Bird Island, Lieutenant William Kidd sat on a small, moonlit beach, with the tide rising all around him. A pelican perched on a nearby rock, staring at him. "What are ya lookin' at, ya stupid fuckin' pelican!"

Long-Haul Bay

La Lune sat anchored behind the dilapidated fort towers of Long-Haul Bay in Nevis. The sky was deep blue with hints of gold; the perfect light to begin the prowl. Silent Sam followed Barns to the edge of the dock, where they crouched behind a cart.

"Inside the wall, past the barracks," said Barns. "The ammunition stores are in there, too."

"When I'm ruler of the Caribbean, I shall give you Nevis," said Sam.

A wherryman's carriage sat nearby, with no sign of a driver. Sam signalled his men and they boarded.

"Viva la Saint-Domingue!" Sam was driving towards the town when another carriage approached. "Shit! Quick, look English!"

They looked around inconspicuously as a carriage full of English militiamen passed.

"I like kippers," said Sturgeon.

"Blimey, kippers are tasty!" Sam agreed.

The militiamen passed by.

"We're lost? How did we get lost?" Sam searched around. "How do ya get lost on Nevis? It's the smallest fucking island in the Caribbean!"

Sturgeon glanced at a man repairing a fence.

"What do we do?" Spike said. "Ask him for directions?"

The carriage pulled up. Sam and his men attempted to rearrange their clothes to appear more English.

"Pardon me, kind sir," Sam began. "Can you help us?"

"What with?" replied the carpenter.

"We're in need of a doctor. Can you point out the hospital?"

Sturgeon groaned.

"What's wrong with him?" asked the carpenter.

"Why do you ask?"

"Is it plague? If so, he needs to be quarantined."

"It's the clap, for Christ's sake," said Sam. "He just needs medical attention."

"If it's a serious wound, the infirmary is up at the fort. Or if it's medicine you need, there's an apothecary in town."

"Much obliged. Aye, aye. Drive on, driver." There was no response, so Sam kicked Spike, who snapped the reins, and the carriage lurched forward.

"Cheery-bye!" Sam waved.

As they neared the infirmary entrance, Sam and his men split up. The two marine guards at the door turned their heads when a whistle sounded. Half-Lovely appeared out of a passageway on one side, with Spike on the other. The pirates grabbed the officers from behind, covered their mouths and stabbed the backs of their heads.

Sam strolled casually through the entrance as the bodies were dragged away.

Inside, the doctor was storing tools as his patients rested on cots. He took a swig from a bottle before heading to the door. Half-Lovely grabbed him, while Sam approached holding a bloodstained knife.

"Oh, lord," said the doctor.

"Yer too kind." Sam licked his fingertips and pushed his hair to one side.

The doctor looked for an escape route.

Spike blocked the only path.

"Help!" the doctor called. "Pirates!"

"We are helping," said Sam.

The doctor put up his hands. "Don't kill me. I'm a doctor."

"Pleased to make yer acquaintance, Doctor." Sam hit him with the butt end of his sword, knocking the doctor down. "Now, where is the German countess? Here, Countess, Countess!"

There was movement behind a curtain.

"Who's in there, a parrot?" Sam opened the curtain. "Hello? Witchy witch?"

The countess rose, covering herself with a blanket.

"Hello, my lovely. Who might you be? Speaken ze frowline?" Sam mocked.

The countess grabbed a bedpan and smashed his head with it.

Sam stumbled backwards, tripping over his own feet so that he hit the floor with a thud. One of Sam's men tried to grab the countess but was shot. Fokman, with bandaged fingers, fumbled for his second pistol, but Spike shot him through the head.

"Shit." Sam massaged his head, then felt something warm running from his nose. He realized he was covered in his own blood. The countess threw the bedpan at him, but he managed to deflect it before it slammed into his head again. *The bitch*, Sam thought.

Spike apprehended her with brutal force, knocking her down and yanking her hair.

Sam staggered to his feet, staring daggers at her. "You're gonna wish you hadn't done that."

"What do you want from me?" she challenged. "Tell me."

Sam knocked her to the floor with his fist. "Consider yerself told, Countess. Bring her and the doctor."

Sam and his men ventured to the Charlestown docks, where Ding Dong was busy lighting a rag stuffed into a bottle of spirits. Fish and Chips were doing the same on the other side of the dock. Soon there were explosions, and *Assistance* erupted into flames.

"Now, there's a diversion, if I say so myself." Sam enjoyed the panic as crewmen scrambled for buckets of water.

After he'd collected his men, they continued along the road to Long-Haul Bay. *La Lune* came into view. The carriage stopped at the dock and everyone got out. Sam jabbed the tip of his cutlass into the doctor's back.

"No, please, I'm a doctor."

Sam jabbed the cutlass in again.

"Don't kill him, I beg you," said the countess.

"You Germans have no character," Sam said. "That's the worst begging I've ever seen." He stabbed the doctor again.

"Ugh! Please stop!" the doctor gasped.

"No talking!" Sam jabbed him again. "I hate it when it does that. A runaway cutlass, what can I say?"

The doctor released a panicked sob. "Don't kill me."

Sam stabbed in again, deeper. "I said, no crying."

"Don't!" Aurora insisted. "Stop!"

"Don't stop?" Sam put his hand to his ear. "She has a dark side. I like it!" The cutlass jabbed in again, and the doctor dropped to the ground. Sam was about to go for the doctor again, but Aurora tugged the doctor to his feet and pushed him along.

At the pier, Sturgeon ran up the gangway to *La Lune*, while Spike led the countess on board. She bolted, trying to escape, but came face to face with Half-Lovely. The countess shrieked as she was seized.

"She screamed again, Doc," said Sam.

Sam stabbed the doctor through the gut with his cutlass.

The doctor let out a high-pitched squeal as he staggered to the gangway. He clutched his side and fell into the water. The countess attacked Sam, clawing at his face. In retaliation, Sam slammed his sword handle into her head. He caught her as she fell, struggling to get her aboard.

"She's well-fed, I'll give 'er that," Sam said. "Just a scratch. See, Barns, ya just gotta treat women right, that's all. A few nice words and a bouquet of flowers, now and then, and a good knock on the head to say, 'I'm thinkin' of you.'"

Sam drew his pistol and aimed it at Barns. His men did the same. "Thank you for yer service, Mr. Barns."

Barns dove into the water, skirting the shots.

Wisdom of Wounds

The sun beamed down upon the Brandenburg fleet, just off San Juan. Prinz Maximilian stood on the deck of *Kurprinz* in full blue steel armor, beaming through the smoke like a beacon. French ships fired at El Morro, while English vessels approached.

"The French line is testing San Juan's defenses," said Rear Admiral Reers, his mustache curling from the sea air. "Many ships, including a man of war and a frigate under an English flag. Our ships are ready to deploy. Something they're aware of as they're maintaining a safe distance to the north."

"Engage the enemy," said Maximilian.

The captain shouted orders, and the battle flags were raised. The fleet sailed towards the French line. The rules of battle were no different for Maximilian, only the terrain. He had never commanded at sea before, but his mother's treachery had forced him to the Caribbean.

Maximilian had fought in the Alps and in the field, even along the coastline, but naval warfare proved more complicated. Aboard, his officers seemed cowardly. Fed up with excuses, he wanted to charge the enemy head-on. All day and night, ships traded shots, traveling the sea north of San Juan.

Two hits struck the Prinz's flagship, and bodies dropped.

"Order all ships to attack," Maximilian said.

"They're out of range again, my Prinz," said the captain. "The French ships have speed, but their guns are no match for ours. I suspect they will retreat. Shall we give chase into the night?"

"The lead French ship is indicating another pass. They're turning to engage," an officer replied.

"You were saying?" Reers said to the captain.

A German officer came aboard, proceeding to the command deck. "Prinz Maximilian, Baron Gretsch has been located. He has the handmaiden, Helena Braunschmidt."

"It's about time," said Maximilian. "Where are they?"

"Aboard *Einhorn*. Both are wounded."

A thin smile formed on Maximilian's lips. "Wounded?"

"Yes, sir, critically," said the officer. "Gretsch is charged with killing the Spanish nobleman Don Medina, on the other side of the island."

"Gretsch killed Don Medina?" Reers said. "There goes our sponsor. Gretsch has caused a disaster."

"I will interrogate them myself. Turn the ship back to San Juan immediately, Admiral," Maximilian ordered.

"The French guns still lie between us."

"Then engage the French head-on," said Maximilian.

Admiral Reers and the captain gave orders. Everyone came to life as men rushed to their stations.

"Inform Count Molke that Helena Braunschmidt is wounded aboard *Einhorn*," Maximilian ordered an officer. "I'm sure he'll have some questions of his own." He wandered to the railing; the battle played out on the horizon. "Cardinal Grimaldi may burn her as a witch after all."

Helena woke to the rumble of a distant battle. She massaged her eyes, uncertain of her surroundings. Full Moon Bay was no more; that future was dead. She rose gingerly. The wound to her abdomen was deep. Helena staggered through her door, which went right by Gretsch's private chamber aboard *Einhorn*. She paused at a bookshelf.

Gretsch approached her. At first, she jumped, then they instinctively reached for each other, before she withdrew. Both felt the sting of their wounds, and they leaned on opposite sides of the hull. Helena felt his eyes invading her, but somehow this was comforting.

"If you are wondering what all the noise is, my ship is guarding San Juan from the French. *Einhorn* is too small to play with the big dogs." Gretsch paused. "I'm glad to see you're well."

"And you. I'm looking for a book to read. I haven't much to do."

"You may like these. They're imaginative." He almost cracked a smile, passing her a few books from the shelf. "Turns out, I've been looking for these books for a year. I never thought to look here. I hardly ever go to sea. I'll leave you to it."

He headed back inside his cabin.

"Thank you." Helena went to her bed. She lay down, staring at the book, unable to read. She closed her eyes and was off to sleep.

It was nighttime when she woke. The room glowed by lantern light. Heavy footsteps approached. Fuchs reported to Gretsch. She couldn't hear their conversation, so she ambled to the doorway.

Fuchs departed and Gretsch appeared.

"Bad news?" Helena asked.

"Little Venice, the port in Lake Maracaibo, was destroyed."

"Are there survivors?"

"There are no reported survivors, sorry. The Spanish say no one lived."

Helena's jaw vibrated.

Gretsch reached for her. She heaved a painful sob and covered her face. The instinct to run seized her, but her injuries wouldn't permit it. Instead, she limped her way back to bed to weep.

Twisted, broken bodies lay under a blanket of smoke and fire. Van Gelder fought off pirates when Barns aimed his pistol and fired. Blood splattered Aurora's face, and then she was hit. The shot burned her backside like a hot dagger. She could hear Sam laughing wickedly.

"Aurora?" said a female voice. "Can you hear me?"

Aurora's eyes opened, and her temple throbbed. She was in her chambers aboard *De Heilige Graal,* wearing a night dress. Someone patted her forehead with a damp cloth. It was Persephone's nanny, Holly.

"Lie still. You got hit on the head," said Holly.

"I got hit everywhere. I feel sick."

Holly reached for a bucket off the floor.

Aurora held the cloth on her head. "How long was I out?"

"You've been in and out since they brought you on board two days ago."

Aurora blinked slowly. "Two days?"

"They bet on whether or not you'd live," said Holly.

"What were the odds?"

"The pirates fought among themselves. Some threatened to kill others if you died."

"Where's Katrina and Van der Hagen?"

"Viscount Van der Hagen's locked up below. They told me to look after you. They said if you die, I die."

"Well, I'll try to live." Aurora peered out the window. "Where's Katrina?"

"They keep her in the captain's cabin," said Holly.

"Do you know her condition?"

There was a pause. "I hear her screams at night."

"They're raping her."

Holly nodded.

"This has gone on long enough." Aurora sat up, the room spinning. "I'll talk to these pirates. They understand money."

"You're not allowed out."

"Or they'll shoot me, or hit me in the head? What more can they do to me? Come on. Let's get Katrina out of there." Aurora saw fresh blood on Holly's back, from being whipped. "Right, you stay here." She grabbed Van der Hagen's walking stick and went out the door, pausing to let a wave of nausea pass. When she stepped out on deck, some crewmen cheered, while others sneered.

"Well, look who's up. It's payday! Sorry about the head, Countess," Sam said. "You were hysterical. You know how women can be. No ill will?"

Aurora gripped the rail, her hands trembling, and she ventured up the stairs.

"What audacity. She can even climb stairs. You win a prize. What does she win, Monty?" said Sam.

Montbars waited for her at the top of the stairs and mimed unfastening his trousers.

"Did you violate Katrina?"

"Me? Of course not," Sam said. "How could you suggest such a thing? Monty did, didn't you, Monty? And the rest of the men too. All but Steeltoad, and I got my eye on him."

"Let her go now, please."

"We call her Kitty. The men like to play a game we call Here, Kitty, Kitty. Sometimes she gets a real kick out of it."

Pain prevented Aurora from going up any further. "For Katrina, I'll pay you whatever you want."

"Word gets around, don't it?" Sam said. "I haven't had my turn yet. A captain's supposed to go first! Shows ya what kinda crew I got, but they'll have to wait their turn for you. Go on in and make yerself at home. I'll be in presently."

Aurora went inside the captain's cabin.

Katrina lay on her side, clutching her knees to her chest. A fresh collection of bruises covered her face, and bite marks swelled on her neck.

"Katrina?" Aurora said softly and sat next to her.

At first Katrina fought her off, disoriented, staring blankly. Aurora tried to be comforting.

"It all starts to look the same, you know," Katrina uttered dryly. "I look in any direction, and I can see her out there. I can still hear her calling me for help."

"I'll get you out of here."

"Persephone, too?" Tears rolled down Katrina's cheeks.

Sam walked in. "Here Kitty, Kitty."

Katrina trembled.

"What do you get when you turn me in?" asked Aurora.

"A free clock. Now, back to bed, Countess. You been up too long, and it's time for your nap, and it's time for me to pet the kitty."

Outside came the crack of a whip.

"You disgust me!" Aurora scowled.

Sam shrugged. "She was told not to let you out. What kind of captain would I be if Monty didn't punish bad behaviour?"

"I have treasure," Aurora said. "I can get all you want."

"That's why we're here." Sam rubbed his hands. "Viscount Van-Cry-Baby's not going to get us the ransom we need to pay all these men. We're all counting on you, Countess. You're the prize. We don't want nothin' to happen to the prize. Now, you go on to bed with Fish and Chips, while I keep Kitty company."

"Don't do this to her, please."

Fish and Chips took Aurora out the door while Sam slinked over to Katrina. He opened a cabinet. Aurora glanced back, seeing a pair of stilettos inside. Sam grabbed his pipe, a pouch of tobacco and a tincture before closing the cabinet.

"Now, we don't want to upset the neighbors this time, do we?" Sam said. "Monty says yer quite the screamer."

Sam gave Katrina the bottle to drink and she poured it all down her throat.

"There, feeling better?"

"I want to kill you so bad," Katrina uttered.

"That's my girl."

Fish and Chips took Aurora to her chamber, pushing her forward. She felt dizzy and nearly tripped through the door.

When evening arrived, Aurora was escorted to the captain's cabin. Sam sucked on his clay pipe as Holly set the table and slaves carried in a roast pig. Van der Hagen sat at the table, dried blood down the side of his head, sick and silent. Montbars brought in Katrina. She was barely conscious as she was propped in a chair. Her head lolled to one side.

"Ah, the guest of honor, Kitty, my own countess," Sam said. "And the court jester over here." He indicated Van der Hagen. "Cheer up, Zonny. Katrina fancies me; she don't admit it, but it's true. As luck would have it, I need all of ya in here. Bring us more wine—oh, and Cognac for the countess."

Holly was slow to respond, so pirates grabbed her and dragged her out the door.

"Good help is hard to find," Sam snorted. "Soon we'll be at San Juan. We hear it's a real war zone up there, and you being so popular, we're being followed by more than a dozen ships. Almost time to shed some ballast."

"What do you mean?" asked Aurora.

"I mean, eat up. You never know when it's yer last meal. Make the most of it." Sam ate swiftly, but nobody else touched the food. "What is this? Come on, Countess, you never missed a dinner in your life. Why all the sad faces?"

"Do you ever see the faces of the people you hurt and kill staring at you when you try to sleep at night?" Aurora asked.

"You just cursed me, didn't you?" Sam said. "Good for you."

"Maybe you'll see me burning to death in your dreams."

"Oh, I do. But they crush witches now. It's the latest thing."

"Or, crush me to death. I've seen that. Have you ever seen eyes popping out of someone's head? I have." Aurora's voice dropped a notch. "I'm going to haunt you for the rest of your life. I am a witch, after all. You never know what surprises I may have in store for you."

"Since you're not eating, won't you join me on deck for a show?" Sam scraped his chair and stood.

His men forced all of them up and out on deck.

Sam ran upstairs to speak with Montbars.

"Are you sure about this?" Montbars asked. "If there are ships ahead, we'll be surrounded."

"Just you watch where yer going and send *La Lune* ahead to take a look."

"Slasher Al's old ship, *Bloody Mary,* and Tom Jones's *Cymru* to the northeast." Montbars indicated.

"Bring out the wench," said Sam.

"*La Lune* will go out ahead. Steady as she goes. Remain on course," said Montbars.

A red-haired woman was brought up from the lower decks.

"Meet another guest of honor: Atia, or, my personal preference, Racy Red," Sam presented. "Yer on a royal galleon now. The Countess Aurora of Calenberg is on board. Be on yer best behavior."

"Ya brought me up here to meet the countess?" Atia replied.

"That's your friends joining the party out there. What did you name Al's sloop? *Whisker Scratches*?"

"*Whiskey Kisses*, in honor of Captain Valentine."

"Art? How is the old stick bug? He's got you wiping tables and pirating on the side? You'd think the wife of a famous pirate would be doing better for herself."

"Lord Admiral Seele," Fish began, "the enemy ships are out of sight."

"We have a little surprise lined up for you folks." Sam waved to his men. "Look here! All right, men, we have too many mouths to feed. Every one of ya, pick a darkie and make 'em walk the plank!"

Pirates ushered terrified slaves and crewmen on deck. Fish and Chips dragged out Holly.

"Over the side with them," said Sam.

One slave was pushed over and splashed into the sea. Pirates forced the rest over the side and shot at slaves who latched onto a rope and clung to the side of the ship.

"Why are you doing this?" Van der Hagen asked.

"Too many mouths to feed. Your countess does tend to eat a lot," said Sam.

"Captain, please no!" Aurora said.

"Captain? Have you no respect? I'm admiral now. You rich Borgias have no respect for those of us who work for a living!" Sam grabbed Holly and threw her over the side. She hit the ratlines, falling face first on a rat-board, unconscious. Sam used a walking stick to push her into the water.

"You bastard!" Katrina broke free, attacking Sam.

Aurora joined in, and they managed to knock him down before Montbars and others restrained them.

Sam rose, red-faced. "That won't happen again. Take the prisoners inside. Get them out of my sight!"

They were all hauled away.

"Fish, you and Chips go pick up the Capitaine," said Sam. "It's time he joined the party."

Whiskey Kisses

Miles Gladstone clung to the mast of *Whiskey Kisses*, feeding rope to Grymes, who reworked the lines. The wind picked up, and he clung harder. Zoe worked above, stitching the sails. From this height, Gladstone thought he could see *De Heilige Graal* sailing east to San Juan.

"Stop, it's ripping!" Grymes said.

"Where's zit ripping?" asked Zoe.

"From the clew iron."

"It needs another mainsail. It must be fixed."

"That's the last of the cloth," said Gladstone. "Unless you want us to start undressing."

"I will if you will," Zoe offered.

"How many men are sewing?" asked Grymes.

"Five. Well, four and one woman," said Gladstone.

"Christ, take it down," ordered Grymes. "Them ships are getting away."

"It's her," the lookout called. "The redhead. And it looks like they're throwing something over the side."

"Atia?" Gladstone scrambled for his telescope. A red-haired woman frantically waved. "It is *De Heilige Graal*."

"How can you tell from 'ere?" asked Zoe.

"She's got fire damage, and I can see *La Lune* in pursuit," said Gladstone. "I think we have found *De Heilige Graal* after all. And there's Major Paine's *Rascal*. Follow that ship!"

"Well?" Grymes indicated the sail.

"Right! Fix the mainsail, and then follow that ship."

When the sun sank on the horizon, the sky lit up orange and purple. *Whiskey Kisses,* with *Cymru* following, chased the flotilla of ships following *De Heilige Graal* through a chain of islands.

Gladstone hid at the bow, smoking his pipe. His shoulders relaxed and he took a deep breath.

"Help us!" came faint cries.

"Did you hear that?" Gladstone said.

Crewmen glanced around.

"What's up at the bow?" Grymes said.

"It's just us," Gladstone replied.

The plea for help came again.

"And someone else," Gladstone added.

"What's going on up there?" Jones said.

Zoe came out of the forecastle, smoking a clay pipe.

"Hey, no smoking on deck," Gladstone said.

Zoe shook her head. "I heard someone calling for 'elp."

"Dead ahead," Grymes said. "Someone's in the water."

"How many?" Gladstone asked the lookout.

"Say about ten."

"Maybe Atia and others jumped over?"

"All darkies," said the lookout.

"All what?" Gladstone said.

"Slaves or Indians."

"We can't stop," said Grymes. "We gotta get up to speed."

"Prepare to stop," said Jones. "Man overboard!"

Crewmen rushed around, getting the ship ready to stop and rescue the people in the water ahead.

"All stop. Prepare to drop anchor! Ready the boats," ordered Jones.

"You're making a mistake," said Grymes.

Crewmen raced to the rowboats.

Jones grabbed a lantern and leaned out. "There, Miles, directly ahead."

Gladstone checked with his telescope.

"They were thrown over to slow us down," said Grymes.

"All the same, prepare to take them aboard," said Jones.

"It could be a pirate trick."

"We'll be quick," said Gladstone. "It may be Ekene or Fatima."

"Deploy the boats and search for survivors," said Jones.

Heads bobbed on the water's surface, and soon they were hauled into the boat.

"They have wounded. Mr. Gladstone, prepare the forward compartment for triage," said Jones.

Gladstone and Zoe rushed inside. Zoe wiped down the crew table, while Gladstone sorted through the medical supplies. Thankfully there were items from the apothecary in Port Royal. Strangewayes Brand Laudanum, Strangewayes Brand Dwale and Strangewayes Extra Sleep Formula. "Good thing Atia didn't know this was here." Gladstone slid a tincture of Strangewayes Bliss Formula into his pocket.

When Gladstone ventured back on deck, a woman was passed aboard.

"Anyone we know?" Jones asked.

"I don't think so," said Gladstone.

"You are a doctor, can you 'elp her?" asked Zoe.

"You're a doctor?" Grymes said.

"Well, sort of. I do doctorly things," said Gladstone. "Let's get her inside."

They delivered her to the triage.

"You must have seen wounds like this on the battlefield?" Zoe patted Gladstone's back.

"Battlefield?" Grymes stared at Gladstone.

"Aye, Strangewayes plantation was a hell of a battle."

"That's on Jamaica?" Grymes asked.

"Aye, and Port Royal—now, that was a battle."

"That it was, Miles," Jones agreed. "Now, we both set bones before. What would Doc Strangewayes do?"

"He'd get his face covered in coca-leaf powder. You're going to be all right," Gladstone said to the woman. "Do you understand? Squeeze my hand for yes."

She squeezed his hand.

It was after dawn, and Gladstone's tired red eyes couldn't focus any more. He fastened the last of the bandages around his patient's head and jaw. The woman was now asleep.

"You really are a doctor," said Zoe.

"Aye, that's right. She's my patient now."

"Can she breathe?"

"Yes." Gladstone freezed, thinking he forgot something. "Of course, she can breathe." He adjusted the fabric.

"How will she eat?"

"With some difficulty. Someone's going to have to chew her food for now. We'll let her sleep—and me, too."

"Aye, get some rest, Miles," said Jones. "You earned it. Now, let's go get Atia. Mr. Grymes, follow my lead."

"Aye," said Grymes.

"Clear out now," Gladstone insisted. "Let our patient rest."

Jones and Grymes departed.

Gladstone and Zoe lay down together on a cot.

"How will you change the bandage?" Zoe asked.

"I haven't figured that out yet." Gladstone yawned.

The patient woke, groaning. Gladstone took her hand. Tears ran down her cheeks. Something in the sky, however, caught Gladstone's attention. "Excuse me a moment." He took the telescope from his vest hanging on the cabin door.

"What tis zit Miles?" Zoe said.

"A bird." Gladstone went up on deck. "There's a bird, and not just any bird. The Capitaine's broad-biller! He's following Atia."

"The dark broad-biller?" Jones looked.

Minuit zoomed towards an island, disappearing behind palm trees.

"It's a black bird. It could be any black bird," Grymes said.

"That bird is one of a kind," Gladstone asserted. "I'd know him anywhere. It's Minuit. I'd bet on it."

"That bird follows our Atia like Marc Anthony after Cleopatra's twat," Jones said. "It's called a Broad Billed Parrot, and probably the last of its kind. It's on the trail of Atia."

Gladstone whistled and tried various bird calls, with no results. Then Jones and Grymes chimed in. Nothing.

Zoe whistled and shouted in French. "Hey you, pretty bird, over 'ere."

Minuit changed course. He swooped around and landed near Zoe and nibbled at her dress.

"He is 'itting me on."

"Well, you said he was pretty," said Gladstone.

"He's got a message." Jones took the parchment from Minuit's leg bracelet. "It's from the Capitaine. He's on Crab Island."

"I'm not going to abandon Red," Grymes said.

"Capitaine won't abandon her," Gladstone said.

"We don't have to," Jones added. "He wants her to wait for him in San Juan. Full on for San Juan, Mr. Grymes."

"Aye, to San Juan," Grymes agreed.

Cymru and *Whiskey Kisses* adjusted their course to sail towards the island of Puerto Rico.

Fatima watched anxiously from inside the ship as Caesar stood at his command post. *Barbarossa I* kept a steady beat, rowing into San Juan Bay. Its flag indicated a slave galley bringing slaves to the city. This tactic was Caesar's plan, not welcomed by his officers. Pirates had met briefly in a Puerto Rican cove to discuss the plan of attack.

Fatima had not been invited to the meeting but heard Caesar arguing with the agha and the raïs upon their return. *Barbarossa I* would reach San Juan first. Under the guise of a slave galley, they would be given priority to land near the fortress El Morro. Caesar also knew the Spanish code system. The Spanish would say the name of a saint and the code response would be the place of canonization.

Pirate ships paused at the bay entrance, while *Barbarossa I* continued beyond the fortress wall. The plan was to blow up the ammunition storage, thus disabling the fort's ability to fire its guns. Then the pirate ships could enter freely.

Fatima was confined to the captain's cabin but continued to watch. Caesar seemed panicked as they approached El Morro. The Spanish didn't call for the code as expected. Instead, the Spanish called for the ship to stop and be searched.

Caesar ordered the attack and the slaves rowed hard for El Morro. Gunfire erupted. Caesar swung off the ship by rope alone, with two sacks of bombs.

"What the hell is he doing?" Fatima raced on deck.

"Get back inside," demanded the raïs.

"What is he doing?" she demanded back.

"Committing suicide," the raïs said. "This cannot succeed. He went alone. We must abandon this attempt."

The raïs went to the command post, but the agha beat him to it. They argued, shouting conflicting orders to the men. *Barbarossa I* scraped along the fortress wall.

The Spanish fired guns and threw bombs. A curtain of smoke filled the air, and the slaves rowed. The ship began to pull away from the chaos.

"Caesar is blocked," said the agha. "He can't reach the fort."

"He'll be killed," replied the raïs.

"There's nothing we can do. We must protect the ship and leave. Caesar dropped the bombs on the causeway and ran. He's pinned down and can't reach them."

Hands grabbed Fatima from behind. "What's going on?" she asked Ekene.

"Now's our chance—let's go."

"Go where?"

"Caesar is trapped. They can't get him back. Now's our chance to leave."

"No, I'm not leaving. Where would we go, Ekene?" Fatima looked to the smoky shoreline. "Caesar!" She climbed down the side of the ship to the causeway. "Where are they?" Scanning the ground, she followed the barnacle- and weed-covered stonework. Finding nothing, she looked to the water side of the causeway. She hopped down to a lower level and skirted over missing stones until she found a sack with four bombs in it.

Fatima climbed back up and vanished into the smoke. When she found the ammunition storage, Caesar was readying his swords. She climbed up to where he crouched, seemingly praying.

"Fatima! What are you doing here?"

She handed him the satchel of bombs.

"Are the men ready?" he asked.

"The men are cowards."

"Did you bring a light?"

Fatima stared at him in disbelief.

"I jest." Caesar smiled at her. "I have a light." He brought out a burning wick and lit the bombs.

Oars splashed in the water below.

They threw the bombs into the ammunition shed, then dived into the water. The impact shattered the stonework into hundreds of pieces. Burning debris rained down.

Fatima clung to Caesar as he swam them to the ship. Once aboard, he rushed to the command deck.

"Full speed into the harbor," ordered the agha, and slaves again rowed hard.

The fort fired a couple of cannons, both missing the ship. The explosion drew the pirates in, just as Caesar had planned. Soon the harbor swarmed with pirate ships, and *Barbarossa I* was out of harm's way.

"French warships have drawn the German ships far enough from the harbor. We can enter and join the assault on the capital," said the raïs.

"We will have the rest of the fortress by nightfall," declared Caesar. "Fatima, go inside. Tonight, we attack the city. We win or die."

Fatima cursed under her breath as she went to her spot in the captain's cabin. "You're welcome." She peeled off her wet clothes and cleaned up.

Caesar soon entered, slamming the door.

Her heart raced with excitement as he opened her curtain. Fatima stood there naked. "You'll win. I know it to be true."

He approached, a bulge in his trousers. He knelt before her and caught her mouth with his.

Caesar raised her. Her thighs hung over his shoulders, her back against the wall as she raised her skirt. His mouth met her wet femininity and Fatima gasped, gripping a ceiling beam. His tongue probed her, as did his hands. She writhed against him until she spasmed joyously.

By nightfall in San Juan, pirates were pillaging and raping at will. El Morro burned.

"Now take the city," Caesar ordered.

A Janissary waved a red flag.

Caesar and his men swung down to the causeway wall. The agha disembarked with a squad of Janissaries. The raïs followed, leaving a handful of men aboard the ship. Everyone charged up the road into the city.

From the captain's cabin, Fatima observed the chaos. Fires raged and pirate banyans ensued on the city outskirts. Shouts, cries and gunfire carried on the wind. The ship sat mainly deserted. Never had it been so calm.

Fatima opened a drawer to find Caesar's secret pistol. After securing it in her sash, she climbed out the window and clambered down a rope to the causeway. She followed the road towards fiery mayhem.

In a moderately damaged barracks, she found a table littered with alcohol bottles, pipes, tobacco and playing cards. *Caesar's plan would have worked anyway*, she thought. The guards and militia had clearly been drunk when they arrived. Fatima took a taste from each of the bottles.

There came a woman's scream. Fatima wanted to investigate. Undecided about which bottle to bring, she took one in each hand, exiting out the back and venturing up a staircase to the top floor. From there, she tucked the bottles under her arm and climbed up a ladder to the roof. She entered a lookout tower, where she could see the night's destruction for herself. Women and children screamed in the streets. Men cut down defending their homes. A sea of pirates had consumed the city.

Caesar's imposing figure stood out among the crowd like a king. She watched him strangle a man with his bare hands. Alone among all the men she'd ever known, Caesar answered to no one. A nobleman charged at Caesar and ended up having his head cut off with a nimcha sword. She took a large swig of Puerto Rican rum.

Now, that's power, Fatima thought. *Real power*. She gulped back wormwood wine from Port Royal.

By the time she drank half the bottle, Caesar beat and raped an extravagantly dressed girl while her family was forced to watch. This reminded her of all the times she'd witnessed such cruelty at the hands of slavers. Her eyes closed. When they opened again, sunlight beamed down. She stumbled back towards the ship, her head throbbing. She scarcely noticed the dead bodies on the road that she had to step around.

Once aboard, she returned to the captain's cabin, where Caesar was passed out with a half-drunk bottle next to his bed. Caesar's pistol was still tied to her sash. She unraveled it and took aim at his head. She had the power to end his life if she so chose. This lumbering beast of a man was at her mercy. She withdrew, hiding it when he rolled over to face her.

"Where were you?" he woke, trying to focus.

"Just seeing the sights." She tucked the gun away.

"I thought you were gone. I didn't know if they took you or you left."

"I came back."

"Don't leave me again. I need you." He reached out his hand.

"You didn't need me last night." She took it and lay on top of him. "You're a pirate now. You don't need me."

"I need you. My own officers speak a dialect I can't understand. Half the slaves speak languages I can't understand, and neither can the raïs or the agha. You are instrumental in the running of the ship."

"Instrumental?" Fatima cocked an eyebrow.

"I learned the word from you."

"Don't blame me if you sound white." She rubbed her eyes. "Did you kill that girl?"

"Which girl?"

"The one you—never mind."

"No, I didn't kill any women last night. That was necessary."

"Necessary? Did you need a woman so bad or was it something else?" she asked sharply.

"It's revenge. It's control. It's punishing them by defiling their women. You can't understand; you're a woman."

"I understand a lot more than you think."

"No, I think you understand too much. You are so intelligent, Fatima."

"Yes, it's true."

"Yet you are still here with me."

"Where else would I go?"

"You are stimulated by a dangerous way of living."

Fatima retreated to her side of the room and pulled the curtain across to shut him out.

A cannon fired its load. The cannonball soared across the sky, leaving a trail of sparkling dust. The Brandenburg fleet sailed north of Puerto Rico, trading shots with the French fleet. On the flagship *Kurprinz,* Prinz Maximilian toured the lower gun deck to inspect damage.

"Not good enough," said Maximilian. "The French are making us look foolish."

Men loaded the cannons for another shot. An officer hurried down the deck. "Count Molke requests your presence, my Prinz."

Maximilian joined Count Molke, his men and Rear Admiral Reers on the quarterdeck.

"My Prinz, San Juan is under attack from pirates; they slipped in behind us," said Reers.

Smoke billowed from the city.

"I blame you, Admiral Reers," said Maximilian. "If Puerto Rico falls to the French, you'll all be executed."

Later, in the captain's cabin, Maximilian and his staff reviewed maps around a desk.

"The French ships are moving out of range," said Reers. "The whole fleet is sailing north for open water."

"They're not retreating, not with men poised at the fort," said Maximilian.

"No, my Prinz, not retreating. I believe the French fleet will turn around here, gaining speed and momentum from the wind out here." The captain pointed on the map. "Then come back around down here, right to San Juan, with all their guns to bear on the fort and not enough ships to defend the harbor."

"Baron Gretsch's *Einhorn* was of little use," said Maximilian. "What other ships stand between the French and the wall?"

"The English ships *Relentless* and *Sea Horse* broke formation for San Juan," said Reers. "They will arrive before us. By then it will be too late. Pirates are once again advancing on the city."

"In other words, we've been lured away. Take us back to San Juan to engage the French invasion head-on. I'll clear the island of pirates before they can return."

"Messenger ship coming, carrying the Calenberg crest," said an officer.

"*Wunderbar*," said Maximilian. "Have them meet us in the grand cabin."

Once the messenger ship arrived, everyone gathered.

"The ships are slow getting turned and up to speed due to all the hazards in the area," said Admiral Reers. "Also, a flotilla of pirate ships is approaching Puerto Rico from the east. One is said to be *De Heilige Graal*. They may be bringing the countess to San Juan as a hostage. I think it unwise to attack in full."

"*De Heilige Graal* is coming here?" Maximilian's eyes were aglow. "Excellent. I look forward to reuniting with Aurora one last time."

A German correspondent officer entered with police guards, bringing a case of documents.

"What news from Calenberg?" asked Molke.

"News from Transylvania, my Prinz." Count Molke produced a scroll.

"My brother Frederick, what is it? Read."

"Terrible news—your brother Frederick is dead. He was killed by Ottomans. The Ottomans have claimed Transylvania once again."

"Frederick is truly dead." Maximilian waved his fists in the air triumphantly. "*Jaaa*! The eastern front has again opened in war. My mother has no stomach for war; she's a feeble woman. She'll be broken with grief over the death of her beloved firstborn. She will relinquish her authority over the house. She has no choice but to allow me to inherit the title and take the crown. I am crowned Prinz of all Hanover. I am the Prinz of all Germany. Nothing can stop it now. Is San Juan is still surrounded by pirates?"

"A pirate called Black Caesar has El Morro. He's said to be a young African king," said Reers. "The Spanish say he's seven feet tall."

"I've never met a Negro king in combat," Maximilian mused. "I'll kill Black Caesar and save San Juan from pirates. Prepare for ground battle."

"It will be quite an undertaking to transfer the armament so quickly," said Reers. "We could not mobilize in time, should the French ships return. Also, the plunder of French ships in battle could restore the fleet revenue."

"Don't give me excuses. I'll see Black Caesar in combat. I'll have his head. A glorious victory over a pirate occupation will restore your fleet's image. Land immediately," Maximilian ordered.

The captains left, upset.

"Polish my armor," Maximilian said.

Helena lay in bed; a dark figure was upon her. Hands probed her body and a tongue lapped at her breasts. Uncontrollably aroused, she guided the man inside her. At the sight of graying hair, she realized it was Gretsch, but she was enjoying it too much to stop. Drops of perspiration fell on her face and stung her eyes. She squinted and rubbed her eye.

Dodo sat at the foot of the bed with an easel, painting the event. "Ah, tears of joy," he exclaimed.

Helena jolted awake, screaming. Lightning flashed through the porthole, and thunder vibrated the room. She sat up in bed, her tongue recoiling as she spat a bitter taste into the air. "*Scheisse!*"

She rose to look out. El Morro was smoking in the distance; tiny lights flickered along the starry horizon. She cursed and left the room. Gretsch stood just outside his chamber.

"Oh, you. What's going on?" asked Helena.

"French ships are fighting the Brandenburg fleet again. They're closer this time."

"Are we in danger here?"

"Captain Fuchs says we're well out of the way. Put cotton in your ears to sleep and keep the lights out."

"I know the routine, Baron."

"In the morning I'm meeting with the Spanish captain who brought us back."

"Captain Soler?"

"*Ja*, Soler. We'll be discussing battle, but you are welcome to join us for breakfast."

"Breakfast and a show."

"If you wish. The table will be set for eight of the clock."

Gretsch departed, and she went back inside her room to watch ships bombard each other with cannon fire.

Helena was early to the grand cabin, after carefully slipping on a dress and fixing up her hair. A fluttering filled her stomach at the sight of Silvestre Soler. His warm, dark eyes met hers, and he kissed her hand. Dashing in a black uniform with gold stitching.

"You are looking well, *señorita*."

"Thank you." She flushed. "You as well."

He guided her to the aft gallery, where Captain Bohn watched the horizon with a telescope. "Morning, Dame Helena."

"Morning." Helena borrowed Silvestre's telescope. To the north, French warships were taking long-range shots at the Spanish and German ships.

Gretsch arrived. "Captain Soler, Captain Bohn, I bid you welcome."

"Baron, you look, well, you've looked better," said Bohn. "My ship is ready to sail back to St. Eustatius as soon as the coast is clear."

"Are you satisfied with the payment?" Gretsch asked.

"Indeed, thank you."

"So, what are we watching this morning, Captain Soler?" Helena said.

"The baron missed all the fun," said Silvestre. "The French ships of the line made a pass to try and finish off El Morro but were driven back by the Brandenburg navy."

Orders were shouted throughout the ship.

"What is it now?" Helena said.

"The battle's thick," said Bohn. "I'm glad we're out of range."

"French ships are coming in again. Perhaps they want to engage our ships," said Silvestre. "They might be within range."

"Captain Fuchs will inform us if there is any danger," said Gretsch.

Helena stood close to Silvestre, under Gretsch's scrutinizing eyes.

"You see there?" said Silvestre.

"*Ja*."

Flashes came from the sea, followed by billows of smoke.

She stood closer to the windows.

"Stand back, *señorita*, that shot will be close." Silvestre put a protective arm around her.

From the corner of her eye, Helena could see Gretsch shaking his head.

A cannonball hit *Einhorn* at the waterline. A watery explosion pelted the side of the ship, breaking windows and making everyone duck for cover. Helena found herself in Silvestre's arms, while officers and crew rushed around to do damage control.

Gretsch shuffled uneasily, clearly in pain and annoyed.

"Do you want me to yell 'Incoming' next time?" Bohn offered.

"*De Heilige Graal* was seen heading this way," Fuchs reported to Gretsch.

All eyes were on Fuchs.

"She was reported leaving St. Croix the day before yesterday. She was met by two ships, which came out of Charlestown and Long-Haul Bay or Castle Redoubt. They're heading this way, currently southwest of the Virgin Islands."

An explosion came from San Juan.

"The pirates are on the move," said Silvestre. "The return of the French ships is part of a larger plan, I fear. A full-out assault on San Juan, if I'm not mistaken."

"Outstanding, Silvestre," said Helena.

Gretsch grumbled beneath his breath. "Captain, I must determine if Countess Aurora is on the ship and who's in command of *De Heilige Graal*."

"It'll take you a day to get *Einhorn* away from here," said Silvestre. "I'll take you myself on *San Antonio*, Baron."

"Preposterous," Helena said. "He's decrepit."

Gretsch gave her a scathing look. "Thank you, Captain Soler. We'll leave right way."

"I meant, you're in no condition to go. You're not well enough yet."

"I'll follow when she's ready, Baron Gretsch," said Fuchs.

"No, Captain, keep her back out of the way and safe."

Silvestre saluted, giving Helena a smile before departing.

"Wait. I should come with you," said Helena.

"No. Out of the question," Gretsch said.

"You are made of strong metal, my beautiful Helena." Silvestre took her aside to the gallery doors. "This is the best place for you until we return. French buccaneers and Jamaican pirates are not to be trifled with."

"So I've seen. Gretsch will likely send me back with him. Another six months with Max Gretsch will kill me. Just having to look at him for another week will kill me."

"Baron Gretsch said it will be you who decides when this is over."

"What?"

"Your colony is destroyed. You have no other place to go. I was going to ask you later. After the battle. I've been given the post of protecting Puerto Rico and the Mona Passage. I'd like it very much if you'd stay with me in Full Moon Bay."

Helena's jaw dropped. "Stay with you in Full Moon Bay?"

"Don Medina's villa is the logical port for my ship, don't you think? The offer is there. Baron Gretsch figured you'd likely want to be part of the search for your friends. Full Moon Bay is as fine a place as any."

Helena gave him a peck on the cheek. She met his gaze and they kissed.

A rolling concussion of cannon fire echoed, and officers burst into the room.

"I must go," Silvestre said.

"I know. Do come back."

"I hope so." He threw his cape over his shoulder and glided out the room. Helena sighed, smiling as she hurried back to her chamber. She detoured to Gretsch's cabin and knocked.

"Max?" She entered.

Gretsch ignored her as he fitted his armor breastplate, hiding the pain in his face.

"You came back for me in Full Moon Bay, didn't you?"

"I saved your life that day."

"Perhaps."

"Perhaps? Go away, you ungrateful girl!"

"I am grateful. I just don't know how to show it." Helena's hands fidgeted. "Silvestre told me I could search for survivors in Little Venice. That is kind of you."

"*Ja*, I'm sure your aunt Sophie will spare no expense. Since you value Silvestre's company, you may stay here with him if you choose."

"He told me."

Gretsch found his helmet and gloves.

"I'm trying to decide if you were paid to save me," Helena said. "Was it loyalty to Aunt Sophie or love for me?"

"You think I have delusional fantasies of skipping through fields of flowers, holding hands with Helena, the handmaiden of Hanover? I do not."

"But you are?"

"There's just no stopping you, you stubborn girl! You've always been stubborn. I'd prefer if I didn't, believe me."

She stared at him for a moment before making to leave. Then stopped as she searched for the right words. "I'm sorry. I could never love you. Not in that way."

"Thank you, I know! Now get away, you difficult girl!" Gretsch wandered to the window. "Every few years I saw you again, and every time you were disrespectful."

"Every time I saw you, you brought war."

"In the blink of an eye, you were a grown woman. The most beautiful woman I've ever seen. Therefore, I allow you to disrespect me. If you spoke to the Baron of Leipzig the way you speak to me, he'd have you killed. I'm far too lenient with you."

"I feel uncomfortable around you. I hate you watching me all the time."

"You're safer around me than anyone in the world. I could never hurt you. I only wanted to be your friend."

"You have been kind to me, at times." She paused again. "You want to have sex with me."

Gretsch became uncomfortable. He couldn't bring himself to deny it.

Helena headed for her cabin. "That's why we can't be friends."

He hid a subtle laugh.

She went to leave and paused again. "You really shouldn't go; you are terribly weak. I know what I'm talking about. You will bleed inside."

"Stay on board while I'm gone. You're not healed from injuries or your miscarriage, and you don't want another."

Helena couldn't breathe for a moment. She entered her room. "I shall rejoice, should you never return!" Helena slammed the door.

Fama sped from the executive mansion in San Juan across the harbor to El Morro. Cardinal Grimaldi held onto the railing at the bow while Rivero clung to the aft ratlines.

"Prinz Maximilian has landed at the fortress, Cardinal," said Rivero. "We will have you there in minutes. May I say what an honor it has been having you aboard my ship."

"Thank you, Captain. I hear it was you who captured the decoy for Don Medina. She may not have been the countess, but she's a witch. You have done a great service. God rewards those who serve him. We'll soon have the real countess."

Cardinal Grimaldi was rubbing his foot just as the ship ran aground on the beach. He flew off the bow, screaming through the air and crashing face-first into the sand.

"Cardinal!" Rivero said.

Cardinal Grimaldi lay there groaning, slowly trying to get back up, but he was stuck. A wave rolled up and over him, covering him in sand and debris. "Oh, God!" The cardinal coughed up seawater. He struggled; his hands stuck in the wet sand. Then another wave came in that scooped him up and deposited him on the rocky beach.

Rivero ordered crewmen to assist. They helped the cardinal to his feet.

Rivero leapt off the ship. "Cardinal, are you hurt?"

Cardinal Grimaldi limped. "I'll walk it off."

Rivero helped him to the command tent. Inside, Maximilian switched his short-blade sword for a long one and practiced swinging.

The cardinal, with seaweed dangling from his ear, received a cut across the chest. His cassock and shirt split open, revealing a three-inch gash across his left breast. He looked down to see that his cross had been chopped off. "Oh God, oh God!"

"Cardinal Grimaldi," Maximilian began. "I didn't see you there."

Rivero crossed himself several times as he stepped away from the cardinal. "God is punishing you."

Cardinal Grimaldi bent to pick up his cross and lost his balance, falling into Maximilian, who tripped and crashed down on the cardinal in full armor. Officers helped them back up.

"God is punishing you all!" Rivero crossed himself again.

The cardinal checked his injury and pronounced it "just a flesh wound. God's still on our side. It is a test." He rubbed his foot and head.

Everyone removed their hats and bowed their heads.

"Uh, amen," said Rivero. "Prinz Maximilian, the Dutch ship, *De Heilige Graal,* is approaching San Juan. The countess is held hostage aboard. The governor has agreed to allow the ship to land, here at El Morro."

"Then we have Aurora," said Maximilian. "But where's the other pirate leader, Black Caesar?"

"Black Caesar captured the armory, then retreated to the eastern side of the city, out of our reach," said Captain Garcia. "The harbor and the city are surrounded by pirates."

"He's running away!" Maximilian scowled. "Fire before he gets out of range."

"It's too late, the guns won't reach," said Reers. "Governor Carlitos requests you cross to defend the palace."

"Curse him, the dark bastard." Maximilian clanked in his armor. "I didn't get all dressed up for nothing."

"This is the governor's most trusted corsair, Captain Jorge-Miguel José Rivero," said Cardinal Grimaldi. "He captured the decoy, and he's here to capture the countess for us."

"The governor will let *De Heilige Graal* land in the harbor, and I will capture the ship and the witch," said Rivero.

"Then you will be rewarded by God." The cardinal leaned on a chair, but it was unstable in the sand. He fell over, instinctively grabbing whatever he could. Maximilian fell over, crashing into one of the wooden poles of the tent. The entire structure buckled and collapsed on top of them. They writhed beneath the heavy fabric.

"Oh, God!" Cardinal Grimaldi uttered.

"Perhaps God is punishing us?" Rivero said, crawling as he looked for a way out.

"*Scheisse*," groaned Maximilian as he tried to hack his way out with a sword. The blade stabbed into something soft. "Cardinal?"

"It's a test!" the cardinal shrieked.

"God is punishing us!" Rivero tried to cross himself as he dug his way out.

Lovely Bay

Guernsey sat peacefully anchored while Bleedin Art, Freeman and Morris enjoyed fishing off the main deck while sprawled on wooden chairs. Birds chirped and dragonflies buzzed about the bay. The air was fragrant with a mixture of salt and wildflowers.

Stubbs aimed his telescope at the water.

"Whatever it is, Stubbs, we're staying put till I catch something," Art said.

"You caught something here in '58," Morris remarked.

"What'd he say?" Art replied.

"Nothing important," Freeman said. "I'm out of wormwood wine."

"Bring us up another bottle of wormwood wine," Art called. "We're parched up here."

Freyja, now livelier than ever, hopped onto a hanging perch in the shade. She wore a stocking jacket and stretched out her wings.

"That's parched, I said. Thank Mr. Freeman for your new platform," said Art.

"Bach is returning, Commodore," Stubbs said. "In a hurry."

"Ah, viz good newz, I hope," Art said, doing his worst German accent.

They continued to fish while Bach's boat approached. Art joked to his men, as was his habit when suppressing his concern. At one point, he cast his rod and snagged a seagull. "Ah, shit!" The bird thrashed and crashed as Art tried to reel it in.

Bach climbed aboard, rushing over to make his report. He stared as Art wrestled with a panicked seagull.

"What?" Art delicately unravelled the bird. "Ya never seen a man fish before?"

"Your friend the redhead was taken by Silent Sam and his gang of pirates," Bach began. "They killed everyone at

Monte Cristi and took her with them to San Juan, which they intend to sack."

"Sack? Oh no, not San Juan."

"There's word *De Heilige Graal* was spotted in Lake Maracaibo."

"That's the countess, sure enough. Trying to get into Aragua through Little Venice. She won't get through that way," Art said. "So, Atia's alive, though?"

"She was alive, last I saw."

"She ain't been a pirate for a fortnight, and she's got herself all in a knot. Mr. Freeman, please." Art handed over his fishing rod over to Freeman. He and Morris went to work freeing the seagull.

"Captain Stubbs, prepare to get underway, and recall Dietrich with all haste." Art took Freeman's rod and cast it into the water. "Now, where was I?"

The seagull flew off with a shriek, while Freeman and Morris cast lines back out.

Later that morning, Dietrich returned. *Stingray* rowed into the bay, anchoring alongside *Guernsey*. Dietrich swung over on deck.

"Good boy. I got hot news about your German comrades," Art began. "Mr. Bach's reconnaissance has turned up some interesting events. Seems the House of Hanover has some very important travelers coming our way. The pirate Silent Sam and his army of cutthroats has my beautiful Atia, and they plan to harm Countess Aurora."

"The Countess Aurora herself?" Dietrich's mouth slacked. "Coming here?"

"She's in terrible danger," Bach added. "She's wanted as a witch by the Spanish and the church, and she's wanted for stealing the treasury."

"She has the Hanover treasury?" Dietrich said.

"Aye; we're just finding these things out as we pass them along. I'm willing to release you from my service," Art said. "You have a higher duty to your countess."

"Indeed, Commodore, a sworn duty."

"Yeah, I won't keep you. You need to get under way."

"Immediately," Dietrich said. "Where is this Silent Sam?"

"He left Monte Cristi for San Juan, so they say," Bach said.

"He's hot on the trail of *De Heilige Graal;* that's the ship she's on," Art added.

"*De Heilige Graal*?" Dietrich thought a moment. "That's a Van der Hagen East Indiaman, a forty-gunner."

"Just keep my lovely redhead from harm, and I'll reward you. We'll follow with all speed on *Guernsey*. We'll save your countess."

"I will go with all speed." Dietrich swung over to his ship. "Thank you, Commodore Valentine; you've demonstrated true valor today. I shall contact you when I have found *De Heilige Graal*."

"Aye, once more into the breach, dear…blah, blah, blah." Art returned to his chair and fishing rod as *Stingray* rowed away. The sun burst through the clouds. "It's shaping up to be a nice morning. Call Strangewayes up here."

Dr. Strangewayes arrived on deck, off-balance and holding on, pale and foggy.

"Have you got the plague?" Art asked.

"Repercussions."

"It's nearly time to depart, Doc. I was thinking I might put in an order from Port Royal, before we do." Art's voice lowered. "I'm wondering if you still make that Amazon tonic for romantic interludes?"

"Ah, my famous Macho Grande—I'll have Mrs. Beazley include a special gift package," Strangewayes said. "A filly caught your eye, Art?"

"For appearances only," Morris mocked.

"What did he say?" said Art. "We're on our way to save young Atia, Doc. She may be appreciative of her hero when I arrive."

"It's not a hallucinogen," Strangewayes remarked.

"You've met her; it only takes whiskey," Morris replied.

Art couldn't argue with that one.

"We'll be ready to set sail presently, Commodore," Bach said.

"What's yer hurry, Mr. Bach? Dietrich ain't even on the horizon yet. We don't want to be too early; we'll look desperate. Bring wormwood wine. I'm beginning to see what Captain White finds so appealing about morning wormwood." He settled in beside his new parrot. "Never be in too much of a hurry, my Freyja. Good things come to those who wait." Art whistled happily.

Excuse My Sirreverence

Jean-Paul la Roche sat in the dark hold of Silent Sam's hideout home, the merchantman *Servillain*, docked off Crab Island. He contemplated how he could have let this happen and how he would punish those who betrayed him.

"I'm the fucking Capitaine!" he shouted periodically.

The voices outside mocked his calls. They had no idea he was counting voices and checking distances. They were just outside and not on the ship. There were only a few men left; someone made the mistake of leaving only a few guards to watch him, and they didn't watch at all.

La Roche used a skeleton key to open his cell. He crept silently out and peered through a cannon porthole. A rowboat was approaching with a group of men. He squinted. It was Sam's henchmen, Fish and Chips.

"Who goes there?" said a crewman.

"I serve Captain Seele," replied Chips.

"Password?"

"Excuse my sirreverence," said Fish.

"Aye. Let 'em up."

"We're here for the prisoner, on Seele's order," said Fish.

"I'll bet you are," la Roche remarked.

Footsteps came down the stairs to the hold, while la Roche slipped into the unlocked forward compartment.

Fish and Chips arrived and began searching the cells.

"Where'n the hell is he?" Fish asked.

Someone whistled "Frère Jacques."

The two thugs moved towards the flicker of light in the corner, readying their blades. La Roche wasn't there; only a parrot. Minuit poked his head out from behind the water barrels and bobbed his head, whistling.

"It's a parrot," said Fish.

La Roche attacked from behind, smashing Fish in the head with a ballast rock and taking his gun. Chips tried to defend himself, but la Roche shot him through the heart.

Both men fell to the floor. La Roche took the sword from Chips and ran it through Fish's chest, killing him. Then he checked Chips, who was already dead.

"You earned your supper tonight, Minuit." La Roche stripped the bodies of remaining weapons before heading up the stairs.

"It was a shot, I tells ya," a cutthroat said.

"They ain't supposed to kill him," said another.

When la Roche reached the top, an arrow burst through the crewman's chest. A barrage of arrows flew on all sides. Yaguara, a Taíno warrior, and six Carib warriors swarmed the main deck, cutting pirates down. They soon had the ship.

"Capitaine?" Yaguara began.

"It's about fucking time, yes?" said la Roche.

"Yaguara searched everywhere."

La Roche showed a bird whistle and a skeleton key. "The bird found me."

They raided the captain's cabin. La Roche reclaimed his cutlass and pistols before opening the last hold. De Kreep and Cliché stood waiting.

"Capitaine, Yaguara," de Kreep said.

"The boy looks worse every time Yaguara sees him," said Yaguara.

"Good to see you too," said de Kreep.

"How many men do we have left?" asked la Roche.

"Arsenault and la Skunk are on Puerto Rico," Yaguara said. "Black Caesar is poised to seize San Juan. Silent Sam is on his way on *De Heilige Graal* with the countess, dressed as you. Black Caesar still has Ekene and Fatima with him. He has much of the outskirts and many hostages but hasn't been able to break into the governor's mansion."

"That is showing initiative," said la Roche. "That's where we're going."

"Why?" said Yaguara.

"What's wrong, does Yaguara not like Black Caesar?"

"No, Yaguara hates Black Caesar."

"We're not going there to help Black Caesar. I'm going to get what's owed."

"Yaguara's not relieved. Also, Atia is captured. She's on *De Heilige Graal*. Yaguara would rather save Atia."

"Atia will be saved, of course."

"What does Silent Sam want with her?" de Kreep said. "Is she a prisoner?"

"What else would she be? You think she's a spy?"

"No, Capitaine, I don't suggest such things. Your Atia is devoted to you, of course," he said, a note of jealousy in his voice.

"I am not sure. You said Laurens was fucking her back at Tortuga," Cliché added. "Maybe Laurens sold us out."

De Kreep elbowed him in the ribs.

"What? She was? How could she?" La Roche's face blanched. "Uh, not Laurens! Oh, not Laurens de fucking Graaf!"

"Oui, Laurens," de Kreep said.

"When?"

"While we were at Tortuga."

"But when, while we were at Tortuga?"

"The whole time we were at Tortuga, I told you."

"She better not leave me for Laurens, or I kill them both!"

Warriors spoke with Yaguara, leading the group to a beach where ships were visible through the trees. They saw *La Lune* sailing through the islands, heading for Puerto Rico.

Dodo von Knyphausen hated Puerto Rico. The heat, bugs, and Spaniards—it was all too much to take. After all, he was semi-related to royalty. The house of von Knyphausen was a loyal German household, like that of the Braunschmidts. He had lived his entire life with the aristocracy and made a comfortable living painting portraits and designing dresses for the countess. But when war came, Dodo's happy, luxurious life had been tossed into a sea of pirates.

Dodo had found the perfect paradise in Full Moon Bay with Helena, aside from the lizards. It was still too hot, but at least there were slaves to fan him and bring him cool drinks. The Countess Aurora would have loved it. He had hoped they would unite there and had just become accustomed to the idea when their host Don Medina ran Helena through with a sword.

Dodo had been seized by the instinct for self-preservation, and he hid in the bushes in the garden. This was an excellent hiding place until a lizard jumped on him, dropping from the trees. He ran screaming and was arrested by guards. Captain Soler sent him to the infirmary at San Juan, mistaking his panic for demonic possession, while Helena recovered aboard *Einhorn* with Gretsch.

Fortunately, Governor Carlitos of San Juan took an interest in Dodo's work. For weeks, he was a guest at the extravagant mansion in San Juan Harbor. Dodo had all the art supplies he could ever want and a luxurious private chamber. He painted ships in the harbor, portraits of the governor's wife and daughter, and a collection of still-life works.

One morning, Dodo was painting on his patio when a messenger told him that *De Heilige Graal* was coming in. Aurora was on her way. Dodo's newfound happiness was short-lived. Later, Dodo was summoned before the governor to be told that pirates under the French Capitaine had taken possession of *De Heilige Graal* and Aurora was a hostage on board. The day was tense and quiet as Dodo painted the arrival of *De Heilige Graal*.

The ship sailed in under the Calenberg flag, with the brig *La Lune* close behind. Smaller escort ships arrived, passing by the smoking fortress wall of El Morro. The construction scaffolding was in ruins on the upper levels. Tucked in behind the south corner of the stonework, *San Antonio* and *Fama* were at the naval dock. Several Brandenburg galiots and Maximilian's private yacht waited, blocking the east river way to the governor's executive mansion. A Spanish razeé galleon, *Holy Christ*, guarded the great marble landing, next to the governor's private yacht.

The governor and his whole staff arrived on the patio, where Dodo painted the harbor and *De Heilige Graal*.

"Today we witness history," said Carlitos as his slaves carried out his throne and set it where he had a grand view of the harbor entrance and El Morro.

Military and churchgoers gathered on the patio to watch, including Gretsch, Silvestre and Rivero. Gretsch wore a brace of guns and various blades; Silvestre was in shiny armor; Rivero had donned a new ostrich-feather hat.

"*De Heilige Graal's* entering the harbor now," said Silvestre.

Dodo shuddered, as Gretsch and Silvestre stood behind him.

"Paint, damn you, paint!" Carlitos sat heroically on his throne.

Dodo picked up his brush and continued, the hairs on the back of his neck standing upright.

"Do you know this Frenchman?" Gretsch asked Silvestre quietly.

"Only by reputation and gunfire."

"My father met him," Rivero added. "Both as a foe and an ally. His real name is unknown to us."

"Pirates and buccaneers change their names to protect their identities," Silvestre said. "The only pirate raids this French captain can be positively identified at are the attacks on Panama and Puerto Bello in the 1660s and 1670s. He was then pardoned by the English when the war was over."

Dodo continued to paint, his mind on their conversation rather than the canvas. The benefit of being a brilliant painter was that his fingers did all the work, while he devoured the best gossip.

"It's widely known the Capitaine was involved in the raids at Vera Cruz and Cartagena while serving the English as a privateer," Rivero told Gretsch. "Governor Carlitos also gave him a letter of marque, employing him as a privateer for the Spanish. He was known as El Capitaine. There is bad blood between the Frenchman and Governor Carlitos. This Frenchman has no loyalty to anyone but himself. He is wanted everywhere. The bounties on him are insurmountable. He's here to make Governor Carlitos give him a pardon in exchange for your countess."

When *De Heilige Graal* dropped anchor, *La Lune* sailed in.

"The *Holy Christ* is on full alert," Silvestre said.

"That's far enough," Captain Hernández spoke through a trumpet. His voice carried across the water from the *Holy Christ*.

Governor Carlitos rose from his seat. Dodo painted as quickly as he could. This was his specialty. He could paint Aurora graceful and elegant while she danced and frolicked and have the painting perfect by the time she passed out from the Cognac.

La Lune dropped anchor, and the Capitaine arrived on deck.

"I have zee Countess Aurora and the *Holy Grail,* which brought her," came a strange French accent. "I demand to speak with Governor Carlitos."

"Governor Carlitos does not negotiate with pirates," said Hernández. "He does not trust you. I will speak for the governor on behalf of the King of Spain."

"You speak for shit. Tell Governor Carlitos he should have kept his bargain. I will have revenge. If my demands are not met, the countess and all the hostages will die. Bring out the countess," said the Frenchman. A woman in an elaborate dress came forward, a hat covering her face. "My terms are delivered. You have twelve hours, yes?" the Capitaine continued. "Twelve hours—and we kill our first hostage."

"The governor will trust Admiral Longstaff of Port Royal to negotiate release of the countess and the Dutch hostages," said Hernández. "*HMS Relentless* is almost here. Admiral Longstaff will negotiate the release of the hostages."

"We agree to meet with Admiral Longstaff," said the Capitaine.

"Prinz Maximilian demands the countess be turned over to the Brandenburg navy and his authority," said a German official from *Kurprinz*.

"No one demands nothing from Silent Sa—El Capitaine!"

"Is it the countess?" Rivero asked Gretsch.

"I can't see properly from here. She could be on any ship."

"If it's a trick to get pirates into the harbor, *Fama* will lead the assault. Should something go wrong, I want Baron

Gretsch to board *De Heilige Graal* with me," Rivero said to Silvestre. "*San Antonio* will make sure no pirates make landfall."

Rivero left for his ship.

Gretsch stopped Silvestre from following. They spoke off to the side, just out of Dodo's earshot.

Thankfully, I have the hearing of a fox, too, Dodo thought.

"Maximilian will kill Aurora and Helena," said Gretsch. "This will come into play before the day is out. Do you trust this, Rivero?"

"I'm duty-bound to bid you farewell. That is all I can say."

"My duty is to Countess Aurora," said Gretsch. "If killing her is their plan, then I will also perish. Should I die and you survive, please pass on my fondest farewell to Helena."

Silvestre paused. "I think we share feelings for the young lady."

"Her safety is more important to me than my own."

"Baron Gretsch, I have known that since I first met you."

"Give her a happy life."

"I intend to."

Governor Carlitos squirmed on his throne impatiently. "Are you getting all this?"

"Absolutely." Dodo stroked the canvas happily. "Every bit of it."

Silent Sam stood on the deck of *De Heilige Graal*. Atia, by his side, was dressed as the countess, while the real countess stood on the deck below with the rest of the hostages, in a common blue gown.

"Black Caesar has much of the fortress and part of the city," Montbars reported to Sam.

"My Capitaine is coming for ya," Atia said.

"Maybe he's combing his hair," Sam jeered. "He's gotta look good for his grand finale."

"She signed on for this bloody raid in Tortuga," said Montbars. "She's on account, a pirate herself, against the code, if ya ask me."

"You all are framin' him for murder," Atia continued. "You're gonna murder the countess too, I heard."

"You're gonna die alongside yer Capitaine in your heinous killing of the countess," Sam said. "But, until then, what shall we do with her, Monty?"

Montbars pawed at Atia's face and hair. "The Sultan of Tripoli has a generous offer on the table for this one, a hundred thousand worth in gold doubloons."

"A bit pricy, don't ya think?" Sam laughed. "No, I thinks the Sultan will lop off her head when he sees her. She's supposed to be a pure Roman, says a drunk Irishman. She's no Roman, and, she ain't likely gonna pass for no virgin, neither. She's yours if ya want her."

By evening, *Relentless* sat outside San Juan Harbor, *Sea Horse* farther out.

A plank was extended to the damaged causeway of El Morro from the main deck of *De Heilige Graal*. Sam and a handful of men crossed over.

"We have all the leverage we need." Sam grinned.

A longboat approached as the moon rose. Longstaff's man Rodney disembarked.

"Commodore Seele? Admiral Seele! Oh, Lord Seele!" Sam spoke to himself.

"I'm Marine Captain Rodney on behalf of Admiral Longstaff," Rodney began.

"How is Big Dick?" Sam asked. "I am the Capitaine."

"I'm here to begin negotiations for the release of the hostages."

"Right. Oui, oui, oui."

"Do you have the countess alive, Seele?" Rodney asked.

"She's *magnifique*!" Sam kissed his fingertips. "Though the hold is not exactly what she's used to."

Rodney signaled crewmen to bring a chest. They plunked it down on the landing.

Sam's men opened it, revealing a nice haul of gold bits and dust.

"From Admiral Longstaff," said Rodney. "Hoping you might consider releasing the hostages to his charge."

"Tell Dick, he's going to have to do better. We'll take this as down payment," said Sam. "If Dick doubles it, we'll accept."

"I will deliver your terms." Rodney returned to his boat and the crew rowed away.

Sam clapped his hands together. "Payment for the countess, lads! The rest we get from San Juan. Looks to me like negotiations have broken down. 'Tis time to play Wheel of Wench with the bonnie lass."

"She is the wife of El Capitaine," Montbars reminded. "She should die by his side."

"We promised to kill a hostage in twelve hours if negotiations failed, and, gracious me, look at the time. Negotiations failed."

"Capitaine always keeps his word."

"Aye, that he does." Sam grinned. "And look what it got him." He turned his attention to Atia.

Raze it to the Ground

Atia was kept close by Sam's side while an encampment was raised in El Arsenal, part of the fortress of El Morro, under pirate control. Just as in Port Royal months earlier, makeshift stages were fashioned from wood planks. The festivities began for the pirates as the dancer, Cléo, swayed her body provocatively, clicking castanets with her fingers.

Atia carried a painting hidden beneath a sheet at knifepoint.

"You was there for Wheel of Terror, weren't ya?" Sam asked.

"You tried to burn Violante alive with her newborn baby," said Atia.

"You were there! Perhaps it got out of control. We were gonna do a disappearing act—but then you got a body to deal with, and then some. You gotta see this." Sam revealed the painting, which depicted Violante with her legs spread, giving birth in a manger being engulfed in flames.

That girl has been through the mill, hasn't she, Atia thought. *Good.*

"Just like you described!" Sam leant into her, his breath foul. "I captured the event in its full splendor. You see the realism? Blood, sweat and tears go into my paintings. Not my blood, sweat or tears, mind you, but someone's, nonetheless."

"Yer as rabid as a dog that just got bathed," Atia remarked.

"Watch yer tongue, girlie. Just because you're not into me doesn't mean I can't be in you," said Sam.

Atia was bound, gagged and tied to a round wooden table, then propped up vertically, her arms and legs spread to her sides. A sign above her read "Wheel of Terror," with Wheel crossed out and Wench in its place. Various categories included Open Her Box, I saw the Kitty, Woolding Zone and Monty's Choice.

The stage beside Atia featured Aurora, gagged and chained to a chair situated next to a table. The table had three boxes on it, each with a wire leading to a scaffold, then back down the front of the stage, where three handles hung.

Beside Aurora was Katrina, tied flat to a table with various blades rigged to drop on her. Van der Hagen was strapped into a chair with a rope tied around his head, in preparation for woolding.

Sam drew a name from a hat while pirates cheered. "First up, we have Sturgeon," Sam announced. "Sturgeon, come on up."

Sturgeon threw a knife, while another pirate spun the wheel.

Atia did her best not to scream as the knife landed near her head.

"Open Her Box," Sam said. "Pick a handle, Sturgeon. Each handle has a different surprise waiting. Will it be the self-fusing grenade? Will it be the Poison Dart Frog, or will it be the Brazilian Banana Spider?"

Sturgeon pulled a handle, and the box to Aurora's left opened. Nothing happened.

Aurora went rigid.

"Huh?" Sam's mouth gaped. "Where the hell is it?" He picked up the box; there was nothing inside. From under the lid, a spider larger than a hand leapt out and darted up Sam's arm.

Sam screamed, throwing the box as he dove from the stage. Montbars swatted the air, and the pair ran at least thirty feet before stopping.

"Remind me to never again go to Brazil," Sam said.

"Where's it gone?" asked Montbars.

A pirate in the distance ran yelling into a nearby bush.

"It's over there," said Sam.

"Good," Montbars added.

"Oui, oui, oui. Now whose turn is it?"

"My turn," said Montbars.

"It's always your turn."

Montbars, staggering drunk, grabbed a knife. He looked Atia in the eye while he lined up his throw. It landed between her legs—and between two categories.

"Re-throw, re-throw," Sam chanted.

Men cheered, and Montbars was handed a second knife. He took a second throw that landed flush beside Atia's throat. She felt the cold, sharp edge and the warm trickle of blood on her skin.

"That's a kill ya aimed for. You tried for a kill, ya cheeky bastard. What is it, anyway?" Sam looked closely. "It's Monty's favourite. It's woolding time!"

The pirates cheered, but raised voices came from the beach.

Sam and Montbars stumbled over to see a handful of pirates come ashore. Atia recognized some of them.

"Ding Dong Belford?" Sam groaned. "I didn't ring that fuckin' bell. Who invited this lot, Monty?"

"This here's the executive's lodgings," Montbars yelled. "You lot belong with Black Caesar across the bay."

"Where is the Capitaine?" Barns asked.

"What's going on?" asked Wynne.

"We were told that San Juan would be ours," Grubing added.

"It's all here," said Sam. "We have payment for all of you."

"This is it?" Grubing sneered. "Where is the San Juan gold?"

"Where is the Hanover treasure?" Ding Dong, fired his left nostril.

"Laurens said to follow the Capitaine, not Caesar, and certainly not you, Seele. Now, where is he?" Wynne demanded.

"Why do you have the chest and not the Capitaine?" Barns said. "What's going on?"

"Black Caesar had the city surrounded but couldn't crack the egg. As for the Capitaine, come on now, he ain't won a battle since he rode Morgan's coattails into Puerto Bello in '68." Sam paced. "He betrayed you all and ran off with it, is what he's done. He was headed straight for his *Sérénité*. But not to worry, lads, I got it covered. I got Fish and Chips on the way with the frog, as we speak. We'll lynch El Capitaine!"

"We sack the city now and take all," Barns said. "That was the plan. How much did he take?"

"Men, I have the answer, I promise. It's all here, right in San Juan. This is a raid that songs are made of."

"I don't sing," cautioned Wynne. "And what's *she* doing here?" He indicated Atia. "I saw her in Tortuga. She has a ship; she's signed with Laurens for a share."

"She's the wife of the Capitaine. Of course, she was there," said Grubing.

"She's guilty of stealing our booty, along with her Capitaine," Sam said. "She'll face our justice. Women don't go on pirate raids—it's in the code."

"She's on the contract," said Wynne. "She's the daughter of Madman O'Malley. The code applies."

"No, it don't," said Sam. "The same fuckin' code that says women can't go on raids doesn't say women get equal shares or get to defend themselves."

"He insulted the code," said Grubing.

"Shut up, Nathaniel," said Wynne. "Pirates can insult the code. It's not blasphemy."

"She's not a pirate, she's a wench," said Montbars. "A wench who stole from you. Punish the slut."

"She's a spy for Laurens de Graaf, and you know what we do to spies of Laurens de Graaf?" Sam cackled. "You came here to rape and pillage, lads. Why not start with her?"

Anxious for blood, the crowd of angry pirates converged.

"She's got it coming this time," Grubing said.

"You never liked her anyway," Wynne replied.

"I want a piece of her first," said Barns.

"She's mine, keep off!" growled Ding Dong.

"There's plenty for all men. Come now, San Juan is ours. We'll find all their hidden treasures and be rich. They'll sing pirate songs about this raid." Sam waved his arm grandly. "Come now, all of you, gather. We're going to show young Red here what happens to spies. We'll do it in a play. That's it, a play. Atia's going to debut in her first play. But first, some mood setting. Cléo, come here."

He dashed over to grab Cléo, groping between her legs and her bottom, and maneuvered her to the stage.

"There's not a real man here who can resist my Cléo," said Sam. "Come, men, you'll want to see this—the famous Cléo and Ravishing Red, together for the first time."

Cléo was taken off-guard.

Montbars and Spike brought out a tall basket, setting it off to the side.

"Don't make me hurt her, please?" said Cléo.

"I'd never ask such a thing of you. Do Cleopatra, it's yer best dance," Sam said.

"I'm not wearing the right dress."

"You look better in this one." Sam smelt her hair and slid his fingers down her breasts and belly. "You smell so good. I gotta calm the men down before they get mean on me. Do Cleopatra for me. Red's got nothin' on you. You're the real goddess here."

Cléo began her dance, warming up her feet and legs, then her hips. Men gathered, and the musician played slowly.

Atia made eye contact with Cléo; both women were terrified.

"If you got a gift, use it," said Sam. "Begin."

Cléo's costume shimmered beneath the torch lights. Her body shook, contorting into provocative positions. The men pawed at her, and she tried to entice Sam to dance.

"But the ending," Sam said. "You can't forget the ending, pretty Cleopatra. Bring on the ending."

Montbars unfastened the lid to the basket. Cléo tried to leave, but Spike grabbed her. A shiny grey snake jetted out. Montbars ducked away. The snake opened its mouth. Cléo blocked it with her arms, but it lunged at her, its fangs injecting poison. She screamed, but it jabbed again and again. Cléo toppled off the stage.

Next, the snake darted at Spike, injecting venom into his arm. He punched at the serpent, and it bit his hand. He needed little persuasion to try to outrun the creature. This ended unsuccessfully, with the snake piercing his face.

Montbars drew his sword, chopping at the snake while backpedaling. It sprung up, heading for the crowd of pirates.

Sam fell back in his chair, rolled, and ran for the sea.

Cléo lay on her side, convulsing. Foam spewed from her mouth.

Spike dropped to the ground, groaning.

Pirates circled the snake, hacking it to bits with their swords.

"No more fucking snakes or spiders. No more games, Seele," Montbars said.

"Jesus fucking Christ, do you know how much a black mamba costs these days!"

"Ship entering the harbor," said a pirate. "A sloop, it looks like."

Sam dusted himself off. "Ah, here's my Fish and Chips with our Capitaine. Right on time. The night's not over yet."

A boat rowed in towards the shore. Nine silhouettes with familiar hats came into view and the pirates gathered.

"Oi, Red, you still alive? You'll never guess who's combing!"

Atia blinked blearily.

Sam and Montbars stood over Spike.

"Is he gonna make it?" asked Sam.

"I think not," said Montbars.

"He's strong. A shilling says he makes it."

"The woman took most of the poison. You're on."

Spike collapsed and died.

"We didn't shake on it," said Sam.

"That's a shilling!" snapped Montbars.

"Bring Fish and Chips up here," said Sam. "No evening is complete without Fish and Chips."

The figures approached. It appeared Fish and Chips were bringing the Capitaine, but Atia recognized the figures of the Capitaine, Yaguara and de Kreep.

"You missed Cleopatra's beautiful asp, but not to worry, Capitaine, I have your redhead, so we're going to play another game." Sam paused, realizing. "It really is the Capitaine!"

Sam's men aimed pistols at la Roche's head, while the Frenchman's cutlass hovered at Sam's throat.

Yaguara and de Kreep aimed weapons at the pirates.

"I'm in command now. I have the ships, and now the countess," said la Roche

"Certainly appears so. I'd say you're right," said Sam.

"Enough of your games," la Roche snarled. "Release the hostages and send them back to their ship. The countess stays with me."

Pirates cut the bonds of the prisoners. Some of Wynne's men took Van der Hagen and Katrina to a boat. De Kreep limped over to a trembling Atia to help her down from the wheel.

"We must stop meeting like this, *mademoiselle*," said de Kreep.

Atia exhaled heavily, and they shared a short kiss.

"Who paid you?" la Roche demanded. "Who paid you to betray us?"

"Big Dick hired Silent Sam to frame you for the murder of the countess," said Atia.

"Why would they want to kill their own countess?" La Roche scowled.

"Her cousin Maximilian wants her dead," said Atia.

"Who cares," said Montbars. "Hostages are worth nothing anymore. I couldn't give the governor of Maracaibo away in '85. I say, kill them all now."

"I have a bounty of treasure to divide among us all," said Sam.

"Given to him by Big Dick's man," Atia said. "I saw it."

"A Port Royal pirate hunter—that proves it. You men are misled by Sammy the fucking Seal while others do all the work," said la Roche. "I was put in charge of this raid, and I am in charge now. We do not kill hostages; we make them pay."

Pirates cheered, waving their weapons.

"Don't call me that," Sam hissed. "No one ever calls me that."

"Everyone calls you that, you slick-shit weasel," Atia scoffed.

"Seele and Laurens are in with Port Royal slavers," said la Roche.

"Laurens betrayed him. Sold him out to this lot. I bear witness; it's why they wanted to kill me," said Atia.

"Laurens de Graaf betrayed me in so many ways. He will regret it," la Roche said bitterly. "I'm taking over, yes? Follow me. We sack San Juan, and we take the spoils for ourselves and leave nothing for the Spanish, the English, or Laurens de fucking Graaf. Hear me, Carlitos?" he yelled. "Your city is mine, now. You should have stuck to your bargain! Men, raze San Juan to the ground!"

Aboard the *Holy Christ*, the crew manned battle stations in San Juan harbor. Pirates were on the attack. Iglesias called the officers to an emergency meeting in the captain's cabin. Inside, Captain Hernández snorted white powder and perspired profusely as slaves helped him into his armor.

"Captain." Iglesias saluted.

Hernández spun around, his eyes glowing red. "Men, this is it. The pirates are on the move. They have the witch, and the forces of evil are upon us. But we shall prevail! We shall never fall to the unholy heathens; God will protect us. We save San Juan tonight!"

Hernández buried his face in a giant white mound on his desk. He inhaled deeply and raised his head, shaking it side to side. He roared, and his head dropped like a stone. Poof! A cloud of powdery residue filled the room.

Iglesias and the officers brushed their faces. When the dust cleared, their captain remained face down in the dune of coca-leaf powder.

"Captain Hernández?" Iglesias shook him. No movement. "He's dead."

"Pirates are attacking!" the lookout called.

"Holy Christ!" said Iglesias.

Pre-dawn light crept over La Fortaleza, the executive mansion in San Juan. A Spanish fast galleon burst into flames in the harbor. Dodo fell off his chair and the bottle of Puerto Rican rum he had nursed throughout the night slipped from his hand. The magnificent oil painting of Governor Carlitos and the arrival of *De Heilige Graal* sat nearby, drying.

Guards ran down the hall outside his room. "Wake the governor!"

Dodo stumbled onto the terrace. Pirate ships glided towards the estate. Pirates stood on the decks holding torches, chanting, "San Juan, San Juan." Canoes sped across the harbor.

On the balcony above, Carlitos and his aides rushed out.

"What is happening?" demanded Carlitos.

"I might ask you the same question," Dodo said.

"The governor's mansion is under attack," an officer called. "Man the defenses."

Pirate ships fired their guns, blowing up a cannon on the gun deck of the governor's mansion. A cannon fired back but missed.

"I should have gone to Italy." Dodo gathered his easel and paints. "By any chance, can I get paid now?"

"Pirates are already on shore!" a guard yelled before being shot.

Pirates disembarked at the executive landing.

"This wasn't supposed to happen," said Carlitos. "Where's Rivero? The Capitaine said he would take revenge; it's the Capitaine!"

"*Fama* and *San Antonio* are on the move," said an aide. "Rivero is heading for *De Heilige Graal*."

"Order him here at once," Carlitos said. "Defend the estate."

"Pirates have landed," said Captain Garcia.

"Call Maximilian for help," said Carlitos. "This wasn't supposed to happen!"

In the harbor, the *Holy Christ* erupted into flames.

"We've lost the *Holy Christ* and San Juan! Destroy the evidence!" Carlitos ordered.

Guards used a torch to light the painting. It went up in flames.

"No!" Dodo shrieked. "Not my best work!"

Boats full of buccaneers and pirates landed on the shore below; pirates scaled the walls. The lower level was seized.

"We must evacuate," Carlitos said.

"We are surrounded," said Garcia.

"Hurry! Barricade the doors and windows," the aide said.

"Where is Rivero?" Carlitos paced back and forth. "This is his fault."

"Rivero has two ships fighting to regain control of the landing, but there are just too many. Pirates are winning on all sides. Governor Carlitos, you and your family will evacuate inland when I secure us a route."

An explosion from inside the palace had them all ducking for cover. The governor, his family and staff ran through the smoke.

"Should I not come too?" said Dodo.

"Close the gate," ordered Captain García. "Retreat inside!"

The gate slammed shut, bolted before the servants could enter, leaving them to the pirates.

"The place is surrounded," the aide said.

The governor and his family were whisked away through a private exit.

"I'm left with the refugees!" Dodo whined, following a line of servants along a passage. They eventually arrived at the docks, where pirates were landing on all sides. The servants scattered, while Dodo tried to hide between some barrels.

A well-dressed man caught sight of him. "You, there!"

Dodo tried to run, but his easel dropped, and he tripped over it. He was surrounded. "*Hallo*," Dodo began. "I'm a painter. Just a painter."

"You are the painter? Aurora's painter?"

"I only work for her. I do paintings!" Dodo gave a shaky laugh. "I make her look good and slim, I don't worship Satan or dance naked. Well, not often, and never of my own accord. I'll testify against her!"

"You are the painter. Come with me," said the well-dressed man. "I have a ship. I can take you to safety."

"Safety? *Ja, Ja, danke*! Lead the way."

Dodo was assisted to his feet, easel back in his hand.

"I'm Reyning, and this is *De Fortyun*," the well-dressed man said. "I'm glad we found you; you're very important."

"I always thought so." Dodo followed him aboard a shiny rosewood ship with Dutch patterns on the sails. Dodo handed his easel to a crewman. "Here, you carry it, *danke*."

Swarms of pirates came and went all around them.

"Lucky they don't see us or hear us," said Dodo.

A pirate gave him a toothless grin as he went by.

"That was nice," Dodo remarked.

"You are safe. These pirates are after Spanish gold, not simple painters," said Reyning. "But we must leave."

"I must have a tonic before I can sail," said Dodo.

"No problem." Reyning led Dodo inside, where slaves waited. "Treat our guest as royalty. They'll see to your needs."

"I don't suppose you have any caviar?" Dodo asked.

No Place for Ladies

San Juan harbor was a cluttered, fiery ruin, with pirates raiding and ships battling in the harbor. *La Lune* was anchored near El Arsenal, while *De Heilige Graal* raised its anchor. With limited crew available, only a handful of boats slowly pulled the huge East Indiaman away from the causeway. Skirmishes broke out between pirates loyal to Silent Sam and those loyal to la Roche. Arsenault rowed in with buccaneers and Indians.

"Protect my investment," said la Roche to Atia. "Take the countess to the ship."

"Aye, aye, *mon capitaine*," she spoke sharply. *Your investment?* She thought. *It was my bloody idea to get the bloody countess in the first bloody place!*

"Stay on the ship with her." La Roche told de Kreep. "And stay out of this. You're a cripple, yes?"

De Kreep escorted Atia and Aurora to a rowboat.

Silent Sam and Montbars tried to reach the countess but were held back by la Roche's men.

De Kreep and Atia rowed to *La Lune*. As they reached the ship, a boatful of pirates, with Silent Sam and Montbars, rowed for *De Heilige Graal*.

Dark clouds rolled in with rain and thunder from the east, while smoke still hung in the air. Atia could see *Whiskey Kisses* and *Cymru* at the entrance to the harbor. The tiny figures of Jones and Gladstone peered across the water with telescopes.

That's me loyal crew! Atia brightened.

Cliché was on *La Lune's* deck, waiting. He helped de Kreep aboard first. They conversed in French.

Atia pushed off with the oar and rowed. Aurora assisted as well.

"What are you doing?" de Kreep called.

"Sorry, love, but I gotta leave ya," Atia huffed. "This ain't a place for ladies, and ya know it."

"She has a point, yes?" Cliché said to de Kreep. "Your decision."

"Let her go." De Kreep blew her a kiss. "This is no place for ladies."

Atia and Aurora rowed through the smoke. "My ship is this way. Past the wall. Row."

"I don't see it. Are you sure?"

Cannon fire lit up the harbor. Many ships emerged, firing at one another. German galiots attacked.

"Row faster!" Atia's heart raced.

"We'll be run over before we get there," Aurora said.

Smoke parted like a curtain as *Barbarossa I* appeared.

"Is that your ship?" Aurora fumbled with the oar.

Caesar stood at the bow, shouting in his native tongue.

Atia trembled at the sound of his voice.

"Someone you know?"

"Black Caesar."

"*Scheisse.*"

"Atia!" Jones called.

Cymru cut through the smoke behind them.

"Get the countess!" Caesar said to his men. The great galley glided to a stop.

"Jesus," Jones exclaimed. "Black Caesar."

Cymru sailed fast, and a rope ladder was thrown over the side. Atia grabbed it and signalled the countess to follow. Aurora faltered halfway up, so Jones's men brought her up the rest of the way.

"Close quarters!" Jones said.

Men drew swords and Grymes rushed to Atia's side.

"Get ready to fight for your lives, men," said Jones.

The oars of the galley clattered against the oars of the ketch. Caesar shouted at his men.

"Surrender the women," said Caesar.

Atia lifted a white scarf from one of Jones's men. She ran to the boat's edge, waving it.

"What are ya doin', lass?" Jones said.

"We surrender."

"We do? Are you sure?"

"Aye, we surrender."

Caesar swung across on a rope, through the smoke onto the deck. Two Janissaries followed, brandishing nimcha swords.

"So, it's a choice between Black Caesar and Maximilian," Aurora said.

"From what you've told me, it's our best bet," said Atia.

Aurora gawked at Caesar. "What is that?"

"Crisp's monster, Mandingo," said Atia.

"That be the pirate Kabaka," Grymes exclaimed.

"Black Caesar, as he's known now," said Atia.

"Well, I'm glad we cleared that up," Jones said.

"I claim the countess as my hostage," Caesar boomed.

"Fine, take her," said Atia.

"What?" Aurora blanched.

"We're all on the same side," Atia said.

"I'm taking you, too."

"I thought ya might. Ya work for the baron who took over for Crisp, do ya not?" asked Atia. "Is he paying you?"

"Come with me now, or I'll kill all of you," Caesar said.

"Is this the part where I die trying to defend my goddaughter?" said Jones.

"No. This be the part where you go back to the Swiftsure for a mug of ale and wait for me while I go have a word with Crisp's successor," Atia said. "I'll see ya back there."

"G-good plan!" Jones clapped his hands. "I like it. I'll see ya at the Swiftsure."

"You too, Grymes, go on. I got business with Black Caesar and his master." Atia's throat went dry as Caesar's men ushered her and Aurora aboard.

"Put them in yokes and fetters," said Caesar.

Atia shrunk in the presence of this monster. Never had she been this close. One step closer to avenging the death of her da and uncle. *I've got him right where he wants me*, Atia thought.

A Gloomy Shade of Death

Silent Sam climbed aboard *De Heilige Graal* on the port side, while Montbars surprised the crew on the starboard side.

"Search the ship and get her up to speed," Sam ordered.

A door opened, and Sturgeon brought Katrina and Van der Hagen on deck.

"Puerto Rico is off my ten best travel spots," said Sam. "Miss me, Kitty? You wouldn't believe the day I've had."

"Spanish! It's *Fama* and *San Antonio*," Montbars said. "Close quarters action!"

The ships collided into *De Heilige Graal* on each side. Rivero swung across with his officers, while Silvestre boarded from the other side. Spanish soldiers quickly overpowered the pirates.

"Find and protect the hostages," said Silvestre.

Sam and Montbars pushed Katrina and Van der Hagen back inside to the grand cabin. Once there, Van der Hagen turned on them, his fist slamming into Montbars's nose. Blood jetted. Katrina tried to run, but Sturgeon struck her. In the blink of an eye, an axe flew into Sturgeon's chest, and he dropped dead. A German in a steel breastplate retrieved the weapon.

Sam raised his hands, backing into the corner where Katrina cowered.

"You're my special girl, Kitty. Just you and me."

"Surrender your hostages," Rivero demanded.

"Never," Sam replied.

"Where is Countess Aurora?" asked the German.

"This ain't her?" Sam said. "Shit."

Katrina shrank away from Sam, her hands behind her back.

Montbars fought with Van der Hagen for control of a sword.

"Let the girl go and surrender," said Silvestre.

Sam rubbed Katrina's shoulders. "Y'know, you and I got off on the wrong foot. I want ya to know, I'd consider marrying you, maybe, someday, if you get us out of this. I'll send you all on your way. What do ya say?"

Katrina stabbed him in the ribs with a stiletto. At first Sam didn't even feel it go in. Then came the burning sting as a second stiletto entered the opposite side. Instinctively he hit Katrina upside the head with the butt of his sword—again and again until she fell to the floor.

Montbars won the sword from Van der Hagen, just as Rivero and Silvestre cornered them.

"Surrender or die," said Silvestre.

Montbars relinquished the sword. "I surrender."

"Answer. Where is the countess?"

"I wouldn't be here if I knew, Captain."

Van der Hagen fell to his knees, reaching for his daughter.

Sam pulled out the stilettos, blood gushing. "We're even."

Montbars surrendered all his remaining weapons.

Silvestre tended to Katrina, who had blood pouring down the side of her face.

"It was her fault." Sam spat. "It was her own fault!"

"Where is the German witch?" Rivero asked.

"The Countess Aurora," the German added.

"She's not aboard this ship. The French Capitaine captured her. They took her on another ship," said Van der Hagen. "Hold on, my darling girl."

"Where are we, Papa?" Katrina slurred.

"San Juan. You'll be fine. You'll be fine, now."

"We must find Persephone," Katrina said. "She's gone to the village after dark again."

"You rest, dear. Persephone's fine." Van der Hagen held her tight.

"Can you take me home now, please Papa?" she uttered. Life drained from her face and her eyes dimmed.

"Remove those filthy bastards from my ship!" Van der Hagen wept.

Spanish soldiers dragged Montbars and Sam out on deck.

"She had it coming," Sam gasped. "I can't go like this. Monty, kill me, run me through. I want it said that I was killed by Montbars the Executioner."

"She killed you."

"You bastard! Kill me, please!"

"You look dead to me, yes?" Monty impersonated a French accent.

"Now you have a sense of humor. Fuck you, Monty!"

"Hey, Sammy's dying," said a pirate.

"He was stabbed by a girl," Montbars said.

Sam sobbed, spitting up blood as the last of the men were rounded up.

"Take the prisoners to my ship," said Rivero.

The German staggered, hardly able to stand. Silvestre assisted him. "Let's get you back to *Einhorn*."

Sam felt very cold. He tucked his knees to his chest. "What a world, what a world. No room for pirates...anymore...Monty." Sam stared blankly and exhaled his last breath.

Guernsey floated in Lovely Bay as fluffy white clouds blew overhead. Bleedin Art sat fishing off the deck of the captain's cabin, sipping wormwood wine. Behind him, his new parrot Freyja was being tended to by Dr. Strangewayes. Art peered over the railing. A familiar swift ketch, *Alley Cat*, approached the bay.

Morris and Freeman oversaw the taking down of tarps over the decks, with Bach's assistance.

Art's fishing rod went limp.

"Bach, come here and tend my tackle," Art said.

Bach absently cut a strip to attach to the hook and ended up cutting his hand. "*Scheisse*. Freeman, stop, I'm cut."

"We can manage from here," Freeman replied.

Blood dripped, leaving a trail, as Bach entered the captain's cabin to see Strangewayes.

"Wait yer turn." Art patted Freyja's head. "What's the prognosis?"

"Excuse me," Bach said.

"A bit of skin rash," said Strangewayes. "From the sweater, perhaps. We could try another material?" He noticed Bach bleeding. "You're in luck; I have just enough time to fit you in."

"Mind the Persian rug," Art remarked, glancing down at the carpet he had acquired from Cherry Red's Boutique after Cherry's sudden death during the pirate raid at Port Royal. "You can't be done out there yet."

"I'll write him a doctor's note," said Strangewayes.

"Freeman said it was fine," said Bach.

Stubbs came down the stairs from the poop deck and entered the cabin. "*Alley Cat* is here, minutes away."

"Elliot, with my ointment. I anticipate my rendezvous with my fair Atia, and perhaps the Countess of Calenberg."

"If she's anything like the last two German beauties, I would like to meet her," said Strangewayes.

"We'd all like to meet her. I shall be at my utmost in the presence of the countess. I ordered a few things just for the occasion."

"Ah, the Strangewayes Brand Macho Grande Manhood Stiffener. I sent a letter to Mrs. Beazley requesting a few things be sent to aid with romantic endeavors."

"What happened to doctor-patient confidentiality?"

"Oops, I forgot that Mr. Bach can speak English," Strangewayes said.

Morris entered. "The countess is going to fall for him, too, is she? Send us some laudanum—that oughta put her in the mood."

"I heard that one, Morris!" Art said.

Freeman also entered. "The diving bell is up, and the boom secured."

"Fine, prepare to receive supplies from *Alley Cat*," said Art.

"We're on it, Commodore, sir," said Freeman.

"The wind has ruined my day, anyway. Captain Stubbs, get her ready to sail. Dietrich's found our quarry."

By evening, crates and barrels were being loaded by lantern light. Captain Elliot came aboard with a pouch that he handed to Art.

"What took ya so long, Elliot?"

"Good things come, Commodore. White wanted something delivered to you, as did Violante Hayze."

"Violante Hayze?" Freeman and Morris said together.

Art rummaged through the bag, checking through letters and scrolls.

"Morris wants to know how Violante is," said Freeman.

"First things first. Where's my ointment?" Art asked.

"The package from Mrs. Beazley, please, Captain Elliot," Strangewayes said. "It should be wrapped with the label Strangewayes Apothecary."

Elliot handed over a small box with a note attached.

"This it?" Art said, crestfallen. "That's it?"

Strangewayes read the note. "I'm afraid I may have given Mrs. Beazley a bit too much information. She sent a substitute."

"What did she send me?"

"Here's five bars of charcoal soap. Her advice on wooing is to start by washing off that repugnant smell."

Art winced. "What'd I ever do to her?"

"I could use some soap," said Bach.

"Get yer own." Art broke the seal of another letter. "This one's from my newest head wench, Violante; she was poisoned. So much for Scarcliff's protection."

"Poisoned?" Strangewayes said. "Is she well?"

"She's well enough to write a letter, it seems, Doc. Hmm, Big Dick has been bad, however. Longstaff and Lady Beeston have been very bad. Making plans for our countess behind Captain White's back."

"What kind of plans?" Bach said.

"Bad plans, Mr. Bach, weren't you listening? Now, let's see what the president of the council wants of us." Art pulled the wax seal off another letter. "That's in poor taste. He wants us to proceed with the insurance investigation. He's located Crisp's successor, Baron de Klauwen, from the Barbary Coast. His flagship's in Samaná Bay. Prepare to get underway, Captain Stubbs."

"Aye, sir."

"You're in luck, Herr Bach. We're going to Samaná Bay."

"What?" Bach blanched. "Where the kraken lives."

"Not to worry, Mr. Bach." Art grinned. "Perhaps you can lull it to sleep with a clarinet."

Barbarossa 1 rowed into the sunset and away from Puerto Rico. Fatima stood by Caesar on the command deck with the raïs and two other officers, shivering in the wind.

"We're entering the Mona Passage," said the raïs, glaring at her.

"Turn southwest. Look for two small islands," Caesar said. "Fatima, go inside and get washed up. There are new clothes for you in there. The baron wants you fresh and clean."

Fatima headed inside.

"I know you betrayed me," Caesar snarled to the raïs. "Fatima is not to be harmed or touched by anyone, understand?"

"I'm the one who is loyal to Caesar."

"She's the loyal one."

"I don't betray you; she clouds your judgment. You should drop her off somewhere."

"You touch her, you die."

Fatima smiled to herself before entering the captain's cabin. A trunk sat on her side of the room. She found an assortment of linen dresses inside, plain in comparison to the jewel-toned Eastern fabrics she currently wore.

Caesar entered.

"You shouldn't have," said Fatima.

"Our benefactor wants you presentable."

"Benefactor?"

"The man I work for. The one who owns both of us."

"You can't be owned. You're Caesar." Fatima groped between his legs.

"Later. It's not that simple. If you want to be freed, do as I say. I'm taking the countess to Baron de Klauwen; then I am to be freed."

"Can you free me?"

"Baron de Klauwen can free you," Caesar said. "I'll be owed for this as part of my compensation, I will claim you as mine and free you."

"It's not that simple. You said so."

"Come with me. I will speak with this countess."

They ventured down to the hold. Thunder boomed in the distance as the door opened to reveal two women in iron bonds, their ankles in fetters, clamped to an iron bar, and their necks in collars with hooks.

Fatima stopped cold at the sight of Atia. They had met at Strangewayes Plantation long ago and became friends.

"Yer lookin' well, little one," said Atia.

"You know her, Fatima?" asked Caesar.

"Yes, Caesar, we're friends."

"She is worth one hundred thousand in gold to the Sultan of Tripoli if it's proved she is of pure Roman descent."

"A what?" Aurora scoffed. "Her? She's red!"

"Watch yer hooks, missy." Atia deliberately smacked into Aurora's neck brace.

Caesar towered over the countess. "Is she not?" He put a blade to Atia's throat.

"She could be," Aurora interceded.

"Please don't, Caesar," said Fatima. "She's my friend."

"She isn't Roman." Caesar withdrew the weapon.

"No, she's not. I don't know of any Irish Romans; she might as well be the kraken," said Fatima.

"You still got some Port Royal in ya, Fatima," said Atia.

"Will you let her go, Caesar?" Fatima pressed.

"Baron de Klauwen wants her. I trust you are comfortable, Countess?"

"Everyone here has a terrible sense of humor," said Aurora.

"I remember you," Caesar said to Atia.

"Aye, I remember you, too," Atia said.

"Where do you know him from?" Aurora asked.

"This monster is one of the men who killed me da and uncle. I killed the other."

"Oh."

"You shoulda seen what I did to Slasher Al," Atia continued.

"You did me a favor," said Caesar. "Maybe my benefactor wants to thank you."

"Maybe he does."

"I'll have guards bring you up for dinner in an hour."

"As a guest or a course?"

Caesar took Fatima's arm and escorted her back out onto the deck. The hatch closed.

"What will the baron do to them?" Fatima asked.

"It's not for us to say."

"Atia's my friend. I don't want her hurt." Fatima's hands slid up, groping his bulge. Caesar took her into the captain's cabin and slammed the door.

Einhorn

The German warship *Einhorn* headed away from Puerto Rico under a strong wind. Baron Gretsch limped along to his cabin, feeling his guts imploding. He collapsed onto the corner of his bed and tried to unfasten his bloodied breastplate. His heart leapt and sank simultaneously when Helena entered.

"Aurora?" she began.

Gretsch shook his head. "I lost her."

"But she's alive?"

"I don't know. She's a pirate hostage. That's the last I know of her. There are a hundred ships out there and a grand island. If Maximilian found her, then she's already dead."

"This is how I said you'd come back."

"Get out."

"Let me help you."

"I'm fine."

"You came back. That must count for something. Your Captain Fuchs had the ship sailing fast all day," Helena chirped. "I was very impressed. We'll find her."

"Please leave me." Gretsch sighed. "Why don't you join the search on deck?"

Helena departed.

Gretsch closed his eyes, aching. As he pulled away his armor, his hands shook and stung. Once free of the soiled battle clothes, he bathed, dabbing off the blood. When his door burst open, he quickly covered himself.

"Max, I saw her!" Helena exclaimed. "Aurora is on a ship out there."

Gretsch pulled himself up. "What makes you say so?"

"I saw her." She pulled at him. "Come."

"I'll be right there."

Helena raced out of the room.

"A thousand boats around San Juan, and she saw her," Gretsch mumbled as he slid on trousers, a shirt, and his boots. He found Helena on the quarterdeck with Captain Fuchs.

"So, where is she?" Gretsch had his telescope ready to humor her.

Helena pointed to a ship in the distance.

"That one?" Gretsch pointed to *Barbarossa 1*, a lateen-sail Mediterranean-style ship rowing northwest. "Black Caesar's ship. I saw it in San Juan. It's leaving the harbor by itself."

"*Ja*, I saw her. I saw Aurora myself. She's with a red-haired girl. I know what I saw, Max."

"I believe you did." Gretsch gave her a faint smile. "Captain, Helena saw the countess on that ship."

"It's far away—are you certain?"

"*Ja*, that ship," Helena said.

"Captain, I don't recognize the flag," said Gretsch.

"The flag is new. That of a slaver merchant in the service of the East India Company. They're exempt from many laws. She's probably allowed to leave San Juan."

"Captain Fuchs, follow that ship," Gretsch said.

Einhorn rode colossal waves in the middle of the Caribbean. Gretsch tried to ascertain their position, but howling wind and rain pelted his eyes. "Anything?" he asked Fuchs.

"*Barbarossa 1* is gone," the captain replied. "She may have outmaneuvered us and turned back. Or perhaps she went straight. She's faster than we are."

Gretsch cursed under his breath. He remained at the bow, futilely peering through his telescope. After several hours, a crewman approached, telling him, "The captain wants you."

Gretsch ventured inside to the grand cabin, where Helena and Captain Fuchs were having dinner.

Helena was quiet, barely eating, while Gretsch filled a plate.

"There was a ship to the northwest, spotted a short while ago. It could be the ship we're following," said Fuchs. "Should you choose to follow that ship, she's heading right for Cape Engaño. The eastern tip of Hispaniola is known for dangerous reefs. This place is famous, for in 1502, thirty-two ships were lost to the reefs in a storm like this."

"What do you recommend we do?" asked Gretsch.

"We're so close," Helena spoke softly, "she can't get away now."

"I could bring us closer west to Hispaniola," said Fuchs. "From there, we stand a chance of spotting her without being too close to reefs. But I don't recommend approaching Hispaniola."

The remainder of dinner was silent until Helena excused herself to go to bed.

The next morning, *Einhorn* tossed and turned in the waves. Gretsch and his officers continued to scan the area for ships. Helena joined them, clad in a raincoat.

"You should be inside, please," said Fuchs.

"May I look?" she asked.

"There's a ship to the west, somewhere," replied Gretsch. "We saw it a while ago, by a small island."

"We've lost sight of her behind Isla de Mona."

Helena took the telescope from her jacket and aimed it ahead.

"You can't see anything," Gretsch said.

"You're right." Helena returned the telescope to her pocket.

By late afternoon, the sky lightened, and the wind diminished. Helena stood beside Gretsch as both continued to search.

"Is that it?" Helena pointed. "I see a ship."

Gretsch and Fuchs trained their telescopes to the haze. A crack of lightning lit up the sky.

"It's the galley. It's Black Caesar's ship," said Fuchs. "Well done, Helena."

"*Ja*, Helena, well done," Gretsch said.

"Captain, can you catch her?" said Helena.

"I'll try. Bring us on her. Intercept course. Wait inside, please, now."

Gretsch gave Helena a smile before she retreated to her chamber.

Fuchs continued to follow *Barbarossa I* with his telescope. "She's going into Samaná Bay."

The next morning, Helena rose at sunrise and went to the grand cabin for some stew and a hot drink. Her stomach fluttered; she felt as though they were very close to finding Aurora.

A crewman knocked. "Baron Gretsch is calling for you."

Helena rushed out to investigate. "Max, what is it?"

"I thought you might want to see this. Whales."

"Whales?" Helena surged with excitement. She went to the rail, just as a humpback burst from the sea not three hundred yards away. It rolled and plunged back down into the water, leaving frothy, churning foam on the surface.

"Did you see that? *Scheisse*! I've always wanted to see a whale." Helena looked in the opposite direction. "There's more of them!"

"Many," said Gretsch.

"Fantastic. But Aurora?"

"We're stopping here. We lost Black Caesar's ship in this bay. He's hiding in somewhere," Gretsch said. "The captain doesn't want to go too deep into the bay. There's a small town over there. I'll go ashore and find out what they know."

"May I study the whales?"

"You shouldn't be on deck," said Fuchs.

"Let her indulge her interest," Gretsch said.

Helena went inside to collect drawing materials, then studied the amazing creatures, taking notes and making illustrations. Nearby, a whale jumped from the water and landed, sending a mighty white splash over the deck.

Helena screamed joyfully beneath the spray. "This is incredible!"

"She should really be inside," said Fuchs. "We're at general quarters. This is not appropriate."

"I know," Gretsch said.

"What are those big pink things?" Large, protruding, pink tube-like things, briefly appearing out of the water as the whales rolled over each other. "They're mating. Fantastic!"

"Won't she get in trouble for drawing that?" said the captain.

"She's always in trouble," Gretsch mused.

"What if it goes off when it's aimed at you?" said a crewman.

The men laughed, and so did she. They made large-penis jokes at her while she sketched a diagram.

"Just ignore them," said Fuchs.

Gretsch wandered by, examining Helena's drawings.

"A calling of yours, whales?" Fuchs asked.

"And giant penises." She laughed.

Fuchs returned to his command post without another word. Helena and Gretsch pretended not to notice each other smile.

"She can sketch mine," said a crewman.

"Are the men bothering you?" asked Gretsch.

"Max." Helena pointed. "How tall would you say that penis is?" She held up the quill. "It's so big."

Gretsch's face reddened, and he limped away.

Helena continued to draw, expanding her subjects to include various seabirds. She was left alone for a few hours to do as she pleased. Gretsch and the captain conversed, while longboats were deployed.

Gretsch approached her. "You should go in and have something to eat," he said.

"Can I come with you to the town?"

"No. You stay inside, with the windows closed. General quarters are enforced from here."

"I had a wonderful day. Thank you." Helena went inside.

Gretsch took one of the longboats to Samaná Town. He thought of Helena the whole way there, losing track of time in the process. His chest ached whenever they made eye contact. Her warm brown eyes haunted him, until the stench of fish woke him from his daydream.

Gretsch stopped at a squid vendor. "The pirate Black Caesar, do you know of him?"

"Everyone knows Black Caesar. His ship went by yesterday. Not here, back there."

Gretsch followed the man behind the corner, as the merchant made sure no one was watching.

"Black Caesar is much feared here," the merchant continued. "His reputation in the Florida Keys has everyone terrified. If you enforce the law, then God be with you."

"Where did Black Caesar go?"

"His ship rowed in fast, under oars all the way to the end. Into the forbidden zone."

"What is the forbidden zone?"

"It's an area forbidden for anyone to go. Before, it was Maroons and Taínos who ruled Samaná Bay, then the Samaná Bay buccaneers, and now it's Black Caesar and a Dutch baron."

"Baron de Klauwen?"

The merchant nodded. "The baron came in on a large galley, bigger than any Spanish galleon. It lies at the end of the bay, in the Yuna River. They call it *Dionin*. Only well-armed slave galleys come out and go in. Anyone who goes there does not come back."

"What happened to the Maroons and the Samaná Bay buccaneers?"

"There are many tribes of Maroons inland. They stay away from the bay now. The buccaneers moved on. The name made them too easy to find."

Gretsch handed over two shiny gold coins in thanks before returning to *Einhorn* and immediately reporting to Captain Fuchs in the grand cabin. Helena was already there, sitting next to the window, her hair blowing in the breeze as she watched the ships on the horizon.

"Close the window and come here," Gretsch said.

Helena locked the window and joined them.

The captain spread out two maps of the area. "What did you find out?"

Gretsch pointed. "It is said the galley went to the end of the Yuna River. It could be a trap. I have sent for Captain Soler. Though his ships may be engaged."

"Silvestre." Helena perked up.

"There are hundreds of ships scattered and fighting north of us and all the way through the Mona Passage," said Fuchs. "There's a storm coming, just to complicate matters. So, Helena, be so kind as to lock up and secure the cabin."

On deck, Gretsch scanned the surroundings while the captain went up to the quarterdeck.

"Bring up the anchor," said Fuchs. "Take her out into the bay."

Helena lay in bed, unable to sleep with the lightning and thunder. Then there was cannon fire, and Gretsch entered the room to fasten on his breastplate, with its silver wolf and Calenberg crest.

"What is it?" asked Helena.

"Pirate ships. We're surrounded."

"Are we fighting or leaving?"

He strapped on his gun belts, swords, and daggers, with a battle-axe over his shoulder. Come with me." Gretsch guided her down below deck to a small compartment filled with tightly secured barrels.

"Don't leave me in here," she said.

"You must hide. I will come back for you shortly." He gave her a pistol. "You only get one shot."

"I'll make it count, then."

He hesitated before leaving the room. For a split second it looked as though he might kiss her. He tried to speak but couldn't get the words out. Gretsch shut the door behind him.

Helena crouched within the barrels.

The ship vibrated and there was a loud scraping of ships' hulls. *Einhorn* jolted. Helena was hurled, then tossed, before rolling along the floor.

The door to the compartment opened—Gretsch rushed in. She slid her arms around his shoulders, and he carried her out.

"Max?" Helena said.

"The ship is stuck on a reef."

The floor shook, propelling Helena from Gretsch's grip. Water sprang from cracks in the hull, and she was flung into a pile of debris in the corner.

"Abandon ship!" called Fuchs.

Helena found Gretsch, who was slow to get up. She slid her arm around his waist, aiding him to the main deck. They were sprayed with water, and *Einhorn* spun on her side, propelling men into the violent surf. Even Captain Fuchs was swept off the deck, vanishing into the waves.

Pirate ships were closing in, deploying grappling hooks. Helena shivered when she saw Ding Dong leap aboard, brandishing guns.

Gretsch shielded Helena as Ding Dong fired. The shot hit Gretsch's armor. There was a hole in the back plate, where blood ran down his arm.

Waves crashed over the main deck, and Ding Dong was swept away. *Einhorn* collided again with rocks and this time tipped over completely.

Helena was thrown over the rail, landing hard on the water by the rocks below.

Gretsch landed beside her, with a resounding, metallic thud. He clasped her hand as a wave propelled them both upwards onto the rocks. The bow of the ship just missed them and rolled the other way. Gretsch tossed her forward. She clawed her way up the embankment, while Gretsch slid back down.

"Give me your hand." Helena reached for him. "Come on."

Pirates emerged on the ship's deck.

"Go on," said Gretsch.

Another mighty wave pummeled the ship, casting pirates overboard.

Helena reached for Gretsch again. This time he slipped away beneath the current. When the water receded, there was nothing but the sparkling metal of Gretsch's armor sinking into the abyss below.

"Max!" she shrieked. "Gretsch!"

Einhorn flipped back in the opposite direction, with no sign of life aboard.

She crawled on her belly up the muddy hill and into nearby bushes. Below, she could see Samaná Bay town. At the outskirts, pirates dragged the dead hulk of *Einhorn,* using various ships and cables, to a nearby cluster of mangroves. Pirates interrogated the townsfolk, and by nightfall they were all drinking and singing in the town square. Helena, who leaned on a branch as she watched, collapsed against a tree a few hours later and fell asleep.

Bird calls woke her the next morning. Groggily, she rose, her eyes following pink and gold reflections to an estuary that reminded her of Full Moon Bay. She was scarcely aware of the tears rolling down her cheeks.

A ship glided through one of the channels. Too tired to run, she merely watched. A man dressed in Venetian velvet stood on deck, peering through a telescope.

"By the gods!" Helena uttered. "Dodo!" She waved. It took all her remaining energy to holler one more time before hitting the ground.

The first thing she noticed was the gentle rocking from a ship. A soft, dry bed cradled her aching body. Lantern light reflected against the stained-glass window of a captain's cabin.

"She's waking," said Dodo. "Helena, you're safe with me."

A man entered the room and removed his hat.

She could scarcely focus on his face.

"She doesn't look well," said Dodo.

"Are you Helena Braunschmidt?" the man asked.

She nodded.

"I'm Captain Reyning. You are safe on my ship, *De Fortyun*. I work for Van der Hagen's partner. He's expecting you. You'll be protected."

"You're going to be well, Helena," said Dodo.

Helena's voice failed her. She stared at the stained glass. A heavy cough made her body shake.

"Get some rest; we'll talk later." He spoke privately with an officer.

She coughed again.

"She doesn't sound well, either," said Dodo.

"Did you find Baron Gretsch?" she managed.

Reyning shook his head and departed.

She fell back to sleep.

The following day, Helena and Dodo sat chatting in the captain's cabin. They periodically glanced out the window whenever they thought they heard chanting. Charred trees stood along the banks.

Helena was furious with Dodo for running off when Don Medina had stabbed her, but she knew that, had he not done so, he probably would have been killed himself. She sat back on the bed and yawned. "Where is he taking us?"

"Something bad is coming. I know it," said Dodo.

Helena exhaled heavily and went outside.

"Where are you going?" Dodo said. "Get back here."

Helena went upstairs. Black smoke was rising from an immense operation. Dead humpback whales littered the banks, being chopped up by slaves. On the fields beyond, on the Samaná, hundreds of slaves were busy harvesting crops.

Helena ventured forth. "Just where are you taking me? I thought you said I was going to Van der Hagen's partner."

"We are. All is well," said Reyning. "Take her below and keep her there."

Men seized Helena.

"Am I a prisoner, Captain?" Helena said.

"For your own safety, until we reach the river. This is a dangerous area."

"So I've noticed," she muttered as she was escorted below.

Into the Lair of Dionin

Aurora and Atia were dragged from the hold of *Barbarossa I*. A thick stench hung in the air, a smell of rot and decay—death. Aurora gagged, and her iron collar snagged on Atia's.

"Be careful with that," Aurora said.

"Ya mean the great pointy iron rod keeping us locked together?" Atia pursed her lips. "I'll try my best, Countess."

"What were you before you were a slave?"

"I was born a slave. Then I was a wench, then a pirate, and now a slave again."

Rows and rows of chained slaves were being herded into longboats.

"What is this place?" said Aurora.

"I think we're sailing into hell, Yer Highness," replied Atia.

They floated on the Yuna River, through a tree tunnel, into a swampy lake covered in bright green lily pads.

Caesar emerged on deck with Fatima by his side. They passed lateen sails masked behind the trees. Several smaller galiots had formed into a flotilla around a huge wharf. Then, a giant galley hidden at the end of the swampy waterway came into view. Its nameplate read *Dionin*, and the serpent figurehead had long fangs and red eyes. Various carvings and patterns made the ship look like a great snake.

Barbarossa I dropped anchor at the wharf. *Doppelsöldner* mercenaries chanted an old Germanic war song as they lined the decks. Some wore blue armor and feathered hats and carried long arquebus guns. Others wore morion helmets and brandished *zweihänder* swords, pistols, and crossbows. They performed an elaborate march to the beat of a drum.

"That's quite the welcome," Atia remarked. "I've never seen a ship like this before."

"I have. In the Mediterranean and Baltic Sea," said Aurora. "Whole armies can be transported on ships like this."

"You do get around. Those men look like yer type."

"Those men are called *Doppelsöldner*. Elite German mercenaries."

The march ended abruptly; each man stood at his post.

"Just as long as you speak the language," said Atia.

As evening loomed, it was their turn to be loaded onto a vessel with Caesar. Once the boat was lowered into the water, slaves rowed it to a dock next to the snake ship. At their approach, curtains were opened in the aft windows and lantern light beamed down upon them. The glass doors of the gallery were opened, and a silhouetted figure glided into the light. A man with sunken eyes, dressed in a woolen purple cloak and embroidered hat, grinned at their approach, revealing pointed teeth. He rubbed his hands together before vanishing back into the shadows.

A tall, gaunt, almost rat-like henchman approached. "Take off the shackles," he told Caesar. "Welcome, Countess Aurora, to the Garden of Eden. I am Orlok. Please join our celebration in your honor. Bring the other woman."

"I've been called that before," said Atia.

"Silence." Caesar unlocked the two women. "Go up."

The women massaged their wounds as they climbed a unique flight of stairs to the main deck.

"Baron de Klauwen apologizes for Caesar's treatment of you. It will result in a deduction from his compensation. Your wounds must be cleaned," said Orlok. "Baron de Klauwen offers his hospitality. Your quarters are waiting."

They navigated the maze of *Doppelsöldners* before entering a passageway into the ship.

"You will clean up in here," said Orlok.

"Will we?" Aurora said.

"The baron believes women should always be clean before dinner." He led them past many slaves to a room with a large copper tub full of water. Clean dresses were hanging in a wardrobe.

"Those are for me to wear?" Aurora said.

"For *us*," Atia said. "Unless Mr. Orlok likes to get fancy once in a while."

"A pleasant anecdote." Orlok grinned widely.

"I'm the countess. I'll pick first."

"I hope the sizes will fit. Make yourselves comfortable. The baron will be ready after sundown." Orlok slinked away.

Aurora and Atia both took advantage of the tub.

"I've never been so dirty in my life," Aurora said as she scrubbed away the grime.

"Clearly you've never been to Port Royal," said Atia.

Once bathed, they went to the wardrobe. Aurora reached for a dark green dress.

"That dress don't suit ya," said Atia. "You really want to wear that one?"

Aurora scrutinized the garment and handed it over. "Looks too Irish, anyway. Go ahead."

"Something wrong with Irish?"

"Not at all. Someone has to be the wench, right?"

"We're going to get along just fine."

Atia laced up the dark green dress with embroidered gold accents, while Aurora tried a red one.

"Now I look like the Princess of Poland." Aurora checked herself in a mirror. "I hate the princess of Poland!"

Aurora found another, a gold one with fancy beading on the skirt. "Better." Atia helped lace up the back.

They could see the ship below, where slave women were being brought out and offered to Caesar.

"You suppose that's part of his payment?" Atia asked.

"For bringing me here, possibly. It's common in the east to sell women."

"It's common everywhere." Something else caught Atia's eye. Another ship had anchored nearby, and a longboat was being rowed in. "It's Reyning."

"*Ja*, it looks like it's going to get stormy, but surely dinner is inside," said Aurora.

"No, Reyning. He's a Dutch ship captain who gets around in these parts," said Atia. "His ship is *De Fortuyn*. The sneaky bastard deals in slaves."

"Oh yes, I heard the name back in Tobago, I think."

"You heard right. Tobago and Barbados are his home ports."

Summoned to dinner by a slave, they passed through glass doors into a grand stateroom, where a banquet table was laden with food. Fabric-lined walls were decorated by many oil paintings, including one that resembled Dante's *Inferno*.

When Reyning arrived, he brought with him Helena and Dodo.

Aurora nearly fainted at the sight of Helena. "Thank Nerthus, it's you, Helena!" Aurora rushed over and they embraced. "I dreamt of you."

"I know," said Helena.

They laughed and embraced again. Aurora struggled not to cry, while Helena fought to stand upright.

"You have no idea what I have been through." Aurora brushed away her tears.

"What *you've* been through?" said Helena.

"Little Venice was destroyed," Aurora gasped. "I saw it. I saw Catharina. They're all dead."

"I heard."

"Dodo!" Aurora suddenly noticed him. "Have you been with Helena the whole time?"

"For an eternity since we left Hanover. We were with Baron Gretsch."

Aurora's face soured with distaste. "You came here with Baron Gretsch?"

"I know. I'll never recover," said Dodo.

A shadow slid across the wall, and then Baron de Klauwen stood behind them, his long, gray fingers intertwined. "Countess Aurora of Calenberg."

Dodo nearly collapsed at the sight of the baron.

"Yes. I'm Countess Aurora of Calenberg."

"Caesar was not to treat you unkindly. He will be punished," said the baron.

"Punished with twenty virgins?" Atia questioned.

"Atia Crisp, we finally meet," said the baron

"Atia la…O'Malley, if ya please, Baron. You're Crisp's partner from the Barbary Coast?"

Baron de Klauwen bowed his head. "We have much to discuss. Please make yourselves comfortable." He turned to

Reyning. "You earned your payment. The first full shipment to St. Eustatius is ready to depart."

"The payment was satisfactory," said Reyning. "There are many ships entering the bay behind me. Pirates have the German ship, *Einhorn*."

"You were followed; it was unavoidable," said the baron. "There is also a ship out of Port Royal north of the Samaná, a merchantman called *Guernsey*. Do you know this ship?"

"Her captain is a man named Stubbs. He sailed with Morgan the famous buccaneer. He regularly ships for Valentine Shipping."

"Arthur Valentine, who bought slaves from Crisp?" The baron's eyebrow cocked. "Our presence here is revealed earlier than expected."

"Shall I meet *Guernsey*?"

"No, you must deliver the slaves on time. My men will meet Captain Valentine. It's time to let Port Royal know that the Garden of Eden is open for business."

Reyning waved his hat to the women before heading to the door.

Dodo stirred and was helped to the table.

"We're staying here, then?" Helena said.

"You're safe now, Helena, you and the countess." Reyning left.

"Not to worry, missy, Captain Valentine's a friend of mine," said Atia.

"As my guests, you are under my protection," said the baron. "Come, my pretty ones, dinner awaits. You must replenish your bodies."

Hunger got the better of them, and they sampled the buffet. Various meats, fruits, cakes and other pastries sat on silver trays. There was also a platter devoted to lemons— lemon wedges, lemon tarts, lemon cake, and lemon pudding. A slave brought out a large salmon garnished with lemon slices.

Baron de Klauwen poured them each a drink before he sucked a dark liquid from a cup shaped like a skull. "Eat, please. If this is not to your liking, I have a wide variety from all over the world."

"Cognac?" Aurora asked hopefully.

"Of course. Orlok, bring Cognac."

"Finally, someone with taste."

Orlok presented her the bottle for approval.

"*Ja, ja,*" she said.

Orlok poured the contents into a glass, unblinking.

Aurora drank back the whole glass and cleared her throat.

Orlok paid no mind and left the bottle on a side table.

"Another glass, please, Orlok," Aurora said.

Orlok snatched the bottle and delivered it.

After refilling the glass, Aurora smiled while his expression remained vacant. She swiftly grabbed the bottle. "I'll hold onto it."

"Orlok, nectar," summoned de Klauwen.

Orlok ventured to the cabinet to retrieve a crystal decanter filled with thick red liquid. After pouring the baron's drink, Orlok seized a lemon off the table and gnawed it ferociously.

"Forgive me for asking, but I assume you brought us here intentionally?" Helena asked.

"Indeed, Helena Braunschmidt of Hanover, you are under my protection." Baron de Klauwen's eyes fixated on Helena, making her shuffle uncomfortably in her chair. "The slave trade has replaced piracy as the most lucrative business in the New World. I'm a partner and longtime associate of Calenberg. You are safe here."

"How did you come about all this, Baron?" Aurora asked.

"I made a fortune on the stock market. I sold all my tulip plantations before the crash."

"The whaling and the slaves are yours, too?" asked Helena.

"Only twenty-three and such a knowledge of metals, chemicals, and the stars." The baron continued to stare. "A naturalist as well now, I hear—a superior woman."

"What do you want with us, exactly?" Helena asked.

"You speak with authority. Some would call it insolence," the baron replied.

"I've had a very rough journey; forgive me."

"You were difficult to bring here. But, well, worth the effort, I think."

"My handmaiden is of particular interest to you, Baron?" Aurora interjected.

"She is." His rat-like teeth formed a demented grin. "It is said that, when only a small child, the Countess Aurora of Calenberg was switched with the daughter of a Braunschmidt knight, for her protection. They were never switched back."

Dodo indicated Helena. "So, you're saying that she's the countess?"

"Preposterous," Aurora scoffed. "An absurd fantasy."

"Please go on," said Helena.

"You have a scar on your chest. Between your breasts."

"No."

Everyone stared at Helena's chest.

"Fine, then, yes, I have a scar there."

"The real Countess Aurora was stabbed in the heart at age one, but survived, leading to the rumor of witchcraft from a very young age."

Helena's fingers caressed the scar. "How would I survive a stab in the heart?"

"It is legend. The blade broke in two. Sophie's knight was a surgeon. He took the blade out from your ribs."

Helena's mouth gaped. "Maximillian Gretsch."

"No, it can't be," said Aurora.

"Look at the painting of Aurora as an infant. Then see the family portrait five years later, when young Aurora's petite brown eyes inspired poetry."

Aurora unintentionally batted her big brown ones.

"It makes sense; I'm more intellectual than you," said Helena.

"Watch it, Braunschmidt!" Aurora's face reddened. "Were you there?" she asked the baron.

"He was," Helena said. "I remember."

"You couldn't possibly remember if you were only two," Aurora said.

"One," corrected Helena.

"I supplied the slaves for that battle," said de Klauwen.

"Even if it is true, and it's not, I'm not going to be a handmaiden," said Aurora. "Forget it."

"I don't want to be a countess, anyway," said Helena.

"What?" Aurora belched, backfiring the Cognac. "Why not?"

"I hate all your friends."

"*Ja*, that's true," said Dodo.

"I didn't mean to offend, Countess," said the baron. "I couldn't resist. Please accept my apology for my prank."

A ghoulish advisor came in and whispered in the baron's ear.

"There are rescue ships coming from Calenberg," said the baron. "Quarters have been prepared for each of you. Orlok will show you. Have a pleasant evening. I'll see you tomorrow, when you're refreshed."

"Thank you, Baron," said Aurora.

"*Ja*, thank you, Baron," said Helena.

The baron departed while Orlok escorted everyone to their rooms.

Atia was shown to her room. It had a small cannon port, a window overlooking a promenade, a red and gold rug, and a canopy bed with red silk pillows.

Atia brought out a small pouch from within her dress and withdrew from it a clay pipe, some tobacco and a flint with which she lit it. She inhaled deeply. When she finished, she opened the window and climbed out.

Above her, guards kept a watchful eye. She strolled along casually, glancing up, and when she saw the guards were distracted, she blew a bird whistle.

"What is that?" came Aurora's voice.

Atia followed it and climbed around a spiral pillar.

"It's the bar wench; she has a whistle," said Dodo. "Bugs, pirates, Indians and heat aside, I'd never get used to the scent of death here. I want out. Can we go back home now? I rather miss Hanover. The Caribbean is pretty, but I've seen it."

Aurora stuck her head out the window of her room. "Atia? Well, this is cozy. He's got us all together."

Aurora and Dodo climbed out.

From behind the pillar on the opposite side, Helena emerged. "He's not even worried about us escaping."

"Escape to where?" Dodo said.

"Exactly," Helena said.

Smoke wafted through the trees, given off by the flickering torches of the slaving operation. Across the pond, waterlilies glowed white beneath the giant moon.

"Here." Atia brought out a wooden box with a silver spoon. "This stuff helps me think."

Aurora inspected the white powder. "Oh, that'll do!" She snorted some up each nostril. "Where did you get it?"

Aboard *Cometa,* in the captain's cabin, Laurens de Graaf tore his room apart. He ripped all the drawers from his desk and threw them on the floor. He then proceeded to knock over statues and yank paintings off the wall.

"Where the fuck is it?" he shouted.

Nigel and the other officers stood at attention in the corner, wincing and grimacing as everything was dismantled. Even the parrot Henry V flew out of the room.

"Where the fuck is it?" Laurens barked. "Where the fuck is it!"

Back aboard *Dionin*, Aurora took another snort up each nostril.

"It's arse hole tax." Atia brushed her nose, shivering. "Other countess?"

"No, not for me," Helena said.

"She's not a countess," Aurora insisted.

"Suppose he's right?" Dodo said. "Suppose Helena *is* the countess?"

"Suppose I kill you?" Aurora shot him a look.

Helena studied the moonlit, petal-covered lagoon, while Dodo partook of the powder. He shook his head, making strange faces, then ran off, sneezing.

"How do you suppose he feeds all the slaves?" Helena said. "Do they eat the whales, or is all the food brought in?"

"Maybe the baron's eating his slaves," Atia suggested. "Cannibalism happens around here."

"Or fish?" Dodo added, looking ill as he returned to them.

Atia handed the powder box to Helena, who dug in the silver spoon and snorted.

"*Wunderbar*, this is enjoyable!"

"You mean to tell me you never tried it before?" Aurora's pitch rose. "What happened to the stuff I bought for you?"

"You snorted it all."

"Oh."

Helena sniffed some more, and she gave a bemused frown, massaging her scalp and temples.

"Are you liking it?" Atia asked.

"Where's my head?" Helena said.

Aurora took the box and sniffed. "Oh, gods!"

"*Ja*," said Helena.

"Yeah, that's it," Atia replied.

An iridescent dragonfly landed on Dodo's arm. He stared at it, mesmerized by its brilliant colors. "I'm hallucinating a beautiful fairy on my hand."

"Coca-leaf powder is not a hallucinogen," Helena said. "That's a real bug."

Dodo yelped and shook his arm until the dragonfly flew off into the night.

"It's nothing to be afraid of," said Atia.

A dark object swooped by, snatching the dragonfly and soaring off towards the dark treeline.

"What about that?" Helena said. "Should we be afraid of that?"

"What? What did you see?" Dodo asked.

"Something dark and fast. Like a bat."

"You're joking. She's joking," said Dodo. "Oh, look at the treeline and the ship! I have to paint this. Helena, be my model for a sketch."

"Not me. Not now. Use her." Helena indicated Atia.

"Paint a wench?"

"Thee wench," Atia corrected.

"Consider it an illustration of the underprivileged Caribbean wench," said Helena.

Dodo's nose pointed up. "Illustrations are beneath me."

"What a strange place this is," Helena said to Aurora. "Gretsch was grotesque until I met Baron de Klauwen."

"I miss the old Gretsch," Dodo said. "What happened to him?"

"He was washed over in a storm, saving me. He saved my life when I got run through with a sword. The crazy old bastard saved me twice."

"How'd ya get run through with a sword?" Atia wondered.

Helena walked away without a word.

They waited for over a minute.

"Is she coming back?" Atia asked.

"I suppose not," said Aurora. "So, paint me where?"

"When the sun comes up," said Dodo. "Where does the sun come up?"

"In the east," said Atia.

"Which way is that?" said Dodo.

Atia shrugged. "Who am I, Ferdinand Magellan?"

After another minute, everyone dispersed. Dodo went to organize his art supplies, Aurora went to try on the dresses, and Atia climbed back inside her room, leaving the window open.

Atia tried the bird whistle again.

"*Ma chérie*," said Minuit.

Atia jumped and turned around. "I *thought* that was you, pretty boy."

Minuit nibbled at the fruit bowl.

She patted his head and checked the leg bracelet. "Do ya have something for me?" She unrolled it. It wasn't instructions, but questions, such as: how many guards inside with weapons?

Atia thought a moment and went to steal a bit of parchment and charcoal from Dodo. She then wrote her responses and put them in the bracelet. After Minuit's meal, she took him to the window. "Wait here."

Atia checked for guards, but none were looking.

"Now."

Minuit took off, camouflaged by his dark feathers.

A cold breeze from the east sent chills up Atia's arms. She stared at the clandestine operation deep within the trees and shook her head. "By the pricking of my thumbs, something wicked this way comes."

Bay of Arrows

De Heilige Graal sailed through the Mona Passage at sunrise. Within the orange glow travelled four Brandenburg galiots and several warships. Prinz Maximilian's yacht raced ahead of the pack. He stood on deck in jewel-encrusted Prussian blue armor, peering through his telescope. A smoke trail caught his attention, and he followed it to a ship.

"That's an East Indiaman," said the captain. "It may be *De Heilige Graal*."

"Intercept course," said Maximilian. "Full speed."

"Oars, double time," said the captain.

The men rowed until exhaustion set in. An hour later they closed in. The ship's figurehead of a haloed Virgin Mary and the nameplate revealed it all.

"That's it! We found it," Maximilian said.

Later in the morning, the yacht and the galiots came alongside *De Heilige Graal*. Maximilian and his men scaled the side ladder with difficulty, wearing heavy armor. They scoured the deck, finding the navigator at the ship's wheelhouse.

Maximilian cornered the navigator. "Who's in command?" He drew his sword. "Answer."

"My Prinz," said the soldier, Krieger. "The ship is all but derelict. Her captain and the officers are dead. Just the owner, Van der Hagen, and a few crewmen and slaves are alive. It's like a ghost ship."

"What about the Hanover treasure?"

"We searched the ship thoroughly. We are very confident the treasure and countess are not on board. The ship has been searched by pirates, buccaneers, and the Spanish. There's nothing left but a charred hull. Viscount Van der Hagen is in the grand cabin."

Maximilian went inside the smoldering ruins of the once-proud ship to find Van der Hagen sitting across from his dead daughter. "Viscount Van der Hagen, you have my sympathies," said Maximilian. "Where is Countess Aurora?"

"She is not aboard," said Van der Hagen. "The big black pirate took her."

"Black Caesar, *ja*. Where did he take her?"

"My fleet, like your Brandenburg fleet, is insolvent. I've sold it all to Baron de Klauwen. He was going to pay a king's ransom, and my daughters and I were going to live the rest of our lives in Curaçao." Van der Hagen paused. "I was going to have a government office in Aruba. But that's not going to happen now. They're taking Aurora to Samaná Bay. He betrayed me, you see."

"Like you betrayed Calenberg?"

"I ask God for a merciful death. My house is gone, my daughters are gone, I have nothing left."

"Then go die how you see fit, Viscount Van der Hagen." Maximilian turned to his men. "Black Caesar has taken her. Back to the boats, on the double. The treasure could be there, as well as the countess. Order the fleet to follow me to Samaná Bay."

At dusk, Maximilian ventured on deck. He had changed into a long black justacorps with delicate gold stitching and a frilly white cravat. A message flashed from one of his galiots from Puerto Rico.

"It's the cardinal and Count Molke," said the captain.

"All stop," said Maximilian. "Bring them aboard."

The oars were raised, and a plank readied. Soon the ships converged. Count Molke and Cardinal Grimaldi crossed over.

"Don't look down, just walk straight across," advised the captain. "Quickly now."

The cardinal's foot slipped on the plank.

The count stepped back as the cardinal fell backwards onto the boat. For several seconds, Cardinal Grimaldi lay unmoving, until he finally shrieked with pain.

"Well, help him up," Molke instructed the crewmen, before boarding the yacht.

The cardinal whined, reluctant to move. Crewmen put him in a makeshift stretcher and carried him aboard.

"Prinz Maximilian, we have something for you," continued the count. "Cardinal?"

Crewmen propped up the cardinal next to Maximilian.

"I bring an invitation." The cardinal checked around.

A Spanish officer handed over the cardinal's case. "Is this what you're looking for?"

"Thank God." Cardinal Grimaldi opened his case and handed over a parchment with de Klauwen's seal.

Maximilian took the parchment, but it slipped from his metal glove. He overreached trying to catch it and punched the cardinal in the face. Clank! The cardinal groaned.

Count Molke held the invitation up while Maximilian read.

"Invest in slavery. Invest in the future," said Maximilian.

"The Garden of Eden Slave Emporium," said the count.

"It's a major development in Samaná Bay." The cardinal cradled his bleeding nose.

"Samaná Bay is where Countess Aurora was taken," said Maximilian.

"Baron de Klauwen has the countess and her handmaiden in his possession," said the cardinal. "She's a guest on his ship."

"I accept Baron de Klauwen's invitation," said Maximilian.

Guernsey sailed south through choppy whitecaps and beneath angry, rolling clouds. Bleedin Art and his men stood on deck as the Samaná drew closer. Dr. Strangewayes arrived, clinging to his raincoat. Beyond, *De Fortuyn* seemed to appear from nowhere, rowing out of the bay, followed by a slave galley.

"What do ya know, it's Reyning," said Art.

Morris put his palm up to the sky. "No, it's not."

"*De Fortuyn*, Reyning out of Samaná Bay," said Freeman. "With a slave ship and escort."

"Reyning taking merchandise out for sale," said Art. "I'd say Baron de Klauwen is open for business."

"Where do you suppose he's going?" asked Strangewayes.

"San Juan, maybe, or the Leewards," rasped Morris. "I can't count how many ships there are over there."

"Well, I can count the ones over there in the Bay of Arrows," Freeman said.

They trained their telescopes to *Cymru* and *Whiskey Kisses,* anchored behind cays in a bay off the starboard side. *De Fortyun* and the slave ship sailed by the other way.

"Reyning's doing well for himself," said Stubbs.

"He's all cack," Art said. "Stubbs, take her in for a look-see around the point into the bay. Mr. Freeman, why don't you and Morris take some lads to go see Tom Jones tonight."

"Aye, sir. I ain't seen Tom Jones for a fortnight."

In the evening, *Guernsey* dropped anchor behind the point, shielded from the wind. Lights danced upon the sea's surface from the steady flow of ship traffic to the west. Two longboats delivered men to *Guernsey*: Freeman with Jones in one and Morris in the other, with many of Atia's crew.

"Permission to come aboard, Captain Valentine, or should I say *Commodore*?" Jones began.

"It's admiral, the moment you sign up," said Art.

"We have wounded," said Gladstone.

"Is the lady a slave, Mr. Gladstone?" asked Stubbs.

"She's registered crew; I signed her up meself."

"Where is she from?"

"Uh, during all the fuss, I forgot to ask. Her jaw is broken and she ain't talking."

"My patient, Admiral?" Strangewayes said.

"Your patient, Doctor," Art replied.

Strangewayes assisted the injured woman into the triage at the forward compartment.

Freeman and Morris escorted Jones up to the quarterdeck.

"Join me inside, Captain Jones," said Art.

Inside the captain's cabin, Freyja, now wearing a little woolen vest, climbed up a miniature ladder to a compartment fashioned to look like the aft cabin of a ship.

"What's happening in Samaná Bay, Jones?" Art asked. "Where's my pretty Red?"

"Black Caesar's got her, and that countess they're all lookin' for. Took them all the way into the bay."

"Some of us want to follow," Grymes said. "Black Caesar will do her like her old man, you know it."

"And you are?" Art queried.

"Grymes. Captain Red's first officer."

"*Captain* Red? I didn't think she'd take pirating this far. Well, Mr. Grymes, wait outside. Captains only."

"Beggin' the admiral's pardon, I'm acting captain of *Whiskey Kisses* until Red's return."

"Right, right, right. So you are, Captain Grymes. Well, Jones was right not to be too hasty. Samaná Bay's a deathtrap."

"We saw Reyning's ship pull out with a lot of slaves," said Jones. "He's tied in with this baron."

"If only we could stop him and see what he's up to," said Art. "Perhaps he has the countess?"

"It's illegal to stop a slave transport," said Stubbs.

"But he may have the countess and our Red."

"Aye, what if she's on that ship now?" Grymes shifted position.

"Captain Grymes, would you be so kind as to follow Reyning's ship and find out where he's going?" Art said. "It can't be far; a galley like that can't take enough food for a long voyage. Find out if he has your captain."

"Aye, I'll find her."

"On your way, then."

When the cabin door clicked, Art continued. "That's better. Now, while Captain Grymes follows Reyning to the Leeward Islands, we can focus on where they are."

"Where are they?" Jones asked.

"Baron de Klauwen has them. For what, I don't know."

"Hostages?" Bach offered.

"Hostages ain't worth shit anymore," said Morris.

"Morris has a point," said Freeman. "She's not worth the fuss as a hostage. She must know where this treasure is, or they'd have chopped her long ago."

"Maybe it's a German conspiracy and they're comin' to whack her," Morris added.

"What'd he say?" Art wondered.

"Nothing important," Freeman said.

"What's our situation to the west, Captain Stubbs?" Art asked.

Stubbs peered through the curtains with a telescope. "A whole lot of German ships coming this way."

"Germans comin', Germans goin'," Art mused.

"They're coming for their countess, and they don't look happy," Freeman said.

"Are we friends with the Germans?" Morris mumbled. "I lost track."

"We're friends, last I checked," said Art. "Mr. Bach is my ambassador to the Germans."

"Suppose Morris is right. If they start a fight, it will get Atia killed," Jones said. "Someone's got to go into Samaná Bay and make contact with Baron de Klauwen and get her back."

"Captain Jones just volunteered to visit Baron de Klauwen," Art said. "This is working out well, isn't it?"

"Me?" Jones said aghast. "Well, the Lord hates a coward."

"Didn't think you was religious."

"It's never too late."

"Well, my fleet is coming together. Now, if you'll excuse me, I have a bird to tend to, and you all have jobs to do," said Art. "By the way, where is *De Heilige Graal*?"

"She's still out there in the Mona Passage," Jones said. "Not making good time, if you know what I mean, but coming nonetheless."

"Dietrich was all set to go after her when he spotted the wreck of the Brandenburg ship, *Einhorn*," Stubbs added.

"Let me know if she's sighted. Providence tells me she's comin' right to me."

After *Guernsey* anchored off Cayo Levantado in Samaná Bay, Art smoked a Cuban cigar on the deck of the captain's cabin. On a nearby beach, the hull of *Einhorn* lay on its side. *Stingray,* alongside longboats and a group of men, was trying to refloat her. German ships rowed by, ignoring their presence. Jones's *Cymru* arrived alongside of *Guernsey*.

Art finished his cigar just before a knock came at the door.

"Come," said Art.

Jones, Bach and Stubbs entered.

"Thanks, Tom, for the kind visit. Them Germans got no manners at all," Art said. "Oh, sorry, Mr. Bach, didn't see you there."

"Admiral Valentine, Prinz Maximilian is among them, with a special invitation from Baron de Klauwen," Bach said.

"So has Bleedin…Admiral Valentine." Jones removed a letter from his pocket. "This got delivered to me. A boat met us about halfway in. Nice bunch, a bit pale for around here, though."

"Where's your invitation?" Art broke the wax seal.

"Do I need an invitation? I didn't make the guest list."

"Call Dietrich in, Captain Stubbs. I'll go in on *Stingray*," said Art. "Follow me in, but nicely. Mr. Bach, I have a letter which needs delivering. Gentlemen, this is our way in."

Up in Smoke

Helena sat on the balcony of Aurora's chamber aboard *Dionin*. Dodo was painting Aurora in a white gown with embroidered flowers. Behind them, hundreds of emaciated slaves were being whipped and force-marched.

"I'm not sure of the background," Aurora said.

"They'll be happy little trees. That's it, happy little trees," Dodo assured.

Helena picked away at the remnants of lunch. Her stomach churned. Every one of her senses was telling her that they were in danger. Ships were arriving through the tunnel of trees. "There are ships coming."

Aurora and Dodo turned to look, while Atia appeared from her side of the balcony.

"I see them," Aurora said.

Helena aimed a Braunschmidt telescope, then handed it to Aurora.

"It's the Brandenburg ships. I recognize them." The color drained from Aurora's face. "Maximilian's yacht. He's here."

"Not a rescue but an execution squad," said Helena.

"May I?" Atia took the telescope. "They're not all Brandybergs. I see *Guernsey* out there, too. It's Bleedin Art. Don't know about you three, but I'm countin' on being rescued."

"Who?" Helena said.

"Bleedin Art. The slaver with a heart, is what they say. It's his advertisement. He was a pirate who turned to slave trading. He owns the tavern where I work."

"I'm no more enthusiastic about meeting Bleedin Art than I am about seeing Maximilian," said Helena.

"Hold on—I thought this Max fell overboard," Atia said.

"My guardian, Maximillian Gretsch, is who you're referring to. This is Prinz Maximilian," Helena said.

"Once more?" Atia said.

"My cousin, Prinz Maximilian, a real *schmerz im arsch*, intends to brutally murder us," said Aurora.

"So, Maximilian's the one with a kettle on top?" Atia remarked. "Take no offense, should I distance myself from you lot for a while."

"He will not take us alive," Aurora said. "The three of us will commit suicide before we're taken by Maximilian."

"The three of us?" Dodo said. "Uh, a painter is like a peasant; I should probably go with the wench. Would you like a painting, Wench?"

Atia glared at him. "You ain't comin' with me, Dodo."

"No one is going anywhere." Orlok appeared at the window.

Atia's hand patted her chest. "Gave us a fright."

"Follow you to where, miss?" Orlok inquired.

"To the privy," Atia snapped. "The painter's a peculiar little bastard."

"You are expected this evening at the presentation," said Orlok.

"What presentation?" Aurora asked.

"Your presentation."

"May I decline? I'm not feeling well," said Helena.

"She always declines," Aurora said.

"The women will attend the presentation and wear the dresses provided." Orlok revealed some sheer fabrics. "The artist will paint the affair. It will be most grand. This is not a request."

"That's not a dress; it's a veil." Helena could see her hand through the fabric.

"I wouldn't wear this to a costume ball," Aurora said. "You can see everything. No."

"*No* is no longer a word you may use," said Orlok.

They were ambushed by strong men, who came at them from all sides of the balcony. The women and Dodo were forced to their knees.

"What is this?" Aurora demanded as her dress was being torn off. "What are you doing?"

One gripped Dodo by the collar.

"Fine, fine," Dodo raised his hands. "I won't make trouble."

"I have never been so insulted," Aurora scoffed. "I'm a countess!"

"Not anymore," said Orlok.

"I don't know what yer all so surprised about." Atia was now completely naked. "I've only been expecting this the whole bloody time."

All of them were marched to the room with a copper tub. The women struggled and swore, until female slaves arrived with cosmetic items.

"Shave their mounds, make sure they're clean and presentable," said Orlok.

"Not the quim!" Aurora's face reddened. "I can't believe this! Do you know how much it itches growing back?"

"If you use wax, you get less of a rash," Dodo said.

"*Ja*, if we must do this, beeswax would be preferable," said Helena.

"I could save the mold and hang it on my wall." Orlok laughed giddily.

Helena cringed.

"Give the women plenty of drink," Orlok instructed the slaves.

"Good idea," Aurora said. "Give the women drink."

"And me," Dodo insisted.

Glasses of a pale-yellow liquid were served.

"What is it?" Helena took a glass.

"Something to make you more comfortable. When they are presentable, take them to the grand stateroom." Orlok departed.

Muscular men stood guard while the women were shaved, everywhere except for the hair on their heads. At first, Helena kept her knees together, until one of the men pried them apart. A woman slave shaved her with a blade.

"How do we get into these situations?" said Helena.

"Ya mean this has happened to you before?" Atia replied. Am I permitted to go to the privy?"

A guard escorted Atia across the room to a curtained area.

The slave woman set down the folding blade before sorting through perfume bottles. Discreetly, Helena swiped it, tucking it under a cushion. A guard noticed and seized the weapon.

Upon return, Atia gestured to Helena's stomach. "That's one hell of a porthole."

"Don Medina did this to me; he didn't want me carrying his child."

"I guess not." Atia leaned around to see the scar on Helena's back. "He ran ya right through."

"Oh, Helena." Aurora's eyes bulged. "You mean you were?"

Helena tried to leave the room, but slaves held her back.

"I'm sorry." Aurora squeezed Helena's hand.

Atia indicated the scar on Aurora's bottom. "That, I'm not the least bit surprised at."

"It was done by an Englishman they call Two, or Tew. The fool shot me by mistake."

"Right, by mistake," said Atia.

Cosmetics and jewelry were applied to the women. Atia had green eye paint and crushed charcoal powder around her eyes, while Helena and Aurora's faces were brightened with gold dust and their eyes darkened with dark grey ore.

Helena felt her pulse quicken. A sick realization filled her stomach. "Breeding stock."

"What?" Aurora said.

"Breeding stock. It's no different here than it is on the Barbary Coast or under the Ottoman Empire. This is what they make slave women wear in Arabia and Istanbul and Tripoli. We're going to be sold as breeding stock. Dodo, remember the paintings?"

"One of my teachers came back with renderings he made when he was on a ship in the Barbary Coast. He did several paintings of Ottoman princes and noblemen, and they all had dozens and dozens of women, all dressed like this. They sell them and rape them and torture them all they please."

"Aye, we get it," Atia said.

"Atia, do you know Black Caesar?" Helena asked. "Have you met him before?"

"Black Caesar is one of the men who killed me da and uncle."

"*Scheisse.* I was hoping we could reason with him."

"Reason with that?" Aurora laughed.

"Clearly, he's a slave in all this, too. Look how young he is. See him up close, he's barely Atia's age."

"I'll kill Black Caesar meself when I get the chance," vowed Atia.

"We must find a way out of here. Can you be civil to him?"

"Be civil to the man who killed me da? Is he gonna believe it?"

"No, of course not."

"Like I said, Bleedin Art's a friend of mine," said Atia. "We gotta get word to him that I'm—we're here. I'm sure he'd like to see what's going on."

"I don't know what's going on." Aurora shook her head.

"A shilling says I leave with Bleedin Art," asserted Atia.

Helena half laughed and half cried. "I almost expect Gretsch to show up and save us. But I know he's not out there."

"Took a liking to the old troll, did you?" Aurora asked.

"No, can't say I did. But I wish he was here now. I said he was vile, but he never made me dress up in a mosquito net and show off *meine fotze* in public."

Helena went to the porthole. The clouds rolled by as Orion shone through. They would have to make their move soon. She would rather die than fulfill the destiny being forced upon her. "Tonight, we fight our way out, or die."

At sunset, Bleedin Art emerged from his cabin freshly washed, in a blood-red suit with gold stitching, an ostrich feather hat on his head, and a shiny black walking stick in hand. He met Morris and Freeman on deck. They were festooned in their best finery.

Stingray glided towards them.

"Admiral, you've never looked better." Stubbs handed Art a telescope.

"Thank you, Captain. Any new contacts to report?"

"Two more ships entering Samaná Bay; Spaniards this time."

"See Morris, Spaniards. We're allies now," said Art. "This meeting will go splendidly. Dietrich's with me. He speaks the language."

"But they're Dutch," said Morris.

"Admiral, that's what Bach was supposed to be for," reminded Stubbs.

"He's delivering mail." Art passed the telescope to Morris. "Tell me that's not your old ship, *Lamb*."

"*Lamb*?" Morris looked. "Son of Rivero! It's her, all right. I'd know those lines anywhere. She's under Spanish colors."

"So, where's Cole?" Freeman asked.

"He didn't give it back to them," said Morris. "I'm for hoisting our colors and finding out."

"Still want to go in there, Admiral?" Freeman said.

"We're under parley in port," Art said. "What can happen in front of all these witnesses? The Prince of Calenberg himself is attending. But just in case, load the twelves with bombs, the sackers with rounds and the swivels with grape shot, quiet as a mouse."

"What's the signal?" Stubbs asked.

"Signal?" Art said absently.

"You ain't gonna need a fuckin' signal," Morris said.

"There won't be trouble; we're all allies. This is the grand alliance come to life in front of our eyes—the Dutch, the Spanish, the Germans and Britons united under a common ideal: slavery. You'll know the signal when you see it, Captain Stubbs. Just come in shooting if I'm in trouble."

"Aye, aye, Admiral."

Once aboard *Stingray*, they sailed up the Yuna River, trailing behind German galiots. Light permeated the trees, illuminating a tunnel. Once through, the mighty galley *Dionin* came into view. Her snake figurehead sat fiercely at the bow, sporting long fangs. The rest of her was white, with red sails and serpentine carvings. *Doppelsöldner* mercenaries lined the decks by the hundreds, guarding every entrance.

"Sure you don't want to rethink this?" Freeman pressed.

"The baron doesn't spare any expense on security," Art said.

"I thought only Dewar and Llewellyn had gatherings like this." Morris ogled the naked slave girls on deck. "I could get used to it."

Stingray anchored and a longboat was deployed. Art and his men landed at a wharf, following the lead of the German delegates and Cardinal Grimaldi, a former resident of Port Royal, being carried on a chair.

"So that's a German prince?" Morris rasped.

"Looks like a German prince to me," said Freeman.

"How do you know what a German prince looks like?"

"What else would a German prince look like? Kapitän Dietrich, is that a German prince?"

"That is Prinz Maximilian of Hanover."

"In full armor, going to the ball," Art said. "He's a dunderhead."

"He has his own hair; that counts for something," Morris added.

A large wooden sign hanging nearby stated: *Welcome to Baron de Klauwen's Garden of Eden Slave Emporium*. A pale, gaunt figure stood waiting as music began in the background.

"Welcome to Baron de Klauwen's Garden of Eden Slave Emporium," the gaunt man began. "Soon to be the largest supplier of slaves and indentured servants in the West Indies. I am Orlok, your master of ceremonies."

The Germans were escorted up a grand staircase to the main deck, where musicians played, and other guests mingled. A small boy in eastern fabrics and a turban welcomed Art and his men. "Please follow me." They ascended the stairs. Lanterns lit the deck, illuminating the stained-glass doors to the grand stateroom.

Art and his men were led to the side gallery window.

"Right by the privy. Maybe I will have a drink," said Morris.

"Let's not be rude, Morris. Wait for our host," said Art.

Baron de Klauwen entered, in a shimmering gold cloak, rubbing his skeletal hands together. Mild applause stirred from the crowd.

"We are pleased to announce the signing of a contract with our new partners, the Fuggers Bank," said Orlok. "This will ensure that slaves are brought to Germany."

"Countess Aurora of Calenberg is here," said Maximilian. "She stole from the treasury of Hanover, a large amount that has not yet been recovered. She was taken by the pirate Black Caesar."

"We have just what you're looking for. Right this way, Prinz Maximilian, let us converse privately." Orlok motioned for the baron's private, curtained box.

The auctioneer took over for Orlok, ordering a round of slave girls for bidding.

"Prinz Maximilian, welcome," began Baron de Klauwen. "I haven't seen you since you were a small boy."

"I have no time for small talk," said Maximilian. "Where are Aurora and her handmaiden?"

"Impatient as ever. I have the countess, but she has no treasure. She has nothing at all. Ask her yourself. Bring them," the baron instructed the guards.

"She'll tell us where it is," Maximilian said.

"She must confess to its location, by any means necessary," said Cardinal Grimaldi. "We know it wasn't aboard *De Heilige Graal* or the Dutch ship the handmaiden travelled on."

"It is our belief that Aurora does not know the location, nor does the handmaiden, nor the wench," said Orlok. "We suspect the Hanover treasury was moved separately and Aurora herself was the decoy. Six vessels carrying the stonework of Calenberg Castle to Jamaica, contracted not through Van der Hagen shipping, but through Valentine Shipping, in Jamaica."

"I was not aware of the contract with Valentine Shipping," said the cardinal.

"We were not aware," said a German official.

"I smell Mother!" Maximilian hissed.

"Where are these six ships?" asked Count Molke.

"Ask him," said Orlok. "That's Valentine, there."

"Admiral Valentine, at yer service." Art removed his hat and bowed. "Prinz Maximilian, your mother indeed signed a contract with Port Royal. Our acting lieutenant governor purchased the castle to house the new Port Royal Bank. Each stone carefully removed and numbered to be reassembled across the bay from our beautiful city. Come, see for yourself."

"We don't wish to exclude Port Royal, Admiral Valentine. Captain Slazerelli was also a partner, with a fifteen percent share," said Orlok. "He was to transport slaves to Jamaica, but he couldn't make it. You could take his place. The East Indiaman, *Sainte Andrew*, arrived in St. Eustatius weeks before Aurora reached the islands."

"These ships must be searched, starting with *Sainte Andrew*," said Count Molke. "Governor Carlitos has the authority to issue a letter of marque, ordering the confiscation of Valentine's fleet."

"Rear Admiral Reers, ready all ships for immediate departure to St. Eustatius," said Maximilian.

"The Prinz of Pewter hasn't the authority to stop my ships," Art said. "The Brandenburgs carry a letter of marque on Spanish, pirates and the French by declaration of war. It's illegal for you to stop an Englishman. Aye, it's piracy if you stop my ships. But as it is, I'm here to do business. I'm willing to negotiate a new contract with Calenberg."

"Admiral Valentine is also a guest," the baron reminded. "Your disagreements will be resolved in time, and the treasure recovered. Let us speak of the future."

Atia, Aurora and her handmaiden entered, all wearing transparent veils and bound together with leather straps.

"They're naked," exclaimed the cardinal.

"They certainly are." Art couldn't help but stare at Atia and the other two women. "Go on and have a drink, Morris, we're among friends."

"Aurora of Calenberg," Orlok presented. "Charged with witchcraft. From nobility to piracy and now slavery."

"They're for sale?" Maximilian queried.

"Not for sale. These three here are for investment," said Orlok. "Women to mother a new line of slaves. Rabota slaves, for specific breeding, to create the perfect slave for all occasions."

Voices murmured throughout the crowd. Slavers and officials spoke with Maximilian.

"Excuse me, gentlemen, but the wench belongs to me," Art said.

"I'm loved, as you can see," said Atia.

"The Irish girl? We have the original signed indenturement, with an arrest warrant. The baron owns the whole family," said Orlok. "Do you have the signed release form and freedom documents?"

"Crisp's estate is in the courts in Port Royal," Art said.

Orlok revealed documents. "The baron inherited all of Crisp's estate by order of King William himself; notification of this has been sent to Port Royal for your courts to see. It's in the mail."

"Ah. Well, that does change things a bit."

"A bit?" Atia scoffed.

"Okay, a dram."

"What are they all saying?" Aurora said.

Orlok readied pages for the prince to sign. "Prinz Maximilian has the authority to have Aurora indentured as a criminal. An arrest warrant from Governor Carlitos also for Helena."

"How dare you!" Aurora's cheeks flared. "I'm a countess."

"I won't allow it," said Dietrich.

"Easy, Fritz," said Art. "Max the Prinz has yer leash, and so do I."

"We have everyone present to make it legal throughout all Germany," said Baron de Klauwen. "Count Molke, the Governor of Calenberg, and Cardinal Grimaldi, who represents the Vatican and is standing in for Emperor Leopold of the Holy Roman Empire. A new dawn for a new Germany: Prinz Maximilian, Elector of Hanover."

"Countess Aurora is no more and can legally be burned as a witch, should the Prinz so choose," said the cardinal.

"She claims to be the countess." Aurora indicated Helena.

"What? Me, a countess? With these dishpan hands?"

"The price for Aurora and Helena would cover the cost of your expedition to find the Hanover treasure," said the baron. "If you sign to have African slaves brought into Germany, I will have the Calenberg treasure restored in full at my expense."

"If she's sold into slavery, then we would not run the risk of making them martyrs," said a German.

Maximilian nodded to his staff, while Baron de Klauwen glided to the podium, licking his lips. "By selective breeding, we will create the perfect slaves for all occasions. Caesar shall breed with all three to create specific bloodlines for each."

"Excuse me?" A look of horror spread on Helena's face.

"Caesar and Helena shall create perfection—offspring of intelligence and strength beyond compare," said the baron.

"Caesar and Helena," said the painter. "Oh, dear."

"Then, what's that make my wench?" Art queried.

"The Sultan of Tripoli has retracted his offer. She's now breeding stock."

"I was freed, sir," said Atia.

"Atia will create new lines like no other. Fast breeding and full of energy."

"I might as well be the one to ask, but what happens to us if we refuse?" asked Helena.

"Do not speak," said Orlok. "You cannot refuse."

"The sedative should have kicked in by now," the baron remarked. "Oh, where did all the virtuous women go? I'll supervise the seeding myself."

Atia recoiled. "Need we be so formal?"

"Tonight, for your entertainment, Caesar will have them while the rest of us watch. The painter can paint the unions," said the baron.

"I've been in trouble for painting things like that," said Dodo. "Maybe another time."

"I'll have some more to drink now," said Atia.

"Is there an alternative?" said Aurora.

"If ya have whiskey, I'll take that, too."

"Refreshments," Orlok ordered.

Slaves brought in pastries and cakes, with lemon tea. Musicians played while female slaves danced erotically.

"Orlok, nectar," said the baron.

Orlok retrieved the liquid.

"We grow and raise our own food here," said Orlok. "*Dionin* is completely self-sufficient."

"You certainly have a lot of lemons," said the cardinal.

"Helps digestion, a proven fact."

"The sweetbreads are exquisite. What is it made with?" The cardinal took another mouthful.

"Local game," said Orlok.

Baron de Klauwen sat down and drank his thick red liquid. "The farms on the island are raided frequently. The buccaneers lived on wild pig and feral animals. Samaná Bay, once the lair of the kraken, now is the slave capital of the world."

"The kraken is legend, of course," the cardinal said, laughing.

"Your religion has given you a narrow view," said the baron. "The kraken did exist; the caverns below us are bottomless. This whole bay was once its lair."

Orlok leant in next to the baron. "Remember, don't insult the Christians."

The baron hissed and waved him away, claws extended. "The kraken fed on the humpback whales, which came here to mate. The mighty Dionin, an enormous snake, fed on the kraken. All things consume to survive. We all eat each other. If the kraken is gone, then it leaves the humpbacks for us."

"Do you believe the kraken may still exist?" asked a Fugger banker, who was writing on parchment.

"The locals say the kraken exists," said the baron. "It feeds on the humpbacks. Why are you writing that?"

"Well, I'll have to investigate why the insurance company agreed to the emporium if it may have a kraken."

"What?"

"Indians, buccaneers, now the kraken." The banker shook his head. "I'm certain the insurance company would want all the facts."

"Should it return, we have a steel net across the bay," Orlok said.

"To capture the kraken? What would you do with it?" asked the cardinal.

"Consume it. What else? Keep it as a pet?" The baron chuckled. "I have considered that, but it would be difficult to contain. If life cannot be controlled, it must be destroyed."

Atia gave him a contemptuous look.

Maximilian signed documents while occasionally giving Aurora a cold glare.

"Aurora and the handmaiden are now the property of Baron de Klauwen, until sale or death," said Orlok.

Officials and slavers spoke in their native tongues.

Caesar arrived on deck, clad in bright silks, his chest bulging. Highly polished swords and knives hung off the belt around his waist. Two well-armed Janissary guards accompanied him, alongside Fatima.

Maximilian sized up the imposing opponent.

"Welcome Caesar," said Orlok.

"He's a wanted pirate," an official said.

"Caesar is pardoned by the government of Port Royal under the Act of Grace law."

"Once a pirate, always a pirate," said the banker.

Morris raised his glass. "I'll drink to that."

"We could try an arrangement with Caesar and see how it goes?" Aurora offered.

"Caesar may now claim his prize," said Orlok.

"If the payment is right," Caesar said. "Right now, it's not right. I want Crisp's bill of sale for Kabaka. All the records. And I want a signed declaration of freedom before I sign."

"I want, I want, I want," the baron mocked. "Very well. Bring Caesar's documents to sign. A couple of drinks in you and you get ugly."

Maximilian stared at Aurora. In turn, she stuck her tongue out at him.

"On behalf of the Vatican, I'm authorized to invest," said Cardinal Grimaldi. "I have here the indenturement into slavery record for Aurora and Helena, signed by the Elector of Germany, Prinz Maximilian."

"What is Port Royal's investment to be?" Art chimed in. "We have three landowners here tonight and another on board *Guernsey*. Let's talk shipping rights."

"Thanks, Art," Atia jibed.

"Told ya never to call me Art, wench."

Atia gave him an icy smile.

Baron de Klauwen spoke privately with Orlok for a moment.

"What's fifteen percent going for?" asked Art.

"Captain Slazerelli committed two hundred thousand weight in gold," said Orlok.

"And you believed him?"

"Do you want to buy in?" Orlok said.

"I want to buy the chubby one," Morris said.

"They're not for sale, Morris; they were just sold for breeding stock." Freeman pointed to the other women. "They're for sale."

"Hell, I'll breed 'em all, sign me up," said Morris.

"Are we permitted to use the privy?" Atia asked.

"Take her to the privy," the baron told the guards.

Guards unlinked the women. Helena hunched over. Atia squeezed her hand before being escorted away.

At the far side of the deck, Dietrich caught Art's attention.

"What's got you smiling, Fritz?" Art asked.

"Mr. Morris, he's drinking, fast," said Dietrich.

"Aye, wars tend to follow when Morris drinks," Art said quietly. "Don't be too concerned about his reflexes. He nearly captured the Cagway single-handed in '55, and he was legless, absolutely legless. Just try and keep up with Morris when he's had a few, I tell you."

"A little dissension in the ranks," Freeman said. "Caesar doesn't like taking orders from the baron, and Maximilian's not likely to leave here without taking them with him. He's all but foaming at the mouth."

"What's Caesar mad for?" Morris grumbled. "He gets paid to fuck all these women and he doesn't know if he wants the job?"

"So, am I to understand your investing is a ruse?" Dietrich said.

"Chivalry is not dead, Kapitän Dietrich. We'll not leave without your countess or my wench." Art rejoined the procession. "So, Baron, as I understand it, if Caesar agrees, he stands to be a full partner in all this?"

"Yes, that's in the contract," said Caesar.

"Hmm. That's going to take some doing; legally it can't be done," said Art. "Then there's Prinz Thanks-a-Million over here and his type over in Hanover. How will they explain their union with an African slave?"

The comment incited argument among the Germans and slavers.

"Caesar can retire to a castle on top of the Samaná with the rest of his wives," said the baron.

"I will not stay here with these fat women," Caesar said. "My contract is fulfilled. I am to be freed, it was agreed."

"I can make you the richest man in the world." The baron extended his claw-like hand. "All this is only the beginning. You will have full control of the slave trade through the Caribbean. You can have a hundred women if you want. Port Royal, Curaçao, San Juan, will all respect you. These women were specifically selected for you. They are each perfect in their own way. You may have them now, Caesar."

"Now?" both Aurora and Helena said.

"Now?" Caesar frowned. "Here?"

"Now, now!" The baron curled his boney fingers into fists.

"Have the countess, first." Maximilian gave an evil grin.

"I think I'm going to need something a bit stiffer," said Aurora. "The drink, I mean."

"The other one," said Caesar.

"Oh, *scheisse.*" Helena massaged her face.

"Absolutely not." Aurora stepped between them. "He will not touch her."

"She's been run through with a sword," added the painter.

"Dodo's right. I've been stabbed; he witnessed it," said Helena. "A wound to the abdomen. Childbearing right now would kill me. I can show you the scar if you like, please?"

Baron de Klauwen slithered over for a closer look at her wound. She trembled as his nail tickled. "She speaks the truth. She may not be able to reproduce. Let's hope not. That would be tragic."

"Well, I can't have you hurting my Helena, so I'll do it myself," said Aurora.

"Her ass is all shot up," offered Dodo.

"That's what the coca-leaf powder is for," said Aurora.

Caesar guzzled the contents of a pewter mug before slamming it down. He went to Aurora, setting her up on a table's edge. His fingers groped between her thighs.

"I can't watch." Helena peeked through her fingers.

"I've had this dream before," said Aurora.

"As have I," said Helena.

Atia was groped by Caesar upon her return. He resumed drinking. Men clapped or stomped their feet, chanting "Caesar, Caesar!"

"Caesar will now penetrate them all," the baron commanded.

Strong men forced Atia, Helena, and Aurora up onto a platform.

Dodo readied his paintbrush and patted the sweat from his brow.

"I don't want to mate with Black Caesar," said Helena.

"*Ja*, you do," said Aurora.

"Not under these circumstances."

"I'm just relieved he likes girls," said Dodo.

Caesar joined them. He pawed at Atia, brushing his protruding manhood against her. Atia grabbed a knife from Caesar's belt and lunged.

Fatima struck Atia with an oil lamp.

Atia instinctively slashed with the blade, catching Fatima's arm. Blood spilled.

"Seize them! Seize them!" the baron shouted. "Disgraceful behavior!"

Caesar grabbed the knife and smacked Atia to the floor.

Guards forced Helena and Aurora down by their hair.

An enraged Dietrich was held back by Morris and Freeman.

"Everyone, remain calm," said Orlok. "We just had a slight accident; there's no cause for alarm. Have a crab puff."

"I'll kill the wench myself this time," said Caesar.

"Not until I say so," the baron reprimanded.

"Fatima is hurt," said Orlok. "Take her below to the infirmary."

"She is mine. I'll take her to my ship," said Caesar.

"No, she goes below with the slaves."

Guards whisked Fatima away.

"Tricksy Atia." The baron sneered. "Crisp always underestimated tricksy little Atia. I may have to cut off your hands. I will not tolerate insolence from any of you."

"She's mine—you said so," Caesar said.

"Keep your place, mighty Caesar. You will be king again, but you are not yet free. There is no port in the West Indies or East that will have you without my authorization. Every government will continue to hunt you as a pirate and a slave if I so choose. I won't tolerate any disobedience from any of you. Clean them up and double the sedative."

Guards seized the women, roughly escorted them away.

"Thank you all for the lovely evening," Atia said.

In the lower decks of *Dionin*, guards took Fatima down a long passage to the bow. Chains and various lines ran out of oversized portholes to the outside, where there was a mangrove swamp nearby. Fatima clutched her bleeding arm as they brought her to the infirmary. A faint rotten smell hung in the air. A round, bald doctor in a cloak examined her, a collection of blades hanging behind him. He started to unlatch a hatch in the floor.

"This one's to be mended," a guard said.

"She is a runt," the doctor snarled as he abandoned the hatch. "Oh, very well. The baron knows what he's doing. Put her in there."

Gunfire erupted from above, and the guards went to investigate. The sounds intensified and the doctor was distracted. Fatima took a machete off the wall and slipped into the shadows. Memories of when she was little surfaced. She had once hidden for over a day on a huge slave galley like this. But she also remembered what they did to her when she was caught. *Don't get caught.*

"Now, lie back and be still," the doctor's voice said from behind the bulkhead. "Where did you go?"

Fatima came at him from behind and hacked the blade into the doctor's head. His body dropped instantly. After heaving out the weapon, she bound her arm in cotton, using her teeth to tighten it. Fatima ran back through the ship to a hatchway and scurried down a flight of stairs. Her foot slipped on the last step and she fell hard on the orlop deck. The lowest deck on the ship, where she hid as a child. She searched the benches; they were staggered between two decks, with a small space between them where she could slip in between. Footsteps clanked above her, and soon they came downstairs.

Fatima climbed out of an oversized porthole into the misty air. Shots rang out, to and from the trees. A body fell, splashing into the water.

A voice yelled in German, "We got one here."

On the outside deck above her, *Doppelsöldners* searched, their guns cocked.

Fatima tucked herself against the hull. Shots erupted from the jungle. Spears and arrows flew from the trees. She secured the machete around her waist, climbed back through the porthole and squeezed between the decks. The stench from the infirmary was magnified. She followed a dark passage to another hatchway. Smoke wafted from it, and a faint light peeked through the darkness.

Fatima followed the sickly-sweet stench of decay. Flies vibrated through the pile of corpses and dismembered body parts. Vomit surged to Fatima's throat at the sight of skinned slaves hanging from hooks. At the room's center, body parts, butchered like slaughtered pigs, sat on a blood-stained wood block.

Fatima stumbled out of the way, spewing. She found the nearest porthole and jumped out. Splash. She remained underwater as long as she could, screaming inwardly. Shots snaked past her and sank to the bottom. She surfaced cautiously, aware that she had landed in the midst of the fight between those in the trees and the ship. Fatima tread alongside *Dionin*'s massive hull towards the stern.

The celebration in *Dionin's* grand stateroom was interrupted by the sound of gunfire but soon resumed as their hosts assured everyone that all was well. Bleedin Art stayed off to the side of the crowd with his men, his palms sweating. The situation in Samaná Bay was far from well.

"The Germans don't know what they're in for," said Morris.

"And this Baron de Klauwen's bitten off more than he can chew," added Freeman.

Art knew it was time to go. *Where did they take my Raving Red?*

A far-off explosion drew everyone's attention. The sky glowed and a fizzling spark burst through the air. There was another explosion to the south. The *Doppelsöldner* colonel arrived to report to Baron de Klauwen. "Indians, east up the Yuna and to the south, the Caba Road; larger in scale than last time, Baron."

"Remain calm," said Orlok.

Caesar got himself a drink while Maximilian and his group argued with the slavers.

"No, it's Indians all right. Taínos and Maroons," said Morris. "They're angry, too. It's a major offensive, not some skirmish. I think we're in for a helluva fight if we don't get out now."

"What he say?" Art said.

"He said it's Indians, lots of Indians," Freeman translated.

"Everyone remain where you are. I shall return in a moment," said the baron. "Those pesky Indians! My soldiers can handle this. It will not spoil our evening. Have a crab puff."

"I am done here," said Maximilian. "Bring Aurora and Helena; they're coming with me."

"They belong to me. We have a contract," said the baron.

"The Germans have ownership until payment is made," Art added. "What's their condition?"

Baron de Klauwen took a gulp of his nectar. "Bring the Calenberg women and the wench."

Guards returned with Atia, Helena and Aurora, all three looking exhausted. Atia's left eye was swollen from where Caesar had struck her.

Dietrich stepped forward. "I won't watch them be treated like this any further. You do not own Countess Aurora, nor Helena Braunschmidt."

Guards drew their weapons.

"The privateer, is he Brandenburg?" asked Maximilian.

"I'm *Korvettenkapitän* Roman Dietrich of the Braunschmidt schooner *Stachelrochen*, serving Calenberg and duty-bound to protect Countess Aurora."

"Oh, I'll go with him," said Aurora.

"She's coming with *us*," said Maximilian. "They both will."

"They belong to *me*," hissed the baron.

Caesar clasped his throat, struggling to breathe, then collapsed to his knees, doubling over in pain.

"Something on the tip of yer tongue, Caesar?" said Atia.

"What's wrong with him?" asked a Janissary.

"Perhaps a crab puff didn't agree with him?" said Art.

"He's been poisoned," said Freeman.

"By who?" Caesar spoke weakly.

"You'd be surprised what an angry wench is capable of," Atia said.

"You!" Caesar could barely lift his finger.

"Aye, little ol' me. You killed me da and uncle. And like Slasher Al, I got you."

"You wench!"

Atia bowed with an exaggerated arm gesture.

"Everyone, there's been a slight change in plan," said Orlok.

Caesar's head hit the floor.

"What a strange turn of events," Art mused.

"What did you use, wench?" the baron demanded.

"I'm sure it was arsenic, or maybe hemlock. Or was it belladonna, I don't know, is he blue?"

"He was the last of his kind," the baron said.

Caesar pleaded for help, reaching for the baron. Baron de Klauwen ignored him and sized up several strong male slaves, rubbing his chin. "Oh, it's no good, none of them are suitable. You ruined everything, you stupid wench. You must carry his line. Orlok, cut off Caesar's testicles. We must resort to artificial seeding."

Orlok and two guards approached a pleading Caesar, who tried to crawl away. Maximilian and his group laughed.

"My doctor has a remedy which could save him," offered Art.

"It's no use—look at him. Pathetic. It won't get here in time. I will never find a new stud of his size and strength." The baron paused. "Cut them off."

"Let me," offered Maximilian. "You can keep Aurora if I can cut Black Caesar's balls off."

"The wench may already be with child," said Caesar.

"Explain," said the baron.

"I heard it from Wynne and Grubing in San Juan. She was had by Laurens de Graaf in Tortuga."

Horror filled Baron de Klauwen's face. "Laurens de Graaf had you in Tortuga!"

"He did?" both Freeman and Morris said.

"He did?" Art sounded disappointed.

"Not Laurens!" The baron's fists hit the air. "Bastard! Backstabbing bastard! Did he seed you?"

"Ask Laurens." Atia paused. "Sure. So did my husband. I've been seeded and fertilized aplenty. So cut the bastard's balls off, for all I care, but it may do you no good."

The baron grabbed Orlok by the scruff of the neck and stared into his face. "Husband?"

"I, I was not aware."

"Idiot!" The baron slapped Orlok across the face. "Have you bled since?"

"I was just in a bloody pirate battle, mate. I bled plenty."

"That is not what he means," said Aurora.

"Do you Germans have any sense of humor? I know what he means. It's not something I wanna discuss."

"Kapitän Dietrich, take the women into protective custody," said Art.

Art's men drew guns. Dietrich went to Aurora and was shot through the heart—it wasn't clear by whom. He staggered.

"Remain calm," said Orlok.

Windows were blown out. Art and his men shielded themselves. The floor vibrated and paintings fell off the wall.

Dietrich fell dead.

"Told ya," said Morris.

Then everyone in the room was panicking, scrambling to leave as the ship was pelted with gunfire.

German soldiers were fighting off Maroons at the aft decks. More windows shattered. Native warriors adorned in war paint and leaves swung onto the ship using vines and ropes. Art, Freeman, Morris, and Bach fought hand-to-hand with swords and guns. Arrows flew.

"That took a sharpshooter with a long-range musket," said Morris.

"It's buccaneers," said Freeman.

"Orlok, take the women below," ordered the baron, before summoning one of the German mercenaries. "We can no longer trust Caesar's men to stay loyal, now he's gone. Liquidate the Janissaries."

Soldiers escorted Orlok, the women and Dodo below.

Art and his men were pinned down while German officials and slavers dropped dead trying to flee. Maximillian and his men fought their way out in the opposite direction.

Fatima scarcely kept her head above water as she kicked and thrashed. Once clear of *Dionin's* hull, she reached a wharf. She pulled herself up and then collapsed, trying to catch her breath.

Barbarossa I was not far away. Janissaries were fighting Maroons on deck when a hailstorm of shots from *Dionin* shredded the upper decks. The raïs was shot through the middle and fell, while the agha and the rest of the officers were shot off the deck. Ekene and others jumped over as an explosion obliterated *Barbarossa I.*

Oars deployed from *Dionin*, rowing it to safety.

Fatima lingered behind the companionway; the machete still tied to her waist.

Ekene swam to her.

"Fatima," Ekene called.

"Where is Caesar?" Fatima asked.

"I don't know. Are you hurt?"

"He's eating them."

"Who?" Ekene said. "What are you saying?"

"The baron is eating his slaves. Hundreds of them. The hold is full of them."

Ekene stopped cold. "Caesar is there."

Caesar staggered on *Dionin's* deck, struggling to breathe. He tumbled over the railing and splashed into the water.

"He's shot or hurt," Fatima said. "Go get him."

"Fatima?"

"Please hurry, Ekene."

Ekene reluctantly dove in. He struggled to keep Caesar's head out of the water. Fatima waded into the shallows to assist. They maneuvered Caesar's huge frame to the shoreline.

"Caesar?" Fatima checked him. His eyes rolled into the back of his head, while his tongue and lips swelled blue.

"He's alive, barely," said Fatima. "Poisoned by deadly nightshade. It's a Port Royal favorite."

"Is there an antidote?" asked Ekene.

"Yes, on *Guernsey*. Strangewayes will have activated charcoal; it'll soak up the poison," said Fatima.

"We can leave on *Guernsey*," said Ekene.

"Back to Port Royal?"

"We can't stay here."

"I can't swim, anyway," Fatima said. "I'll stay here with him."

Ekene swam towards *Guernsey*.

Fatima took Caesar's head into her arms and forced seawater down his throat to make him vomit.

Below deck, Helena, Aurora, and Atia stepped around dead bodies. The lower cabins were being converted for combat, loaded with cannons.

"I don't want the Germans or Valentine near my women," declared Baron de Klauwen. "Take them to the caves until this is over. Set some of the slave girls free to distract the men."

"Caves?" Atia said.

They came to a capstan that operated a mechanical lift sizeable enough to hold six people.

"Get in," said Orlok.

"Down to a cave?" Atia said.

Shooting erupted nearby. The baron and Orlok took cover. Native warriors with axes and spears were met by guards. Maximilian returned in full armor with a squad of soldiers, shooting their way on deck.

Helena pulled Aurora and Atia into a passage behind the capstan. A maelstrom of arrows began to land. Dodo stumbled after them, terrified.

"We go now," said Helena.

Aurora gave her a look. "Where?"

"This way." Atia led them back to the hatch leading out under the promenade deck. Dodo trailed, still clutching his easel and satchel of paints and brushes.

"Leave that behind! You're going to get us caught," said Atia.

Dodo froze, breathing rapidly.

Aurora couldn't get by. "Dodo, keep going!"

"I said, leave it," Atia snapped.

"No. It might be useful." Dodo wept. "When I'm back home in my garden painting pretty trees. I love painting trees. I want to go home and paint trees."

"What's wrong with him?" Atia asked.

"It happens sometimes. I know how to deal with this." Helena took Dodo's easel and smashed him over the head with it. He fell flat on his face, unconscious.

"Good thinking," said Aurora.

Helena in turn led the way, leaving Aurora and Atia to pick Dodo up by the arms and drag him forward.

"Is he still alive?" Atia said.

Dodo moaned.

Helena came back, ready to knock his head on the deck.

"He's out, he's out," said Aurora. "Don't kill him."

Sudden screams—from women and men—froze Helena's blood. The bodies of the cabin boy and a naked slave girl smacked the rail on their way down to the water.

"Kill them all, and take everything," said Barns.

"I want the handmaiden," said Ding Dong.

Helena sat gripping her knees, believing that Ding Dong had perished alongside Gretsch when pirates seized *Einhorn*.

"She'll die, I'll make sure of it," Ding Dong continued.

Helena remained frozen.

"Don't you lose it, too. I'm not certain there's another paint stand," Atia said.

"We have to get going, you said," Aurora pressed.

"I see Art's ship. You'll like Art once you get used to the teeth," said Atia. "We can swim for it. Come with me. Swim for *Guernsey*."

"I can't take this anymore." Helena rose. "Shoot me now."

"Get down." Aurora yanked her, just missing an arrow.

"Not Bleedin Art. I'm finding the Spaniard, Silvestre." Helena scanned the bay.

"What's with you and this Silvestre?" Aurora pried.

Movement nearby. Maximilian aimed his gun at Helena and fired. She ducked, but the top of her shoulder was left bleeding, and she fell against the hull. Atia and Aurora dragged her back into the shadows.

"Damn it, just grazed her," said Maximilian. "Keep them pinned down. You go that way; you go that way. Get them."

The women swung Dodo from the promenade over a rail and climbed inside a passage.

"Easy, not so loud," said Helena.

"Are you well?" Aurora asked.

"*Ja*, fine. Why do you ask?"

Below them, soldiers and crewmen readied cannons. They heard the thumping of feet on the deck above.

"What happened?" Dodo stirred. "What's that thumping?"

"It's Maximilian. He's found us," said Helena. "He's coming down here to kill us all. Look, he just shot me."

Dodo fixated on the blood running down Helena's arm.

Maximilian drew nearer, and Dodo nearly fainted.

Helena crept away down the deck in the dark.

"I'm really hating the way she does that," said Atia. "Where's she going?"

"It's Aurora, get her!" said Maximilian.

"Pirates!" shouted a soldier.

Shots rang out. Maximilian fell back, wounded. Barns and his men advanced, hacking and slashing with swords. Maximilian stabbed Barns through the shoulder. Barns hurled himself out of a porthole to avoid being run through.

"Coward," said Maximilian. "Which way did she go?"

Helena found a rundlet of gunpowder and scattered the contents all over the deck.

"Helena is there—get her," Maximilian said.

Helena grabbed a torch and threw it. Flames jetted across the deck. Crewmen and soldiers raced to put out the fire.

Helena retreated.

"We lost them!" Maximilian stomped his feet.

"We have the painter," said a soldier.

Helena stumbled into the dim forward compartment. Her shoulder stung as blood dripped down her arm. She peered through a porthole, hoping there was a connection to the decks, then recoiled when she realized she was directly under a privy. She hesitated before climbing out. A scream came from above, then a shuffling from behind her.

She was not alone. Ready to fight, Helena turned to see…Gretsch's metal breastplate! Then a heavy, painful hit to the head knocked her down. When she recovered enough to open her eyes, it was Ding Dong looming over her, wearing Gretsch's armor.

"I found you." Ding Dong cleared his nostrils.

"What happened to the man who wore that?" Helena asked.

He bent her over, face to the wall, tearing her translucent veil. "This old thing? I've had it for years. Like it?" Ding Dong unfastened his trousers. "I've been looking forward to this."

"So have I." Helena braced her feet against the wall, toes digging into dirt and rock. Her eyes shut and her body went rigid. She pushed backwards with all her strength, doing a backwards frog leap. The back of her head met something hard and unyielding—his face. He groaned, falling backwards.

Helena twisted her body and grabbed the knife from his belt. He yanked her hair, exposing her neck, intending to cut it with the blade in his right hand. But Helena eyed a gap in the armor just under the armpit and stabbed him there repeatedly. Blood cascaded all over her. His body went limp against her, and she pushed him over. She removed his weapons and unfastened the breastplate. "I'll have that."

Helena hauled the plate with her to the hole's entrance.

Aurora and Atia stood not thirty feet away.

"There you are," said Helena. "Let's go."

Orlok and two guards appeared out of the dark behind them. Long, white fingers wrapped around Helena's throat. Nails dug into her skin. Baron de Klauwen's foul breath made her gag. He sniffed her, appetized by her blood-soaked skin. "You are a very stubborn girl. It's the caves for you."

Dr. Strangewayes snuck outside, onto *Guernsey's* deck, for a peek. An arrow flew by, and he felt as though he were back at his plantation in the Blue Mountains when it was attacked by Maroons. He ducked instinctively.

Guernsey's crew successfully fought off pirates. When things died down, there was a splashing sound. Stubbs and two officers raced down from the quarterdeck, guns aimed.

"Friend!" a familiar voice spoke. "Friend!"

Strangewayes investigated.

"Who goes there?" asked Stubbs.

"Our captain needs medical assistance," said Ekene.

"It's a bloody battle," said Stubbs. "Who's your captain?"

"Kabaka."

"You jest; it's a trick. Ready the guns."

"No trick. He's poisoned. We're asking for your help."

"Help Black Caesar? Piss off. We shoot in thirty seconds."

"Hold your fire." Strangewayes arrived. "Nobody shoots. This man is unarmed. You cannot refuse."

"Doctor," said Ekene.

"Ekene."

"You know this slave?" Stubbs said.

"He's in my employ," said Strangewayes.

"Bring him up," Stubbs said.

Ekene climbed up the side. He and Strangewayes shook hands, while crewmen and officers were quick to aim guns.

"Stand down," said the doctor. "What do you require?"

"I bring a message from Fatima. She wants charcoal. Caesar's been poisoned with the nightshade. He's dying."

"Fatima's with you? Captain Stubbs, the girl he speaks of is also in my employ. We must retrieve her."

"*Guernsey's* not going any further, and I cannot spare the men nor boats until we have the admiral back. I wouldn't for the likes of him, anyway. Ya have wounded to tend, so hurry up with this and get back to work."

"Aye, sir. Now, for the activated charcoal. You'll need a few things to go with it."

Strangewayes went below to gather a kit for Ekene while crewmen watched him. The doctor returned with a small crate of jars.

"Ah, this is it. Strangewayes Brand Emergency Stomach Cleansing Formula. Ingest whole jar and wait. You will soon have a very real outcome. Yes, that's self-explanatory. Now, when you're done, can you and Fatima swim back out here?"

"Fatima doesn't swim."

"Oh, right. Well, if you can find your way back, do it. I'll never be able to talk these gents into coming for you, so you'll have to come to us."

"I'll try to find a way." Ekene climbed down to the water.

"Ready a boat," said Stubbs. "I'll need volunteers to go aboard *Dionin* to retrieve the admiral."

Men whistled and quickly went about their work.

Bleedin Art's gums bled as he picked his teeth, bending a silver toothpick. The battle outside shook the hull of *Dionin*, while he and his men hid beside the stained-glass door to the forecastle, avoiding as much of the battle as they could.

Morris reloaded his gun behind the staircase. "Reload now while we have the chance."

Freeman joined him, applying pressure to his bleeding left arm. "And medical aid, if it's not too much trouble."

"Where the hell is Stubbs?" Art stuck his head out.

"If this ain't enough of a fuckin' signal, what is?" Morris rasped. "Keep your heads down."

Art's hat flew off, and he ducked back down. He retrieved it and assessed the hole. "Had to look."

Morris peeked, mumbled something, and stumbled back, rubbing his knees, swearing under his breath.

"He says we're gonna have to fight our way out," translated Freeman.

Bach arrived through the doors to find his crewmates aiming guns. They raised their hands.

"Retreat is a foregone conclusion," said Art.

"No, it isn't," said Bach. "The Germans are winning."

"You play the bloody clarinet!" said Art.

"I don't think all the Germans are on the same side," said Morris.

"Them soldiers have been all over the world, Morris," said Freeman. "They specialize in defending against attack. And, you said it yourself, it's got castles and towers."

"I see lightfooted soldiers, sharpshooters and Indians in the trees," said Morris. "It's the bloody buccaneers next, I tell ya. Who else can coordinate pirates and Indians?"

A guard tower exploded, and then another. Men on fire leapt to their deaths. The main deck was bombarded by another wave of pirates: Silent Sam's men, including Half-

Lovely and twenty well-armed cutthroats. The few remaining *Doppelsöldner* mercenaries defended.

"Retreat this way," said Freeman.

Art's men made a run for the main deck.

Fama and *San Antonio* rowed in, firing guns at the shoreline. Rivero and his thirty men swung across, followed by Silvestre with his fifty. They fought hand-to-hand with pirates, Indians and buccaneers.

"This way." Morris ran aft.

Art and Bach turned to Freeman for translation, but he was already running. They followed through wafting smoke, choking and firing at pirates, picking them off one by one.

"The Spanish are coming to help us," said Bach.

"Be my guest, Bach," Morris chided. "That's no Spanish corsair down there; that's Rivero, a pirate. He ain't on their side, and he sure as hell ain't on my side, either. I killed his father."

"*Ja*, Spanish tend to take those things seriously," said Bach.

"Don't they, though."

Near the mainmast, Rivero met an injured Barns. They duelled, demonstrating formidable skill.

"Let's shoot 'em both," said Morris.

"Not in front of the Germans," said Art.

On the stairs to the quarterdeck, Silvestre, with his rapier and dagger, came face to face with Half-Lovely and his cutlass. They battled. Silvestre was faster, but Half-Lovely's cutlass was fiercer. Another pirate jabbed Silvestre in the back.

Silvestre fell to the main deck and was slow to get up.

Half-Lovely pursued, swinging his cutlass. It was deflected by Maximilian's sword, and the Germans plowed through the pirates. Maximilian parried and dodged Half-Lovely's blind side, keeping him turning. Half-Lovely jabbed Maximilian's side, but the blade didn't penetrate.

Shots were fired.

"Hey, Pewter Prinz, get down," said Art.

Maximilian ducked out of the way; Art's men unleashed a hailstorm of shots. Half-Lovely was hit in the head and chest. A soaking wet Barns used him as an uncomplaining shield that aided him as he leapt overboard again, letting the body drop into the water.

Stubbs and a handful of crew landed at the wharf.

The *Doppelsöldner* colonel and Rear Admiral Reers met, having the entire deck surrounded.

"Drop your weapons and surrender," said the *Doppelsöldner* colonel. "All of you."

Art's men raised their hands in surrender.

"Anyone moves, kill them all," said Maximilian. "Where is Countess Aurora?"

In the Caves

Atia shivered as she was forced into a mechanical lift powered by slaves. The group was lowered, descending into darkness. Everyone shuffled uncomfortably, and Orlok yanked the chains holding the women and Dodo together.

"Like a virgin's *fotze* in here," said Aurora.

"Smells like one," Helena remarked.

The lift clunked as it hit the bottom. They stepped off and the basket automatically went back up.

"Uh, I can't go much further," said Atia.

"You killed my Caesar, Atia—do you know how much that's going to cost?" said the baron. "I invested a fortune in him. Fortunately, as he fell overboard, I can still claim him on my insurance."

"Did you intend to free him?" asked Aurora.

"Of course not. Free Caesar? He wouldn't know what to do with himself."

"The way I see it, he outsmarted all the best pirates in the Caribbean, as well as the English, the French, the Spanish and the German Navy," Aurora continued. "He's a juvenile. You said yourself he won the prize. I'd wager that pirates, Indians and slaves would follow Caesar rather than you, Baron."

"I brought you here. I did. Caesar has no mind of his own. Everything was going according to plan until that horrible Valentine intruded. Remind me to kill him later, the meddling fool."

The roar of water thundered above the vertical caves. Before them sat an underground lake and waterfall that shimmered green and blue beneath the lantern light.

"What's that sound?" said Atia.

"Thousands of tons of water all around us," Helena offered.

Atia's jaw clenched. They were herded forward into a series of dark caverns where water rushed all around them.

"Are we not stopping?" Atia said.

A work area lit with lanterns lay ahead. Slaves pushed water barrels along a channel.

"What are you doing with us?" Aurora said.

"Take them to the treasure chamber, where Maximilian can't find them," the baron told Orlok. "He's another fool, a stupid, arrogant fool. This whole day is gone to cack because of stupid fools."

The baron left the way they came in.

Orlok and the guards took the women deeper through twisting, narrow channels. Lantern light revealed Taíno pictographs and petroglyphs on the walls. They came to a narrow bridge where water rushed on both sides.

"We're not goin' that way," protested Atia.

Orlok dragged her by the arm as they crossed beneath a waterfall. Pinpricks of light seeped in, igniting the water. Helena paused to admire the spectacle but was pushed on.

Atia shuddered; the walls were closing in, and the sensation of being buried alive instantly crept up her spine. Broken wood beams, ladders, rigging, and barrels littered their path. Body parts and skeletons were interwoven in the wall, indications of people buried alive.

Atia came face to face with a protruding hand. "What the hell."

"It's a hand." Aurora looked ill.

"Someone was buried alive," said Helena.

Atia clutched Helena's arm. "Someone just put it there as a joke."

"A joke, sure."

Then they felt a tremor, followed by the sound of a rockslide somewhere in the distance. The rush of water reverberated around them. Their path narrowed, leading beneath another waterfall and alongside streams of mud.

"Do you live down here, Orlok?" Atia laughed nervously.

"Looks like there are frequent cave-ins," said Helena. "People die all the time down here, buried alive."

"I hate yer fuckin' guts, ya know that, sister." Atia's legs slowed.

Orlok pulled her hard, towing her.

Atia stumbled.

Helena caught her. "You were saying."

"I said ya remind me of my sister. She was a pain in the arse, too."

"I must admit, you're doing well for someone with an aversion to confined spaces."

"It's the walls closing in that gets to me. I've been buried alive—twice."

"Twice? Well, that can have an after-effect."

"Third time lucky?" Aurora said. "No, that came out wrong. So, why is it called the treasure chamber?"

"Cause it's full of kraken dung!" Atia remarked. "They use it for keeping treasure."

"Laurens de Graaf's treasure," Orlok said.

"I figured it was for the Hanover treasure," Atia said.

"No, this is where Laurens de Graaf kept his treasure for years. He just sold all this to the baron."

"You're being nice to us," said Aurora.

"You might be down here for some time."

They came to a place where an image of men fighting with spears and arrows against a giant squid-like creature appeared on the wall.

"Wait," said Helena. "Look at this."

"It's the kraken," said Atia.

They found ancient ruins, stone blocks connecting to stair-like structures.

"This is said once to be the home of the kraken," said Orlok.

"Well, if it was only said once, then we shouldn't believe it," Atia said.

"You can lower as much line as you want into the water. You'll never reach the bottom. This is where I leave you."

"Here?" Atia and Aurora said together.

"I suppose you are bait for the kraken." Orlok cackled. "I'd eat you. Goodnight, Countess." He left through a narrow passage, taking the light with him. The guards followed in due course.

"Orlok, don't leave us here like this!" Aurora said.

Atia screamed and clawed in the darkness, trying to find the opening by which he'd left, but he had vanished so quickly. She slipped on wet rock; there was a splash and Atia was engulfed in cold water. She flailed between panicked gasps.

"Where is she?" Aurora said.

Helena, too, fell forward on the rocks and plunged into the water.

"Here, here!" cried Atia.

Atia eventually found Helena's hand, and she latched on. Arms linked, and the women managed to climb up and huddle together on the muddy edge. The three clung to one another in the darkness.

In a dark mangrove forest, Fatima held Caesar's head in her arms. The weight of his shoulders made her legs to go numb. She whispered in his ear, describing what she saw on *Dionin*. He moaned in pain and sobbed periodically. She loved this enormous, helpless beast and wondered if there could be a future for them or if they should die together here and now.

The gunfire had mostly ceased, and Germans were arresting pirates.

Fatima's thoughts turned to Ekene. He could have been killed or captured. She knew Ekene loved her, and she'd taken that for granted, but she no longer loved him.

A twig snapped, and Ekene emerged from the weeds, carrying a small crate of jars.

"I never doubted you." Fatima embraced him.

"Is he still alive?" Ekene asked.

Caesar moaned.

"There's a note from Strangewayes in one of the jars," said Ekene.

Fatima read. It was all things she knew. Poisonings in Port Royal were a regular occurrence, accidental and intentional. She had become familiar with many methods for dealing with poison.

"You must trust me," Fatima told Caesar. She found the activated charcoal and forced some down his throat. He vomited black tar. "Just a few more days of this, and you might live."

He finished spewing.

"You're ready for another helping." She put more charcoal down his throat.

Ekene pulled her arm and took her aside. "He'll live or die now. Come with me."

"Where?"

"Away from here. Doc Strange is on a ship out there. I'll help you swim."

"I don't swim. Besides, I can't leave him right now."

"Him? He murders people and rapes women."

Fatima couldn't help but look back at Caesar.

"Come with me," he pressed.

"No, I'm not leaving him. You go, Ekene."

"Fatima, I really don't know who you are anymore."

Caesar coughed, trying to speak. "Help me kill de Klauwen."

"You can't get up," said Fatima.

Caesar rolled over, pushing her aside as he vomited again.

"Why did you come back for me?" Caesar asked.

"That would have left the agha in command, and he's terrible." Fatima opened one of the jars. She made him swallow and caressed his face. "I love you. Why will you not have me as your bride?"

Caesar's eyes met hers and his giant hand stroked her cheek. "Help me up."

"You shouldn't."

Caesar gripped some tree roots, trying to rise, but doubled over, vomiting. Fatima laid him back down and cleaned him up as best she could.

Just before dawn aboard *Dionin*, Bleedin Art and his men were on their knees, held at gunpoint by ten armored German soldiers. On the bright side, Art's knees weren't hurting at all; in fact, he felt invigorated. They were all gathered in the grand stateroom, its shattered glass doors lying in pieces on the deck.

"Order your men to pursue the Indians and pirates who attacked us," said Baron de Klauwen to the *Doppelsöldner* colonel.

Orlok entered as the colonel left.

The baron clattered his nails together impatiently. "Now, where are Caesar's balls?"

"He fell off the deck before we could extract them," said one of his ghoulish aides.

"Damn, I wanted those balls! This enterprise is not going as planned."

"Baron, a messenger aviso is at the wharf."

A Brandenburg correspondent holding a case arrived. He conversed with guards before being let in.

"What are they saying, Mr. Bach?" Art asked.

"A priority message from Hanover."

An argument erupted among the Germans, the banker, and a slaver. Baron de Klauwen and Orlok got involved.

"What the sprekenzy is going on, Bach?" Art said.

"A messenger ship from Hanover was sent to find Baron Gretsch, but he's not here. There's a very important message from Calenberg. Count Molke and Maximilian are to be arrested, by order of the electorate of Hanover."

The German officials reviewed the message with Cardinal Grimaldi. Art inched closer, trying to get a glimpse.

"I demand to know the charges," said Count Molke.

"The charges are conspiracy, corruption, treason, and more," said the correspondent.

"I smell Mother!" Maximilian snarled.

"These orders are legally binding, Prinz Maximilian. Your mother is in full command of Hanover, by your father's own declaration."

"He regained consciousness." Count Molke looked as though he just ate a lemon. "Preposterous."

"This means the countess is not yours to sell, my Prinz," said the German official. "There can be no contract with Baron de Klauwen."

Maximilian stomped, rattling the floorboards beneath the weight of his armor. "This is only temporary. Soon I will rule over all Germany."

"I will bring our case to the emperor," said Count Molke. "Your mother doesn't stand a chance against the Holy Roman Empire."

"That's for the court to decide," said the correspondent. "Count Molke is to be extradited to Hanover to be executed."

Count Molke sulked. "Sophie is overstepping her authority."

"By order of the emperor," clarified the correspondent.

"I have no choice but to obey, my Prinz," said Admiral Reers. "Arrest Count Molke and escort the Prinz to his ship."

"Damn you, Mother!" Maximilian threw his steel armor glove. It bounced off a side table, making contact with Cardinal Grimaldi's groin. The cardinal fell forward, cupping himself. "Oh, God!"

"By order of Sophie, Elector of Hanover, the charges against Countess Aurora are dismissed," finished the correspondent.

"She cannot be sold into slavery and must be freed," said the German official.

"Release the countess; she's coming with us," said Reers.

"The contract is signed and permanent," said the baron. "Cack, what else can go wrong tonight?"

"*De Heilige Graal* is approaching," said Orlok.

"I should punish Van der Hagen for being late and losing the countess. How soon is he expected?"

"Not long."

Heads turned as a flickering light entered the estuary. *De Heilige Graal* sailed in, her sails at maximum, torches lit on deck.

Gunfire erupted from the trees and surroundings.

"It's buccaneers, I tell ya," said Morris.

Freeman sniffed the air. "Grenade!"

They dove for cover as a crackling object zoomed by. Then came the explosion. The men were concussed on the floor.

Art's ears rang as he choked on sulfur smoke. "Thanks, Humpy."

Buccaneers arrived, fighting their way inside.

"Told ya," Morris said.

An imposing dark shape blocked the exit and a large hand gripped the polished door. Caesar stepped heavy inside with Fatima under his arm.

"Caesar!" The baron grinned, clasping his bony fingers together. "My Caesar returns, very much alive. Oh, rejoice."

"You never intended to free me." Caesar pushed Fatima aside and moved gingerly towards the baron. "You lied the whole time."

"Guards, kill them," said the baron.

A barrage of arrows entered. Guards fell and Taíno warriors seized the aft deck. Art and his men kept their hands up, staying hidden in the corner. Meanwhile, Orlok ran for the exit and Fatima slashed the back of his head with her machete.

"You wanted to cut me up," said Caesar. "You betrayed me."

"Of course not," said the baron. "I would never."

"I heard you tell them to cut off my balls," said Caesar.

"I had to make other arrangements." The baron shrunk back.

"Other arrangements!" Caesar looked to Fatima. "Tell them what you saw below."

"He's eating slaves." She repeated this in various languages.

"You ate people tonight." Caesar laughed dryly.

Everyone held their stomachs; some gagged or vomited.

Art smacked his lips. "I never thought I'd have anything in common with l'Olonnais."

"Not crab puffs?" Morris uttered.

"No, Morris, not crab puffs," said Freeman.

"How were the sweetbreads, Cardinal?" Caesar asked. "Makes you a cannibal, don't it?"

"But I had no idea he was eating his slaves, I swear," Cardinal Grimaldi protested, crossing himself. "A-and, they technically aren't human, are they?"

Caesar's hand clamped the baron's throat.

Baron de Klauwen grinned almost giddily.

"Kill him," said Fatima.

"I want something from you, Baron. First, where are the hostages, the German women and the wench?"

The baron's face soured, and he reached for a dagger.

Caesar squeezed the baron's feeble wrists together with only a few fingers.

"I'll put fifty doubloons on Black Caesar," said Freeman.

"I order you to let me go," said the baron.

Caesar's hand trembled around the baron's throat.

Outside, *De Heilige Graal* drew closer.

"It's comin' right at us," said Morris.

"Time to go, Admiral," said Freeman.

"Where's the countess?" Art asked.

Caesar twisted the baron's wrists until there was an audible snap and his hands hung limply in their sockets. The baron shrieked and collapsed to the floor. "They're in the caves."

"Not the caves out in the bay," said Stubbs.

"No, beside the ship; there's a hole. It leads to the caves. They're in the cave, the one Laurens used to keep his treasure in."

"Yaguara knows the cave he refers to," said Yaguara.

"Captain Stubbs, go with him," said Art.

Stubbs rounded up Freeman and Morris, pausing at the door.

"May we?" Stubbs asked Caesar.

Caesar nodded.

Art enjoyed watching the baron suffer. He thumbed through papers on a desk.

"Time to abandon ship, Admiral," Bach said.

"Where is the paper that frees me?" Caesar demanded.

Art searched. "It's all here. He left it all to you, Caesar. All it needs is the baron's stamp. Ah, here it is." Art lit a red candle and dripped wax onto the document and pressed down the seal. "Now witnessed by these noble creatures."

Caesar forced the Fugger banker to sign the document.

"That's that, nice and legal." Art poured wax on another area and stamped. "One there for good measure on the correction. There ya have it, Caesar is now yer official name, and all that is Crisp's or Burghill's or Baron de Klauwen's now belongs to you."

"No, no! My Caesar, listen," said the baron.

"Baron de Klauwen claimed four hundred slaves lost overboard in one month alone on his insurance," Art continued. "Now we know Carlitos of San Juan and Reyning of Tobago are equally guilty. Caesar is entitled to fair compensation." Art's teeth gleamed as he drew his sword. "Baron de Klauwen, I arrest you for insurance fraud. Caesar, you have uncovered a major crime organization. Port Royal will pay you handsomely for your service in shutting it down. You buccaneers know the Capitaine has a longstanding commission in Port Royal."

"Capitaine is not here," said Caesar. "I'm in charge here."

"He's the Capitaine's lieutenant." Art indicated Arsenault.

"I'm here for the Capitaine's wife," said Arsenault.

"They took her below, into some caves. We're tryin' to get her back for you," said Art.

"De Klauwen? De Klauwen. De Clown, remember?" Morris said.

"Morris, have you been sipping that Strangewayes shit again?" Freeman asked.

"No. Remember Panama? Baron de Klauwen, we knew him as De Clown. He shipped slaves to Henry Morgan for the raid."

"I remember now."

"De Clown? Hmm." Art puzzled. "How'd I miss that? The Dutch investor who backed Morgan at Panama. Now he's invested with Laurens de Graaf in Samaná Bay."

"So, Laurens is behind all this?" Arsenault said.

"Impossible. The Capitaine would have known, and he didn't," said de Kreep.

"He doesn't know much at all, it seems." Arsenault exhaled heavily. "While we've fought against slavery, our own leader is building a slave capital like Port Royal. Our worst enemy, in our own backyard."

"Laurens was slave smuggling through Samaná Bay to the Spanish, by way of San Juan, right?" Morris said. "The

Spanish have to buy their slaves from the English. Made law by the Royal African Company, the King of Spain, and King William. De Klauwen had close relationships with Modyford, Molesworth and Morgan, and the governor of Tobago. They had those pretty Dutch ships that looked like shoes. That's where it started, way back in the day. He's the peculiar little chap that never got off the boat. We called him De Clown."

"What'd he say?" Arsenault asked.

"He said yes, Laurens is smuggling slaves to the Dutch and English for Baron de Klauwen under a Dutch flag," Freeman translated.

"Laurens is a traitor," said Morris.

"Laurens was always a traitor," said Art. "First time I met him he had Spanish colors."

"I'm sure we can all die reassured that we uncovered the truth, but it don't make me feel any better," said Freeman.

"Why are you complaining?" Morris said. "We knew it was in a trap."

"I say parley," Art said. "We join forces and get the women out."

Outside, *De Heilige Graal* burst into flames on a collision course.

"She's not stopping," said Freeman.

"Abandon ship, Mr. Freeman," said Art.

"Abandon ship!" Freeman bellowed.

Almost everyone ran to the nearest exit.

Art turned to Caesar, who was staring into Fatima's eyes. "Pirating is no longer a lucrative profession. Leave slavery to the slavers. You ought to try real estate. This whole bay and the Samaná are soon to be the insurance claim of the century. Sell it all now and be on your way. This will all belong to the Spanish or the French, if or when the war is over. It makes the most sense to sell now."

"Sell it to who?" said Caesar.

"I'll make ya a deal, Caesar. I'll take it off your hands for all the gold dust I'm carrying. A bit less than the going price, mind you, but I'll take these legal pages with me to Port

Royal and file them with the proper authorities. You'll be legally free and pardoned from piracy, free to sail into any port."

"Don't listen. He's lying," the baron muttered.

"Make your choice," Art persisted. "You got a second chance at life here. Time is running out."

De Heilige Graal closed in. Fire raged below deck and the crew jumped overboard. Wood ground together, splintering. *De Heilige Graal's* hull split, and the forward mast burst into flames, falling on the baron's vessel.

Art extended his arms. "Prices are falling!"

"I free you, I free you!" Baron de Klauwen exclaimed. "My beloved Caesar, don't do this to me. You are mine! My great beast. We will rule the slave trade, you and I."

Caesar wrenched the baron. The baron's back snapped like a dry twig. As a final gesture, Caesar placed the baron in his plush chair at the head of the table.

"I'll give you everything!" the baron pleaded.

"You already did, Baron." Art swiftly gathered documents from the desk. "Pleasure doing business, Caesar. Stop by the Feathers some time. Now, every man for himself." Art tucked the case and scrolls under his arms. His long legs propelled him from the room, just before it all went up in flames.

Art caught up with Morris and Freeman en route to the dock. "Wait, my knees," Art called.

They didn't wait. Art followed as his men evacuated down the gangway to the wharf. They readied a longboat as *Stingray* approached.

Rivero stood on the poop deck of *Fama* as she passed by. "Morris!" Rivero drew his sword. "There he is."

Art accelerated down to the wharf as Freeman and Morris were about to shove off. Morris tried to hide his face from the passing Spanish ship.

"John Morris, you killed my father!" yelled Rivero.

"Oh shit!" said Morris.

"Keep going!" Stubbs said. "Admiral, glad you could join us."

"I always pride myself on timing." Art accelerated past them and found a seat.

Rivero drew his pistol. "Surrender, Morris."

"We're all under parley, here, Captain," Art called. "Onward."

Rivero shot at them. "You can't hide Morris."

"I can sure as hell try, asshole!" Morris dug his oar into the water.

Fama snagged on cables and debris from *Dionin* and couldn't follow as Art and his men rowed away in the smoke.

"I'll get you, Morris!" Rivero's voice echoed across the water. There came a colossal blast and *Dionin* exploded. Its fiery carcass rolled over, along with that of *De Heilige Graal*.

Sunrise on the Yuna River was obscured by thick black smoke. The sun was a dark bronze ball on the horizon. Everyone evacuated, and longboats littered the water. Some people were scouring the shore for survivors.

Art awaited the search party from his cabin deck. Outside on *Stingray*, the crew sat somberly, having a private service for Kapitän Dietrich. Soon, a boat cut through the smoke. Stubbs, Morris, and Freeman rowed without enthusiasm and boarded Art's ship in silence. They made their way into the cabin.

"The countess and my Red?" Art said.

Stubbs shook his head. "The cave has collapsed. If they're down there, they're dead. We ain't going to find nothing."

Art turned to Freeman and Morris for a second opinion.

"No one's comin' out of that cave alive. There's no way to get in," Freeman said.

"I'll go down there and find out for myself," Morris insisted.

"It's suicide, Morris," Freeman said. "A pointless suicide. They ain't down there."

The German galiots emerged from the smoke.

"Everyone on deck." Art led them out.

As the ships passed each other, Maximilian stood on the deck of his yacht, his armor dented with jewels missing.

Art's men readied their guns.

"Where is Aurora?" Maximilian asked.

"Your countess was buried alive by the cave-in," replied Art. "The buccaneer and my best men say there's no hope the countess or her handmaiden survived."

Maximilian's fists shot into the air. "*Wunderbar!*"

"Excuse me, but my lovely Red was with them."

"The wench?" Maximilian blew a raspberry. "Whatever treachery you and my mother are involved with, Valentine, I'll find out. You haven't heard the last of me."

"Your mother's calling you, Prinz. Think you best be headin' home now, know what I mean?"

"We do. We have business to tend, my Prinz," said Reers. "Let's not have any further incidents."

Maximilian's upper lip reared as his galiots rowed out, disappearing into the black smoke.

Bleedin Art's hands trembled against the railing while he gazed out at smoldering, charred hulls, the ruins of *Dionin* and *De Heilige Graal*. *Cymru* and dozens of boats searched the land and water for survivors. "Come on, girly, where ya be at?"

Caesar tested a rowboat, while Fatima waited on shore with a sack. The rowboat sank immediately, and Caesar jumped out. He grumbled, staggering over to Fatima. Nearby, *Guernsey* bustled with activity and *Stingray* lowered more boats.

"I'll buy a ship off Valentine." Caesar trudged along the shore.

Fatima yawned, hurling a sack of plunder over her shoulder. "Don't trust him."

"Who, Valentine?" replied Caesar. "Of course not."

"There are more boats. Let's go away, me and you. I love you. Why won't you have me as your bride?"

"My mother was small, like you. My father said she died in terrible pain when giving birth to me. I won't allow the same to happen to you."

"But you don't care if you hurt women. I've seen how many you hurt. You like it."

"Other women are not like you," said Caesar. "They're like that fat countess."

A longboat wasn't too far away. Just as men appeared, blocking the way, Captain Stubbs called, "Bring them over." Fatima nearly fell, and Caesar stumbled forward. They were transported to *Guernsey*.

"Ahoy, Black Caesar," Stubbs said. The men at the boom rigged a hoist.

"Admiral Valentine said payment is everything you have in your chest," Caesar said.

"The rest goes in the bank in Port Royal, just like we agreed," said Art.

"Fatima needs to see your doctor," said Caesar.

"No." Fatima shook herself awake. "I'll stay with you."

"Are you not friends with the doctor?"

"He's tending wounded," said Art. "But as they are acquaintances, I'll allow it." Art turned to an officer. "Call down to Strangewayes—another patient."

"Go aboard." Caesar lifted Fatima out of the boat, setting her on deck with her sack.

She hesitated. Ekene arrived on deck.

"Your service is fulfilled," Caesar told Ekene. "You and Fatima are free. It's agreed."

Morris and Freeman brought out a chest and handed it down to Caesar. He took it as if it were as light as a feather.

"I want to buy a ship," Caesar said, setting the chest down.

"I got nothin' to spare," Art said sympathetically. "Ya got no crew, anyhow. There's bound to be a boat about still seaworthy."

"Permission to continue the search, Admiral," said Morris.

"Right you are, Mr. Morris," Art said.

"You won't find them here," Caesar told them. "The caves go on for miles."

"Where?" demanded Freeman.

"There is an underground chamber, but not here."

"Other chambers? Where?" barked Freeman and Morris.

"I want a boat. Like this boat." Caesar indicated the longboat on which he stood.

"If you know where the countess and my wench is at, I'll give ya that boat," said Art.

"Out there behind the trees. The painter got it right. The tall one at the end has a hole. A cave going down. The next rock over has a chamber underwater, where there's air. There are passageways to these caves."

"You're saying the women could still be alive?" Freeman said.

"If they lived, that's where they might go. It all floods when the tide comes in."

"I want payment in my account and this boat. Also, the redhead for what she did to me."

"If she's alive, she belongs to me," Art asserted.

"I'll see you in Port Royal someday."

"Until then."

Dr. Strangewayes appeared on deck, sniffing and shaking his head while a trail of white dust followed him.

"The doctor's ready," an officer said.

"Fatima!" Gladstone came on deck in a hurry. They rushed to greet her as she lost her balance. She was caught by Gladstone. She glanced back at Caesar.

"Go get medical attention," he said.

"You'll wait for me?"

"Yes."

Gladstone and the doctor carried her below.

Art and Freeman also ventured to the triage. The painter, Dodo, sat on a barrel, nursing his head, with a broken easel by his side and a few paintings behind him.

Art eyed the painting of a landscape with trees. "Can I be of service, lad?"

"I'm waiting for surgery," said Dodo.

Art pointed to the rocks in the painting's background. "Where'd ya see this exactly?"

The chattering fell into the background for Fatima while her arm was stitched. Her eyes closed, and she reflected on the past several months with Caesar. She was back aboard *Barbarossa I*, in the captain's cabin, then on the command deck, hidden beneath the canopy.

Fatima awoke to find herself in a cot on the gundeck, next to several other people. She got up and scurried out.

Gladstone caught her arm as she reached the foot of the stairs. "Hold on, Fatima, I got you."

"Caesar!"

"Caesar left yesterday," Gladstone said. "You're free of him."

She broke away and ran up on deck, drawing immediate complaints from officers.

"It's all right," Gladstone spoke soothingly.

"Not right." Freeman stomped over. "What's she doing up here?"

"Where's Caesar?" Fatima insisted.

"He left yesterday," Freeman snarled. "Now, if ya don't mind, Mr. Gladstone, we have a countess to find."

"Caesar!" Fatima screamed at the top of her lungs.

Gladstone and Ekene dragged her back down to the triage.

Atia stared at the water, which had a hint of sparkle on it. Her nails dug into her leg. Aurora held her close, trying to keep them both warm. Helena sat nearby, investigating what she called a "mysterious light." It seemed to have been weeks, not days, that they had been in the dark.

There was an explosion of water, and then the three were dragged down onto the rocks, hitting their heads and being battered and bruised. They clung together, treading water in the blackness until, feeling around, they found a flat rock above the surface to sit on and helped each other up.

"*Scheisse!*" Helena bawled.

"It's no use," said Aurora. "There's no way out."

Atia screamed, her voice reverberating off the walls.

"Oh, shut up," said Helena.

"I can't stand tight spaces," Atia cried.

"I can't stand screamers," Helena said.

"Neither can I," Atia continued. "It's just, of all the ways to go, I go out like this. I'm going to die in here."

"The tide is certainly coming up," said Aurora. "What was the kraken, again?"

"Who are you asking?" Helena muttered.

"You're the one who knows these things," Aurora said.

"Shut up and help me find a way out," Helena snapped.

"Don't talk to me like that, I'm a countess!"

"There is no way out!" shrieked Atia.

The word *out* vibrated through the caves.

"Yes, there is a way out; we just have to find it," Helena insisted. "By the way, thank you for stepping in for me. Black Caesar would have killed me."

"Anything for you, dear," said Aurora. "Our only chance now is with the wench's slaver, Blood Art."

"Bleedin' Art," Atia corrected.

"Whatever you say," said Aurora.

"I saw something, a light perhaps," said Helena.

"You banged your head; you're seeing stars," Aurora said.

"Not even the stars remain constant," Helena said. She dipped into the water with a splash and disappeared.

"Oh no. Did she go?" asked Atia.

"I hate it when she does that," said Aurora.

They waited and waited.

Atia brought her knees to her chest and rocked. "How long can she hold her breath?"

"How long has she been gone?" Aurora wondered. "I should have counted."

"About a minute."

"Helena!" Aurora screamed. "You get back here!"

A shiver jolted down Atia's spine.

Aurora's voice bounced off the walls of the cave. After a minute it died down.

"Maybe she got out," said Atia.

"She can be so resilient," Aurora said. "She climbed the Matterhorn once—well, halfway at least, but you know what I mean. Maybe she got out."

"Maybe it's just one of her disappearing acts," said Atia. "She does it a lot. She can be very difficult."

"She did that to the young man who proposed to her once. It took him half an hour before he finally asked if she was coming back. I told him probably not."

Atia and Aurora embraced, shivering in the cold damp.

Deliriums and a Diving Bell

Bleedin Art chipped a tooth waiting for the German ships to leave. He instructed the crew to pretend to have trouble sailing, wanting the Pewter Prinz and his ships to leave first. *Stingray* and its crew remained under Art's command, half from Little Venice, now homeless with no captain. Longboats pulled *Guernsey* to a chain of rocky coral cays. The last one was cone-shaped. Some of the men explored them in longboats.

"The hole is too small for your diving bell," said Freeman. "We're back to where we started."

Yaguara, de Kreep, and two Taíno men arrived by canoe.

"Yaguara, you actually managed to get Maroons and Caribs to work together?" asked Arsenault.

"How did you do that?" Freeman asked.

"Yaguara told them the Samaná Bay buccaneers would return if Baron de Klauwen wasn't destroyed. Nobody wants the Samaná Bay buccaneers to return, and nobody likes Baron de Klauwen."

"Who won San Juan?" asked Art. "Is the Capitaine hanging from a noose?"

"No, the Capitaine's passed out drunk on Crab Island. Yaguara wants to know what you're doing. The diving bell's too large for the cave."

"That's what we said," muttered Freeman and Morris.

"Exploring some caves while we're here," Art added. "This is where Laurens used to keep his booty."

"A misconception," said Yaguara. "Laurens has booty everywhere. These caves connect to the ones collapsed in the river. If Atia and the German women escaped death, then this is where they'll be."

"So, how do you propose we go down and find out?" Freeman said. "You gonna swim down and see for yourself?"

"Yaguara smoked too much when he was young."

Taíno men agreed to scout the cays. Upon their return, they spoke with Yaguara.

"We found an underwater cave," said Yaguara.

"Watcha waiting for, men?" Art called. "Let's do some diving."

Atia sang. "Lullay, lullay, la, lullay my dere moder, sing lullay. Als I lay upon a night alone in my longing, me thought I saw a wonder sight, a maid a child rocking. Lullay, lullay, la lullay—"

Aurora seemed to recognize the song and joined in. Eventually they broke into an argument over the lyrics, which ended abruptly when voices came out of the darkness.

"Uh, who was that?" asked Aurora.

"I think they're speaking Indian," said Atia.

A voice answered. The two voices spoke to each other, then fell silent.

"*Hallo*," said Aurora.

"It's the cave people, come to eat us," said Atia. "They're all cannibals here."

"*Hallo*, I am Countess Aurora."

"They're gone. I saw a shadow underwater. They swam out."

"You can't see," said Aurora.

"I can see better than you, obviously," replied Atia. "There's a way out down there. Countess Two was right."

"Then we should follow them out. She sent them back here to get us. Let's go."

"Down there, in the water?" Atia paused. "I'll wait here."

"Helena found a way out."

"Aye, I will. Give me a while, first. Maybe those men are coming back with help."

"Or maybe with cutlery. You're right, Wench, they're all cannibals here."

It was night when men turned the capstan, lowering the diving bell into the water. Bleedin Art had studied the painting for what felt like hours. The location matched perfectly.

"Three stations are set up underwater. We'll move them from station to station," said Stubbs. "Each one has enough air enough for ten minutes."

"Ten minutes if they ain't breathin' too hard," Morris said.

"And then what? After an underwater trek they're gonna swim up, all smiles, and wave?" Freeman growled.

"No, they go into the diving bell and then we bring them up," said Stubbs.

"That'll go over like the Tower of Babel. The cave's too narrow for the diving bell."

"Not in the cave; beside the reef. We walk them underwater using sacks of air, into the diving bell," said Morris.

They continued to argue. Art remained silent. With the help of the buccaneers and the Natives, he hoped the women stood a chance.

Atia slipped in and out of consciousness. She felt Aurora slip from her arms. Lantern light filled the cave and Dashiell Dupris was there with Taíno men connecting fat leather tubes to sacks. Atia felt Dashiell's mouth against hers; then he poured liquid down her throat. Colorful flashes came out of the rocks.

A sack was placed over her head. She fought it, but she was too weak. She woke in another cave. This time a barrel with a leather suit attached was fitted over her. A little window had been cut out. She felt sand between her toes as she was guided along. Bright orange, green and purple flashed nonsensically before her. Figures walked ahead of her in the murk. Everything blurred when she took her first breath of smoky sea air. She thought she saw Art, before passing out.

Atia could see her ma drowning, sucked off a ship in a hurricane, before being smashed beneath the waves. Atia herself nearly drowned as she was sucked into the icy current as brackish water filled her nostrils and throat.

Atia emerged in a tunnel. There were explosions above her, causing a cave-in. A hand reached into the dirt and found hers. It was her da, Cormac O'Malley. "You'll not go from me sight, only from me view."

Atia's skin crawled, and her stomach burned. Her heart pounded as poison killed her. There was blinding light and the taste of whiskey. Someone spoke to her, reciting poetry. Bleedin Art read to her in Mrs. Beazley's spare bedroom as she recovered from the blue death, belladonna.

Atia lost track of how many Shakespearean plays and sonnets she heard. She could hear one now. "Shall I compare thee to a summer's day? Thou art more lovely and more temperate: rough winds to shake the darling buds of May." She began to recite along and became aware of the bed she lay in. She felt the night dress she wore and the blanket that covered her.

"So long as men can breathe or eyes can see, so long lives this, and this give life to thee," Art finished.

Atia opened her eyes. "Haven't heard that one for a spell."

"Easy, love." Art held her hand. "You're safe now."

Atia tried to focus, through the blinding headache. She massaged her face and caught a glimpse of Aurora, bandaged and asleep on a bed.

"Will she recover?"

"I expect so. Come, you need fresh air, food and water."

"What about Helena?"

"Not yet. Still searching."

Atia was led to the captain's private deck. A chair with plenty of cushions waited, and she sank into it. She relished the hazy sun, taking deep breaths. The breeze felt like silk against her skin. On a perch, Minuit and Freyja napped next to each other.

"Art," she said.

"Admiral Valentine," he corrected.

"Thanks for coming for me."

"No ship could sail fast enough. I'll always come for my whiskey kisses girl."

Helena searched the never-ending system of chambers. She encountered a chain of underwater islands and purple coral reefs. Iridescent fish swam in and out of porous volcanic rock. Some areas she could only swim in and out of again. Cracks of light would appear but led nowhere. Other areas had no light at all. It made little sense.

Helena reached the forlorn conclusion that she would never get out. Exhaustion prevented her from taking another step, and she collapsed, half in and half out of a tide pool. Tears coursed down her cheeks. "Everything we do has consequences. Everything." She would end her life against the rocks, leaping from the highest point.

"It's not like you to give up." Gretsch climbed the rocks.

Helena jolted. "Gretsch! Max Gretsch. How did you get in? I thought you were dead."

"There is no stopping you, you stubborn girl."

Helena woke on the rock, alone. Water rose around her, and a flicker of light came from beneath the surface. She dove in to investigate. It looked like a lantern. It illuminated a hole in a rock, and she swam into it, only to get stuck. She kicked and clawed trying to dislodge herself.

Breaking free, she kicked hard to reach the surface. When she broke through, she caught sight of someone holding a lantern. She pulled herself up the rocks, her hands reaching for the light. She fell, exhausted. As everything went dark, she felt hands all over her.

When she stirred, a light temporarily blinded her, then she saw the diving bell and native men. She tried to speak, but her voice was gone. Everything went dark as if eternity enfolded her in its arms.

Helena found herself floating amongst luminous mist and twinkling celestial bodies. She plucked a star and cradled it in her hands. It got brighter and brighter, its warmth surging up her arms, radiating to her whole body. It got so bright, she shut her eyes.

Helena woke to a man with a crooked nose examining her. "This is the handmaiden, then?"

Fatima loomed over her. "Yes, that's her."

The following afternoon, Helena ventured on deck.

Silvestre loitered, leaning on a walking stick, his arm in a sling. His swollen, bruised face lit up at her approach.

Helena thought she was still dreaming as he kissed her.

"Are you ready?" he asked.

"I will say goodbye." Helena crossed to the deck, to Aurora and Dodo.

They all kissed and embraced.

"The captain says we're getting underway," said Aurora.

"I have to do this now." She brought out a garland of flowers and a wooden plaque that bore a list of names, including those of Katrina and Persephone Van der Hagen.

Aurora tossed the items in the bay in commemoration.

"I suppose you're also staying in the grand cabin," Aurora said. "It's charming but small."

"There's something I need to say," Helena said. "I'm going with Captain Soler."

"What are you saying?"

"She's leaving," said Dodo. "She hasn't had enough of Puerto Rico."

"You never saw Natalia's body," Helena said.

"There was a rumor Natalia might still be alive," Aurora agreed. "Somewhere in the West Indi jungle."

"We have to go find her."

"I saw for myself—there's nothing there."

"I'm going to look for her," Helena insisted. "Maybe she's sitting in a cave somewhere. I know what that's like."

"You are stubborn. I wish I could go with you."

"You can."

"Come with me." Aurora took Helena's hand. "We'll send the Indians in your place. I'll fund your expedition from Port Royal."

"With him?"

They looked to the upper deck, where Bleedin Art smiled at them, his huge teeth glistening.

"Valentine. He's quite charming in his own way," said Aurora. "At least his ship is fully stocked with the best Cognac. Of course, that never appealed to you, did it."

"Write me as soon as you get there."

"I will."

"And send money."

"I will. You go find Natalia."

"I have an excellent guide." Helena smiled. "His name's Yaguara. He knows the area better than anyone, they say. He's one of the men who found me in the cave, and he knows Natalia. I also have a translator, the girl, Fatima. She also knew Natalia in Port Royal. Nerthus couldn't make it clearer. It's fate."

"You don't believe that stuff."

"I have to go, now."

"I'll dream about you."

"I know you will."

Aurora gave Helena one more peck on the cheek, and they parted ways.

Silvestre escorted Helena to the boat and they were rowed to *San Antonio*. Once aboard, she watched from the captain's cabin as *Guernsey* sailed away. Silvestre entered with someone. A smile formed on her lips but faded when she saw Rivero. They bowed to her.

"Helena, you remember Corsair Jorge-Miguel José Rivero."

"I'm so pleased to see you," said Rivero. "I'll never forgive myself for what Don Medina did to you."

"Likewise."

"I hope your countess is faring well."

"The countess has sailed, Captain Rivero."

"Countess Aurora is on Valentine's flagship," said Silvestre. "She's sailing out now."

"Oh, no, not Valentine. You mustn't."

"What do you mean?" Helena queried.

"Valentine—he's a no-good pirate and is in the service of the Jacobites."

"So?" said Helena.

"Oh, no, no, no," Rivero said. "The Jacobites want to murder her so her title can pass to one eligible to marry into the Stewarts. You cannot leave her in the hands of a pirate like him."

"I suggest we warn her at once," said Silvestre.

"I'll set out right away," said Rivero. "We will follow her."

"I'll follow you," said Silvestre. "Not to worry, Helena. I'll have your countess back safe."

Helena walked away.

"Is she coming back?" Rivero said.

Silvestre shrugged.

Art stood on deck, adorned in his blood-red suit, watching *San Antonio*. Atia stood next to him in a deep red dress with black lace, a parasol in her hand.

"I bet that one's the real countess." Atia said, indicating Helena.

"The handmaiden, love?" Art replied.

"I'll bet ya. Eventually it'll be revealed."

"Really?"

"Aye."

"You're on. How much?" Art patted his jacket pocket. "I'm a bit low now. What makes you think so?"

"Wench's intuition."

They strolled along deck.

"So, where will you mail the letter to?" Art asked.

"Tortuga. I don't think Crab Island has post. Capitaine's bound to show up there, sooner or later."

Gladstone and Jones paid their respects.

"Take care of yerself, lass." Jones gave her a hearty hug. "Stay out of the piracy trade."

"Where will you go from here?" Atia asked.

"I'm taking this lot to *Sérénité*," Jones said. "Gladstone and Ekene. Fatima, too, but she split on us. Went with Yaguara and the other countess. It's not too late; come with us, it wouldn't be the same without ya. Besides, how am I supposed to tell your brothers yer goin' back to Port Royal?"

"I'll tell 'em meself, and you keep my place for me at *Sérénité*."

"Will do."

Atia turned to Gladstone for a hug.

"You used to run into my arms," he said.

"Let's do it again, and you can give me a running start."

"You're really not coming with us?"

"That dream's long over for me, love. You go on. You've found yourselves a beautiful home, now go live in it." Atia gave him another hug. "Have a drink for me in Carlena Bay."

"I will."

Atia spent the afternoon watching *Cymru* sail out of the bay.

Aurora and Dodo came out of the grand stateroom after the third course of their lunch.

"Oh, where will I find such a devoted handmaiden?" Aurora moped. "I'll worry about her getting into it with the natives. Or natives getting into her."

"At least she's away from Cardinal Grimaldi," said Dodo.

"Where is Cardinal Grimaldi? I assume he left with Maximilian."

"No, they left him behind."

"Admiral Valentine, do you know what became of Cardinal Grimaldi?" Aurora asked.

Meanwhile, in a jungle in Hispaniola at the top of a cliff, Cardinal Grimaldi was tied by his arms and legs to two palm trees that had been bent over to form an "X". The Fuggers' banker and another slaver were tied in the same way.

A tribal priest with a machete sliced the bonds holding the trees with the slaver attached. The trees sprang apart, tearing the man to pieces, hurling parts through the air. The villagers cheered. The tribal priest moved on to the banker. Body parts flew through the trees.

Cardinal Grimaldi's turn came. "We can work this out," he stammered. "I'm a man of Gaawwdd—"

Art thought for a moment and then shrugged. "Haven't the foggiest, Countess, but we'll let you know if we hear anything."

"Pity about Captain Dietrich," Aurora sighed. "I would have liked to have known him. He served me loyally, I hear."

"He met you plenty of times, by his account."

"Ah, good to know." Aurora contrived some tears as she nodded to the crew. "What became of Black Caesar? You know, in all this I couldn't help admiring his determination. In a way, he's like my Helena."

"Black Caesar was released to his own devices, per my agreement with him, and paid a king's ransom," Art said. "Was the chest heavy enough?"

"Full to the rim," said Stubbs.

"Caesar won't get very far on that, I'm afraid. Pesos are just not worth what they used to be." Art took a deep, satisfied breath. "At least all the assholes have left the Samaná."

"Please join us for refreshments in the stateroom, while the ship gets underway, Countess," Atia said.

Aurora and Dodo, easel in hand, went inside.

Art leant into Atia. "Let's not overdo it just yet, my lovely."

"Trust me, Art." She stood on tiptoe and put her mouth to his. This caught him off-guard, and he shuddered happily. Too soon she pulled away but gave him a mischievous wink before following the countess.

"Set sail for Port Royal, Captain Stubbs," Art ordered.

"Aye, aye, Port Royal."

"By way of the Bahamas, methinks."

"Aye, sir."

A wide grin filled Art's face as he strolled inside.

Guernsey sailed around the Samaná, turning west, into the sunset.

The End

About the Authors

MJL EVANS wanted to be a writer since she was ten years old and in 2014 she finally got her act together and pursued her dream. She is the co-author of No Quarter: Dominium, No Quarter: Wenches and Search for the Holy Grail. A huge fan of Monty Python, Red Dwarf, and other BBC shows, her time is devoted to acrylic painting, photography and catering to her senior cat and of course, writing.
You can connect with MJL Evans on Instagram at @mjlevans or meganjlevans@gmail.com

GM O'CONNOR is a visual artist, illustrator and writer who dabbles in guitars, acting, and sometimes wildlife rescue. A movie encyclopedia, he's a fan of sci-fi and history. He is the co-author of No Quarter: Dominium, No Quarter: Wenches and Search for the Holy Grail. He hopes one day to bring the No Quarter Series to film and/or graphic novel.
You can connect with GM O'Connor on Twitter at @gm_oconnor or noquarterseries@gmail.com

If you enjoyed this book, you may also like the ebook and audiobook editions of

No Quarter: Dominium – The Complete Series
and
No Quarter: Wenches - The Complete Series

If you have any feedback/suggestions or would like to sign up to be a beta reader please contact us at:
noquarterseries@gmail.com

or follow us on Facebook at:
https://www.facebook.com/noquarterseries

www.ingramcontent.com/pod-product-compliance
Lightning Source LLC
Chambersburg PA
CBHW031026030726
47497CB00004B/1026